I0736178

TOOTH

AND

CLAW

BY

MICHAELA THORN

Published in the United States by
Not a Pipe Publishing, Independence, Oregon.
www.NotAPipePublishing.com
Cover by Michaela Thorn
Art by Michaela Thorn

Trade Paperback Edition

ISBN-13: 978-1-948120-58-6

DEDICATION

To Poppy and Grandma Geri,

you will always live on in my heart, my soul,
and my stories.

TOOTH

AND

CLAW

Who trusted God was love indeed
And love Creation's final law
Tho' Nature, red in tooth and claw
With ravine, shriek'd against his creed

-"In Memoriam," Canto 56
by Alfred Lord Tennyson

ONE

BAMBI

The wolf is fast like a bullet. She zigzags between cedars and firs. Branches and straggly roots scrabble to catch her, but she vaults over them effortlessly. Not one step is out of place. She is as much a part of the forest as it is a part of her.

She's fast, but *I'm* faster.

Uneven soil kisses my paws. A canter echoes in the wake of every stride. The wind sings with the woods: a whisper in the pines, a rustle in the underbrush, wings fluttering, and murmuring waters ahead.

Digging my nails into the dirt, I lunge forward and race beside her. The chestnut wolf glances at me. Shadows waver across fur. One dark brown iris oozes adrenaline. Wordlessly, she dares me to catch her.

A break in the trees bathes us in sunlight. A creek cuts through the woods, rolling across pebbles and stones. In its tide is the sky. Interspersed across jewel blue water, white clouds hug rocks and kiss the shore. They waver beside our misshapen reflections as we splash through the stream, sending droplets in every direction.

We run back into the woods, over a boulder, a rotted log. Wherever she goes, I'm right behind her until she weasels beneath a collapsed tree. I dive after her, and hastily wriggle out from under. She's gone.

The wind stills, but the tall grass shudders in the aftershock of her. When I breathe, lilac and lavender mix. Intoxicating. I know her scent. I sink low and follow the trail.

A crow caws overhead. It soars across a thin beam of light and steals the day on its wings. Its shadow casts down through the leaves. Its twisty talons are claws scrawled on bark, curling over dirt and rock to puncture my paws. The crow passes. The sun shines again.

Apprehensively, I creep forward.

Where are you, Lilac?

The trees thin. Between branches, in the far-off distance, the green mountains are tinged blue. Row after row they lose pigment until it's impossible to separate alp from azure sky. The tallest ridge grazes the sun. The storytellers call her Dreamer. What other name do you give to the mountain trying to touch the stars?

There's a rustle ahead. Something small spasms in the shadow of a tree. I inch closer, sniffing. Lilac and lavender are corrupted by the scent of blood. My eyes sharpen.

It's a mink. Its leg twitches, repeatedly grazing the low-hanging branch of a bush. The leaves chatter, thunderous against the uncharacteristic quiet all around. Every individual hair on my pelt stands stark. The woods are never quiet. Especially not on a midsummer afternoon.

My ears lie flat. A breath brews in the pit of my chest as a shudder quakes through my legs. I get on my haunches, and whine at the mink.

All it does is twitch, twitch, *twitch*.

The wind shifts the leaves. Sunlight casts across its dark, matted fur. A gash splits its neck open. The summer-baked soil guzzles its blood, starved for moisture. The mink's limbs convulse. They're quick, short spasms, a frantic attempt to run from a death that already came and bled it dry.

What happened to you?

The gash is too cleanly cut. It must've been a knife. Which means...human hunters? This far into the forest?

I glance around and hastily backtrack. Wherever Lilac is, I need—

She surges into me from my left. We tumble down a hill. Yapping, scrabbling, and snapping teeth turn into laughter, wrestling, and noisy kisses. We're a naked mess tangled at the base of the hill.

When I stare back up the knoll, Lilac cups my cheek. I start to say something, but she muffles it with her mouth. She kisses me thoughtless, empty of everything except her. As she reluctantly pries her mouth from mine, I push for more. She presses a long, dark finger against my lips with a grin.

"Macy, Macy, Macy." She skims her nail down my neck and plays with my beaded necklace. It was a gift from her. "Didn't anyone ever tell you not to wander off into the woods alone?"

A laugh bubbles out of me. "I was chasing my girl-friend, but I lost her."

She mirrors my smirk.

I say, "Have you seen her anywhere?"

She sucks air between her teeth. "What's she look like?"

I sweep a hand through her dark tangles. "She has wild black hair. Pretty brown eyes. Oh, yeah! She's also super into lanky redheads!"

She gasps. "What a coincidence! *I'm* super into lanky redheads! Does she love rolling around naked in the grass, too?"

I shove her shoulders, rolling on top of her. Her laugh is eager and beautiful. She doesn't fight me when I pin her wrists.

"You are such a loser," I tell her.

"You love me."

"Miraculously."

"Pfft!"

She pushes me off, and hops to her feet. One hand on her hip, she extends the other toward me. I take it.

She pulls me up. "C'mon, girly, we're late."

I groan.

"Bambi, stop!"

"I don't want to go." I complain.

"Your evaluation isn't even until tomorrow!" She tugs me homebound. "We can't sit here and kiss all day. As much as I would *love* to."

"We can try!"

She lugs me a little farther with a laugh. Jogging ahead, she shifts back into a wolf. I lag a bit behind. The beast inside prowls anxiously, ready to take my limbs and run.

I glance over my shoulder. The mink flashes in my head, accompanied by a bolt of fright.

The wolf takes control. I dart back home. There's no fun in our running this time. It's a dutiful dash toward the future.

We leap over her cabin steps, and into her open door. Our nails leave scratches in the wood, but our calloused, dirty heels are immune to the splintery planks when we shift again.

Lilac shakes her arms out and skips happily into the next room. She returns wearing a shapeless, hand-stitched dress. The sloping neckline reveals the golden beta symbol tattooed beneath her collar bone. It's grander than the two, bronze omega symbols stamped on my chest. I rub them like it'll ease the shame.

In her hand is my green slip dress. She tosses it at me. "Don't look so miserable."

"That's hard to do." I deadpan as I pull the dress over my head. "They don't call me Macy Miserable Braddock for nothing."

She snorts with amusement. "No one calls you that."

Of course she doesn't understand. "If I fail tomorrow, Lilac—"

"That's tomorrow." She folds her arms. "Today is to-day. Can you wait to ruin the fun until *after* the RAE please?"

I scoff through my nose, and march past her. She sighs before following me into town.

Hydrilla isn't on the map. It's tucked away in the un-charted forest lands of the North Maine Woods, masked from prying satellite eyes by impenetrable leaves. Far, far away from modern human culture, too deep into the woodland for any intelligent hiker to stray, it's the perfect abode for my people.

I drudge through our unusually hectic home toward the testing chambers. The entire city is abuzz with this summer's trials. The pathways are dappled in shadows cast by lofty foliage. Troves of shifters move in and out of shade. They babble about where they're needed next, or what task they've yet to complete. Everyone's preparing for Friday, and the ceremonies that follow the RAE.

The Rank Alignment Evaluation was established by the very first Alphas after the shifters defeated the vampires centuries ago. Pack-mates (the shifters yet to take or pass the RAE) are required to take it at age sixteen. They earn their rank in the pack and do their part to safeguard the Earth as a full-fledged adult. It's our duty.

America is made of six packs: Sage, Agave, Poppy, Knotweed, Foxglove, and my pack, Bloodroot. Each is ruled by two Alphas of either sex. They interact with powerful humans to sustain our secrecy. Assisting them, are the betas. They're a small pool of elite champions, fated to one day battle for the Alpha rank. Below that is the civilian rank, the deltas. Teachers, healers, artists, everything. But the omegas?

They're lower than dirt. A meritless mixture of the pack's most inept and dangerous. Criminals aligned with the incapable because incompetency is as irredeemable as murder. All omegas lead lives of servitude.

Tomorrow is my Rank Alignment Evaluation. My *third* Rank Alignment Evaluation. A hot wash of humiliation flushes my body from head to toe. The symbols on my chest *burn.* They're a reminder that I won't have a fourth chance.

Just breathe.

Lilac slips her arm around my waist. "Did you sleep okay last night?"

I shoot her a look.

I've been plagued by insomnia for years. It never goes away. It just weakens or intensifies, depending on the moon. She *knows* that. And *I* know this is another of her trademark attempts at halfhearted optimism.

She pouts.

I sigh. "No."

"You always have a hard time closer to the full moon." She bumps my arm with hers. "But it'll pass. After tonight, you can hibernate with the other animals."

"In the middle of summer?" I poke her arm.

She grins. "Well, a doe like you needs her sleep."

I laugh under my breath.

We follow the path to the testing chambers. A pair of massive doors protects the tightly wound labyrinth burrowed inside. Each door bears one half of Mother Nature's symbol, the doe. Above it are the words: *Beast, Breath, and Body for Her.*

She speaks to us, messages disguised as soft carols in the wind. Her hands are every tree, shrub, flower, and blade of grass. The animals are her eyes and ears. It's our duty to protect her. We live to serve. An honorable shifter dies to do the same.

Lilac and I slip inside. We lace our fingers together and follow the flow of people to the arena.

A gray-haired man whispers, "There's a trail of dead animals from the southern border all the way here."

The mink's convulsing corpse unburies itself from the depths of my mind. Its fidgeting claws dig into my flesh, and the glaring red gash blinds me. It's all I see for a second.

"A human hunter?" another shifter asks.

"No. They weren't killed for meat or fur. They were...defiled."

An uneasy knot twists in my belly. Lilac catches my expression and pulls me further. The gossip surrounds us.

"A vampire?"

"Can't be. Aconite isn't missing any citizens."

"Another coven maybe?"

The knot in my stomach tightens.

Vampires. The Man in the Moon's children birthed from his scorn. After being bested time and time again throughout history, they're now confined to their walled-in cities, known as covens. Each coven is guarded by our gammas, the militaristic rank between beta and delta.

However, vampires are unruly creatures. Some claw their way out to hunt for fresh blood, violence, revenge. We call them rogues. Most shifters are lucky enough to never meet one. I wish I were so fortunate.

"Let's go." With one last tug, Lilac pulls us through the swarm.

Sunlight pours in from the colosseum's open roof. Several verandas have been tunneled into the walls. Shifters lean over the edges with their hands braced on the beams, ogling the spectacle below. On one of the lower balconies, Alphas Althea and Garth exude royalty.

"It already started!" Lilac releases my hand and squeezes through a pair of engrossed men. She rests her elbows on the banister, and eagerly bends over the rail. She lets out a giddy cry of excitement. I drag my feet to stand next to her.

A horde of wolves snarl below. All their pelts are matted with blood, oozing from grisly claw and teeth marks. They all must've taken on the challenger—the auburn wolf at the center of the fray—one by one. A howl ricochets through the colosseum. Slowly, they retreat to the edges of the arena, where they dip into the caves.

The competitor returns to her original shape. The knot in my stomach tightens. Alanna Hyland. She's one of the older pack-mates, just like me. She failed the RAE two times already. This is her last chance, too.

I careen closer.

Her sweaty, contused skin glistens, and her hair is a damp, knotted mess. Her shoulders rise and fall; her chest swells and collapses; her ribs push and pull against skin; she makes and unmakes fists. Immediately, my body resurrects memories of bone-breaking fatigue.

"We missed the first phase." Lilac pouts in disappointment.

"She passed at least," I say.

"Everyone passes the first phase," she remarks.

I dig my nails into my arms.

Another howl signals the next trial. Unlike the first phase, which focuses on the most instinctual shifter skill of all, transforming, the second emphasizes complete mastery of your Grounding and Marrow Mark.

Every shifter is born with both. Marrow Marks are where Mother Nature touched our souls and gave us life. They age with us until our bodies are decorated in her artwork. Mine is a scarab beetle stamped between my shoulder blades, and spindly threads branching down my body. Lilac's is her namesake. Alanna's is a butterfly.

Groundings are the souls of powerful, deceased shifters, who bind us to Mother Nature. Some are from ancient times, others from more recent eras, but no two living shifters share one. Without them, we can't morph or harness our Marrow Marks.

Four opponents enter the arena, one from each tier, excluding the Alpha rank. They all hold a bowl of paint. Gold for the beta, red for the gamma, silver for the delta, and bronze for the omega. The highest rank she defeats is where she'll be placed.

My heart hammers at the sight of one of Alanna's opponents. Lily Dexter.

"Your sister's one of the testers?" I demand, wide eyed.

Her hair is pulled up in a tight ponytail. The wild curls twirl disobediently behind her head. They're all topless, but none are as proud as she is, despite her arm. It's been a year. Her Marrow Mark has grown over the stump. Orange and purple lilies.

Your fault echoes in my ears.

Lilac glances at me.

"I didn't know..." My breath hitches. "I'm glad she... How *is* she?"

She doesn't look at me. "She's healing."

"I—"

A third howl vibrates through the colosseum. The omega lowers his bowl to the ground. He dips his hands into the metallic liquid, and swipes bronze across his chest. He wets his hands with more paint and then stands. The other three testers retreat to the edge of the arena.

Alanna's shoulders sag before they straighten. She pulls in a breath and closes her eyes. Her Marrow Mark shines gold.

Lilac whistles with the crowd. "Who's her Grounding?"

"Azad," I say.

"Never heard of it."

The omega springs forward. Alanna stumbles away, unprepared. Her shine disappears. He nearly catches her arm; he nearly stains her skin bronze. She trips, falling out of his grasp. The crowd roars when she lands in the dirt. They're louder as she scrambles away.

Her faded glow builds again. Vivid yellow petals peel away from her skin. They flutter freely in the air, creating a storm of butterflies. The cloud of insects intercepts the omega's second approach. They nearly swallow him up. He leaps away. Dozens of shallow cuts redden his arms.

Alanna struggles to get up. Every motion is made difficult by exhaustion. *Just beat him,* I think. *Just win.* But there's another fight after this, and another after that. I chew the inside of my lip. *Mother Nature, just win.*

The butterflies circle back to Alanna. They dance around her and perch themselves on her limbs.

Breathless and bogged down, she swings an arm forward. The swarm rushes the omega.

He jumps out of the way. Finally, he plaits his skin in light too. From his faintly glowing Marrow Mark, ethereal maroon snakes detach themselves. They're flickering ghostly serpents. They burrow into the dirt, and worm through it like tree roots.

One lunges at her ankle. She steps aside and waves her hand again. Another attack.

This time he isn't as fast. He's caught in the cloud, and nearly falls over. Alanna sees her opening. She chases it. Sprinting nearer, she parts the swarm of insects to reach him. One of his snakes attacks her ankle again. It wraps around the delicate bone, strong enough to stagger her.

Her focus is broken. The butterflies begin to crumble. The omega emerges from their golden ashes. His glow flickers. She can't find her footing soon enough, trapped on a collision course with him. The crowd is desperate. Everyone roars until his hand touches her heart, branding her. Their voices are swept away by the wind.

"Oh no," I whisper.

Alanna glances at the handprint on her chest, bottom lip quavering. The weight of her future sends her to her knees. She wails as she claws at the paint until bronze is mixed with blood.

TWO

HUNGRIER

"That was pathetic," Lilac mutters.

A wave of disappointed murmurs echoes throughout the arena.

I hang my head and watch as Alanna wrestles with the gammas dragging her out of the colosseum.

I look away. "Can we go now? I don't want to stay for the other trials."

She nods. Protectively, she hugs me into her side as we retreat back where we came. Once we're outside, she looks at me with concern.

"You know you're gonna pass tomorrow, right?" Lilac reassures. "You've trained all year for this. There's nothing anyone can say or do that will change that, Bambi."

"She trained all year too."

Lilac purses her lips together. She switches the subject, like always. She never has to acknowledge the bad. "Are you having dinner with your parents?"

A groan rises from inside me. "Unfortunately."

"Meet me by the lake at midnight."

"Lilac."

"Please?"

Her puppy eyes win me over. "Okay."

She smiles, bumps my shoulder, and walks me to my parents' cabin.

Vines scale the walls and burrow between planks. It's forged from warm brown logs, with sparkling windows—probably polished by an omega. Leaves plaster the roof like tiles. It's not the grandest cabin in Hydrilla, but it's bigger than my measly cave-carved dwelling. Dad's time as a gamma earned them a lot of favors.

It's welcoming enough, like the distant homes nearby. Unfortunately, my despairing parents lurk inside. I love them, but they're desperate I pass tomorrow.

"Midnight." Lilac reiterates as she slowly backs away.

I smile meekly over my shoulder. "Midnight."

Then, she's gone.

Unease consumes me. It's not like I'm the only person in the world who's ever wanted to skip dinner with their parents. The only thing that keeps me from fleeing is the fact that Mom and Dad are crazy enough to hunt me down.

As I enter the house, I'm hugged by toasty warmth. I breathe in as the familiar scent of roasted hazelnuts greets me. Light swims through the windows, bathing the plants lined beneath each one. Every vase and jar thrive as the result of Mom's famous green thumb. It's like this all over the house.

I close the door behind me and make my way to the main room. The floorboards are made from a different, lighter wood than the walls, which are a much rosier bark. All the tables and shelves have been populated by mom's plants. There's a desk reserved in the corner for Dad.

He's a burly man with a gut, seated on the handmade futon at the center of the room. I inherited my height from him, but not his strength. He's also to thank for my crimson locks, fair complexion, and sunset eyes. Fortunately, I didn't receive his bear-like figure or features.

Some of his old gamma comrades call him Grizzly. I never figured out if it was because of build, or his Marrow Mark: a dark, indigo bear's paw stamped over his heart. It whirls all over his body like Celtic war-paint.

He rests his feet on the coffee table, his nose buried in his trademark notebook. He doesn't even notice me. He's like that, cursed with a terminal case of tunnel vision. It's not until I snap my fingers that he finally looks up. His pale, freckled face wrinkles with a smile. He automatically tucks his journal aside.

"There you are, Macy." He crosses the room to wrap me in a hug. I inhale his woodsy scent. "We've been waiting for you."

"Yes. We have."

Sucking in a sharp breath, I turn to face my mother.

Kathleen Braddock stands in the doorway to the kitchen. She's a much steelier creature than Dad. She's pale, blonde, and sharp. Her hair is pulled back in a tight bun to accentuate the faded mark of a vampire's claw. The poorly healed injury stretches diagonally across her face, over one of her eyes.

Her frosty cobalt Marrow Mark is a clematis blossom. It sits atop her right hand, with vines that sprawl the length of her arm, twisting and twining like loose braids. It's gorgeous. She is too, under all the grief. All that anger.

I pull my bottom lip into my mouth, and nervously wave. "Hey, Mom."

"You were supposed to be here ten minutes ago, Marcine." The criticism is jagged. "You always do this. You can't be late to your evaluation tomorrow."

"Yes," I say. "I know, Mom. Sorry."

She stares out one of the windows. With a sigh, she softens. Regret flickers in her eyes. She swipes a stray hair out of my face, touches my cheek lovingly, and motions for us to join her in the kitchen. Not an apology, but close enough.

Mom plucks a few blueberries from the fruit bowl on the counter and pops them into her mouth. She turns to the oven and gloves her hands with mitts. Dad takes one of the plates from the fridge and sets it on the table. I join him, grabbing a smaller platter.

"So...what did you guys do today?" I fill the quiet.

"We helped the Dexters," Mom says as she retrieves the food from the oven.

"They were doing the beta ceremony, weren't they?" I ask.

"That's right," says Dad. "They mostly did the heavy lifting. A few of the other families were handling the guest list and the seating."

"It was better than assisting the deltas." Mom snorts.

"None of them are any real fun, except maybe the Alpha ceremony." he reminisces. "But the gammas come close. I remember quite a few from before I retired. It's always busy work with the deltas."

Mom frowns. "Everything would all be done sooner if the omegas weren't off needlessly preparing their own ceremony."

"Is it really a celebration?" I take the stack of plates and silverware she offers me.

Dad grunts at my question. "If anything, it's more like a condolence ceremony."

Mom laughs under her breath. "'Hi, hello, welcome. We're sorry, too.'"

Her words are unintentionally barbed. She doesn't mean to wound me, but, given that neither of my parents ever suffered the spiritual bumbling I do, their empathy is clouded.

I eye Mom's profile. Her scar. Which is worse? Omegas or vampires? Memories bombard me. Vampires. *Definitely* Vampires. At least the omegas are useful.

Immediately, shame washes over me, followed by fear, and then desperation.

I won't fail the RAE tomorrow.

I place the last piece of silverware. Dad brings the dish from the oven, and Mom walks beside him with a few glasses and a pitcher of ice water. We all take a seat.

"Enough of that," Mom says. "I've been starved all day. My mouth is watering after cooking this deer. It was quite the catch, Rochester."

"I can't take all the credit." He cuts into the roast. "Weston helped hunt. Brought home a stag of considerable size himself."

"Have you heard about that trail of animals?" I ask.

Quiet overwhelms the table. Dad's hands hover over the roast. I regret asking.

"The hunters think it's a human," Dad says, "but it doesn't feel right. Humans don't leave corpses lying about."

"I heard..." I chew my lip, then lean across the table. "Some people say it might be a vampire."

Mom's expression turns severe. Dad sets his knives down, takes her hand in his, and nods. "The killings are brutal. There's no purpose in it all. No mercy or gratitude. Whoever's to blame is doing it to cause harm."

Or send a warning, a dangerous thought trespasses. I shake myself free of it.

"...I'm not sure it's a vampire," Dad says. "There haven't been any rogues since February, and they were quickly apprehended."

Mom whispers. "An Eidolon? Like your brother...?"

"It's possible." Dad grunts. His nostrils flare.

My eyes sink to my plate.

The Eidola are shifters who've lost themselves to their animal instincts. Many omegas were once hellish warriors whose minds were overcome by their beasts. They're living phantoms of who they once were.

I remember when my uncle began to fade. By the time anyone caught onto his condition, his mind had irreparably deteriorated. My aunt refused to sanction his demotion, denying he was ill at all. He often wandered away, his whereabouts unknown, and frequently forgot to pray before his hunts. His prey was slaughtered, without purpose, mercy, or gratitude. He eventually went missing, discovered weeks later smattered in dried human blood. It was the final straw.

We don't really talk about him anymore. He's dead to us, to anyone, except my aunt and Dad.

"Enough." Dad decides as he piles slices of meat onto our plates. "No more of this conversation. The hunters are working with the betas to resolve the issue. It's all taken care of."

"Yes." Mom agrees.

She exhales, and shakily serves us each a helping of fruit. The ladle wobbles in her grasp. I take it and do it for her. She frowns at me. It's somehow thankful and agitated at the same time. She feels weak, inferior, but I love her too much to let her struggle

"That's not enough, Marcine." She scrutinizes my plate.

"Yes, it is, Mom..."

Dad talks around a mouth full of food. "You should eat more, Sweets. A strong Grounding needs a strong body."

I'm Grounded by the revered warrior Aimil MacAdaidh, said to have made mountains tremble with her howl. After Mom's accident, I lost touch with Aimil. It's humiliating, infuriating. I don't know which is worse: that I'm inept at all, or that Mom blames herself.

She steeples her hands, eyes stern. "It might be strong, but strength is hardly an asset without restraint."

My throat tightens. It's hard to swallow, but I force myself to. All their attention is on me now. I can't look weak. They'll attack my mediocrity, as if their criticism will stomp it out.

"I'm doing better," I tell her, eying my plate.

She straightens and leans forward, abruptly hopeful. "You've reconnected with your Grounding, then?"

Her eyes are penetrating. I've memorized that look. It rifles through me, searching and searching for an answer she wants. *Tell me,* it begs, heavy with the hopes and dreams I'm doomed to shatter.

"For the most part."

A cricket chirps outside. It's louder than either of their breathing. Their gazes burn my skin.

"What does that mean?" Dad asks.

I play with my food. "I still have to work out a couple of kinks."

His brows knit together. Mom grimaces. Are they disappointed or scared? It's hard to tell. Probably both.

"The important thing is that I'm better than I was before." I rush to explain. "Lilac's been helping me, so I won't hurt anyone again."

Mom's shoulders slump. "Let's hope so. We don't want another incident like what happened with her sister."

I shrink into my seat.

Dad adds. "Or another omega in the family."

I mumble. "I'm not going to fail…"

THREE

MIDNIGHT

My voice disappears for the rest of dinner. By the time we're done eating, I nearly bolt for the door. They wave goodbye as I eagerly flee. Once I'm out of their sight, I run as desperately as I've wanted to all night, all year, all my life, as if a sprint will lead me away from my troubles.

I bound from the marked trail, deep into the forest, and tear my clothes off, anxious to abandon any constraints. I'll come back for it all later. Right now, I belong to Mother Nature.

My heartbeat quickens. Electricity sparks in my veins. It coats my skin. My limbs grow, shrink, and change in whatever way they require. My hands and feet morph into paws, face strengthened by attentive ears, a snout veiling knife-like teeth, and a downy pelt. I'm not an anxious, clumsy young woman anymore.

I am the beast; the wolf. My senses are keener. My pulse is faster. My thoughts are rapid. My emotions are raw. I'm under the Earth's spell.

The moon and its twinkling kin send dull rays of grayish light through the canopy of leaves. It graces the forest floor, and reveals branches, acorns, and pinecones. Brambles and thickets are tickled by nightlife. The taste of earthy air dances across my tongue.

I catch the familiar scent of the lake and take a sharp turn. As its dark waters come into view, I ease to a trot.

Mother Nature sings in the wind. The thumping in my chest slows. The wolf is lured back inside my soul, imprisoned again. Rapidly, I reshape into the woman I was before.

I shiver under the moonlight. I rub my arms as a breeze sweeps by. It smells like lilacs.

A stream of ethereal petals teems from behind me. They rollick, wispy, delicate, and beautiful. The glimmering storm swirls up and around my body, but never touches me.

I glance over my shoulder to see Lilac inching closer. In her wake, bushels of her namesake flower sprout from the Earth. They multiply with every step, and frame her like she's a goddess whose most mundane actions breathe life. In a way, she is.

Her Marrow Mark shines against her dark skin. The lavender tattoo starts at the nape of her neck and twists down and around her body.

She's indescribable, but if I had to use words as paint to create a picture of her, I would equate her to every meadow, mountain, waterfall, sunrise, and sunset. And I would still include a disclaimer because words cannot do her beauty justice.

"You always have to make an entrance." I tease.

"It's my one and only talent." She grins that cheeky smile of hers. "You can't complain."

"Try me." I challenge.

Now that she's closer, she reins in her Marrow Mark. The tattoo's shimmer dims, then disappears. The petals and plants fade, too.

"You're lucky I grabbed your clothes on the way." She digs into her bag slung over her shoulder and pulls out my underwear. "Also, you left these at my place last night. Where'd you get 'em? They're nice—mostly because you're not wearing them, but whatever."

I swipe them from her. "My *other* girlfriend bought them for me."

"Tell her she has poor taste." She snickers, then laughs when I flip her off. "I'm just glad you didn't toss the necklace. It took forever to make."

I twirl it around my finger. "I don't want to break it."

"Try fewer naked sprints." She chuckles.

She ruminates for a few seconds. I cock my head at her, concerned. She's notorious for her impulsiveness, not forethought.

"So," she finally says, "I know dinner didn't go all that awesome. Running bare-skinned through the woods is never a good sign. *Super* horrible timing considering tomorrow..."

"Mother Nature, no!" I groan. "Don't remind me about that now. I just calmed down!"

"Hang on!" She interrupts me interrupting her. "I've got an idea."

"Oh no."

"It's a good idea!"

"That's what you said last time"—I point a finger at her— "and we ended up with poison ivy *everywhere*."

Lilac pauses at that, then folds her arms defiantly. "Well, yeah, that was poor planning on my part. But you didn't recognize it either!"

With a sigh, I wave for her to go on.

She's pleased. "We should head east toward the river junction. Do some stargazing!"

I must look doubtful, because she opens her mouth to defend herself. I speak before she has the chance. "My RAE is *tomorrow*, Lilac."

"Exactly!"

I frown. "I don't want to risk the rest of my life for a romantic night under the stars."

"But... but... it'll get your mind off it." She uses her famous puppy eyes. "I thought you'd like a break from constantly worrying about something."

The puppy eyes intensify. I groan again, louder this time. I can't help it. A softer, more appreciative smile tugs at my mouth.

"Fine."

She cheers at my compliance.

FOUR

THE MONSTER

We head east. She skips barefoot up a steep hill. At the top, where the trees open to a valley of rivers, she pulls me down to lay beside her. We gaze at the moon, hands intertwined. He glares back.

The teachers say the Man in the Moon was gravely jealous of Mother Nature's love for humans, her first and finest creations. His jealousy led him to infect their corpses with his bitterness, creating a twisted version of "life." That was how the first vampires came to be. They had no purpose other than to inflict pain and spread their scourge.

Horrified, Mother Nature went to the strongest warriors, asking them to defend her creations. In exchange, they were endowed with the vicious power of her beasts. Her wolves. Did the Mother know that, thousands of years later, her army of protectors would be diluted by people like me?

Stop.

I won't fail tomorrow. I can't lose everything. Mom and Dad would cut me off like they did my uncle. I would be an orphan of circumstance. And what about Lilac?

I glance at her. She stares at the stars. Her gaze is an endless universe. We've been close since we were pups, chasing each other's tails. We don't always mesh. She isn't always there. Sometimes, when I need her most, she runs away. I don't know if that's okay but having her at all is better than saying goodbye.

I close my eyes, letting the wind soothe me. Too soon, however, the melody fades and dangerous questions roar within the silence.

I squeeze her hand. She squeezes back.

"Lilac." I murmur.

"Yeah?"

I hesitate. Stay quiet, let things be, or speak my mind and pollute her bliss with my worries? My traitorous heart compels my persistence. "Tomorrow..."

"Uh huh."

"If I fail—"

"You won't."

"—alright, well, in case I do..."

"Macy." Lilac whines. "You're not going to fail, okay? We came out here to have fun. *For once.*"

I jerk my hand out of hers and sit upright. She glowers at me, propped up on her elbows.

"No." *Stop talking,* I tell myself. My mouth works against me. "I have to know, okay? My entire life changes tomorrow. Maybe for better, maybe for worse. You don't get that because you've always been great at everything. I *haven't.* If I fail tomorrow and become an omega... what would happen to us?"

The words scald the roof of my mouth as if they're laced with acid. Lilac doesn't answer immediately like I wish she would. She takes her time. She *thinks* about it. She ponders the same thing I do every time the scenario comes to mind.

Omegas aren't allowed to further their bloodline. They're sterilized and prohibited from romantic interactions outside of their own rank. The pack cannot condone competent shifters becoming infatuated with incapable partners.

"You won't fail," Lilac states.

She's firm but not confident. An excruciating difference.

"Are you saying that because you think I can do it?" I demand. "Or because you don't want to hurt my feelings?"

She looks away. "Don't make me say it."

A stabbing pain punctures my chest. "Are you *serious?*"

She closes her eyes.

"Really?"

The forest is dreadfully silent. It waits for her response.

"After everything, all these years, it ends if I fail?"

She grimaces. "That's how it works."

That *is* how it works. That doesn't make it hurt less.

I'm wounded, and that makes me stupid. I open my mouth, as frustrated as I am pained, but a scream overpowers my voice. It's raw and shrill, a wail for help that ricochets between the trees. It burrows into my heart.

We jump to our feet and share a look. There's no terror in her stare. Just strength. I wish I could say the same. I wish I could blame the cold for my trembling, blame the wind for my goosebumps, and blame the dark for my fright. Shamefully, I tear my eyes from hers.

"Was that... was that a human?" I stammer. "Why would a human be this far into the forest?"

I cautiously retreat in the opposite direction of the scream, eyes peeled for anything. I'm almost thankful the scream was so far away. My Grounding is dangerous in desperate circumstances, hard to control. It does more harm than good. Without Lilac, I'm helpless.

I want to go home.

Lilac's on a different page. Her stare is locked in the direction of the screech. "I don't know..."

"It has to be an animal, right? A deer or something." The words quiver out in a hushed whisper. I'm surprised she hears me at all.

"Sure didn't sound like a deer..." Lilac studies the trees. She climbs branches and runs miles with her eyes. "How far away do you think they are?"

"Too far." I clutch her arm. "We need to go."

She doesn't budge. She's caught up in things beyond me, beyond us.

"Lilac." My voice breaks from the weight of my fright. "Lilac, *please*, we have to—"

Another shriek. My imagination resurrects the mink, and gruesomely slaughters it all over again. It screams like the woods.

My knees wobble. I tug her again, but her feet are planted.

"We have to go!" I plead. "It's not our responsibility!

Finally, she looks at me. She *glares* at me. For the first time ever, we aren't equals. She's my superior.

"*This* is why you're an omega." she snarls.

I gape at her. My whole body wants to shrivel up.

She pries herself from my grasp, then bounds toward the shriek.

"Lilac!" I yell. "Lilac, *don't leave me!*"

The trees swallow her. Her footsteps fade. I strain my ears, but she's gone. I'm all alone. Fear creeps up my spine. It whispers in my ear. *Run.* I burst into a sprint.

The pines blot out the moonlight. Their shapes blend in with the shadows. The canopy of leaves is a starless, black sky. It's too dark. It's too quiet. My heartbeat is deafening. I run until several warm, malty glows bloom ahead.

Lilac has to be there. She couldn't be anywhere else! I almost call her name but stop myself. Whatever made that creature scream might find me too. I run into the light.

Relief, then realization.

At the center of a small clearing, a mob of people circle a crumpled man like hungry vultures. He's a mess: bruises, blood, and gore. The grass around him is soaked in his blood.

Panic pulls me a step back.

He's hefted up by another man dressed in a tattered, leather duster, eliciting a ghastly groan. His body sags weakly in his tormentor's arms, and his head rolls on his shoulders.

"My knife." His captor precariously balances his body, extending his open palm.

One of the others hands him a blade. Almost tenderly, he swipes the captive's hair out of his face, guiding his head back to expose his—

The tortured man sees me. There's so much hurt in his eyes, but worse: there's hope. Someone came. Someone came, and he doesn't know how unfortunate he is that it's me.

That spark of short-lived optimism is stomped out by the knife brought smoothly across his throat. His blood cascades down his chest like a sanguinated waterfall. The killer opens his arms. The man slides down to his feet. He gurgles, grasping at his neck.

My stomach tries to climb up my throat.

I take another step and try to tear myself from the scene, but I'm pulled in by another pair of eyes. They're gray. Stormy and dark. The eyes of a monster.

But monsters are supposed to be obvious. They shouldn't smile or laugh. They're supposed to look as immoral and evil as their actions. Yet there he is: normal, until you see the dead man lying at his feet.

"Look at this." His tone is even, the kind of voice that could be mistaken for soothing if it weren't for the menacing impact of each word.

Fear blots out everything but his mouth. I watch the way it moves. With every syllable, his bloodied fangs peek out from behind his lips. I look at the others. All their faces are smeared red, and they all have the same smile. The one that says *look, dessert!* Their fangs catch glints from their flashlights clutched by veined hands and gangly nails. Those too are mottled crimson.

Vampires. *Rogue* vampires. The ones that scrape and claw their ways out of the covens to hurt and kill people the way they hurt Mom.

The Monster steps over the corpse. "A stray dog's wandered in on our meal."

They all leer at me.

My feet are anchors. The same tether tying the soles of my feet to the Earth has stitched my airway closed. My body aches to run. I need to run. I know what happens when you cross the wrong vampires; I was raised by a woman whose face bears a vicious reminder.

The Monster licks the blood off his knife, tucks it in his coat pocket, then purrs. "It's shaking."

He's right, but I can't rein in my own trembling.

"Oh." A malicious smirk tugs at the corner of his mouth. "Cute. It's paralyzed. Who's in the mood for dog meat?"

Before any of them have the chance to make good on their word and a meal out of me, a momentous storm of petals spills from the adjacent line of trees. A second wave follows, and then Lilac herself.

"Another one!" one vampire shouts.

The petals sever into streams. They chase the vampires, who all duck and jump out of the way. All of them, except the Monster.

For the first time outside a classroom, I see blood magic at work.

The Monster rolls up his sleeves. Horizontal scabs break open and bleed dark, dark scarlet. He extends his arms. The blood in the soil answers his call.

Rain, waterfalls, Groundings; I've seen it all, but none have ever been as swift, strong, or *disturbing*. His blood mixes with the dead man's. Swirling shades of crimson twist into a shield against Lilac's Grounding. It absorbs the ethereal petals easily.

They frantically fight against their crimson cage, but the currents keep them pinned in the undertow. He flicks his wrist and the barrier splits into several even smaller streams, now imbued with Lilac's own might. He sends them her way at a speed too fast to match.

A sudden, quaking fear snips the steel thread holding me captive. I launch into a sprint.

The knife.

Where is it? I saw him put it away. Grab it. Hurt him. *Where?* My view is clouded with the image of the blade brought across the man's neck.

Throat.

Someone calls an unfamiliar name. Not mine. I clutch his jacket and reach for his pocket. The Monster catches my wrist. I gasp and reel back. He yanks me in front of him.

My eyes widen at the sight of one of Lilac's attacks bolting towards us.

The world stops.

She stands unscathed and empowered on the other end of the clearing, close to the trees where she can escape at any time. The blood previously aimed at her puddles on the ground. She avoided the attack.

This is why I'm an omega.

He pins my hands behind my back with one of his. The other grips my hair. He yanks my head back, pressing a volatile kiss into the side of my throat. My skin crawls. His breath is hot against my jugular. His laughter is mocking beside my ear.

Lilac pulls her petals back. They spin around her in slow lethargic circles.

"I'll kill her, and I'll kill you," the Monster promises.

"There are more of us." Lilac lies in a rush. "They're on their way."

He snorts and twists my hair. It tugs the individual strands. If he pulls any harder, they'll rip right out. I hiss through gritted teeth.

I yank at my hands, but his hold is unbreakable.

"I dislike liars." His grip tightens, eliciting a grunt. The bones in my wrist grind. I struggle more, but the pain gets worse and worse.

Something familiar stirs deep inside my chest. My Marrow Mark glows, faint and stifled.

Lilac holds her hand out. They all flinch. It's not that kind of gesture. "I'm not lying!"

"I don't believe you," he barks. "It doesn't matter. Neither of you are worth more than a night's dinner."

He violates my skin with his mouth. More kisses against my jugular. I writhe away, but there's no running from his fangs. They taunt my skin, but they don't bite.

I'm not sure which is a fouler torment: the fact that he's going to kill me, or that he hasn't done it yet. He mocks us by drawing it out, giving me ample time to remember the lessons burnt into my memory by dozens of instructors. It was always the same rhetoric, repeated in every class.

We live longer than humans, vampires live longer than us, but their bite is poisonous to shifters. It will infect any human with their curse, but it will always kill us.

It was always the same images, too.

Dead shifters sprawled across medical beds with bold, black lines attached to particularly gruesome segments of their corpses. Descriptive blurbs about the wounds and the venom's effect. Nightmares for weeks about being cornered and killed by a vampire. They got worse after Mom's attack.

The electricity in my limbs intensifies.

"Stop! I'm a beta!" Lilac jumps forward a step. "The pack will look for us!"

"Ah." He smiles against my throat. I shiver. "So, you were lying."

She gasps. "No..."

Every labored breath is swift and shallow, and my mouth is dry. There's a weight in my stomach, and a blockade in my throat. My heart pounds.

It whispers to something wild, dangerous, and unpredictable inside. My Grounding is awake. Memories of Lily's shaking fingers painted red flicker in my head. I've been so cautious since then, but maybe that's what we need right now. Something wild, dangerous, maybe even unpredictable, but it requires a trigger...and there's one thing that could do that...

I eye the Monster in my peripherals.

"How am I supposed to trust a word you say?" All the life is gone from his voice.

She gapes at his question, then looks at me. There's an apology somewhere in her gaze. It's mirrored by the one in mine.

"Please." Her petals slowly disintegrate.

I try to shake my head at her, but he ruthlessly stabs his fangs into my flesh.

The entire world is burnt to nothing. I'm consumed by an inferno. Its sluggish flames destroy me, but they destroy the safeguards too. Power pushes past pain. My chest swells with vengeful lust, then my limbs. It pounds beneath my skin, its cage, and finally explodes from my Marrow Mark.

The Monster and all his men yell as they're tossed against the trees. They clamber to their feet, sharp nails dug into tree bark, bleeding and shocked. One doesn't rise. They call for him, but he doesn't move.

They stare at me. They're scared. So am I.

Lilac's gone.

Good.

My Marrow Mark flares. It erratically shifts between blinding and dull as long, emerald fronds bleed from my skin. They move like lightning outside my control.

As my Grounding combats the vampires, my body fights the fire. It's in my chest. My heart betrays me, spreading the poison. It sears the inside of my veins, bakes my blood, my muscle, my bone. It's in my arms and my legs, even my fingers and my toes.

The clearing is fuzzy and far away. The vampires disappear into the woods. Without their proximity, my Grounding shrinks. The stems are too close now. They attack me instead.

I stumble unevenly towards the tree line, but the fire defeats me before I get there. I dissolve into powerless and paralyzed pieces. On the ground, blackness creeps in from the edges of my vision. The moonlight fades away and the leaves go dark. Everything is almost gone when someone turns me onto my back.

It's Lilac. She's crying, shaking my shoulders. The fire is worse where she touches me. I want to tell her to stop, but my lips won't move. The sound I manage to make feels less like a word and more like a wheeze. She says something, but I don't hear her. I think I shake my head. I try to, at least.

The shadows leave a pinhole for me to view the world through in my final seconds. *That's right. These are my final seconds...*

What a pitiful death.

It'll be a sad funeral, but not because I was a magnificent shifter. No, it'll be sad because I never achieved anything. My friends and family will mourn how little I ever accomplished, how unskilled I was. They'll receive condolences, both for my death and my lacking life.

I try to say Lilac's name as the darkness takes over. I have to tell her I love her before I go, but the words don't come out.

The last thing I see is her transformation into a wolf, and her cold snout nuzzling under my hot arm is the last thing I feel before the fire makes even that impossible.

FIVE

LEECHES

It all comes in flashes. Vague combinations of colors and shapes; muddled sounds, voices, and faint sensations. Some are clearer than others.

Trees speed by. I'm bounced atop something. Soft. Furry. A wolf. *Lilac*. There comes a weeping howl, trailed by many more. In the distance, the wind roars a dark, ominous song. It calls out to me.

My parents' faces mix with the dreamlike visions. Their expressions are blurry, but I see pain. Mom sobs.

Dad, too. That must be his hand holding mine. It's so big and warm. They say something, but it's too jumbled.

Lilac reappears. She's sadder now. Her parents are at her side. They clasp her arms and gently pull her away. I try to reach for her. My body won't move.

In between familiar faces and long, maddening stretches of blackness, come other images. Skeletal hands, limbs, and bodies claw to the front of my mind. Bones try to break out of skin; hungry mouths stretch wide, bloody fangs bared; a crimson moon.

The flashes stop. The fire burns itself to near nothingness, leaving only its ghost: a hot and barren feeling in my throat. That's all there is for a while.

Eventually, the nothingness is disturbed.

The world shakes and shudders in slow, sweeping movements. Is that gravel pattering the underside of a car? A tire roving onto asphalt? Vibrations humming? The booming clatter of heavy metal? And those are brakes, aren't they? They let loose a screech, abruptly ending the assault on my senses.

I open my eyes. Darkness persists.

A door slams and voices ricochet in the air. Their muffled conversation is carried by echoing footsteps. They amble past but come to a halt nearby, hidden in the shadows. A third voice is carried closer from the distance.

Who are they? I wonder.

Monsters, my fear answers.

Terror holds my breath captive.

A pillar of light splits the darkness. It's slim at first, but fattens and scares the shadows to the farthest corners of the room—the back of a truck? I try to hide as well, but my body is manacled to the ground. It must be the darkness pinning me! I yank on my arms and legs. Not darkness. Metal bands.

A man's hulking silhouette emerges from the light, doused in black. His shoulders are broad, and his meaty hands spur countless memories of my own puny fingers wrapped in another's.

Dad?

My eyes adjust. It isn't Dad, but they look close in age. His black hair is pulled back into a high bun that show-cases his prominent, straight nose, and his almond shaped green eyes. A well-trimmed beard heartens the sturdy shape of his jaw. The sleeves of his faded, green flannel are rolled up his elbows. His arms are marred by a step ladder of scars.

A green pocketknife is hooked to one of his belt loops. No Marrow Mark?

He motions to one of the figures behind him. The shackles release me from their biting grip.

My arms tremble as I lift myself up. They ache. It's mostly tolerable, with one exception: a shooting spider web of pain on the side of my neck. I touch it. My fingers are met by heat and gauze.

"I suspect it might scar." He gently breaches the uncomfortable silence.

I stare at him through my hair. With a close-lipped smile and amiable eyes, he eases closer. He cautiously extends a hand to me. I thoughtlessly take it. He opens his mouth again, and his fangs poke out.

Fear explodes in my chest. It throws me back, away from the stranger, fueled by the gasoline burning in my neck. The ache spread thin throughout my body is suddenly outmatched by memories of visceral pain. All I see are fangs framed by wicked sneers. I'm a captive again, a victim, a corpse, a meal.

He lags closer and blabbers poisonous words. I won't let him hurt me like the others.

Still, he's adamant. He holds his hands up like I'm a feral animal. He gives me another misleading smile.

Leech.

"I understand why you're afraid." He attempts to reason.

I snarl.

He whispers. "I promise you, you're safe."

"Stay away." I croak, but the words aren't right.

My mouth feels foreign. I run my tongue across my teeth, startled by my newly sharpened canines. They were *always* sharp, but it's never been this extreme; this piercing; this chilling.

My neck sizzles with the memory of the Monster's fangs.

That's not possible.

My past instructors echo in my head, *a vampire's bite always kills us.*

Except, I'm not dead! I press one of my elongated fangs into my fingertip. The coppery flavor of blood scorches my taste buds. I shake my head. *No.* Blood trickles down my finger. Denial transforms into unnerved rapture.

"This is a shock," he says too compassionately. "It undoubtedly—"

"What *is* this?" I slam my fists on the floor.

He takes a step. "If you would please—"

"*What is this?*" The mightiness of my yell is shrunk to a hoarse squawk.

He grimaces solemnly. "You've been turned."

"That doesn't make any sense." I deny. "I'm a shifter."

He shakes his head. "I know it's hard to understand. If you come with me, *calmly,* I can correct your confusion."

"You're lying."

"Do your fangs lie as well?"

Glowering, I look down at my Marrow Mark. It's the symbol of my dedication to Mother Nature, to the Earth.

Vampires are the polar opposite of everything I am. They're children of the Night, abusers of the world's magical energy, hungry for and empowered by blood. They're kept far, far away from human society, from shifters, from innocent people, and still they seek to do harm. Now... I'm one of them?

The universe presses in on me. I slump under the weight.

"What's your name?" the stranger asks.

"Macy."

"I'm Valberg Marshal." He offers another one of those smiles. "Will you please come with me, Macy?"

He holds his hand out once more, light glittering in from behind him. His words are honeyed with lies. He's can't be genuine. He's a vampire. A trickster. But what other option is there?

I take his hand. He pulls me out of the van, onto my legs. They're heavy, almost numb. My ankles feel unstable, and I'm worried one of them might snap. If not, then maybe a knee.

Valberg supports me as he leads us through an indoor parking lot. The ceiling is supported by concrete pillars and checkered with white, rectangular lights. They singe my eyelids with fading flashes every time I blink. The ground is unnaturally smooth, as if every possible lump has been paved from its gray surface. I miss the gravel and the dirt.

We're outnumbered by cars and trucks. A door slams behind us, and I glance back. The truck I was delivered in revs to life. The metal garage door opens with a clatter loud enough to rival it. The truck disappears down a road flanked by night, dry grass, and trees.

"Where are we?" I rasp.

"A long way from home," he attempts to joke.

I narrow my eyes. "And how far is that?"

"Arizona."

During our early studies, shifters learn each of the states and which ones belong to which packs. Of the five packs, Arizona is overseen by…

"Knotweed?"

He chuckles under his breath. "You figured that out quite quickly. I should've expected as much. Shifters are always well-versed in their own culture."

"Yeah, well." I shrug. "I'm not as familiar with vampire culture. What coven is this? The only Knotweed facility I know about is Amianthi."

Amianthi is one of the largest vampire covens across the world, renowned for its strict shifter administrators and even stricter laws. Unlike most covens, which are built like towns, Amianthi is more like a prison. The worst of the worst vampires are sent there. They're the most scheming, underhanded the Man in the Moon has to offer.

It's a testament to shifter power that those monsters could be restrained. Children are taken on field trips to admire the facility, and even adults visit to be swept away by the valor and prestige.

"That I expected." He laughs. "However, no. This is a smaller, more modest place. Welcome to Devil's Trumpet."

"How inviting," I mutter under my breath.

"Your people are responsible for that," Valberg says, his tone more educational than snappish.

I ignore him. If vampires wanted the right to name their own cities, then their ancestors shouldn't have betrayed Mother Nature. But they did, and now they huddle together in covens named after poisonous plants.

Valberg guides me to a door guarded by two gammas.

They remind me of Dad. He wore a uniform like theirs. I always thought it resembled human military garb too much. Probably because they have to travel so much more than the average shifter. Their Marrow Marks radiate dim light where they're visible.

My mother used to sparkle as she sang me to sleep. That was before her attack. Dad did the same when he read to me. Lilac was by far the easiest to catch. There have been lots of nights her naked body lit up in the dark.

This is not that kind of glow. It's enough to catch the eye, not enough to blind. An unspoken threat. For the first time in my life, a shifter makes me uneasy.

I study the one nearest to me as we cross the threshold from garage to hallway, but shame averts my eyes. Even that is too much, apparently, because the gamma snatches my arm and throws me forward. My heart jumps. I lose my shaky footing, and nearly fall to the floor.

Valberg catches me. He's much gentler. It's a disconcerting contrast.

He holds a hand up to the gamma, shaking his head. She doesn't flinch, but she doesn't advance on him either.

"That's enough," he declares. "Your job is to *defend*, not defile."

He ushers me further into the hall where two more leeches wait.

The woman is short and plump with a hooded brown gaze. Her raven black hair is cut in an uneven A-line. Her prominent round features are sharpened by her pointed chin and dramatic eyeliner.

In comparison, the man is towering, but slender. His braided platinum hair tapers at the breast pocket of his pale-blue dress shirt. His sleeves are rolled up to mid forearm. They're mottled in several scars like Valberg's, but his are faded and white, not puckered and pink.

The woman spots us and smiles warmly. "We were just debating if we should come get you."

"Didn't trust my abilities?" Valberg chuckles.

"Quite the opposite." The other man fiddles with the motley jewels around his neck. "We just did not trust the shifters to comply so easily."

Valberg snickers.

My chest swells with the pride of my people, sturdy and strong like the trunk of a tree. It echoes into my limbs, my branches. A remark wells in my throat...but it's tempered by that gamma's fingers. They were steely and cold like the Monster's.

I don't say anything. Guilt follows.

The woman scans me. I scowl at her.

"I'm sorry," she says. "Your people aren't kind to new-comers, but apparently neither are we. I'm Pyera, the Lady of Devil's Trumpet. This is Cleon, the Lord. We're...the vampire equivalent of Alphas, minus *most* of the politics." She gestures to Valberg. "You've already met our Grand Enchanter. He also helps oversee new arrivals."

"Your Alphas would not consider his presence synonymous with leadership," Cleon says, "but he helps keep the coven afloat."

"Come." Pyera sidles down the hall. "Let's continue this conversation elsewhere."

The rest of the building is quiet, or maybe they purposely lead me down isolated hallways. When we do cross other vampires, whose invasive eyes cannot be averted, Cleon and Valberg frame Pyera and me like a barrier. Pyera opens one of many doors and holds it open for me.

Almost as a rule, everything is black, gray, red, or a cousin of the three. The walls are black, lightened by silver filigree patterns. The glossy hardwood floor is similarly dark, but tinted red. It reflects the golden lights above. There's a desk at the center of the room. There are books everywhere. Photos, random trinkets and collectables, and several vases of roses.

"Have a seat," Pyera says as we file into the rose-scented room.

Cleon pulls one of the chairs from the side of the room. He motions for me to sit. I cautiously study him, his fangs, the chair, before I finally obey. He leans a leg against the desk, where Pyera settles.

Behind me, Valberg speaks softly to someone. I turn around to see who, but they scurry away. The door is shut with a quiet sigh, and the Grand Enchanter glides closer, a steaming mug in his hand. He gives it to me.

I flare my nostrils. "What is it?"

"Tea," he says. "For your throat."

I stare warily into the rich brew. I inhale deeply. My skin pricks with a giddy wave of electricity. Every hair stands straight. My head spins and my throat blazes. How long has it been since I drank or ate anything? The memory of berries is flavorless compared to this. My lips are magnetized to the warm, white glass.

Sugary bliss pours into me. I groan in satisfaction. The fire and ache waver. Then they scorch ten times stronger. I let loose a desperate growl. I need more, so I tip my head back and guzzle it all. More, more, *more*. There is nothing else. No air. No thoughts. No world. Then there's no tea left. My lungs seize.

I lurch forward with a ragged gasp for air. Streaks of reddish-brown slide down the sides of the mug. I lick it clean. I need *more*.

"More," I echo.

"I'll have someone deliver another cup." Pyera lifts the phone from its hub on her desk. Into the speaker, she says, "Hi. I need someone to run up a cup of tea, please...? Uhuh. Yes. Spiked."

"Spiked?" I glance at the mug. "Like alcohol?"

"No." She fights a frown. "Spiked like blood."

"*What?*" I throw the cup. It shatters on the floor, a dozen pretty pieces glistening under golden lights. "You made me drink blood?"

Pyera barely nods. "Your body requires it."

"You made me drink *blood!*" I rise from my seat.

"Macy, please," she begs.

Valberg puts a hand on my shoulder to gently guide me back down. Cleon grabs a broom and dustpan. He hastily sweeps up the mess I made, looking neither surprised nor bothered. They do this a lot.

"Your body requires it," Pyera hurries to say. "It's essential you get those nutrients this soon after your metamorphosis."

"I don't care!"

"We do." Her softness shushes me.

I slouch in defeat. Valberg retracts his touch. I mutter, "How do you know my name?"

She folds her hands in front of her. "Alphas Althea and Garth gave us your file."

I glance at her. "Just tell me what's going on."

"I know this is all very confusing," Pyera says.

"Understatement of the century." I snort.

Her lips turn up, marginally amused.

"How is this possible?" I demand. "It's not supposed to be."

"It was never *im*possible," Valberg says. "Most of your people are uninformed, but your leaders are certainly aware. I suspect your doctors as well."

I glower. "Why wouldn't they tell us?"

"I suppose that's a hard question to answer." He rubs his thumb over his elbow. "We could attribute it to many things. Racial tensions, the power of misinformation, the uproar the truth could cause...the list is too extensive to recite, frankly."

"That doesn't make me feel better," I tell him pointedly.

"We are aware," Cleon interjects. "I doubt anything will. You will have to get used to it."

I glare at him.

"That's why we're here." Pyera warms the mood. "Our goal is to make your transition as seamless as possible. We look after and protect each of our charges, and now you're one of them. If you need anything, then we'll do our absolute best to provide it."

"Alright," I say instantly. "I need to contact my parents."

They all share looks of sadness, and I know I won't be going home any time soon.

"I'm serious," I reiterate.

Pyera sighs. "We.... can't allow that."

A rush of anger twists my voice. "Didn't you *just* say you would do your best to give me what I need?"

"Allow me to elaborate." Cleon holds up a hand. "We will provide you what you need within established boundaries, but we cannot overstep the guidelines that have been put in place by *your* people."

"What are you talking about?" I dig my nails into my palms. My stomach twists in knots.

Pyera stares at her hands, and Cleon clears his throat. They send each other a glance out of the corner of their eyes before turning to me. The Lady makes inescapable eye contact.

"You can't contact your family, your friends, or anyone from your life before because...as far as they're aware, you're dead."

Her words crack like lightning and sting like a whip. The puzzle pieces don't fit together. It couldn't have been more than a day ago! I ate dinner with Mom and Dad. I raced through woods around Hydrilla and held Lilac's hand. A few hours at most! They have to know I'm alive!

My eyes trickle with tears. I blink them away.

"What about the Alphas?" I cling to my last string of hope. "They sent you my file. They know I'm alive. They won't let you keep me here!"

"Miss Braddock, it is they who sent you here," Cleon says in a milder voice. "Whatever their reasons, you, and those like you, are secrets they cannot afford getting out. That is why you are here. Devil's Trumpet is an underwhelming coven about 3,000 miles away from Hydrilla. You will never be discovered by another shifter here."

"What about the gammas?" I motion to the door.

"They've sworn a vow of secrecy," Valberg tells me regretfully.

"So...What?" I demand. "That's it? I get swept under the rug?"

The Enchanter purses his lips, eyes tight with sadness. "That's not the case."

"It seems that way!" My fury encases tender heartbreak. "Why didn't they just kill me?"

Pyera frowns. "Why don't they kill any vampire? Why keep us locked away? Your people worship Mother Nature, the giver of life. Why would they take what she gave you?"

"Like you know anything about *giving life*," I snap.

Her grimace deepens. "We'll do our very best to accommodate you here, Macy, but we are prohibited from allowing you any access to the Packs."

I stand, fists clenched, muscles taut with unkempt emotions. All I want to do is find somewhere secluded, and hide, safe from the world and its maiming truths.

"Where am I supposed to go?" I growl.

"We have already prepared an apartment for you," Cleon says. "It has been paid for and stocked by the coven. We hope it is suitable, but if you have any complaints, we will be happy to listen, and, with any luck, oblige."

"I'll show you the way," Valberg says.

"Thank you, Macy, for...*trying* to understand. It will get easier, I promise..." Pyera says as I turn toward the door. Her voice is a consoling hand on my back. "Before you leave..."

Valberg's hand hesitates on the doorknob. His face is a war of logic and apprehension.

"...You should wait for that second cup of tea," Pyera finishes.

My body is wrought with eerie temptation. I more than need it. I *want* it. The fire burns hotter. I shiver in disgust.

"No." I stare at my feet.

"As you wish." There's a frown in her voice.

"This way, Macy." Valberg holds the door open.

I follow him into my new existence.

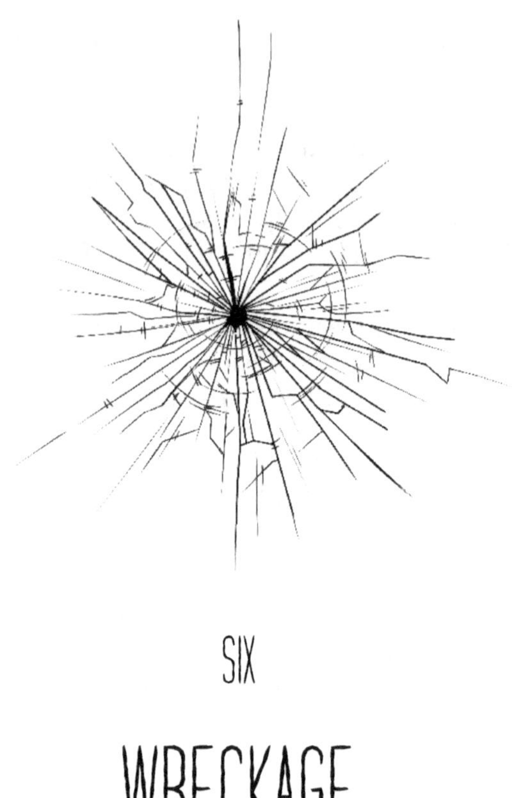

SIX

WRECKAGE

I clutch the keys and run my other hand along the wall. Cautiously, I edge further into *"my"* apartment. The cold, hardwood floor creaks. It's all too clean, untouched, distant. It's all mine and yet none of it is.

Eyes closed, I count to three. The empty loft is still there. So am I. Traitorous tears threaten to fall.

"Macy," Valberg says from the doorway.

I don't look at him.

"You need time." His voice softens further. It lingers as if to say *I know it hurts, but you will heal.*

A silent snarl twists my upper lip.

There's an odd clatter. I peek over my shoulder. He withdraws his hand from the table beside the door.

"A cellphone." A phantom smile flickers on his mouth. "The Lord, Lady's, and my phone numbers are all there. Have you ever used one?"

I shake my head.

"I'll stop by tomorrow. I'll bring food and walk you through it." There's a lengthy pause. He wants me to say something; I want him to leave. "It's time I go."

Yes, it is. "Okay."

"Whatever you need," he reminds me.

He waits for a response but doesn't receive one, so, with a sigh, he shuts the door. Then it's just me and my grief caged in this apartment. By shifters. Not vampires.

The Alphas know, and they don't care. My entire life has been dedicated to Mother Nature, the Earth, to serving her soils and worshiping her spirit. I studied with the other pack mates. I listened to their lies—I *believed* them—and here I am. Macy Braddock. A vampire. A leech. Less than an *omega*. Alive, when I should be dead.

I wish I was.

A scream splits me in half. I am two parts: fury and sorrow. I hammer my fist into the wall. The keys bite into my palm. Heartache swells under my skin. It needs out, and, if I don't bleed it from my body first, it'll burst free.

I become a storm. Chucking the keys aside, I kick over tables, chairs, and shelves. There's a clock—ticking, ticking, laughing, laughing. At me. I tear it down to stomp on it. I throw open the cabinets, shattering plates and cups on the floor. Toothy shards of glass are strewn about, fangs hungry to tear into my flesh.

In the bathroom, I knock everything off the counters. Toothpaste, bars of soap, brushes, and hand-towels. They clatter a frantic beat as they plummet and hit the linoleum hard. "Essentials," but none of it is essential to me.

My reflection pulls me in.

White lights glare down on her. She's covered in bandages and bruises, cuts, and scrapes. She breathes raggedly. A sheet of sweat glistens on her forehead. Her eyes are red and puffy. Her cheeks are wet. The fire in her eyes is nearly put out.

She wears Mother Nature's artwork. *I* wear her artwork.

I watch my reflection, waiting. My Marrow Mark will come to life. It'll glow brighter than it ever has because I am a *shifter*. My soul harbors a beast, a wolf, the power of the divine Earth. I was born to serve. Mother Nature wouldn't strip me of that privilege, so I concentrate.

"Aimil," I murmur. "Aimil, please."

I dive into the depths of my broken spirit, looking for any sign of her, the beast, or myself, but, when I open my eyes, I only see a mistake. I grimace at her, at *it*, until I can't look at it any longer.

I barge into the bedroom, ripping the sheets off the mattress. The pillows leap away in fear. The entire frame wobbles.

I dart back to the bathroom and climb onto the counter. My fingers shake as I cover the mirror. The sobs return. She's a stranger with my face, my Marrow Mark, my body: the echo of a stolen life. I hate her.

Once she's hidden, I stumble from the bathroom.

Monstrous sorrow unfurls. It crawls out from under my skin, and, with its heavy hands, embraces me into its dark core. All alone with my sadness, I collapse in the middle of the wreckage.

On the wall, rays of sunshine glitter gaps in the blinds. It's diluted by the tinted windows. Tinted for my *protection*. How ridiculous. I was kissed by the Earth and the

Sun at birth, and now, were it not for shadowed glass, the day would burn me to my bones.

I lift a hand. Light grazes my fingertips like a breath of familiar warmth.

I will find a way home.

SEVEN

NOCTURNAL NORMAL

The Wall is colossal. It surrounds all of Devil's Trumpet. Some nights, I creep along it, searching for a crack to chip away at.

The gammas are well versed in vampire rebellion. My unabashed but ill-conceived attempts at insurgence are nothing more than a meager hassle. It's insulting. But, after a month of trying and failing, my personal revolt devolves into hopelessness.

And, what if I did escape? What would I even do? Run? Like always? I don't have the paws to carry me anymore and the wind hasn't sung to me in weeks. Even if either were still present, where would I go? Mom, Dad, Lilac; they all think I'm dead.

I follow the sidewalk back into town.

The coven isn't *entirely* hideous. Sidewalks snake between low-rise buildings crammed closely together, and trees scatter in plots along the pavement. They're detached from the woods on all edges of the coven but kept company by radiant streetlights.

The occasional car zooms by, and throngs of people saunter along sidewalks, passing mismatched storefronts. Locally owned businesses neighbor larger franchises, the result of shifter negotiations with well-connected, influential humans. Among the mingling cultures, the occasional shifter shop asserts itself.

The Desert Willow is one such lounge.

Off-Duty gammas lounge behind doors barred by a sign which reads *Shifter Only Establishment*. They tip their heads back, bouncing their shoulders with laughter. I envision the youthful image of Dad seated among them, flaunting his freedoms behind windows in Aconite, a Bloodroot coven. Does he know about people like me?

I sigh through my nose as I enter Cinnamon's Café.

The cramped red and white diner welcomes me inside with a chime. Scattered about booths and tables, vampires chatter. Their voices tangle with static-warbled music, the television behind the counter, and the loud clangs and clanks from the kitchen.

As I stand in line, waiting for it to dissolve, I catch movement in my peripherals. In every corner, sleek white cameras watch us. Their tiny red lights blink, a message from the gammas in Morse Code. *We're watching, always and forever.* I glare into one.

"Miss?" The cashier catches my attention.

"Oh!" I startle. The line is gone. I rush to the register. "Sorry!"

"The usual?" His smile is oddly genuine. "Spiked?"

A frown twitches on my mouth. The searing heat in my throat burns. I nod my head without meeting his eyes. His smile turns reassuring as he takes my cash, and rings me up. I sign the receipt before he bustles to fill a Styrofoam cup for me.

Taking it, I settle into one of the empty tables, glancing at my phone. Luc should've been here by now.

The Lord, Lady, and Grand Enchanter all made it a habit to visit me during the first few weeks. Cleon was the least eager to stop by. He isn't the doting type. But Pyera and Valberg visited more frequently, though Pyera tallies the highest number. She likes to cart me around on errands. Usually, we take a detour to the mall.

Although they've all done their best to help me *"acclimate,"* it's clear they aren't best suited to handle me. Enter Luc. According to Valberg, he's another shifter turned vampire. We're rare, but apparently the Alphas like to congregate us in a select few covens. Apparently, that's supposed to help acclimation, too.

I stare at the door. Hopefully, he'll alleviate my discomfort about sitting alone in a café full of vampires by appearing from thin air. No such luck.

There's a prickle on the back of my neck. Eyes. Watching me. That's normal. Vampires stare. So do gammas. *Everyone* does.

Across the room, a vampire with a red beanie slouches alone in a booth. He watches me, unabashed even after I spot him. *Just another vampire*, I tell myself. My gut says otherwise.

He exudes something terrible. Something dark. There's a predatory glint in his gaze. *Dangerous* is written across his scowl.

A stranger moves between us. Uncaring, he leans forward. A silver crescent moon dangles from his neck. There's a red tint to it.

I stand, cup in hand, and dart out the door—right into Luc.

"Whoa!" He braces both my arms. His blue eyes sparkle with amusement. "Where are you off to, Tenderfoot? You're not standing me up, I hope!"

I glance at the boy. He stares at his hands, frowning deeply. I turn back to Luc.

He cocks his head at my expression. "What? Aren't you happy to see me?"

"You're late," I grumble as I shake loose of his grasp. We move away from the door.

He swipes a hand through his auburn hair, and smiles. His crooked nose makes it lopsided. "Thought you might need a little more time to put on your big girl pants and smile."

I can't help but grin. "Did you get lost or something?"

"I was distracted." He produces a crumpled napkin from his pocket, and hands it to me. A string of numbers is hastily scribbled above a girl's name.

"Samantha? Isn't this the third girl in two weeks?"

He rubs the back of his neck. "Uh, yeah. But Sam has beautiful blue eyes, Macy!"

"Your weakness," I snort.

"Your sarcasm borders on searing," he says.

I stare at the paper a moment longer. Lilac dashes through my thoughts. We were never strangers. When our fathers were young, mine saved hers from dying at the hands of a crafty rogue. After that, they shared an unbreakable bond. So, Lily, Lilac and I all grew up together. Come adolescence, Lilac and I sought romance elsewhere before we found affection with each other. A pang of overwhelming sadness invades my heart. I hand back the paper.

He frowns. "You okay?"

I chew my lip. "Yeah, sorry."

"You don't look too hot. You've been feeding, right?"

"Yes, Luc." I raise my cup prove it.

"You've been drinking the blood Val brings you, right?"

"Yes, Luc."

He holds his hands up, then jabs my side. I swat at him. "It's just hard to tell sometimes with those ten-ton bags under your eyes!"

"What would I ever do without you?" I laugh. "Always inflating my ego."

He snickers before genuine concern softens his face. "For real, what's up?"

"I'm just tired," I say. "I haven't slept well since I got here."

Then again, I haven't slept well since I was a kid.

"Huh." He strokes his scruffy chin. "Do you have nightmares? Or do you just have trouble falling asleep?"

Both. Falling asleep is hard enough. But when I do, the Monster haunts my dreams. They're the kind of nightmares I only remember in blips and glimpses, but never entirely.

I rub the scar on my throat. "Why does it matter?"

He says, "Valberg could make you something to help."

"He can do that?"

"Dude!" He jumps in front of me. "He's not called Grand Enchanter for nothin'. He can charm almost anything—well, anything the Pack says he can. Trouble falling asleep? Wham! A sleep enchantment stronger than Nyquil."

"He's that good?"

"Oh yeah!"

"Even with all those restrictions?"

"Yeah!" he says. "Val is a by the books kind of guy, anyway, but he can work some crazy magic around those rules."

I feel the Monster's breath on my throat. "That's scary."

"What?" Luc looks surprised. "Nah. Honestly, they restrict him too much.

I purse my lips. "You aren't just born with the ability to manipulate blood without a few limitations, natural or imposed. Sometimes the rules don't even work."

His lips turn down. There's unspoken irritation in his eyes. I ignore it.

"So, I was thinking..." He changes the subject. "It's about time I introduced you to my some of my friends...or, well, one of them."

I bite my lip to hold back a smirk. "I was about to say I wasn't sure you had more than one."

He grips his shirt like he's been wounded. "She strikes again! I need to start carrying Band-Aids whenever we hang. It's starting to hurt."

I chuckle at him.

"You've been cooped up in that apartment for too long," he says. "It's about time I show you all the wonders of vampire civilization."

"I'm fine," I joke. "I've got things I need to do anyway."

"Right." He grins. "I bet it's hard to find time away from sulking around your apartment."

"I only sulk half the time." I tip my chin up.

"And the other half?"

My shoulders sag. "I've been trying to reconnect with my Grounding.

"Oh."

"Have you ever reached yours?" I ask him, but his silence says it all.

Aimil has always been there, roaming the deepest segments of my soul. I may have been too weak to utilize her, but there was never a moment I didn't sense her. Without her, I can't serve the Earth.

"Don't worry," he says, picking up on my stormy thoughts. "It'll get better."

His smile isn't optimistic. It's gloomy. We both know I probably won't ever shift again. The word *probably* is but a spark of futile hope.

"Are you ready to go?" he asks

"Go?" I shoot him a look. "Aren't we here?" I motion to the café.

"Oh, Macy, you gullible thing, Cinnamon's was just a ploy to get you out of the house!" He grins. "We have somewhere else to be."

"You said Cinnamon's the other day," I say sternly.

"I know what I said." He concurs. "I lied."

I give him a look. "Okay, great. Then where are we going?"

"The library," he declares with his chest puffed out. At my lack of response, he deflates like a balloon. "What's that face for?"

"Nothing!" I hold my hands up. "I've just never been a big fan of books."

"I guess it's a good thing we're not checking anything out," he grumbles.

EIGHT

RAVENS, EAGLES, AND BULLS

The library is *big. Really* big.

All the windows scale more than one story. A tower stands a level taller, topped with a glass dome. It catches and refracts glints of moonlight like a crown. Inside, the orderly aisles are endless. Each bookcase is embellished with thin, sloping metal bands, and crammed tightly with books. There are so many. I doubt even the oldest vampire has read them all.

The library itself is divided into three sections. To my left, *Fiction* and to my right, *Non-Fiction*, each guarded by a gargantuan archway with its name embossed across the top. Straight ahead, *History* is nestled at the base of the tower. Another archway bears its name.

"Fancy, huh?" Luc's smile is small, amused. "I thought you'd like it."

Gawking I nod and walk a little further. He tugs my arm before I get far.

Startled, I demand. "What?"

His smile grows. He shakes his head. "We have to check in first."

"We do?" I ask. "Isn't that weird? We never do that at Cinnamon's."

"Maybe it's weird somewhere else," he says, "but it's normal here. The gammas need to keep track of everyone in case anyone goes rogue. It's better than the collars. Or the trackers. Some old vampires still have theirs."

I follow him to the front desk.

"Also," he says, "we *do* have to at Cinnamon's. We all sign the receipt for a reason."

I look at him uncertainly. "But we used to be shifters."

"That's not a good thing around here." He points to one of the many gammas stationed about. I hadn't noticed them before, but now I see them. Everywhere.

The woman at the desk looks up from the book in her hands and studies us. Her beady eyes narrow into a scowl. I purse my lips.

"We're here to sign in." He gives a friendly smile.

Her chilly demeanor perseveres. "Are you teaching her how to read?"

Luc laughs it off but it's not funny.

"Excuse me?" I lean forward on my elbows.

"It's just a question, dear." The woman claims in a honeyed voice. "Shifters are known for their brute strength. Not their intelligence."

"I know how to read." I inform through gritted teeth. "But *thank you* for your concern."

She rolls her eyes, looking back to Luc who is so rigid he might shatter. "Someone already checked you in. You'll both have to sign."

I glare as she hands him a tablet. It's like the ones the gammas carry. It flashes a prompt, asking for a signature.

"No problem." Luc agrees while I choke on a million and two snide remarks.

He scrawls his name, then hands it to me. It sits strangely in my hands, so I set it down on the desk to write. I make sure to print my name precisely, so each letter is stubbornly perfect. I slide it across the desktop.

"I know how to write too." I enlighten her. "In case you were worried."

"Oooookay." Luc grasps my arms and steers me away, spewing apologies.

I shrug his hands off, gaping at him. "Stop saying sorry! I'm *not* sorry."

"Yeah, I know *you* aren't." He hisses. "But we're the ones who're outnumbered here, Macy."

"That lady was being rude," I exclaim.

"Yeah, she was, but that's something you have to get used to. Some vampires aren't keen on shifters, former or present."

"Well I'm not keen on them *ever*." I bite back.

He looks me in the eye. "You're one of them, Tender-foot."

I glance away. We cross into *History*.

Nestled in the tower, the walls are lined with shelves instead of windows. They climb all three levels to the dome. A walkway wraps around each of the upper levels. People sit on the steps, lean over their books, or against the wooden guardrails. Others browse for anything that might pique their curiosity.

The ground floor is more of a common area.

A tan-skinned, chubby rocker sits sideways in one of the Queen Anne Chairs. She spots us, and waves excitedly. She smiles wide, parading her fangs and creasing her teak wood eyes. Freckles scatter across her button nose, from which a gold septum piercing hangs.

Luc waves back and I give a shyer gesture.

"Macy, this is—"

"Circi." She hops to her feet, honey blonde pigtails bouncing. She extends a hand. I shake it. "Luc said something about a new cub. It's nice you've come out of your wolf den."

"So he talks about me." I grin wryly.

A devious smile flirts with Circi's mouth. "Oh. All the time."

I laugh. "Nothing too honest?"

Luc bats his eyes at me. "Only how cruel you are. All those rebuttals are daggers to the heart."

Circi snickers. "Riiight. No. He's gushed about you like you're a puppy. He's got a new shifter friend. He's so excited." She pats his head.

He swats her hand. "Don't sell me out!"

"Sorry, Luc." I nudge him. "You're not my type."

His groan becomes a laugh. "It's just nice having someone other than Terces around."

Circi's eyes go big with curiosity. "Actually, how is that old bat?"

"Who?" I ask.

"She's the coven's resident psycho..." She taps her chin. "Well, one of them."

I lean closer. "There's more than one?"

Luc gives Circi look that says *cut it out.*

"She deserves to know." She shrugs flippantly.

"Yeah, but—"

"I also *want* to know." I interject.

Luc tips his head back and flings an arm over his eyes. He motions for Circi to continue. "Fine. But not all vampires are like this. Okay, Macy?"

I turn back to Circi. "Fill me in."

"Oooh, Luc, you know I love when you bring me gossipers." She rubs her hands together. "Terces is weird. I heard she wasn't always like that, but she's been making people's lives harder for as long as I can remember."

"How long has she been here?"

"Twenty years," Luc says, lowering his arm.

Circi rests her elbows on her knees. "Her favorite pastimes include long, creepy walks through the woods, trespassing at shifter venues, *vandalizing* said venues. If she didn't talk to herself and threaten random people, I'd join her"

"Charming." I scoff.

"That's me." She grins. "Princess Charming."

My mirth morphs into cautious curiosity. "Why is she like that?"

Luc clears his throat and strokes his thumb across his eyebrow.

"What?" I look between them.

Circi whispers. "The Sunlight Chambers."

Anxiously, they glance over their shoulders and huddle closer.

"They're these cement cellars with iron bars over the top." Luc clarifies. "Cages, I guess. Gammas used to throw vampires in there. They'd leave them out during sunrise...You know, so the sun..." His breath hitches. "Usually, they covered them up fast."

"But not Terces." Circi sours. "They left her out for hours..."

Stiffening, I stare at my hands. I imagine my skin—red and pocked with welts, dripping like candlewax. Bile brews in my stomach. I squeeze my eyes shut and shake myself loose of those images.

Luc gingerly touches my shoulder. "Terces was the last one. Covens all over were trying to get the Chambers decommissioned. That was the final straw."

Circi throws herself backward in her seat, arms flung out. "Terces Redloh, driven insane by shifters just like all the other whackos. One day, we'll all be crazy."

"One, there aren't *that* many. And, two, no we won't." He places a hand on his chest. "I, for one, am very sane and plan on staying that way."

She scoffs. As she looks at me, her eyes are drawn toward the entrance. "Speak of the devil."

Curiously, I glance over my shoulder. Luc does too. We both snap forward immediately. All I need to see: hoodie, red hat, dark hair, darker eyes, a crescent moon necklace that glitters crimson under the skylight. This time, I notice the pocketknife hooked to his belt. Goosebumps pebble my arms.

Did he follow me all the way here?

No. Of course not. But I feel his eyes. Again. I shudder.

Luc eyes me. "Macy?"

"Who *is* that?" I ask under my breath.

"Nico Navarro." Circi snarls. "Aka resident psycho number two."

Luc's face twists with uncharacteristic ferocity. "Has he bothered you?"

"I saw him earlier, but he was just...*staring* at me." I chew the inside of my cheek. "Like I was *food.*"

Luc growls. He dips his head marginally closer. "Don't mess with him. He's bad news."

Yes. It's written all over him.

Circi touches the top of my hand. "*Really* bad news. He's reclusive, violent, temperamental, holds a grudge, and has a disturbing obsession with knives. It makes sense with his mommy-daddy issues. Just last year he..." She glances at Luc. "Nevermind. You'd just think the Man in the Moon would have better tastes. But for whatever reason, he made that guy one of his soothsayers."

"I'm sorry. Soothsay...what?" I fumble.

"There's this legend," says Luc, "that because the Man in the Moon is seated in the sky, he sees all possible futures for the Earth. Good and bad."

"The Prophet of Fortune," Circi says, "and the Prophet of Misfortune. One for the good, one for the bad. Nico got lucky. He sees the good futures."

I squint at him, head cocked. "Shouldn't that be *Mother Nature's* job?"

"You know how it goes. She sees through the animals around us, so her sight is limited to them. They say he'd let her perish, but his creations, us, reside on her Earth. So, he gives two vampires the gift of divine foresight. He's done it for...I don't know how long. When one of them dies," Luc explains, "the gift of foresight is passed onto someone else, but the Man in the Moon didn't choose another soothsayer when the last one died. Or if he did, no one's come forward."

"How come I haven't heard of this before?" I furrow my eyebrows.

Luc smiles gently. "I think we've established the Packs aren't always forthcoming with information."

I rub my tired eyes. Whatever. "So, Nico is one of the soothsayers. Despite his reputation. That's—"

"Totally shitty, right?" Circi says. "Not to mention, he's not even a Pureblood. Not that it matters, but the Prophets have only ever been Purebloods. Kinda sucks that the one thing specific to us is..."

Luc gives her a look. She purses her lips.

Pureblood. The vampires that are born, not bitten. The elite among the dirt. Luc: bitten. Circi: Pureblood.

Luc's eyes are cold. "Just stay away from him. He's not worth the grief."

I spare a glance at Nico. He's focused on the book in his hands. His knuckles are white against his brown skin, contorting the paperback.

Luc gets to his feet, jarring me. The skin around his eyes flexes as he thinks, faraway.

I study him. "Are you okay?"

"Yeah…" The agitation on the edges of his expression softens. "I need some food; it's not too late to hit Cinnamon's again is it?"

"You just want to hit on that girl again." Circi glares at him suspiciously.

He wags a finger at her. "I found a new love of my life. Thank you very much! Besides, Macy is the one in need of a pretty girl." He nudges me. "I'll help you snag some digits. Not to toot my own horn, but I'm a great wingman."

"Tell that to my high school boyfriend." Circi rolls her eyes. You know, the one I didn't have. Because you scared them all away."

He shushes her.

"I was there earlier." I shrug. "I think most of the girls are too busy fawning over you to care about me."

Circi gasps. "Lucas!"

"I'm irresistible!"

I scoff. "Irresistibly smackable."

He clutches his heart.

"I do like the idea of watching you flounder, though." I grin.

She lifts her hand. "I second that motion!"

He mimics us under his breath. "Have a little faith, you guys."

NINE

DAWN

I wake up hyperventilating, sheets stuck to my sweaty body. Only two sounds breach the unnerving silence: the frenzied resonances of my own shallow breaths and my pulse, drumming in my ears. I sit up and glare into the dark.

Where are they?

The Monster and his pawns are nowhere to be found. There's no sign of their fangs glinting in the darkness. No laughter. No blood. No clearing. Just me and my bedroom.

The knife?

Whose throat was it again? It *was* the human's, right? Or was it mine? I tentatively prod my smooth, unmutilated neck. A shaky sigh tumbles off my lips.

Another nightmare.

It's my first coherent thought.

Calm down is the second.

Frail hope dashes in my chest. My fingers skim to side of my neck. The scar grates against my fingertips.

I close my eyes. The nightmare springs to life in my mind. My eyes burst open.

Okay. No sleeping yet. I stare at the ceiling and pick out patterns in the stippled plaster, forcing myself to breathe steadier. Eventually, a great heaviness weighs on my limbs. I sink deeper into the mattress.

The nightmares resurface. *Stay awake,* I tell myself, but my mind is fuzzy around the edges. I fight against the strain to keep my droopy eyelids open. They slide shut anyway.

Is Lilac asleep right now...? No. She always sneaks away at night, seeking new adventures in the woods. Mom and Dad are definitely in bed. Their searches for fun and mischief under the cover of night ended long ago.

I wonder if they saved any of my things. Lilac must have. Maybe that shirt she stole every time she spent the night. Maybe one of my blankets. She always fell asleep bundled up in the bright yellow one, nose nestled in fabric, content as she dreamt. I smile.

I venture from phantasm to phantasm, or maybe they're memories. All those dinners with my parents I used to hate, feel so much more blissful. At Lilac's home, Lily's frostbitten demeanor thaws to lukewarm acceptance, and Lilac chases me through the woods. We heal the old wounds of our love. We apologize for all the ways we've hurt each other. Her lips are a dream within a dream.

Lilac.

She pinches tiny beads between her fingers, whittling finite designs. She offers for me to try. I fail but her laughter consoles me.

A gust tousles her hair. It sings to me. I almost mistake it for Mother Nature, but her carols are tender, affectionate. This is darker. It grazes my skin less like a mother and more like a lover, calling from some place outside these reveries.

Drawn closer to the boundary of sleep, I drift through muted green and pastel brown trees. They move like water, bend like an impressionist painting, and eventually open into that familiar clearing.

This isn't the first time I've visited this week, or even tonight. It *is* the first time I'm not plagued by immediate fear. The human, the blood, the Monster: they're all missing.

The wind beckons me to the center of the glade. There's a voice in its current. A touch, too. I smile at the way it cradles me. It plays with my hair, making fiery strands dance to its haunting hums.

I close my eyes.

There's a promise hidden in the chanting. Whatever gift it might offer, I want. Another draft swivels up my body. It brushes beneath my chin, guiding my face to the sky.

Open your eyes, it murmurs.

I'm riveted by the full moon. The singing stops. The entire world is silent, motionless. The moon, the sky, the dreams are all washed away by flashes of a different realm. It's on fire.

Images fight to take hold. They're seared into my memory with cruel detail, and then burnt away so another can scald.

A forest. I barely recognize it. Hydrilla. Consumed by ravenous flames. The fire devours helpless trees until all that's left is ash and smoke.

The wind whispers ominously:

*...hail and fire, mixed with blood, is thrown to the earth...**

A howling wind blows the flames to the horizon. They consume everything in their wake. Once they reach the skyline, they eat away at the heavens, scorching a hole in the clouds. Blue burns like paper. The discolored folds curl away from the rift like dead leaves, bleeding more flashes.

Bony, decayed creatures crawl out from under ancient soils. Then darkness, fear, hunger. My hands scrabble at the dirt and gravel. It's *under* my nails.

—Real life takes hold. My body lurches forward, surrounded not by a catastrophic nightmare, but my bedroom. It's too hot, too tight. Sweat trickles down my spine. The walls are closing in. My blankets hold me captive. —

Jabbering jaws loosely connected to rotted skulls. Skin paled by time; cold skin, cold eyes, cold blood. Ruthless hands look more like claws, shoveling pieces of flesh into their starving maws. Monstrosities.

—Reality returns. I kick off my bedsheets and stumble out of bed. Neither the floor nor my ankles support my weight. My hands and knees hit the cool wood panels. The walls are closer than ever. —

...a great burning mountain...

Alps rise from the masses of monsters, trying to escape the fire but they can't. They're bound to the Earth and therefore destined to burn with it. The fire becomes an explosion. Mother Nature's hand-carved creations are obliterated.

—Clutching the bedframe, I pull myself to my feet. The room shrinks even more. The walls practically push against my flesh. They'll pulverize me. I stagger to the door and throw myself into the hall. —

I crash into murky, red water. No. Not water. Too thick. Too dark. Light can probe the waves of an ocean, river, or lake, but it doesn't breach blood the same way. Only the haziest rays of light infiltrate the red tide. I scrabble toward them, driving my soul into every desperate movement until my head is above water.

I gasp for air.

Reality flickers into place. The tug of war between awareness and hysteria is muddled. The monsters dig themselves out from graves beneath my floor. They break the wood panels and swarm inside. The walls singe and scorch until flames crawl out from under wallpaper.

I don't want to be here.

Dawn's rays penetrate the curtains, a few final hints of night before the Sun seizes the sky. Yes. Sunlight. That will scare the monsters away. Just like when I was younger. It has to.

I book it. Down the hall and across the living room, but every footstep covers an inch and the journey stretches for miles. When did my apartment get so big? Has it always been like this? I try to run faster, but my lungs are exhausted, my legs shaky. I'm limited to fast, fervent gasps, and fumbling steps.

Words loop in my ears, loud enough to drown out the wheezing fiends right behind me. The window's so close. The curtain tickles my fingertips, just inside my grasp, and then my ankle gives out.

My entire body thuds against the floor; hardwood panels become dirt and stone. I glance back, and my heart leaps from my chest.

A ghastly version of Pyera clutches my ankle, trying to drag me into her deadly arms. I kick to unhinge her fingers, but another—Cleon? —grasps my leg. The atrocities swarm like ants to yank me into the pits they rose from.

I kick, scream, and claw at the dirt. The behemoths are too numerous and too strong. Nothing will stop them from taking me.

I'm gruffly flipped onto my back. The Monster. He straddles my hips, strangling me. I scratch at his fingers, but he's so much stronger. His coldblooded, raincloud eyes boil with hate far outmatching my fear.

"The first angel sounded his trumpet." He purrs.

His fingers flex. Everything flickers.

A light touches the darkness surrounding my vision. My chest swells with relief. It's *her*.

Aimil MacAdaidh.

She stands out of reach, a blonde angel without wings. A warrior equipped with a presence that makes the Earth shudder. She glitters brighter than Lilac and stands taller than Cleon or Valberg or Dad. Lightning strikes but it's dull compared to her.

She'll save me. She'll fix it. She meets my eyes, and I want to laugh because it's over. It's over! *She'll fix it.* But she turns away.

She takes her light and the world with her, leaving me behind in the void.

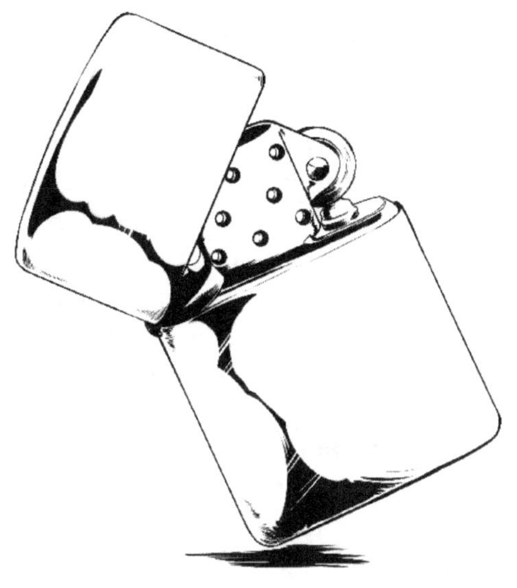

TEN

FIRST RESURRECTION

"Upon the first trumpet sounding, hail and fire, mixed with blood, is thrown to the earth...By the second trumpet sounding, it was something like a great burning mountain that plunges into the sea...The ocean will become blood."

Loosestrife is one of the many shifter settlements nearby the Bloodroot capitol of Celastrus. Through history, it's known for its odd and plentiful quantity of gammas. Regarded as the region's second most beautiful, sturdiest landmark, it's beaten only by the capitol itself. And, as of tonight, beneath the radiance of the full moon, it will be recognized as the first shifter city to burn by vampire hands in centuries.

From the safety of the cliffside, Francis flicks his lighter as he basks in the heat of the gluttonous flames plundering Loosestrife. The grittiest, arguably most rewarding details are too far away to fully enjoy, but screaming shifters are a prize, even from afar.

The explosives sent debris in every direction, brought the mountain to rubble, and ignited the trees. The most treasured spectacle was the blood as it rained down with the hail. He imagines amongst scalded branches and logs are the gory pieces of unwitting shifters.

"How many?" Jeremy asks. From beneath the hood of his sweatshirt, his eyes chart across the charred corpses piled in the valley.

Katherine says, "There must be hundreds."

"I hope so," says Tara. She crouches close to the crag, nudging a stone over the edge.

Jeremy shrugs. "It has to be. They had no idea what was happening."

Francis turns from the burning city, drawing everyone's attention. They're all hungry for his thoughts. He gazes at Orlando, whose usual scowl is replaced by a small, giddy smile.

"It's all thanks to you." Francis' tongue coils around sweet praise like a snake. He opens his arms to the night, a warm halo of light lining his silhouette. "Soak up the sight with me."

Twigs crunch and mud slides under their feet as they approach.

He whispers. "Listen."

One by one, the fire guzzles the trees until it swallows the entire forest. A snarl of thunder overpowers the cacophony of screams and howls. Sound becomes sensation; a pulse teems through the woods.

"Finally." Francis breathes.

He lowers his arms and reaches into his coat pocket. He exchanges his lighter for a vial of blood. Rubbing his finger across the smooth, gossamer glass, he looks at the others. The others produce their own ampoules.

Hunger rumbles in his belly. Need burns in his throat. He languorously licks his lips as he peers into the crimson elixir.

"Kris' death was hard on all of us." He holds the vial to the moon. "We're fewer without him, but we aren't weaker. Like everyone else, he was murdered by a mutt. Stolen by the oh-so-divine Mother Nature." He twists her name into a curse. "They can't hurt us anymore."

Francis pushes the cork open. The scent of aged blood wafts from the glass. His nostrils flare, tingling. The others open theirs. The aroma gets stronger. Francis lifts his to the chaos, a toast to the feeble mutts who struggle to flee a fate they don't realize is theirs.

"However many are dead tonight, they'll be extinct when we're done." He tips his head back to drink their fallen brother's blood. The others join.

In the decimated valley, blood seeps into the blackened river and another roar erupts from the sky.

ELEVEN

DUSK

My eyes ache.

Scratch that. My entire *body* aches, sprawled on my living room floor.

The ground gyrates, and the walls sway. My stomach spins with them. I lie there for a minute, letting the world settle before I push myself up. A shuddering pain vibrates in my brain. I lower my head between my knees, lace my fingers against my skull, and breathe. Slowly, my stomach calms but, when I clutch the couch to haul myself up, it churns all over again.

The furniture is haphazardly strewn about like a crazed wolf stumbled through. Then there are the grooves. Five jagged furrows follow the wall from my bedroom to where I woke up. Many more are scratched into the floor, more frenzied. Somehow their lines bend into shapes and symbols, then words and letters.

Messages. They're messages.

Foggy images surface to the forefront of my mind. Wet lips smack at my ear, trailed by rasps for air. A voice echoes in my head. It's quiet at first, and then it crescendos.

...The first angel sounded his trumpet...

I remember everything.

My brain lags behind my body. I'm at the kitchen counter before I can catch a strand of sensibility. I fumble for my phone. *Who do I call?*

My bloodied fingers and whittled nails know before I do.

It doesn't even ring once before she picks up.

"Macy?" Pyera's voice bursts from the speaker.

"Are you at City Hall?" I'm already headed for the door.

"I—Yes, why?" she demands, jarred. "What's going on?"

"I'm on my way."

"Mac—"

I hit end. Something's wrong. I don't know if it's with me or the world but somehow—by a divine force I've never encountered—I know it's the latter.

Something is *wrong.*

TWELVE

PROPHET

The Lord and Lady's assistants bellow my name down the hall. I scarcely hear them over the footsteps beating on the floor after me. *Gammas,* sense whispers. It doesn't feel right to run faster, but my feet carry me quicker than my heart consents.

"*Stop!*" one yells.

I barge through Pyera's office door. She, Cleon, Nico, and Valberg, all twist around in their seats. On the computer behind them, a newsreel plays my nightmare.

Familiar mountains paint themselves against the sky. *My home.* Its fiery demise for the second time in less than 24 hours. A woman narrates over the catastrophe, but I strain to hear the wind. It's not there.

My legs are frozen, holding me hostage. The gammas restrain my arms and cuff my wrists as office assistants spew frantic apologies. *Struggle. Fight back!* But I can't move.

Pyera bolts up from her desk. "Release her!"

Cleon follows her to his feet. He motions for the gammas to let me go.

They hesitate to unlock their fingers. Pyera growls, upper lip curled to reveal a single, sharp fang. They comply. The Lady waltzes them from the room while Cleon pulls me further in.

"I don't understand," I say in a rush. "I saw that in a dream. Then I get here and it's on your screen? *I don't understand!*"

The door slams shut. Pyera braces herself against it, and stares at me. "What do you mean you saw it in a dream?"

"I *mean* I dreamt of that last night!"

"Wait, Macy—"

"No!" I turn on her. "I'm *not* waiting! I watched the sky burn, and the water turn into blood! Everyone in this room turned into monsters, and that vampire—the one who bit me? He was there!" I touch my neck. "What's going *on?*"

She gapes at me. Her lips move as she struggles to find the words. None come.

"Sit down." Cleon instructs. "Take a breath and tell us everything."

Valberg grabs a chair from the corner of the room. Cleon's hands are soft like feathers as he ushers me to sit.

Nearby, Nico is a curious owl. He stares quietly while I try, fail, and try again to describe last night. They all look perturbed when I'm done.

My stomach seesaws. "What?"

No answer.

"What?" I demand.

Pyera eyes the Lord, who finally speaks up. "Last night...was a full moon. It is when the Man in the Moon is at his strongest, and thus the only time he can contact his two fated Prophets. Nico was chosen at sixteen. Last night, he witnessed everything you just described."

Nico's observes me in my peripherals.

I glance at him.

His eyes are so dark they could hide the moon, and everything else too. The only sign of emotion is a subtle frown on his lips.

Nico Navarro. The Prophet of Good Fortune. The only prophet. Because the second was never chosen. Or maybe they just hadn't been chosen *yet*.

"No." I turn back to Cleon. "No. I'm not the other one."

"Macy..." Pyera sighs.

"No!" I dig my nails into the chair so I don't leap up. "I'm *not*. I'm a *shifter*. Not a vampire! Not a prophet! The moon means *nothing* to me!"

But the Earth means everything. Last night, I watched it burn. All I want is to hold my reality together. The one I was only *just* settling into.

"It doesn't make sense," I say. "The visions were the *same*. I can't be the other one."

"It's rare, but it *has* happened." Pyera breathes gently. Even her mildness crushes me.

"But it's never been this dire," Valberg says, hushed but desperate. He wants me to be right.

"Not once since the start of time," Cleon says, "has it been a coincidence when two vampires shared a vision."

"No!" I practically yell. "I. Am. A. *Shifter*! I didn't want to be a vampire, and I definitely don't want to be a prophet!"

"You do not have any choice," he says in a level voice.

It's a slap across the face. I gawk at him. His soft frown deepens with remorse.

"Macy." Pyera pleads. "Please."

I plead. "I want my life back!"

She's hurt. "I know... But we need you to...try. At the very least."

She massages her temples. This sudden, unexpected burden crushes her. There's fear on her face. Mom flashes in my head. My stubbornness dissolves.

I avert my eyes. "Okay."

"I'm sorry," she says. An apology reserved for me in a room full of people. I let it sink in. She switches back into business mode. "We need to contact the Alphas. They need to know the second soothsayer has been chosen. And our future is in jeopardy."

"Immediately." Cleon nods "Miss Braddock, Mr. Navarro, you will come with me."

"Where?" I ask.

"My office," he says.

Together, they hectically steer us out of the room. Pyera and Val race down the hall together, expressions grim and panicked. Cleon nearly follows them. His jeweled hand twitches, and then flexes into a fist.

He takes forcibly measured steps backward, his calm wavering. "I must retrieve a file. Mr. Navarro, please show Miss Braddock to my office. I will be there shortly."

With that, he darts after the other two.

We stand there for a moment, in shock, as the dread creeps in.

"Y'okay?" Nico scans me, concerned. His voice is scratchy and bland, but there's something there somewhere.

I ignore his question with one of my own, "I'm the second Prophet?"

He nods. "Looks like it."

"You see the better futures?"

"Yep."

"So, I see the worse ones?"

"Bingo."

"But our visions were the same."

"Somehow."

"What does that mean?"

The unbridled truth hardens his muddy stare. "It means we might be SOL."

THIRTEEN

YOU'LL BURN

"His name is Francis Church," Cleon says, seated primly at his desk.

He slides a cumbersome folder across it. Nico and I careen closer to survey the hefty stack of colorless papers inside. A familiar face stares up at us from the first page.

The Monster. A weaker visage. He was so eerily put together that night in the woods. This is a younger, rumpled, broken and bruised version of him, so distinctly unalike, my brain insists they're different people. It's his eyes that eliminate all doubt. They're stormy, vengeful, and malicious, as if he can look past the page. At me. I glare back.

"Careful." Nico warns. "You'll burn the page if you keep scowling like that."

I don't stop. It would be a gift to watch him burn. "Target practice."

Cleon clears his throat. "Until five years ago, he went by Francis Garret. He was the Grand Enchanter of the Veratrum coven in Virginia."

"Bloodroot territory," I say gravely.

The Monster and I come from the same pack. My insides boil.

Cleon says, "Yes. He was as powerful as he was popular."

"I knew he looked familiar," mutters Nico. "He and Val used to be friends in Aconite."

"Indeed," Cleon says.

"Val was friends with *this* maniac?" I can't hide my disgust.

"They studied at the Academy of Blood Magic." He rolls his head onto his shoulder and arches a brow at me. "That's where Grand Enchanters used to study before it was disbanded."

I roll my tongue on the inside of my cheek. "I know what it is." Bending forward, I squint at the picture. "Why did he change his name?"

"He and several others took the name Church following the 2010 Cleansing."

Nico scoffs. I give him a sideways look.

Cleon frowns. "They are the only active members of the Wormwood League."

I narrow my eyes. "The terrorist group?"

"The *vampire-equality* movement *turned* terrorist group," Nico says pointedly.

"That doesn't change what they are now," I say, sharper.

Five years ago, in 2010, a band of activists formed in Veratrum. They called themselves the Wormwood League. Quickly, their ideals spread, branching across the nation. Unfortunately, civil protests became violent revolts in Veratrum. Marches became riots, normal citizens delved into illegal blood magic, shifters were cornered and beaten. The Bloodroot capitol, Celastrus, had no choice but to intervene.

It's been a massive sore spot for vampires. They call it a massacre. We call it a cleansing.

"It is the vengeful product of peaceful protests in Veratrum, yes;" Cleon confirms. "We are aware of six members other than Francis himself."

He turns to another page of headshots. One long finger glides down the page. All the vampires from the clearing, my nightmares, stare up at me. Now, they have names, too. Robin Murphy, Jeremy Wu, Katherine Caldwell, Orlando Scott, Tara Pope, and Kristopher Hanson. Hanson's face brings to mind a bittersweet memory. I killed him the night I was bitten.

"We believe giving up their surnames is some sort of initiation process." Cleon explains.

"Where are they now?" I ask.

"Starting over a year ago," he says, "they all began to disappear. They went missing months apart. At first, we believed it was foul play."

"Why?" I gasp.

"It might have something to do with the fact that they murdered about sixty vampires in 2010. Some weren't even protestors." Nico answers for him in a matter-of-fact tone. Too bad I didn't ask him.

He looks at me, challenging me to disagree. I bite the inside of my cheek and raise a brow. He mirrors it. After a minute of glaring, he gives up. *Good.*

Cleon clears his throat again. "Regardless, that is what many suspected, merely because Wormwood was becoming more radical. They were clear about their desire to incite a rebellion. It would..." A distinctly placid expression washes over his face. "...make sense that the shifters remove them, would it not, Miss Braddock?"

I sink into my seat. "I guess..."

"That was not the case, however. So, the Lord and Lady of Veratrum reported their disappearances. The shifters searched but found nothing. Until a month ago when they supposedly murdered a young shifter woman near Hydrilla, Maine, according to an eyewitness account."

I clench my jaw. "Me."

He nods.

"I don't suppose they caught them after that?" I ask in a flat tone.

Cleon shakes his head. "They vanished yet again. Then, last night they were spotted amongst the chaos in Loosestrife. It was the only settlement to suffer a grievous number of deaths. Enough that the local rivers ran red with blood."

I choke on air.

Cleon stiffens, as though he forgot who I was, and hastily elaborates. "The capitol has taken in the Barberry and Hydrilla residents to protect them from the fire, as well as any Loosestrife survivors."

I sigh in relief. *Mom and Dad are okay. Lilac is okay.*

"The Bloodroot Alphas collaborated with the human government to cover up the incident. An 'unexpected volcanic reaction.'"

Nico's eyebrows sink low over his eyes. "It's that easy?"

"The Packs have always cooperated with human officials to keep our existence secret," I say. "They hide us and our world. We keep them safe from vampires."

Cleon fights off the grimace. He holds a hand up to Nico, who huffs. Cleon moves on. "Pyera received word that local fire control has begun back-burning to hinder the inferno. It's all they can save."

"But they're going to do more, aren't they?" Nico says. "It's great that they stopped the fire and all that, but that won't stop the vision."

I narrow my eyes. "Right now, we need to focus on helping the people. Helping the Earth."

Nico snorts. "I appreciate the hippy bullshit but, call me crazy, I think making sure the world *doesn't end* might help more."

Deep breaths, Macy.

I don't give him the privilege of looking at him. "They'll probably call for a Summit."

Cleon nods with a scowl. "Correct. The Poppy Alphas notified the other Packs last night. One has been called. It will be held in their capitol: Meadowsweet."

"When?" Nico asks, severe.

"September twenty-first."

No.

"*What?*" Nico exclaims. "That's almost two months away!"

"They have to deliberate." I try to reason, pride cleaving me to my people. "It's not easy arranging a global meeting, *Nico.*"

"They deliberated during the Three Kingdoms War, the Mongol Conquests, both World Wars, Vietnam, and every other known historic debacle." He lists, half distressed and half livid. "This isn't one of the visions that can wait. We're talking about a global tragedy here, *Macy.*"

"Enough." The Lord's stern voice echoes in the small room. "This is their game of politics."

"Summits are normally reserved for Alphas and betas anyway." I straighten a second after I speak.

Alphas and *betas*. Lilac blooms in my head. She's color and happiness. She's the embodiment of everything I lost upon being bitten. She's passion, softness, and familiarity. She's *home.*

If we made it to the Summit and made clear the threat of apocalypse, then we could garner the support to hunt, maim, and kill the Monster. And Lilac might be at the Summit. I could find her and explain what happened. She could help me return to the pack. Even after our fight. After everything. I know she won't let me waste away here. Escape tickles my fingers like sunlight.

I look over to Nico. His white-knuckled fists shake. His face is rigid, too; jaw clenched, and teeth gritted. He flicks his eyes at me, then looks away.

I turn toward Cleon. "Is there... *any* way we could attend? If we went, we could sway things in our favor. I'm a shifter. That could help."

"You aren't a shifter anymore." Nico snaps.

I jerk towards him, lips pulled back, snarling.

"We are not sure." Cleon cuts in. "Pyera requested an audience with the Knotweed Alphas. If they agree, she and I will use that time to debate our importance at the Summit. Otherwise..." His eyes move behind me. "Oh. We were just speaking of you."

"Flattered." Pyera sashays from the door. "Our audience has been approved. Thanks in no small part to your doomsday visions."

It's a joke, but the humor is missing. She squeezes Nico's shoulder as she passes him. He relaxes a little. She then pastes a sticky note onto Cleon's desk.

"Alpha Kennedy will be here within the week," she says. "In the meantime, I suggest we dissect your premonitions."

Upon saying that, Cleon opens a drawer, and rummages for a pen and notebook. He sets the tip of his ballpoint on the first blank page and scrawls the date. Pyera sits on the edge of his desk, arms folded.

I raise my brows slowly. "You guys are weirdly in sync."

"You're telling me." Nico smirks.

"So, we know Church is the curator of the events in your vision," Pyera says. "And those events are somehow linked to 'trumpets.'"

"Loosestrife signaled the first one," I say. "Which means there is a second one, and maybe even a third. I think it's a part of a bigger ritual."

"That'd make sense," Nico says, to my surprise. "The world hasn't ended yet. There has to be a sequence. A methodology."

Pyera looks pensive. "Cleon—"

"Already writing it down."

"One more thing," Nico says. "Macy's death plays a role in this somehow."

Throwing my head back, I groan. "Don't remind me."

He isn't deterred. "I saw her die in the vision. She experienced it. That has to mean something. The Man in the Moon never shows you anything for the hell of it. There's *always* something."

"Which means, I need a way to defend myself..." Aimil flashes before my eyes, walking away. "...and maybe that means reconnecting with my Grounding. She was in my vision."

"Perhaps a mentor could help," Pyera hypothesizes.

I nod. "But I don't know where I'd get one around here."

"Valberg could help." Nico points out.

I give him a doubtful look. "He's a vampire."

"And a teacher."

Cleon drums his fingers. "That is actually a fantastic idea. Valberg has always possessed respect for the Earthly Spirit. He collaborated with several healers in the past and learned valuable meditation techniques. Many rooted in shifter medicine."

I chew on the inside of my lip. It's not that I don't think he can help, it's that... I don't think he can help. Meditation has never worked for me before.

"I'll consider it." I offer reluctantly.

Pyera frowns. "I'll set aside time in his schedule anyway. If we want to prevent your vision, it's essential we do everything in our power to defy the future and chart a new course."

"Uncovering Church's ritual should be our main priority until the Alpha arrives," says Cleon.

Pyera's expression turns serious. "Pray to the Night we succeed."

"Pray the Moon answer us," Cleon mutters.

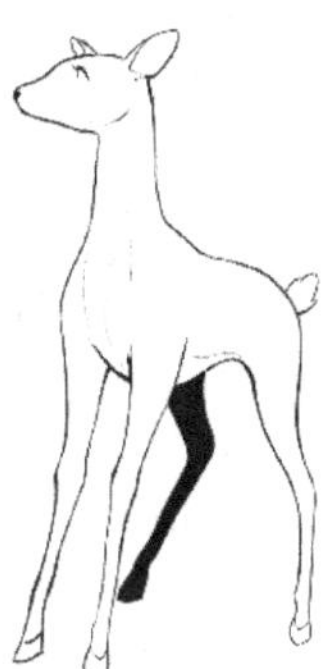

FOURTEEN

MARTYRS

"Nope. Nothing!" Circi slams her book onto Luc's dinner table.

The orange pocketknife at the center clatters to the beat of the vibrations. I place my palm over it, so it stills.

"Hey!" He scolds her. "You know I lost a screw building this thing. You'll bring the whole table down if you keep doin' that."

"At least *that* would be entertaining," she says.

With a sigh, I close my book, and push it away from me. "There really wasn't anything?"

"Not a thing."

Luc sets his book down, too. "That's about another..." He eyeballs the clock on his phone. "...two hours wasted."

Circi tips her head back, groaning. Luc pats her shoulder.

And I thought I didn't like to read...

I reach for her book. *Ancient Rituals and Ceremonies* is stamped across the cover, above some cultish symbols and insignia. The only words larger than the title are the author's name. It looked as promising as any of the others, but none of the paperbacks, hardcovers, or novellas have been helpful.

I toss the text onto our growing stack of self-proclaimed encyclopedias of mysticism. For all their declarations of unseen breadths of work, none so much as hint at a ritual resembling the one from my vision. No mention of trumpets. A few mentions of angels, but none that lead anywhere. In comparison, our pile of helpful books isn't very useful either. Likely because said pile doesn't exist yet.

"At least we know not to look in that one again." Luc exhales, feigning optimism.

Eying our dwindling array of unread reserves, I glance at the clock. 2:56 AM.

It's been five nights since the vision. Four since Pyera sent the visitation request, but we aren't any closer to deciphering anything. Hopefully, one of the others unearthed something, or else we won't have anything to convince the Alpha our presence is needed in Meadowsweet.

I reach for another book, but don't open it.

"Welp." Luc lets out a massive sigh as he stands, eager to be on his feet. "I think it's time we give up on study hall. I'm busting out the comics. We'll die of boredom by daybreak if I don't."

"The what?"

"Jeeze." Circi peeks up from where she rested her head on her arms.

Luc flattens his palms on the table and looms closer. "Don't tell me you've never read a comic book."

I bite back a smile.

He gasps dramatically, throwing himself a step back. "Macy, how are you *alive*? DC is a life essential."

Circi snorts. She tips her chair onto its hind legs, combat boots propped up. "Marvel's better."

He narrows his eyes and points a finger at her. "Don't you start with your propaganda." He turns back to me. "She's just jealous her comic book collection isn't as big as mine."

"Probably because I have a life."

"Hardly!"

He disappears into another room. When he returns, he tosses a magazine at me. I timidly skim my fingers down the cover. It's pretty.

"Beautiful, I know." He grins at me.

"Something like that." I scan a few pages. "Why are you so infatuated with these?"

"'Infatuated' isn't the right word."

Circi pipes up. "Try 'obsessed'."

He sticks his tongue out at her. "It's a hobby. But, little known fact about your boy Luc over here: my life could've been ripped right out of a superhero comic."

I give him a wry look. "You don't look like the sort to wear tights."

"Not outside his bedroom at least," she says.

He gets a proud look in his eyes, forewarning a spiel about the excessive similarities between him and whichever hero he fancies. I teeter closer, practically salivating. Circi senses the same thing. She hides her face in her arms again.

"First of all!" He jabs a finger in my direction. "You disappoint me."

"That's *my* hobby."

Circi gives us a thumbs up, face still buried, communicating *you and me both.*

He rolls his eyes. "*Anyway,* here's the gist of most superhero backgrounds: orphaned as a child and/or a tragic family death leads to their emergence as caped crusader who fights villainy. Most become billionaire, playboy philanthropists." He holds his hands up. "Now, I know what you're thinking: but, Luc, you're not a billionaire, playboy philanthropist. And to that I say: *yet.*"

Circi makes a *pfft* noise.

"I am, however, a child orphaned because of *two* tragic deaths." He touches his heart and gives us a theatrical look. "As a result, I have been imbued with a moral obligation to uphold all that is right in the world."

"So where do you keep the tights?" I ask.

He gives me a naughty grin. "That's for me to know and—"

"They're under his bed," Circi says.

He gasps and swats her arm.

She swats back, smiling devilishly. "It's some costume he bought for kicks a few years ago."

"You always ruin my fun." He pouts.

Snickering, I trace the blocky letters printed across the magazine. "Are you really an orphan, Luc?"

"Oh yeah." His chipper demeanor doesn't even falter. "I was bitten when I was six."

"How old are you now?" I study him. "Twenty-one? Twenty-two?"

"Ooh, twenty-two. Good guess."

I toy with my bottom lip. "Can I ask how it happened?"

"Sure." He waves away my worries with a smile. He tilts his chin down, and that happy smile turns devious. "It's really the most Batman-esque past ever."

"You know, aside from Batman's," Circi says.

I look between them. "...Who?"

Circi snickers as Luc lets out a defeated sigh.

"My parents and I were travelling from Mountain Ash to Baneberry. Sage territory." Luc begins. "We stopped in a human town for the night. I don't remember why anymore. My parents left for...something. Don't remember that either. They were gone for a long time. I was scared, so I went looking for them. Terrible idea."

I rest on my elbows, inclined forward with a concerned ear.

"This is the superhero part," he says. "I found them in an alley after the wind tried to steer me away. There were two rogue vampires feeding from them, and when they saw me, I was next."

"How'd you get away?"

"Blind luck and the grace of Mother Nature."

I swallow nervously. "Your parents?"

His smile finally saddens. "Drained."

Venom requires blood for the transformation to occur. If there is none, the vampiric plague doesn't spread. You just die. Painfully. Had my Marrow Mark not gone haywire the night I was bitten, I would've ended up just like Luc's parents.

"How'd you end up here?" I ask.

"The same way you did," he says. "I was discovered by a nearby gamma patrol, and when they realized what had happened, I was sent here."

Beside him, Circi's cheek rests on her arms, eyes on him. She searches for the same cracks I do, but where I can't find them, she does. Her eyes are trained to pick up on signs I can't.

She says, "He's been my sidekick ever since." It's a joke, but her humor is gentle, meant to take care of him.

Lilac's absence is heavier than usual.

"You guys..." I trail off for a moment. "You guys have known each other a while."

They share a look, messages and memories relayed between them. I avert my gaze to my hands.

"You know..." Circi mindlessly flips through a comic book. "I understand where he's coming from."

I look at her. "Who?"

She shrugs. "That Church dude."

"Uh...what?"

The vision loops in my head. It haunts me when I'm awake, looming at the back of my mind, waiting for dawn so it can latch onto dreams and stalk my sleep. Hydrilla, and its fiery death, scorches my brain. The flames boil my blood.

"You realize he killed hundreds of shifters a few nights ago, right?" I demand.

She says, "Which was *screwed up*, but the 2010 Massacre–"

"Cleansing," I say before I can stop myself.

She runs a tongue over her teeth. "Massacre."

Shooting Luc a glance, I try to send him telepathic pleas for back up. Circi does, too. He stares uncomfortably at the tabletop.

"The 2010 *Massacre* was the *biggest* unjustified killing of vampires in the last two decades." Circi fights to stay level. "Innocent people were caught in the crossfire. There were a lot of upset vampires after that, so even if he's *wrong,* I see why he feels the way he does."

"It was a *cleansing,* and it was necessary."

"When is killing that many people ever *necessary?*"

"There was a rebellion brewing," I say. "We didn't want to hurt them, but the revolt would've forced our hand eventually."

"Did you not hear me?" she hisses. "Innocent people were *killed.*"

"They were rebelling."

She grimaces. "Oh, Grand Mother Nature, forbid an abused people fight their oppression. The shifters would lose their punching bags!"

"We *protect* you!" I insist.

"Is that what you call killing sixty-six vampires in 2010?" she demands. "I bet all eleven children and twenty-four adult civilians felt so protected when they were murdered."

"You guys!" Luc tries to intervene. Too late.

"Those protesters were killing shifters too, Circi." I clutch the edge of the table.

She throws her hands up. "How sad."

Luc butts in again. "Circi—"

"No." She snaps at him. "Hell *no.* They keep us locked up in these covens. They track us like animals. They monitor us every second. Then they beat us when we're down." Her eyes cut to me. "Can you really blame us for being sick of it, Macy?"

Luc holds his hands out to Circi and I. "Macy, don—"

"I'm not blaming you!"

"Well, I'm blaming you!"

"We feed you!" I snap. "You would starve without us. We built entire cities for you. Guard them for you. So what if we monitor you? You want to blame *us?* You have psychopaths like Francis Church who want to kill *everyone.*"

"I'm not him!"

"And I'm not everyone who's ever wronged your people!"

"*My* people?" Her tone is dangerous and disimpassioned. "Did you forget you're a *vampire* now, Macy?"

I glare.

"Didn't they ship you across the country to one of the most unknown covens in America? Did you just forget that you have to sign in and out of everywhere you go so *your people* don't hunt *you* down with unnecessary force?"

"Circi, knock it off." Luc butts in.

"They lied to your family, right?" She rises slowly from her seat. Her hands are flat on the table as she leans forward, nostrils flared. Her septum piercing fogs as she breathes. She's a bull without horns. "You're dead to them because that's better than being a *vampire.* Not only are you a vampire, Macy, but the Man in the Moon picked you, a mutt, a *bloodhound,* to be his second shit-tastic Prophet."

"Circi." He tries again.

"You're a damn vampire!"

I slam a fist onto the table as I bolt to my feet. It wobbles. "No! I'm not!"

"Yes, you *are!*" she yells. "You can't even turn into a mangy dog anymore!"

"*Circi!*" Luc finally gets her to stop, but the damage is already done.

I've suffered Mom's criticism before, even Dad's. They shouted and bickered about how to train me, and then shouted and bickered some more when it didn't work. I've been mocked and degraded for being weaker than everyone else. But I'm not accustomed to Circi's brand of fire. Her heat scalds me; the truth cools the fire.

"What did I ever do to you?" I swallow tears. "What on Earth could anyone have ever done to you to make you so *ignorant*?"

"*I'm* ignorant?" Circi guffaws. "That's ridiculous. How about this, Macy? When a crowd of armed shifters murders *your* mom, you talk to me about who's ignorant!" Her eyes go wide the second after she says it.

Softer, Luc says, "Circi..."

She fights for something else to say. I stare at her, and she stares back. The silence refuses to break. Luc reaches out to her, but she pivots with a huff, then storms out of the room onto the balcony.

"Hey!" he calls after her.

She slams the door.

Pride and ego wounded, I want to argue. I want to defend my people and myself, but more than that, I want to go. So, I gather my things, stuff them into my bag, and head for the door.

"Macy..." His tone is apologetic. "Tenderfoot, c'mon you don't have to go. Let's sit down. I'll bring Circi back in here. You guys can apologize, and we'll get back to reading all these books."

"I'm tired," I lie. "I'm going home."

"I'll drop by tomorrow, okay?" There's a frown in his voice.

I stare at the floor. "Yeah."

In the hallway, my fingers flex around the strap of my bag. I clench and unclench my fists, trying to calm down, but the anger is too hot. It swells in my belly, burns in my skin. It mixes with the hurt and confusion tight in my heart.

Where to? Home? *No.*

I don't want to crawl under the blankets to sob my sadness away. Nor do I want to punch pillows or scream at the quiet. It's all a waste of precious time—time better spent poring over every accessible book.

My feet guide me to the library.

FIFTEEN

A BETTER WORD

I stare at my feet the whole way there, trying to stifle my temper and hurt feelings.

"Hey."

I jump at the voice.

Nico Navarro. He stands at the opposite end of the library's short staircase. He's more unkempt than usual. I cast a look over my shoulder. Is it too late to run back to Luc's?

The wind whispers between us.

"Hey." I rub my arm.

He cocks his head at me. "Do you normally visit the library this close to sunrise?"

"Do you?"

"Yeah, actually." He tucks his hands into his pockets.

I scan him, hunting for any signs of danger.

He arches a brow. "Are you checking me out or looking for my knife? If it's the former, thanks. If it's the latter, then I'll save you the trouble: I left it at home. Pat me down if you want." He grins. He has dimples. "Although, you can do that any time."

It's worth a scoff. "I'm gay."

He sucks in a sharp breath. "My bad."

I roll my eyes, unamused. "Are you here to research the ritual, too?"

He nods.

I scowl. "What a coincidence."

The wind snickers.

"Fate might be a better word."

Not in the mood, I snort.

He motions toward the door. "Want to work together? What's that old cliché? Two heads are better than one?"

"You don't have any friends to help you?"

"No, actually." He bites. "See, there's this trend with assassinations of character. They usually destroy your social life."

I fold my arms. The ethereal doors of the library beckon me closer. Even the wind pushes me in its direction. It howls the word *fate*.

"Fine." I huff and then march up the steps ahead of him.

Inside, I keep an exaggerated amount of space between us. We scour the shelves of the non-fiction section silently. Until, out of nowhere, he says, "I'm not a psycho. Or a whacko. Or whatever."

"Okay..." I say, unsure. The questions must be obvious on my face.

He glances at me out the corner of his eye. "I saw you with Luc and Circi. They like to talk."

I turn back to the boring book in my hands. "Why are you telling me?"

He shrugs, digging his hands in his pockets. "Reason numero uno is because we're Prophets. We're going to work together a lot. I'd prefer if you didn't think I was some malicious psychopath."

I'm not sure what he expects. Whatever he says he isn't, he is, without a doubt, an ass. It's bad enough that I'm the shifter girl chosen by the Moon. The last thing I want is to be the shifter girl chosen by the Moon who spends all her time with the town's local bad-boy soothsayer.

He hides his eyes behind his hair, but I peer through the gaps. There's something sad in his eyes. I hate myself for it, but I offer a sliver of pity.

"If it's any consolation, I'm not sure you're *that* malicious."

His gloomy laugh takes me by surprise. "That's better than nothing, I guess."

A woman's voice gently resounds from the speakers overhead, announcing they're closing soon. We make our way into the main lobby where he pauses. I stop a few steps ahead of him.

"What?"

"I'm gonna grab a few books from the fiction section," he says. "Wanna come?"

"Uh..."

I spare a glance at the front desk, then the door. Beyond it, my apartment waits: empty space between rooms, shrilling silence, half-kempt plants wilting in the dark, reminders of the past sitting alongside memories of the future. All of it waiting to suffocate me.

"...I guess." I reluctantly comply.

The books in this section are much more colorful than the other two departments. I suppose they're meant to catch the eye, but I've stared at so many books since the full moon my eyes glaze over at the sight. Nico, however, is unfazed. We pause multiple times when he's reeled in by a particular novel, and miniature eons pass each time. By the fifth book he browses, puts back, and then picks up again upon second thought, I decide he has no idea what he wants.

One novel catches my attention. I pull it off the shelf. *"Blood Kiss: A Vampire Tale?"*

Nico looks up from the hardcover in his hands. He smirks. "That's a human fad. They're obsessed with us...well, our myth anyway. Same for shifters."

"They...write books about us?" I'm unsure if I should be flattered or unsettled.

"It's profitable."

"Weird..." I mumble, pushing the book onto the shelf again.

"Right?" he says. "There are so many different iterations of vampire lore in their society. They basically worship us."

We move further down the aisle. Pushed against the last shelf is a much smaller section labeled *Major Human Religions.*

"Speaking of worship," I joke, pulling a leather-bound volume from the shelf. It's thick and heavy in my hands. The tabs on the side itch my palm. They're all labeled with strange words and names.

"So...this is what a Bible looks like. It's kind of underwhelming." I note.

He chuckles. "Good thing there aren't any humans around here. You'd be blacklisted by at least six chapels."

"How tragic," I mutter sarcastically.

He places his index finger against his smile, then reaches over to take the book. He turns it over in his hands, and flips through a few pages.

"A lot of them believe in this stuff." He acknowledges, waving to the many religious texts.

"That's a shame." I frown. "No wonder humans treated the Earth so poorly."

The shifters often have to work double-time to sustain what they attempt to destroy, a task which has become harder and harder over time. Their infatuation with modern technology and their disregard for the soils they inhabit has been the cause of many arguments among the shifters. We agree on how to handle omegas, even vampires, but whether we should continue supporting the humans is the topic of heated debate.

"What's the point?" I ask.

He holds up the tattered text. "This is their code of conduct. What's right and what's wrong, but it's all up to interpretation."

"Seems problematic."

"Sometimes." He flips through the book. "Sometimes not."

"If they'd open up to Mother Nature..."

"Macy," he says. "We're on their fiction shelves too."

I purse my lips. "You sure know a lot about them for a vampire."

"You sure don't for a shifter," he says flatly.

Folding my arms, I stare down one of the other aisles. "I liked the woods at home more than the nearby cities."

"I've been outside the coven once or twice." He hands me the Bible to put away. "The history books here aren't too bad either."

"You like to read then?" I eye the book in my hands. "Have you read this?"

"Yes and yes."

"Maybe there's something about trumpets in here." I joke.

We might as well start scouring every book of the fiction section at this rate. It'd probably be as helpful as everything else I've read. With a shake of my head, I slide it back into place. Nico's hand stops me halfway.

At first, I stare at his tanned hand. Strange scars peek out from under his sleeve. They're misshapen versions of the one on my neck. I look at him, grasping for a word, but fall silent at his expression. The Bible steals my attention back.

I gape at it. "You don't really think…"

"I'm a dumbass." He stares at it too. "Wow." He breathes as he grabs yet another book from the top shelf. "I am *such* a dumbass. C'mon. Over here."

We dash to the nearest table. Nico slips into the seat next to me. He flips through the book he grabbed. It's a type of concordance. I stare into it as he races from page to page.

A woman's voice resonates again, but she's background noise.

"Treads, trees, tricks." I read each word stamped in the header of the page. "Trickery, troubled. Trumpets! Hey! Go back!"

His fingers shake but he does as I say. When we reach the page marked by the word *trumpets*, I jab my finger down. Between the words "true" and "trust" are three sections dedicated to variants of *trumpet*. They amass waves of shivers jittering down my spine.

My voice shakes as I read. *"Rev. 8:7 The first angel sounded his trumpet."*

He's a second slower than I am. My fingers curl around the Bible. I skim down the pages until I reach section eight. *The Seventh Seal and the Golden Censer,* and a paragraph underneath that: *The Trumpets.*

"Oh no." I shake my head.

He reads the next pertinent line.

"There came hail and fire mixed with blood. A third of the earth was burned up, along with a third of the trees and all the green grass."

"The North Maine Woods," I say.

I lean closer to the book, finger pressed beneath the words. "Look, there are one, two, three—*seven* trumpets."

My heart hammers. Finally, we have some sense of time, some understanding. It could take ages for Francis to complete his ritual, but my belly doesn't sit well with that statement. No. He'll do it soon. I know it

"We have to tell Pyera and Cleon." I tear my eyes from the Bible, to Nico. His gaze burns with adrenaline.

SIXTEEN

DAY-KISSED

Since it's now approaching 4 AM, Nico dials Cleon. When he doesn't answer I call Pyera. She picks up immediately and orders us to meet her at Cleon's home.

It's well put together. One story with wood panels, tile roofing, and white window frames against dull azure siding. There's a flowerbed of roses. They're the same kind as the ones in Pyera's office. More importantly, the lights are on.

"He's awake." I huff, out of breath. "Pyera must've beaten us here."

"Yep." Sweat beads on Nico's brow. The run was worse on him than me. "Looks that way. Thank God."

We make our way to the front step, where he thuds the side of his fist against the door. I yank his arm down. He looks astonished.

"You don't have to break down the door."

"He's hard of hearing!"

The footsteps from the other side say otherwise. Pyera answers the door.

"So you did beat us." I breathe.

She nods, half amused and half stunned. If I answered the door to find a pair of breathless soothsayers, I'd be surprised too. She waves us inside.

"The Man in the Moon has a poor sense of timing." She yawns at her watch. "Hopefully we can be done by dawn. What happened?"

Nico hunches over against the wall. He braces his hands on his knees. He spares one to point at me. "Ask her."

She leads us into the living room with an expectant look.

I wet my dried lips, tucking my hair behind my ears. "We were trying to figure out the details of Church's ritual. I made a joke about it being in the Bible and, on a whim, we looked and...and it actually was."

"That's..."

"Fitting." Valberg concludes, grabbing my attention.

He and Cleon sit on a blue sofa with throw pillows colored several shades of sapphire.

"Are we interrupting something?" I ask as I sit in a chair Pyera motions to.

"You aren't," says Valberg.

I glance about the three of them. "Do you guys throw slumber parties often?"

Cleon cracks a smirk. "With enough wine."

Pyera slaps his shoulder.

"Actually," Valberg says, "I was explaining what I found to Cleon and Pyera before you two arrived."

"Sorry." I frown.

"I'm not." Nico declares as he strolls into the room. He looks a little better. As better as someone with purple bags and messy hair looks after a sprint like that. He flops onto the armrest beside me. I edge away from him.

"What did you discover inside a Bible?" Cleon asks.

His disheveled locks hang around his wrinkled expression. He crinkles his nose where a few hairs tickle it. Dressed in a sleek robe and socks, the sleepy old man almost looks adorable. If only he was like that all the time.

"There's a part in Revelations called The Trumpets." I start. Nico opens to said section. "It's about the seven trumpets of the apocalypse, and the things we heard in our visions are written *word for word.*"

Nico reads off each of the seven trumpets. The color washes from the others' faces. Even Cleon fidgets. Cleon never fidgets.

I nervously bite my lip. "We've been reading every textbook on rituals and this is the first lead either of us has found. Church is trying to signal these trumpets."

"The first one already came and went." Nico adds. "And maybe the second one too. We saw an entire mountain brought down, and then we were submerged in blood."

"The casualties at Loosestrife were so great..." Valberg trails off.

I nod. Strands of hair fall into my face. "The water turned red."

"Exactly." Nico states firmly.

He and I share a look.

"That's all we have," I say.

"It's weird that it was in a Bible," Nico says, "but it's better than nothing."

"It might not be so strange", Valberg says. "There's always a bit of truth and duplicity in everything. I've been meditating, asking the Man in the Moon for guidance. Tonight, when I woke from my trance, I held a piece of our puzzle in my hands."

He lifts an ancient book from his lap. It's bound in splotchy leather. The words printed across the face are worn, practically unreadable, but it doesn't look like English, anyway. Squinting doesn't make it more legible.

Nico reads my mind. "What does that even say?"

"Loosely translated it says *The Primal Ages* by Dante Hazel."

"That's when it looks like it was written." I mumble. Nico muffles his amusement. Pyera and Cleon shoot us disapproving glares.

"I recognize the name." Nico tries to cover himself. "He was a mute vampire writer, wasn't he?"

"Correct," Cleon says. "He was one of the first Prophets after the Blood War. He was renowned for his written predictions. Alas, history was purged of his image and his very existence. He is barely remembered anymore."

Val drags fingers down one of the pages. "He had an astonishing span of work that stretched well outside prophecies. This book details a part of vampire history mostly forgotten, and consequently debated: the rise and fall of the ghouls."

"Uh..." I hum. "Walking corpses drained by starving vampires? Aren't they a myth?"

"That's the most common interpretation today," Valberg says.

Cleon studies him. "Most believe them to be impossible folklores."

Valberg nods. "Dante thought there was credence to both claims. He believed vampires began as a murderous race, what we now know as ghouls, created when the Man in the Moon cursed human corpses with ravenous blood-lust. They crawled from their graves to hunt humans, feast on their blood, and spread their curse. Their mere presence corrupted the Earth. The plant life wilted, the sky turned black, and the waters boiled."

"In our history, that's when Mother Nature created the shifters," I say.

Valberg smiles at me mildly. "These Earth-bound warriors led a war against the ghouls."

"The Blood War," Nico says.

"Another subject of debate." Pyera's smirk is feline.

Valberg grins. "That it is. You and I can have a rematch another night."

She titters.

He looks at us. "Hazel theorized that the ghouls changed during the war. Starvation quickly overwhelmed them. It drove some mad, and others to the primitive equivalent of prayer."

"That's when the Man in the Moon asked Mother Nature for forgiveness," I say.

"Something like that." Valberg eyes page after page. "He couldn't deconstruct his creations, but he asked that she reach out to them and revive their banished souls. She agreed, but asserted that the new wave of ghouls, what we consider vampires today, would be under her constant watch."

Hence the covens.

The Grand Enchanter's eyes scroll down the latest page, and he recites bits and pieces as he goes. "By *'the seven trumpets of Revelation'* and *'the lunar blood of day-kissed kin,'* the ghouls who couldn't be saved from their madness were buried on a night when *'the gargantuan*

Moon trembled in the Earth's shadow.' Dante hypothesized there might be a way to revive them with a similar ritual."

"What?" I sit up straight. "Why? That's a really dangerous concept to leave floating around."

Valberg scratches his beard. "I suspect he knew this book would be condemned to the Grand Enchanters' archives, which only the most trusted vampires can access."

Cleon pinches his nose. "Even the most trusted people are not immune to corruption."

Pyera breathes. "Val, you think that Church is seriously considering reviving the ghouls?"

He closes his book, folds his hands on top, and stares between his fingers. "That's exactly what I'm saying."

That isn't right. My stomach rumbles at the wrongness of that statement. I didn't see corpses dig themselves out from tombstones. I saw cadaverous versions of Pyera, Cleon, Val, everyone.

"No." I protest. "He's not reviving them." Every part of me tingles. My word is reality, the future echoed in the present. "If everything the Man in the Moon shows us has a purpose, then he's not reviving them. I saw everyone in this room die and then come alive again, thirsty and desperate. I felt *myself* die and become a monster."

"They're being recreated," Nico whispers. His eyes flutter. He knows I'm right.

Pyera stares at her hands as if they've decayed before her eyes. "How?"

"Sounds like eclipse plus biblical bullshit equals doomsday." Nico folds his arms. There's too much bravado in his voice. He's worried too.

Valberg drums his fingers on the book. "Then what about lunar blood and day-kissed kin?"

"What if..." Cleon clasps his chin in thought.

"What now?" Pyera demands. Her confusion disperses when Cleon nods to me. Knowledge is a flower. It blossoms in both their eyes.

I fidget under their gazes. "You don't honestly think…?"

Cleon slowly bows his head. "You were once a shifter. A child of the Earth. Day-kissed, if you will. Now, the Night's blood runs through you."

"You're a sacrifice." Nico exhales.

I'm a shifter. I want to scream it. I want to yell loud enough that the Man in the Moon and the Monster know I will not be a part of this! That I won't die for them. I want to yell loud enough that Mother Nature knows I'm hers. My roots tether me to her! I'm not alive just to die. I want to scream so I don't feel so afraid, so powerless.

A pathetic noise tumbles out of me instead.

"Please." I look around. I find Pyera's eyes. There's so much pain there. It doesn't rival mine. "Please, *no.*"

"*I'm sorry,*" she says.

I bury my face in my hands. She crosses the room to lay a hand on my shoulder. I flinch. She wraps a firm but gentle arm around me. It can't keep me safe.

"What do we do?" I ask. "We have to stop him."

"Staying alive seems a viable option for you," says Nico.

"When's the next lunar eclipse?" Valberg asks.

Cleon pulls out a cell phone to hunt for dates. "It's September twenty-seventh."

I gasp, looking up. "That's not even a week after the Summit."

"If we gain permission to attend, arrive with a battle plan in mind, then maybe they'll support us." Pyera's lips are lined with stress. She still attempts to extinguish our impending freak-out.

"And what would that plan be?" Cleon inquires.

"What if we assembled a group of adept blood mages? The shifters could be our line of defense. We outnumber Church before he signals the final trumpet." Valberg offers.

Cleon ruminates. "It may work, but he is intelligent. Catching him would be no simple matter."

Pyera twirls a lock of my hair around her finger. "We haven't even factored in..."

They go back and forth, and, in no time at all, they forget us entirely.

"Okay!" Nico butts in. "How 'bout this; what can *Macy* and *I* do to stop him?"

Val says, "It's your jobs as Prophets to deliver or deny the future. So, deny it with everything you have."

I sink into Pyera's arms.

After a few seconds of hushed, observable contemplation, Cleon holds up a finger. "There is something we should consider."

"What's that?" Val inquires.

"Should killing Church become necessary..."

"Killing vampires is not an easy feat, Cleon." Pyera holds me tighter

"In the case that none of our plans are successful." He persists. "We should consider the quickest way to strike Church down: venom."

I straighten up.

He's right. A vampire, by some ironic twist of fate, can be killed by their own individual venom. Every vampire has been sampled and those samples have been stored. A bullet or knife laced with it could down a ravenous rogue in *seconds*. In 2010, I heard they used blood magic to combine the entire coven's samples to conquer the rioters.

"Do the gammas still have his?" I perk up.

"I do not believe so," Cleon says.

My heart sinks.

"Veratrum's hospital was destroyed during the Cleansing." He explains. "Most samples had to be recollected. They were still in the process of building back their bulk when he disappeared."

"So what?" I clutch my Pyera's arms. "We're going to get him to bite himself?"

Pyera clicks her tongue. "We're all hardwired with the subconscious instinct not to poison ourselves. It doesn't matter how hard you bite; your fangs won't release any venom. You'll just puncture yourself."

"Then why bring up venom?"

"*Yours* could do it," Nico says.

I narrow my eyes at him. "Elaborate."

"When you were bitten," Cleon says, "Francis injected you with his toxin."

"Yeah, okay. That's Basic Vampire Logic 101."

The wrinkles around his eyes tighten. "During your metamorphosis from shifter to vampire, your body changed. It created a habitat for the venom. Glands and fangs. That said, the venom itself did not change."

I close my eyes. "So basically, I'm the trump card."

"Correct," Cleon says. "And, in a worst-case scenario, your venom would dispatch him in seconds."

"He doesn't have any children?" I try to be *firm,* but it sounds *desperate.*

"Not..." Valberg trails off. His eyes sink to the floor, somber, before he looks up. "No. He doesn't. Regardless, vampires who are born develop their own venom within the womb. It's only those bitten who share venom with their creators."

The urge to scream is unbearable. First, I was a shifter. Then, I was a vampire. Then a Prophet. And now I'm a sacrifice with the ability to end the world, or the Monster, himself. Why? My life never mattered before. I hated it, and now I long for it.

Panic wakes from the depths of my mind. I press my face into Pyera's arms. *Mother Nature, help me.*

BRIGHT EYES

Hints of daylight dye the horizon. Vast darkness turns violet, lavender, rusty orange, and then blazing yellow. The remnants of night protect Nico and me on our way from Cleon's. In the inky black shadows, slowly flushed purple, birds trill awake as the coven settles into its daytime slumber.

Nico digs his hands into his pockets. "I don't want to jump to any conclusions, Macy, but I think you're bad luck."

"You and everyone else." I cross my arms.

He chuckles. It fades into a thoughtful hum. "What do you think?"

I inspect him out the corner of my eye. "About what?"

"About it all."

I let out a frustrated noise. "*I think* the Man in the Moon picked the wrong person to lay the weight of the world on."

He pulls his hood up, obscuring his face in shadows. "There are two Prophets for a reason. Not that I'm a stellar candidate for saving the world either."

"You've got more practice at this."

"Not really." He consoles... *soft,* as opposed to *coarse.* "Good futures are my thing. This apocalypse *puro bla, bla, bla?* It's new for me too." Silence stretches between us until he says, "Y'know, I could help you."

"And how would you do that?" I say, disbelieving.

"Did you know there used to be a boxing league around here?" he asks.

"No." I answer. "Why?"

"I used to compete."

Surprise dapples my features. Perhaps it's my own preconceived notion that athletes, like those in Bloodroot, are strong men and women who stride among bears and mountain lions, but Nico's lean and short stature would've never hinted toward athleticism.

"There was a team in every Knotweed coven up until recently." His fingers toy with the necklace around his throat. "There were annual competitions. Our team won once or twice."

"What happened to it?"

"That's not important." He shrugs. We pass under a streetlight, illuminating his frown. "But you? You just got ten times more important. You need a way to protect yourself now that your Grounding is out of the picture and your life is on the line."

I stop without warning, and, after a few steps ahead, he does too. He turns and cocks his head at me. He swipes a hand beneath his beanie. Strands of his dark brown hair blend with his even darker eyes. *What?* Those eyes ask.

"You wanna box with me?" I say.

"I would prefer the world not go up in flame, meaning you have to stay alive. I wanna help."

My thoughts travel back to Lilac. She and I sparred every so often. It was always beta and omega, and one clearly took it easy on the other. It was more embarrassing than fruitful, but she insisted she was giving it her all. White lies, sure, but still lies.

"One on one?" I ask.

He eyes me. "I can invite Val if it makes you more comfortable."

"I'm more worried about being treated equal," I say.

"What do you mean?"

My voice is firm. "I don't want you to take it easy on me."

Like Lilac did.

The golden radiance of the streetlamp casts orange hues across his brown skin. The stifled embers of a competitor light his eyes. It spurs my own drive.

"As if you won't *make it* easy?" He grins. It's a smug and annoying grin. My fingers twitch with the desire to punch it right now. "No worries. I've got a winning streak to keep up."

"You might be surprised." I challenge.

"That so?" he dares.

I tip my chin up. "Yes."

He holds my eyes for a few seconds, and then looks away with a laugh. He retreats from the light and gives me a lazy salute.

"See you later, Bright Eyes."

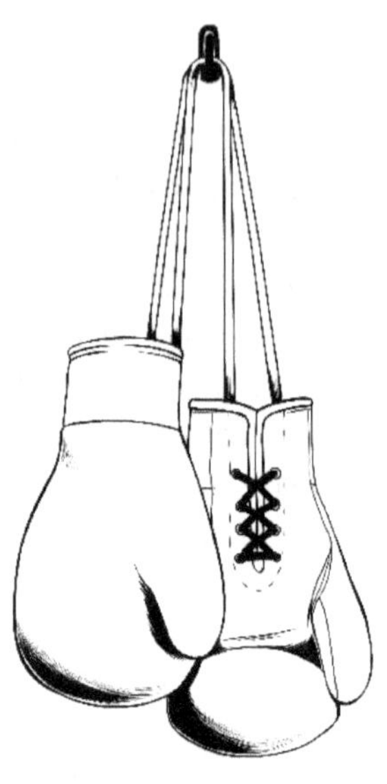

EIGHTEEN

TESTOSTERONE

Luc catches up with me on the way to the gym. Even after I tell him where I'm going, he insists on walking with me. I prepare myself for his vocal disapproval over my agreement with Nico. I wish that's what he had to say.

"It's not the same." I say through gritted teeth.

"Everything got out of hand." He touches my shoulder. "You didn't mean what you said. Neither did she."

I make a face at him. "She seemed pretty serious. But... I don't know. Maybe I misinterpreted the whole *brain-dead mutt* thing, the crap about my life, and that rant about how I'm not a shifter anymore."

He looks away from me.

"Yeah." I scoff. "I definitely misinterpreted *all* of that."

"Okay, okay." He holds his hands up, waving my heated tone away. "That's fair, but it's not like you didn't say anything you regret either."

"That depends. Does *she* regret anything? Is she even sorry? She isn't the sort to have people run errands for her."

He frowns. "I'm just trying to build the foundation of a bridge you guys can cross."

We follow street signs until the gym's roof is visible above low-rise buildings. It's nothing like the library, but it's certainly tall enough to raise a few brows.

Luc heaves a disgruntled sigh. "Macy?"

Here it comes. "Yeah?"

"I know it's not my place," he says. "And I'm inserting myself where I shouldn't, but I'm *really* not sure about this."

"You mean about Nico."

His name waters baleful seeds in Luc's heart. A stone cold, "Yeah," is his only response.

Called it.

"I don't like him." He grumbles.

"I don't like him either, but I don't exactly have a choice, Luc. I didn't ask for any of this."

Luc scoffs. I'm taken off guard by how mean it sounds. I stare at him, trying to understand his bitterness.

"You're acting weird." A realization strikes. My face warps with incredulity. "Are you... jealous?"

I try to reason it away. I must've misconstrued his tone. Every interaction we've shared has been strictly platonic. We've never even flirted because *I'm gay.* It's practically stamped on my forehead in big, bold letters. Yet, I spot a glimmer of green in his blue eyes.

"What? No!" He stumbles, and then frantically gestures with his hands. "Macy, you're like my little sister! You just don't *know* him."

"And you do?"

He opens his mouth, but I hold up a hand. "I know you mean well. I wouldn't be doing this if I didn't have to...But he's the only other person on the planet who saw what I saw, Luc. I don't care if he's an asshole because yes, he's an *asshole*. But I'm not his friend. I'm just working with him."

He averts his eyes.

"Why does it bother you so much?" I lean forward to see his face better.

"It..." He blows air from his nose. He glances up. His face hardens.

A sweaty Nico is seated on the bench outside the gym. He wears a raggedy black shirt with the sleeves rolled up to his elbows. He lowers the water bottle from his lips and stands as we approach. Luc sends him a daggered look. Nico, the duller of two blades, examines him uneasily.

"Valberg's inside." He eyes Luc.

I say, "Luc wanted to talk to me. I didn't bring him to chaperone."

"Don't worry." Luc scoffs sardonically. "I'm not here to ruin your punching party, Nic."

Nico tucks his hands in his pocket, and glares coldly. He says, "The only person I want to punch isn't invited."

"That how you solve your problems?" Luc fires back.

"At least I solve mine."

I can practically taste the testosterone in the air.

"You guys are ridiculous." I push past them and storm into the gym.

Their masculinity contest apparently shattered, Luc bids me a grumpy farewell as Nico catches up. I sign in at the front desk. He then takes the lead and guides me up a flight of stairs

"Is it me or does he hate you more than most people?" I say without looking at him.

His voice is nonchalant. "Short tempers have a way of boiling bad blood."

"You guys have bad blood?" I glance at him.

Maybe I gave Luc too little credit.

"I have bad blood with a lot of people."

Correction. Maybe I gave Nico too *much* credit.

He holds the door open for me when we reach the top of the stairs. The floors are padded and give under my weight. The brown walls are lined by handrails. A few faded green benches hunker by the door, the closest of which is cluttered by some bags, a pair of black boxing gloves, a few other miscellaneous items, and Valberg.

His sweaty forehead and hair glisten under the yellow light. He thumps his leg atop a red cooler as he reads a book. He looks up at the sound of the door creaking. A fresh bruise mottles his cheek.

"Macy!" He brightens. "I'm glad you arrived! I was worried after you missed our meditation session."

I look elsewhere. "Yeah, sorry... I couldn't make it."

He knows I'm lying. He's kind enough not to call me out. "I'm just happy you're here."

Pointedly, I stare at his cheek. "Looks like it. Nico roughed you up."

The Grand Enchanter thumbs the contusion. His eyes tighten in pain but take on a competitive demeanor.

He grins mischievously. "I got him back. Isn't that right, Nic?"

Nico rubs his side. "You got lucky, *anciano*."

"You clearly don't understand the difference between skill and fortune." Valberg teases.

"Oh, I do," says Nico. "At your age? You're *lucky* you haven't stumbled into your grave yet."

I fold my arms, leaning on one leg. "Those are fighting words. Do I sense a rematch?"

His grin grows twice its size. "Sorry. As soon as you stepped into the room he went from competitor to chaperone. But you...?"

He leans past me. Too close. His arm brushes slowly against mine. I level a dry look at him. He winks as he straightens up, boxing gloves in hand. He places them in mine.

"Welcome to the rink, Miss Braddock."

Rolling my eyes, I let the gloves hang around my neck. Unzipping my sweatshirt, I toss it onto the bench. I feel oddly exposed in my green tank top. It's been so long since I've shown off my Marrow Mark.

"Have you ever boxed before?" he asks as I slip the gloves on.

They're hefty and warm. I shake them a few times to get accustomed to their heaviness. It doesn't erase all of the unfamiliarity.

"I've done some hand-to-hand training," I say. "Most of us only worry about combat when we're shifted. Otherwise, we pour everything into our Groundings."

"How did that work out?"

It's a sincere question, so I stifle my annoyance.

"I've never been very..." I search for a word. It tastes bitter. "... *adept* at spiritual training."

Nico tightens the elastic around his wrist. "This should be an easy transition then, shouldn't it?"

Aggravation threatens to win over self-control. *It's okay,* I tell myself, *you get to punch him in just a minute.*

He blows his hair out of his face, and sizes me up. "Show me what you know. We'll test your skills and go from there."

I straighten my stance and guard my face.

Lilac was never invested in our sparring matches. Most days they led to more intimate exercises, and when they didn't, she barely took me seriously. She wanted to help me, but after what happened with Lily, she was distant on many fronts. Here, I don't have a past. I don't even have the same power I did when I hurt Lily. That fact is comforting for the first time ever.

I peer at him over my black gloves, determined. Perhaps he expects something more daring and less steely. He looks mildly impressed for the shortest second.

He's the incarnation of refinement. The residual perspiration from his previous match with Val glitters against his tanned pallor. Left over adrenaline livens him. His bouncing steps are quick but relaxed, agile but restrained.

He glances at Valberg. "Before we start—"

I swing fast, blunt, and hard.

He sees me out the corner of his eye and staggers away with wide eyes. He starts to say something else, so I throw another punch. This one is aimed for his jaw. He swiftly scurries back, and then lunges at me. I barely block his fist with my arms. The force of his swing pushes me back a few steps. I use that distance to regroup. A breath in, a breath out; a step back when he attacks again.

"That was a good block, and an even better evasion! But you're on the defensive."

He lowers his arms as he talks—he does that a lot. So, I jab at him, intentionally missing. He moves to sidestep. My body reacts to a mental blueprint; I kick his ankle out from under him mid-step. He hits the ground with a satisfactory thud.

I frame my hips with my gloves, grinning down at him, less than kindly. "What was that?"

His eyebrows pull together, eyes glinting with a winning mix of aggravation and amusement. A smug smile tugs on my mouth until he sweeps his calf across my ankles, stealing away my ego. Once again, we're on the same level, grappling for leverage. We exchange close-range punches and repeatedly attempt to pin the other. It's at this point that I truly begin to comprehend his advantage. He nearly pins me more than once, and my measly efforts to do the same are quickly broken.

Eventually, he flips me onto my belly, captures my arm, and clamps it behind my back at an angle. The joint burns. My efforts double, triple, and then quadruple as Valberg counts down. My body is too exhausted and contorted. I can't free myself before he reaches zero.

Nico releases me. We each flop away from one another. He throws himself back, and I roll over to stare at the ceiling. The lights leave white lines across my vision when I blink.

We spend a minute catching our breath. Each deep inhalation drains the adrenaline from my bloodstream. The bruises, numbed by the fight, wake up. I ache, feeling daggers and needles all over my body. And to top it all off with a shiny little bow, my throat is scorching for blood. Ugh.

Nico is the first to sit up. He's a little breathless, but better rejuvenated. "Y'know, that was harder than I thought it would be."

"Were you expecting it to be *easy*?" Maybe I shouldn't be surprised. Or offended.

Both must be visible on my face because he laughs. "I mean, it wasn't exactly *difficult*."

I pry a glove off to throw it at him. It wallops his shoulder, making him snicker.

Valberg hunts around his cooler. He pulls two bottles of blood out and abandons the bench. He chortles as he offers his hand and a bottle. I greedily take both. He pulls me up, and I unscrew the cap. I guzzle it down less than graciously as he helps Nico next, who exhibits more self-control.

Blood doesn't heal the body, but it relieves tiredness and thirst. Both currently fray the ends of my soul. I suck in a breath when the burning in my throat is soothed and the heaviness on my shoulders is lifted. Then the shame hits. I glare into the crimson.

"Don't listen to him, Macy." Valberg jars me from my thoughts. "You handled him as well as could be expected."

I jerk my eyes towards him. "You vampires are really horrible about encouragement. *As well as could be expected?* C'mon, Valberg."

The bearded man bellows. "I mean it! You still have your teeth!"

"I went easy." Nico teases.

I tip my chin up defiantly. "So I wasn't the only one holding back?"

He shakes his head, smiling as he takes a swig of his drink. He arches a thick brow at me. "That so?"

"Yeah."

"I guess that means we should have a rematch, huh?"

I give him a toothy grin. "Someone has to kick your ass."

He tosses Valberg his bottle, energized by adrenaline and humor. In his eyes, there's something deeper. Something he doesn't mean to show. Happiness. I squint, surprised.

Valberg takes my bottle too.

Nico and I resume our places.

"Just letting you know," he says, "I'm unbeaten."

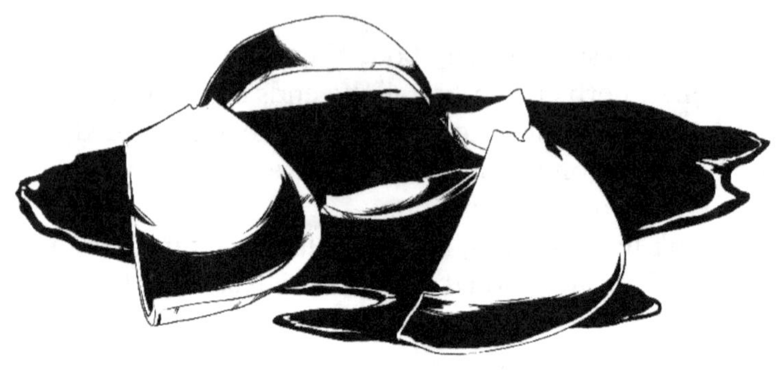

EAT THEIR DELICACIES

A few days, numerous sprints around the track, and several lost matches later, my body demands solace. After over a month of being a vampire, I'm not equipped to handle such exhaustive training anymore. My muscles burn and bruises darken my wet skin.

I hold up an arm. Bathwater drips down my skin in wayward rivers, catching light and emphasizing my bruises. I admire them. They're a visible metric to measure my effort; one bruise = x hours of work. The more welts I get, the stronger I'll become. Eventually, I'll be steely enough to harness Aimil's power.

I soak in the frothy bubbles of my bath. The water darkens my red hair, which floats around my body like vines of seaweed. They're darker compared to the emerald coils of my Marrow Mark. I trace it.

Only nights ago, in a delirious nightmare, viridescent fronds bled from the emerald brands, but that was just a dream. How much longer until I see its luster in real life?

You might not, fear hisses.

I clench my eyes shut. Stubbornly, I think, *Yes. I will.*

It's hard to find an opportunity surrounded by all this noise. Quiet was easy to find in the woods. There were no streets, no cars to rove by in roaring gusts, and if the town's natural noise became too much, all I had to do was wander. The forest would swallow me eventually.

My ears dip in and out of the water, teasing hints of noiselessness. A courageous concept crosses my mind. I suck in a massive breath, and then expel it slowly as I submerge myself underwater. The humming lights and whirring fan become vague distortions, barely audible until any trace disappears.

I search for Aimil.

She always has a habit of hiding from me. Before I was bitten, it sometimes took hours to find her, and there was never any guarantee of communion. And I know why. Despite being her vessel, I have never possessed enough control to wield her strength.

The healers always attributed it to childhood trauma. They would prattle on and on about how witnessing Mom's near-death permanently altered my spirit, and then further hypothesized my actions that day, although responsible for our survival, may have drained me of my potential. *After all,* they would construe, *a child doesn't spectate such cruelty without repercussions.*

At the sight of my parents' concern, they reassured them Mother Nature would guide me to great things if I were diligent and dedicated. And yet, no matter how meticulously I trained, true control always eluded me. Not even Lilac's sister could impart such knowledge.

My chest starts to burn for oxygen.

I wade deeper into my soul. The heavy currents impede my haste. A presence lurks under the waves, too far. Her voice calls out to me and I tread quicker. Frantically, I try to reach her but the tightness in my chest tugs me further and further away.

I bolt upright. The water splashes against the tub. Water dribbles from my face and body like rain, pooling in my open mouth. I push my sopping hair out of my face, blinking the moisture from my eyes. For a second, I saw my Marrow Mark gleam. It's so brief that I soon doubt it was at all. Still, I trace the patterns in my palms, hoping to find some lingering tendril of heat. Nothing.

With a defeated sigh, I lug myself out of the bath.

A restless crackle canters across my skin. I glance over my shoulder at the mirror's shielded but persistent stare. I've contemplated tearing the sheet down to glare at the girl on the other side, but I can't find it in myself to face her. Maybe I will when she looks less like a mistake.

I scowl.

Pyera told me to be at the hospital by ten, so, with less than thirty minutes to spare, I hastily navigate the streets, chasing a shortcut to the Bridge. It's my second favorite place in Devil's Trumpet. But nothing beats the Library.

It slopes over the coven's torpid river. The rails are smooth, sanded and polished by deft hands. Those same hands must've spent hours engraving every miniscule pattern into the columns. I brace myself against the banister to admire the murmuring waters teeming below. The sun's nighttime kin scintillate in its leisurely waves, blotted out by the occasional branch caught in the stream.

Lilac would've loved it here. We would skip rocks across the water like we did when we were younger, and fish stray objects out of the water. I smile. It turns into a sullen frown.

I chart the waterway's course with my eyes. It twists merrily and the coven bends to its will. Not even the wall hinders its passage. It stands sturdy and unyielding to everything but the water, allowing it to weave between stone bars burrowed into the riverbed.

Nestled close to the wall, at the base of a tree, a shadow moves. A gamma? My gut disagrees. They lack the terse stature of a soldier, wobbling, twitching, shaking instead.

Maybe they're a boozed-up vampire, skirting the edges of town. Maybe they're looking for a way out. I don't blame them. Or maybe they enjoy isolated, fidgety naps under trees. *Maybe* I should leave. I like that idea.

The wind kisses the nape of my neck. It pushes through my hair, tickling my jaw, urging me toward the shadow. Not away.

I tiptoe off the Bridge. The figure glances around, but the trees conceal me. There's only silence as I approach, the forest's way of begging me: *Get there, and get there fast.*

She looks like an animal. Her mangled blond hair is knotted, thinner in patches. Her elbows move in and out at strange angles and her spine juts out like boney alps under her shirt. Each movement is chorused by slick, sawing sounds.

My every fiber tries to convince me to go back, but my legs refuse. They guide me closer on wobbly knees. I'm glued to this moment, stuck listening to her ragged breaths and whispers. Mother Nature, what is she whispering?

My voice feels small in the void of night. "Are you..."

She goes rigid.

I try again. "Are you okay?"

Slowly, she turns her head to peer over her shoulder. Skin sags over blistered scar tissue, pocked all over her face and neck, and droops over her one, deep set eye. It moves errantly over my body. Her gaze is heavy on my skin, peeling back my smooth, pretty flesh to take for herself. Protectively, I hug my arms.

Leave, I think, but I ask, "Are you okay?"

She blows a wheeze off her tongue.

"What?" I inch closer, reaching out. "What are you saying?"

My trembling fingertips graze her shoulder. The wind hollers between the trees, telling me, *Stop!*

She pounces up and whirs around, fangs bared. Her mangled face is rabid. She swings one welted hand wildly. Something glints in the dark. Metal. *A knife.* Shock sends me stumbling back into a tree.

In her hand, a half dead squirrel hangs, sawed and stringy. Chunks of meat cling by tissue thread. It swings, its pieces oscillating in her grip. One of the tethers snaps. It *squishes* when it hits the ground. My stomach flips.

"What is *wrong* with you?" I dig my nails into tree bark.

She snarls before fleeing into the dark. Something flies from her coat, and shatters dark liquid close by. The wind shifts the leaves. A thin beam of moonlight illuminates the broken specks of glass on the ground. Another, softer breeze begs me to move closer, but when I take a step the grass squelches. It's black and wet. *Blood.* From an *animal.*

Crouching, I push a few pieces of broken glass together to create the skeleton of a shattered vial. My eyes follow the path the woman took through the woods. *Were you...collecting squirrel blood? Why?*

My back pocket vibrates, resonating down my leg. I wipe my hand on the clean grass, using the other to pull my phone out. The harsh light blinds me, so I shield my eyes. Between my fingers, a text from Pyera reads:

Where are you?

TWENTY

RUN, BOY, RUN

Smoke smothers what remains of Loosestrife. The trees are black and barren. The branches, quills, and leaves are ash, carpeting the forest floor. In the distance, where the haze thins, stands a wall of trees. They were scarred by the fire's nearness, but not it's touch. Beyond them, the forest is alive, guarded by the orange moon.

The wolf, Jaxon, hurtles in that direction.

A shuddering pain plucks its way up and down his ribs. It makes every inhalation painful, every step a trial, and threatens to separate Man from Beast. He clumsily leaps over fallen pines, snakes between firs, but the rogues run behind him, alongside him, ahead of him.

He just has to get to the fire line. There will be gamma patrols, settlements, shifters. He'll run home to Ma. He'll write to Pa and apologize for how they left things. He'll take Miranda up on her offer to live with her in Michigan. Now more than ever, he misses his big sister.

It'll all be fine. He just has to *get there.*

He veers left but one of the rogues emerges from pitch-black nothing. He swipes at Jaxon, so the wolf lunges away. A woman springs from the smoke. She pounces on Jaxon's back. Snarling, he bucks and kicks and propels himself every which way. She tugs over and over on Jaxon's fur until her fingers slip from his pelt. She slams into a tree stump. The charred bark cuts into her arm. The scent of decay radiates from the gash.

The rogues surface from all directions, looming closer, circling Jaxon. He jumps toward each sound they make. So horrible, those sounds: tongues smacking against hungry lips, chuckles brewing in chests, boots kicking up ash and coal as they draw nearer.

"You ran." A silver-eyed vampire says. His eyes match his knife. He strokes it too gently for such gnarled, veiny hands. He's a monster. "What is it you shifters say? *'Beast, Breath, and Body for Her?'* Give everything until your dying breath?"

Jaxon gets on his haunches. Ears lying flat, he pulls back the skin around his teeth and snarls a warning. Jaxon's eyes, emerald like the Earth before the fire, like his sister's eyes, like his mother's, are dark and challenging.

Go on, he thinks, *say it.*

The Monster saunters closer. "Where's your valiance now, mutt?"

Jaxon growls again, but the vampire doesn't care. He wears a giddy smirk as he edges nearer. The others take steady strides toward Jaxon, muttering taunts between laughter. One reaches for Jaxon's tail, so Jaxon whirls around and snaps at him. Another grasps at Jaxon's fur. He nearly snags her fingers between his teeth. Someone pulls on his hind leg. Jaxon kicks the hand away, glowering with menace.

Then, an invisible weight crashes down on him. Jaxon struggles to stay standing, but the vampires tie him up in ropes of blood. They yank on crimson cords, so he falls onto his damaged side. His body convulses on impact. Every ounce of air is expunged from his lungs. He wheezes, tries to free himself of their trap. He jerks every leg and flounders as if he isn't a wolf, but a fish out of water; a shifter in a scorched forest.

They all sneer at him.

The Monster lifts his leg. Jaxon writhes harder as he aims the heel of his boot at Jaxon's ribs. The Monster drops his foot like an anchor.

Crack.

Jaxon howls. It turns into a whine which turns into a scream. The transformation visibly ripples across fur, muscle, and then skin. His injuries draw it out. For minutes, he lies there, coming undone via torturous metamorphosis. When it's over, he's paralyzed by the pain in every joint, bone, and muscle.

The rogues turn him on his back. He roars with agony, making them laugh. They pin him down by his limbs. He yanks on his arms, legs, and bucks his hips, but every movement saps him of breath.

The Monster crouches next to Jaxon. He sets the tip of his knife at the center of Jaxon's naked chest. His struggling comes to an abrupt, petrified pause.

Using his forefinger and thumb, the Monster spins the knife clockwise, counterclockwise, and back again. He then drags it up and down Jaxon's body, tracing the art Mother Nature, fate, and age sewed into his flesh. White feathers, dusted all over him, from head to toe.

Jaxon's muscles tense wherever the knife wanders. A hipbone, a rib, his naval, his collarbone, horribly slow and taunting. Finally, the blade lingers. It draws lazy circles around the Greek symbols on Jaxon's chest. The vampire's eyes are molten hot with mirth.

"A delta." He scoffs. "I would've thought... *omega.*"

Jaxon glares, lips tight. The Monster likes that more.

"Were you a painter? A chef? A stone-carver? Did you gather herbs and roots for the healers?"

He waits and waits.

"Quiet, are we?" The vampire sneers. "It's alright. I was going to cut out your tongue anyway."

Jaxon's nose creases with a growl. His livid green eyes glow with rage. *He* glows. White light singes his flesh as his Marrow Mark burns to life. It sears the vampire's palms. Blisters bubble to the surface of their translucent skin. They yank their hands away, roaring loudly. White doves fly from his body, and the vampires jump away.

The blinding birds sweep low to the forest floor. They spiral around Jaxon, tailed by drafts of ashy air. Their razor-sharp wings slice through blackened bark, logs, and the skin of a vampire who gets too close.

Jaxon rolls onto his stomach, summoning all his strength. He heaves a shout, but it lodges in his throat. His muscles twitch under the invisible weight, but he fights it off. When he finally stands, his thighs burn, his knees tremble, but he *stands.*

The doves shrill like banshees. They cut through the ebony night, teeming away from Jaxon. Their wings are as dangerous as knives, but the rogues move too quickly.

Jaxon is not the first shifter they've killed. They're hunters just like him.

He doesn't care. They'll burn like these woods.

Then darkness descends. It comes from everywhere at once. The weight of the universe threatens to break Jaxon's back. His knees buckle, and his Marrow Mark flickers. He fights to stay standing, but the heftiness grows greater and greater until—his knees hit soil. His spine bends. Mother Nature, it's going to break! He catches himself with his hands. His elbows tremor, then give. He collapses.

The vampires are on top of him again. They pin him on his belly. The Monster strokes a vein twitching in Jaxon's temple, and brushes his dark brown fringe from his face. Jaxon jerks away.

"What magic is this?" he snarls.

The Monster shrugs nonchalantly. "Blood magic, but not the kind you know."

The knife returns, edge rimmed black. The Monster presses the tip into Jaxon's cheek. It's a great and building pressure. The knife indents fat without breaking skin. The possibility taunts him.

His green eyes brim with hot, frightened tears, but he refuses to let them spill. All he ever wanted was to be like his sister. He can't cry now. Not like this.

The vampire pulls a necklace out from under his shirt. He pinches the thin chain between two fingers, holding it under dim moonlight. A cross dangles off it, engraved with finite, particular markings. The grooves are flooded black. It looks like an enchantment, but those are red. What magic *is* this?

The monster smiles, plucking the thoughts from Jaxon's head. "This is the magic your *dog people* took from us. Watch, if I cut you, you'll bleed red."

The vampire leans into the knife. The pressure becomes unbearable. His weight is too much. Jaxon howls, stretching the skin on his face, thinning it. When Jaxon's shoulders quake, struggle renewed, the knife cuts through. Scarlet gushes out from beneath the blade. Salty copper poisons Jaxon's taste buds. He hacks up globules of blood.

The vampires snicker. Their bellies rumble loudly with hunger. Mercifully, the Monster pulls the knife away. Blood dribbles from the corner of Jaxon's lip. Jaxon's arms twitch with residual rebellion, but nothing more.

The Monster licks his bloodied knife. An unseemly moan drips off his tongue. He glares at Jaxon. Rolling up his sleeve, he motions to a fresh cut oozing tar.

"But I bleed black." He swipes his thumb across one of the cuts, and then licks it clean. "And when you bleed black, the night is your blood."

TWENTY-ONE

VENOM

The man at the front desk checks me in, and then pokes a sequence of letters into his keyboard. The doors open nearby. Two gammas stroll out.

They escort me through the beige hallways, which smell like bleach and something sickly sweet. The rooms are mostly empty. A few are occupied, but the gammas jostle me along before I can peer inside.

Vampires, like Shifters, are immune to most human ailments, but there are some sicknesses capable of sending them to an early grave. I read somewhere that, as they age, the protective lining around their glands can decay. They ooze venom, and the vampire dies of their poison.

The most common malady is blood sickness: when they taste fresh blood and become addicted to the flavor, almost feral. It's the leading cause of most rogue cases, aside from outright rebellion.

The gammas hold the door open to a small examination room, guarding either side.

They must expect me to run off. Little do they know, with a month of failed escape attempts under my belt and imminent doom looming over me, I've resigned myself to my fate. I resist sticking my tongue out at one. It's immature, I tell myself. They're just doing their jobs.

Pyera and Valberg greet me inside, as does a vampire nurse, Aurora.

"Where's Cleon?" I reply to their smiles with my own.

"He and our assistants are helping the Embassy ensure Alpha Kennedy's requests are met," she notes dryly.

"She's on her way then?" I ask.

Aurora waves me to a cot, where my legs dangle over the edge.

"That she is." The Lady gets up from her seat. "I actually can't stay either, but I wanted to be sure you got here."

"You thought I'd run."

Her grin is a silent admission.

I snort.

She simpers. "Valberg will stay with you."

Does no one trust me? "Where are you off to?"

Sourness etches Pyera's face. She grumbles, "I've got five bouquets to pick up from a chatty florist on the other side of town. The Alpha requested she be greeted by Butterfly Mist flowers. *Apparently,* they're her favorite."

Valberg chuckles. "Don't let Doretha keep you too long, my Lady."

Pyera aims a finger and a glare at him. "Don't you start, Val."

"Hey..." I grab Pyera's arm. "Before you go."

Her attitude softens. She cocks her head at me.

I tuck a stand of hair behind my ear. "On my way here, I ran into a woman by the Bridge." The skin between my eyebrows creases. "She was torturing a squirrel. Collecting its blood, I think."

She isn't surprised. The corners of her mouth turn down. "Did you catch her name?"

I shake my head. "She had blisters all over her face."

Valberg sighs.

The Lady pinches her nose. "Terces."

I sit up a little straighter. Terces Redloh. The last woman thrown in the Sunlight Chambers. *They left Terces out for hours,* Circi had said. I stare at my hand, imagining ugly welts bubbling up from underneath, remembering Terces' face. My chest tightens.

"I'll have to speak with the gammas," says Pyera.

"That isn't necessary." Val rushes to say.

I jerk my eyes up. "Uh, why not?"

He scratches his jaw. "I'll speak to her. She won't be a problem again."

"Val." Pyera breathes. "You said that last time."

"Last time?" I gape.

"I know." He doesn't acknowledge me. "Just let me handle her. *Please*, Pyera."

Pyera closes her eyes. She flicks her wrist and pushes out the door. The words "There can't be anymore incidents after this" follow her out.

I twist toward Val. *"Last time?"*

He gives me a sullen look. "Terces is... unwell."

"You could say that. Or you could say crazy."

"Macy..." He doesn't say anything else. Instead, he buries himself in the pages of his book. The conversation is over.

"Have you ever given venom before?" Aurora steps between us, cutting through the tension.

I focus on her. "No. I've never needed to."

She smiles and then moves from my end of the room to the other, sorting through a few drawers. "They take a sample from every bitten vampire before they're introduced to the coven. New arrivals tend to be... unruly. Regardless, all vampires are scheduled appointments to build a bulk reserve."

Endless darkness surrounds me as I recall lying in the back of that truck, burning on the inside. I dig through the foggy, half-forgotten memories between when I was bitten, and arrived here.

"I don't remember them..."

She wheels a small metal table to my bedside. Her smile doesn't falter. "No one ever does."

Swallowing, I shift uncomfortably in my seat. "Do they kill that many vampires around here?"

For the first few weeks, I threw myself at any chance of escape, and they beat me back every time. It was easy for them. Laughable. I wasn't a threat, but what if I had been? What if I caught the wrong gamma on a bad day? Or I annoyed the wrong, power hungry gamma? What if my want for freedom was punished with bullets instead of house-arrest?

"Well..." Aurora gloves her hands. "Sometimes, vampires grow weary of their time on this Earth. Their venom can be used as euthanasia. But, usually, venom is reserved for rogues."

If I *had* escaped, I would've been a rogue. It wouldn't have mattered that I wasn't out for blood, revenge, or anything. My only desire is freedom and they would've killed me for it. They could right now. If one gamma went crazy, if I delivered a dry joke at the wrong time, if another vampire rebelled and I got caught in the middle. Even if they just *wanted* to.

I rub my palms. "They...just *kill* them?"

Her hand pauses over her medical utensils. She looks up at me. "Once a vampire leaves their coven, they are considered an enemy to the masquerade. A risk. Very... rarely are they taken in without force. Even more rarely are they taken alive."

"How often does that happen?" I straighten creases in the cot's sheets.

"Not too much." Valberg interjects, having finally stolen his eyes away from his book. He looks kinder, less agitated. "Very few vampires from Devil's Trumpet go rogue."

Because they don't want to or because they can't?

"Fortunately." Aurora nods. She then shows me a small, clear container. There's a fleshy film over the top. "Your venom will be stored in this vial. We won't gather enough for bulk storage today, but the Lady scheduled you a few more appointments. Once we've garnered enough, it'll be used to lace the bullets of a single magazine."

"Just one?"

"Just one." She scoots closer.

"I'm going to ask you to open your mouth. I'll then puncture the skin prosthetic with your fang and press on this part of your gum." She curls her upper lip and points to segment of pink flesh. "Any questions?"

I shake my head.

"Then let's begin!"

Aurora makes the procedure go by fast. We do one fang and then repeat the process with the other, filling the vial with a millimeter. She snaps a lid onto the container and sets it inside a sealed box. Afterwards, she jokingly asks if I'd like a sucker for my good behavior. She didn't expect me to say yes. Nonetheless, I'm rewarded with a bright green lollipop before she leaves, soon to return.

Valberg sets his reading material aside, giving me a cheery look. "You've been adjusting well, Macy. I'm glad."

"Is that how it looks?" I jest, sucker in my cheek. "I guess I *am* dying slightly less inside than before."

He rubs his eyes with one hand, laughing. "Understandable."

"It's not that bad, all things considered."

"Your situation is unlike any other in all of history."

I grin, shaking my head. "Thanks. I almost forgot the odds were stacked against me."

"You aren't alone," he says. "I've noticed you and Nico make a stupendous duo."

"He's a prick."

The man bellows. "Oh, that he is. He has certainly grown into quite the pariah."

"Nice way to say outcast." I pull the sucker out of my mouth. I look at it before glancing up at Valberg. "So... you've known him a long time?"

"A *very* long time." His smile tempers. "Before I became Grand Enchanter, I was tasked with easing the transition of new arrivals into the coven. When he was brought here, he was only a child."

"A child?" I echo. "I heard he wasn't a Pureblood but was he... human?"

"Indeed." Valberg's eyes drop to the floor. "Back then, he was a very fragile thing. It's not my story to tell, but the events that brought him here were horrific. He was so frail and afraid, but..." Valberg closes his eyes, face scrunched. The pain lingers when he opens his eyes again. "He and I are family. My heart aches for what he's seen and hopes for what he'll achieve. It's why I chose him to succeed me as Grand Enchanter."

From prey to pariah to prophet. Like me, from shifter to soothsayer to sacrifice.

"He's come a long way. You've helped."

I kick my feet and knot my fingers together awkwardly. "Uh, thanks?"

He laughs gently. "It *is* a compliment. I meant it when I said you two make a good duo. You've both made incredible leaps since..."

"Since the end of the world popped up on everyone's radar?"

"Yes." He manages a smile. Eyeing the floor, he stares and stares, reliving old memories. Finally, he sighs. "I've been meaning to ask you something, Macy."

I frown. "Aren't you the guy with all the answers?"

"If only," he muses. His face shifts from amused to inquisitive. He rests his elbows on his knees with steepled fingers. "Why have you pursued a physical solution for a spiritual problem?"

Oh. Great. "You mean my Grounding."

"I do."

It takes me a minute to conjure a reasonable answer. I look at the edge of the bed. "Meditation just doesn't work for me. Any time I've summoned her, I was either in danger or at my limits. I don't know any other way to reach her."

He strokes his beard. "I know you avoided the session Pyera scheduled, but if you like, we can try again. I'm no shifter, but I attended the Academy of Blood Magic and studied with your healers. I could guide you to the depths of tranquility and keep you there for however long you need."

A twinge of anxiety pulls in my chest, and I give him the only answer I can muster.

"Rain check."

TWENTY-TWO

EAGLE FEATHERS

A night later, Luc unexpectedly shows up at my door, just after sunset. Apparently, we have plans tonight. I try to weasel my way out of them and back to bed, but Luc drags me into the real world.

"Why was *I* your first choice?" I whine as we stagger down the busy sidewalk, arms looped together.

"You're my trusty sidekick!", Luc says.

"Can I be your trusty bed bug instead?"

Smiling, he nudges my ribs with his elbow. "It's my job to check up on you, Tenderfoot! You're one of my new arrivals."

"Here I thought I was special," I say.

"You are! You're my favorite shifter in the entire coven."

I snort. "Even before you?"

His lopsided smile twinkles deviously. "Okay. Second favorite."

He pulls me toward one of the shops. It's a puny little place, smashed between a jeweler and a thrift store. All three are guarded by gammas. Their eyes follow us. I recoil from the silent threats relayed via glares and glowing skin. These people, these shifters, could and would kill me without sparing a single scrap of regret. It doesn't matter that I was one of them. They have that power.

Luc holds the door to Adeline's Celestial Herbs open for me. A potent mix of roots and spices swallows us. It stings my nose. Dried plants hang from the ceiling, or dangle over shelf ledges beside vials of fine herbs and diced leaves. Elegant, hand-written labels are plastered to every glass or pot, or next to free-hanging roots.

"Name," a gamma by the entrance says. She holds out a tablet with a familiar prompt.

Luc complies. I hastily scribble my name next, eager to move on.

"*Bloodhounds.*" She snarls under her breath as we pass.

I nearly whip around when Luc puts his hand on my arm. I stare at him and see numbness. He whispers. "Let it go."

I don't want to, but I do.

Luc is drawn to a table. Flimsy paper boxes are stacked like pyramids. I pick one up and turn it over in my hand. "Tea?"

"Tea!"

"...Why are we getting tea?"

"There was a new arrival the other day," he says. "He's homesick, and I guess he used to collect tea bags. *So*, we're goin' to buy him some tea."

"Tea bags?"

"Tea bags."

"Who collects *tea bags?*"

"The new arrival!"

"But why?"

"I don't know!" He shrugs helplessly. "You're being pretty judgmental for a nineteen-year-old who didn't know who Batman was!"

"I think your Batman fetish is getting out of hand."

His laugh is big and booming. It sends his head back and makes me smile as I set down the box to pick up another. I scan over ingredients, calories, serving sizes, trying to determine what makes one flavor more collectable than another. My eyes quickly glaze over.

"Why didn't you just bring the new arrival?"

Luc glances up from his box. "I would've. If he wasn't adamant about never leaving his new apartment."

"Sounds like he and I would get along."

"You have no idea." Luc mumbles. "I'm hopin' I can loosen him up some. It's been super difficult, though. Vampirism has a steep learning curve. Especially for humans."

"Does the coven get new arrivals a lot?" I ask.

Luc shakes his head. "We get two or three every several months. Usually, the gammas are pretty good about finding rogues before they hurt anyone."

My conversation with Aurora last night flashes in my head. "Says the bitten shifter to the other bitten shifter."

"Touché." He bumps me, knocking loose my negativity.

"You and Val are the only two who handle new arrivals?"

Opening a box, Luc brings it to his nose and inhales deeply. He holds it out to me to sniff. Lemon and...grape? I scrunch my face at him.

"Yeah." Luc chooses another box as I set the other down. A nostalgic smile touches his mouth. "At first, I just followed him around and helped with cases, then we started splitting the workload half and half." That smile sours. "A little over a year ago, he started taking cases less and less. It's mostly me now."

"That's weird," I say. "Any reason?"

His jaw tightens. "He found another apprentice."

"For new arrivals?" I ask, puzzled.

"No."

I wait for more, but he gives nothing else. With a frown, I edge away, leaving him to focus on his tea mission so I can explore. I run my fingers along the rims of potted plants and the edges of leaves. They kiss my fingertips.

Mom would adore this place. The farmers and gatherers in Hydrilla welcomed Mom any day. Her knowledge of plants, how to care for them, and her innate ability to communicate with the woods was esteemed. When the healers needed specific ingredients for a paste or a tonic, she was always the first person they went to.

As a child, I used to help her water and tend to her plants. That stopped when my parents recruited teachers and trainers to reverse the damage done to my spirit. There just wasn't any time.

Is her life easier without me? No more daughter to disappoint her, let her down, embarrass her. Pain stabs my chest. Sullenly, I thumb some of the plants in front of the main window, overlooking the sidewalk. A few cars zoom by, their whir rumbling through thin glass, as vampires laugh outside cafes, and flood in and out of shops. Gammas patrol the streets. They shuffle people along with loud commands, and sometimes forceful shoves.

Across the road, Terces staggers along, her gaited walk like a discordant dance. She keeps her head low. Her mangled blonde hair falls in unwashed matted clumps, casting dense shadows across her lumpy skin, darkness sinking into deep wrinkles. I can't get last night out of my mind.

"Hey, Luc..."

"Yeah?" He appears at my side.

I say, "Remember what you told me about Terces...? How she's really weird?"

He follows my eyes. "...Yeah."

"Last night, I was on my way to the hospital to give venom samples."

"Val told me."

"On the way there, I ran into Terces." My voice sinks to a whisper. He leans closer to hear me. "She was torturing a squirrel. I think she was collecting its blood."

His auburn brows knit together. He doesn't understand. Neither do I.

"I brought it up to Pyera, right? She was going to alert the gammas, but Valberg stopped her. He was...oddly protective of her. I was thinking maybe... He's Grand Enchanter. Maybe he needs the blood and he had her—"

"Whoa, whoa, whoa!" Luc waves his hands frantically back and forth. "Let me stop you right there. I know what you're getting at, and there's no way that's what's goin' on."

I turn to him. "What other reason is there?"

"Er, Val's just a nice guy?" His wide eyes shrink. "I promise you, Tenderfoot. Val is too by the books."

I fold my arms. "I know he's your mentor or whatever, but don't you think—"

"No. I don't." There's an edge to his voice. "And he's more than my mentor."

"What do you mean?"

His lips flatten into a line. He glances elsewhere for a second, then looks back to me with a sigh. "He's my dad, alright? I know him."

"But you're a shifter..."

"I barely remember that life, Macy." He pulls back the collar of his shirt. Two, sharp red eagle feathers arch over his shoulders and collar bone. I've never seen his Marrow Mark before. It's beautiful. "Other than this, I don't have a connection to my roots. I'm not as attached as you are."

"I'm not..." I shut my mouth. Yes. I am. My eyes scroll his hands and forearms, looking for more feathers. There are none.

"Marrow Marks don't grow anymore after you're bitten." There's a distant pain in his voice.

My heart stops. I massage my green spirals through the sleeves of my hoodie. "I'm sorry, I didn't mean to..."

"It's fine. I was six. Someone had to parent me." He shrugs, relaxing. "I've been a vampire three times as long as I was a shifter. I feel closer to that part of my life than my wolfy upbringing. And I know Val." He places his hand on my arm. "Trust me?"

I look back out the window. Terces is gone. "Okay."

"He pities her," Luc says. "She doesn't talk to anyone but him anymore. I think he feels responsible for her. You know like—"

My phone vibrates loudly in my pocket. I fish it out. There's a text from Nico.

The alpha's here.

I gasp. "Luc, I gotta go!"

"What?" He looks startled.

"Nico just texted me—"

He snorts rudely. He pushes a hand through his hair and twists away from me. "That's great."

I grab his hand. "Luc, the Alpha's here. Don't be like that."

He's tense again, but his expression softens. He frowns at me. "Fine. Whatever. Go."

"Luc." I plead.

"It's fine, Tenderfoot." He closes his eyes. When he opens them, there's a glimmer of his usual positivity. He musters a smile for me. "Go save the word and all that Prophet business."

I smile. "I'm Batman."

"*I'm* Batman!" He laughs.

Releasing his hand, I rush for the door, hastily sign my name, and, on my way out, I glance over my shoulder. Luc waves. As I turn away, that smile decays into something curdled and hurt.

TWENTY-THREE

BRONZE

A pair of gammas lead me through City Hall to the Embassy. Nico sits on a bench outside a pair of doors that are similar to but much smaller than the entrance to testing chambers in Hydrilla. They're not any humbler.

Today, it's framed by two betas. They're discernible by the gold symbols emblazoned on their chests. Of all the tiers among shifters, betas are the second smallest, surpassed by the even scarcer Alphas. Unlike the gammas, who are renowned for their coordination and strength in numbers, Alphas and betas are celebrated for their individual prowess.

They each wear clothes that reveal their Marrow Marks as much as possible. It's a trend popular among all shifter classes, but it's most admired among them.

At the sound of footsteps, Nico glances up. I hurry away from the gammas to sit beside him. He bounces his leg impatiently, but stops when I slide into the seat next to him.

"You almost missed it," he says.

I arch a brow.

"I've been waiting for forty-seven minutes. We're about to celebrate the forty-eighth minute." He taps his phone screen awake. The minute changes. He waves one hand enthusiastically. "Woo."

"You are such a ray of sunshine."

He smirks. "Call me Smiles."

"I like Prick better."

He lets out a crisp laugh. I chuckle, too.

I peek at the betas before I glance down at myself. I fist my hands. The green ribbons wrinkle in my palms. My Marrow Mark will never extend any farther than this. Just like Luc's. But it's still there.

I roll up my sleeves and unzip my hoodie like I have something to prove. I stop halfway. My two omega signs scowl up at me. My hand drops to my lap.

The betas are examples of poise, discipline, and proficiency. I am a product of weakness, irregularity, and clumsiness.

Nico bumps me with his arm, and I jump. Valberg is beside him now.

"Whoa, there. Twitchy much?" His dimpled smirk is lighthearted. He hands me a plastic bottle of cooled blood. "Here. It's a long wait."

"Thanks," I say

He shrugs, tipping his head back to take a swig of his. He wipes his mouth and licks the red off his fangs. "Thank Val."

He waves it off as he sits. "It wasn't a hassle. The assistants were very understanding."

Nico slouches with intrigue. "You used your charm, right? Got it for free?"

"A Grand Enchanter never reveals his tricks."

"*Anciano,* you sly vampire, you."

"Please stop." I shake my head feverishly. "Those implications are traumatizing."

The Embassy door handle jiggles. We all snap to attention.

"Guess we won't be waiting so long after all," Nico says under his breath.

Alpha Kennedy glides out, fluid, graceful. She's flanked by two more betas. I jump to my feet out of respect and excitement. Valberg is much more composed about it, and Nico lags behind, less impressed.

In a lot of ways, Kennedy reminds me of Mom. Her graying blonde hair swallows her, thick and long. Her tan skin is decorated with ashy hyena spots. Her pallor is the same color as Mom's during late summer. That being said, the wrinkles around her coffee-colored eyes are softer. The Alpha knows nothing of grief and anger. She's regal, sophisticated, above struggle.

"Celia, Viridian." Her voice is a breeze. "We're done here."

The two betas move away from the wall and follow her down the hallway. They stop when she does. The Alpha looks over her shoulder at us. My breath hitches.

"This is the second Prophet?" Her question is directed at Valberg.

"Yes," he says.

"Interesting." She arches a brow at me, then disappears down the hall.

"Kill me now." I mumble.

"That would throw a pretty big wrench in Church's plan," Nico says blandly.

I glower at him. "Don't tempt me."

He responds with a smirk.

Both of us turn to Valberg when he opens the Embassy doors. We share a look of apprehension but follow along anyway. It's more like a conference hall than an office. There's another door in the back. It probably leads to a more routine set up for the Ambassador, also known as the Head Gamma, also known as *prison warden.*

And, again, I'm reminded of Mom.

The room is littered with a ridiculous abundance of plants. A prickly cactus is herded into each corner, kept company by smaller pots of flowers. At the center of a round table are several vases of Butterfly Mist. They add splashes of color to the drab room. No butterflies, though.

The Lord twirls one of the flowers in his hand. Seated beside the Lady at the table, he's quiet while Pyera rants, offering the occasional *uh huh* and *I understand.*

"I see it didn't go well," Valberg proclaims.

"That two-faced..." She looks at me. There's a slur waiting at the tip of her tongue. She exhales slowly, working her jaw. "Apparently, Alpha Kennedy isn't sure our presence is necessary at the Summit."

"She claims she is thankful we contacted her." Cleon takes over for Pyera who wrings her hands angrily. "Yet, she asserts that she and the other Alphas in Meadowsweet can formulate a plan without our assistance."

The air in my chest leaves in a single, dejected rush.

We're Prophets! We were chosen by the Man in the Moon to help preserve the Earth. That's the shifter's most sacred vow! And they still throw us aside. I, a *shifter*, was chosen by a divine entity, and this is all I get? Anger bubbles within me.

You're a damn vampire! Circi echoes from my memories.

Nico steps forward.

Cleon holds a hand up. "However, we gave her our notes about your premonitions, as well as the information provided by Valberg. She agreed to bring it up at the Summit."

Nico opens his mouth, but fury claws its way up my throat. "That's *it?*"

The Lord swipes a few strings of hair from his face. "It is. Alpha Kennedy mentioned she will discuss the possibility of our attendance at the Summit. There was no promise."

Pyera lets loose a shaky sigh. "We'll let you know more when *we* know more. I wish we could stay, but Cleon and I are due for a meeting with the local high-stakes poker committee."

"Seriously?" I demand. "We were just barred from attending the one thing we were all counting on and you guys just get to move onto something else? And you expect us to do the same?"

"Macy..." Pyera draws my name out. She looks tired and drained. Angry. But *I'm* angry too.

"We have a coven to run, Miss Braddock," Cleon says.

He tries to be gentle. He extends one hand to touch me, but I move away.

"It's bullshit." Nico's tone drips with venom. "I'm tired of waiting for the Alphas, for you guys, for another cryptic vision from the Man in the Moon. We can't just twiddle our thumbs and wait for the end of the world."

"Did you even *try* to convince her?" I lash out.

"Enough!" Pyera snarls.

Nico and I both swallow our voices.

Her shoulders slump, and she shakes her head. "If either of you two thinks for *one* minute that we didn't argue to the very last second, to no avail, then I'm severely hurt." She glances at Cleon. "We're upset and angry too, but it's our responsibility to run this coven."

Nico stuffs his hands in his pockets. Valberg wraps an arm around his shoulders. Pyera and Cleon get up from their seats and walk around the table. The Lady places her hand on my shoulder. No smile. No soft attempt to quell my anger. Her eyes apologize.

"Can I accompany you on your walk?" Val asks the Lord and Lady.

"What of your enchantments?" Cleon asks.

"You can't put off your clients for too long," says Pyera.

"An hour won't do any harm," Val says. "And I would like to further discuss what the Alpha had to say."

We all file out of the room. Before the three of them depart, Pyera eyes Nico and me. "I'll contact both of you."

"Whatever." Nico growls. He says to me, "I need to hit something."

Me too. "Gym?"

"Gym."

"Maybe all that residual anger will boost your chances." His anger saps his tone of humor.

"That or busting your face will satisfy my violent urges."

There's a glimmer of his usual snide in his smirk. It revives some of my spirit.

"Good luck."

TWENTY-FOUR

GODSEND AND CALAMITY

Nico's gloved knuckles send me to the mat. I heave a frustrated shout, bludgeoning the floor. I thought I had him that time, but I thought that every other time too. I swipe the back of my arm across my damp forehead as he crouches beside me. He extends his now uncovered hands, boxing mitts dangling round his neck, and lugs me up by my wrists.

"That's four," he says, out of breath.

"One more." I pant.

He asks, "How's your side?"

"Who cares? One more."

We've pushed like this for days now. Nights stacked on top of nights, whittled away boxing, studying bible verses, and staying up past dawn, glaring at diluted sun-rays forked across the wall. Hours of rest sacrificed to torture myself with thoughts about the Alpha, the Summit, Lilac, going home, the end of the world.

My weakness congeals inside me. I am never enough. Not as a shifter, not as a vampire, and not as a Prophet.

A yell surges out of me. "This is ridiculous!"

He frowns, cheeks dimpling.

"The Summit was our only chance!" I try to keep my voice level, but I can't. "Now what are we supposed to do? What do they want from us? To just wait? Even longer? For what? And what are we supposed to do in the meantime? Spar?" I rip my boxing gloves off and throw them to the ground. "Church and his goons aren't going to box me. They have knives! They have blood magic! They're going to slice me open and bleed me dry."

"Bright Eyes..." Those deep, dark eyes get a little darker.

"That's what we should be practicing!"

It would feel slightly less fruitless.

He knits his brows together. "I'm not sure that's a good idea."

"How's it a bad idea?"

"You think me attacking you with my knife while you're unarmed is anything *but* a bad idea?"

I clench my fists stubbornly.

"The sun rises in an hour anyway." He snorts at my scowl. "Wow, you're serious."

"I can kick your butt in less than sixty minutes," I say.

"I can kick yours in under six," he replies stoutly.

Neither of us looks away. My anger blazes. His reluctance wavers.

He groans. "Fine."

With a huff, he grabs his pocketknife from his bag and returns to the matt. He wearily sizes me up. A scowl lingers on the edge of his expression. He hates this, but I've made zero progress with my Grounding. We have to look at other ways I can defend myself. More practical ways.

"Keep your distance. You don't attack. You don't turn your back. And you sure as hell don't give me an opening. Right now, I'm top dog." He flicks his blade from its sheath. He strokes the edge with his thumb. "I got the knife; I got the advantage. When I attack, control the knife. Where it does and doesn't go."

"How?"

He lifts his knife. "Grab my arm with both hands. Disarm me."

"It can't be that easy."

"It's not. Don't underestimate your opponent. Ever."

I get into a familiar, defensive stance. My hands are unfurled. Ready to grapple, not punch. When he attacks, it's straightforward. The knife is aimed right at me, but nowhere specific. I grab his wrist and forearm, driving it into my knee. He hisses as he drops the blade. It bounces briefly on the mat.

I snarl and push him away. "That was pathetic!"

Staggering back, he catches himself.

"I'm not going to actually stab you, Macy!"

"That's not the point!"

I kick his knife to him. He glowers as he picks it up, testing the weight in his hands, before he attacks again. This time, he slashes from side to side. The blade cuts the air with a whoosh.

I dodge backward. He matches every step I take, stalking closer. He edges dangerously close. I grab his hand with both of mine. I twist his wrist, but his grasp stays tight on the knife. I twist it more. He lets go with a growl.

Yanking his hand away, he massages it protectively close to his chest. A thin sheen of sweat glistens on his forehead. His hair is a mess, slipping loose from its tiny bun.

"Again." I grab his knife and offer it to him. "Try harder."

He shakes his head, disapproving. "Christ."

For a little while, we practice like that. He attacks in any way he can imagine, and I find more and more ways to counter him. Eventually, after I don't know how many rounds, we relent.

He pushes his sweaty hair back, breathing heavy.

"What about blood magic?" I pant.

He steps off the mat, shaking his head. "Not happening."

"What if—"

"Macy." He snaps. Not sharp. Just tired. "It's illegal to practice blood magic without shifter supervision."

It would be a comfort at any other time. Right now, the restriction shackles me. My head is full of shifting red tides, snaking through the air, easily rivaling Lilac's grounding despite her power.

I pull my sweatshirt on. "Okay. Fine. But... what if? I've seen what Church can do. If him or his followers come for me..."

Nico turns his back to me, staring into his bag. "It has to be fatal."

I barely hear him. "Fatal?"

Turning to me, Nico rolls up his sleeve, exposing the horizontal scars climbing his forearm. They're fresh, overlapping old, faded bite marks. So many bite marks. He draws his thumb over one of the horizontal lines on his wrist.

Valberg said his transformation had been gruesome. I swallow. I focus.

"Make a blood mage bleed," he says, "and you just give them more ammo. So, you have two options. You make it fatal, or you incapacitate them. The quicker, the better." He rolls down his sleeve and nods toward the exit. "C'mon."

At the front desk, we sign our names on the departure list, tended to by a shifter who sneers at us as we exit the main doors. There's a flash from inside. Another one of the gamma's many cameras.

The cold rushes to greet us. I zip my hoodie up. My muscles whine, but I ignore my achy body. We follow the sidewalk quietly for a while. One by one, local storefronts close down, leaving only the streetlamps to guide us home. We come to a turn. This is where we've split before, but like usual Nico doesn't stray from my side when we round the corner.

"Walking me home again?" I ask.

"It's the gentlemanly thing to do."

I roll my eyes. "I forgot. Right after the knife-sparing section in the Prophet handbook, the chivalrous thing to do is walk the loser home."

"You must've skimmed." He grins.

Glancing down, I turn my hands over. My Marrow Mark glares up at me. It demands so much. My Beast, body, and every breath. My blood and soul!

Even after being bitten, I stood by Mother Nature with steadfast assurance, only to be beaten down time and time again. I can't shift, can't contact Aimil, can't use my Grounding. Nothing helps. Then the Man in the Moon chose me to safeguard the Earth in a way more tangible than anything else, but my own people, those sworn to protect Mother Nature and her soils, have betrayed me.

Did they, though? Isn't this just our world? One I was complacent with until it no longer benefited me?

Nico nudges me with his elbow. "You all right?"

I glance at him. "I... I'm just thinking."

"Not fun thoughts," he says softly.

"It's that obvious?"

"Yep." He nods. "You look like someone stomped on a box of kittens."

"I hate cats."

He snorts. "Okay, puppies."

"There you go."

His laugh is mild and short-lived. "Talk to me."

"What are we going to do?" I ask.

"I don't know..."

"I've prayed to Mother Nature. Even the Man in the Moon." I rub the center of my forehead. "I've asked for guidance, for help, for anything. And I get nothing."

That's not quite right. It's not that nothing is working. It's that I'm a failure. I always have been. That's just how my life is.

I empty my lungs with a sigh. "I'm a walking catastrophe."

"Catastrophe is too harsh." He bumps me again. "Try walking disaster."

Somehow, I laugh under my breath. "Thanks."

I sneakily eye him. Luc and Circi's warnings echo alongside my own wariness. My eyes chase the folds of his sleeve. I envision those scars. Where do they end? Why so many? Are they the cause of his rumored violence and anger? Would that excuse anything?

The memory of the Monster's fangs, his venom, and the fire burns the side of my neck. I run my hand over my scar. One scar. One bite. I try to imagine more strewn down my arms. Would the fire build and build? Or would there be a point that the pain becomes so intense, it's almost numb? Valberg said Nico's metamorphosis had been bleak, but...

"What?"

My gaze snaps to his. He stares at me, brow arched.

"Sorry, I..."

"You...?"

I don't look at him for a second. "Val told me you were human once."

Nico stills. I do, too.

He looks torn between being offended and bitter. "He shouldn't have."

"He mentioned that too."

"I guess it was bound to happen." He snarls, upper lip curled. "Everyone likes to run their mouth."

"I'm sorry. I shouldn't have said anything."

"It's whatever."

"Does it bother you?" I ask. "What people say?"

His eyes flit back to me. His mask has fallen, so he tries to hide behind his hair. Pain interspersed with sadness. He looks away. "Depends."

"On what?"

"Who it is. The coven's small. People talk, and most people don't matter. It's the people I care about who..." His lips flatten into a line. "It's the people who turn their backs on you."

"I understand." The raw betrayal of being shunned by my people is a deep, echoing hurt.

Two sharp creases frame his mouth as he frowns. "It's worse when you're the Prophet. Whoever you were before gets lost in the visions and responsibility. And the world either loves you or hates you for it. You're a messiah meant to lead the vampires to freedom. You're an archaic symbol of ineffectiveness because no Prophet before you liberated anyone, and neither will you. But still, everyone looks at you different. Everyone."

What about Valberg? Pyera or Cleon? Are they just people who propped Nico onto a pedestal, while all the others shied away?

"All because of one stupid title." I murmur.

"Exactly. It takes more from you than it will ever give." He scoffs angrily. "All I want is to be valued for who I am, not what I am, y'know? Nico the Prophet, not the Prophet, Nico."

Macy, the shifter. Macy, the vampire. Macy, the Prophet, the sacrifice. Never just Macy Braddock. Never just me. I nod because I get it.

The wind howls an apology. It blows a kiss into my palm and carries it to Nico's arm. I grasp the fabric of his coat. "Nico."

He's taut under my fingers. He clenches his jaw, exaggerating a corded vein in his neck. Slowly, he meets my eyes. A shadowy monster lingers in his stare. It's old, chilly, and somber, and he can't hide it. Dejection, I recognize, because I've felt that way too.

"I get it," I whisper. "And I value you."

A beat of silence passes between us.

TWENTY-FIVE

BAD BLOOD

Although I'm still unsure, after some thought, I decide to take Val up on his offer. Maybe this time will be different. Maybe this time I'll find Aimil. Maybe I'll be enough.

I stop by Cinnamon's for breakfast. Standing at the back of the line, I breathe in deep. I love the smell of hazelnut and coffee, something I learned after living here. Scanning the lobby, I quickly spot Luc and Circi seated by the window. Luc waves at me, but Circi purposefully doesn't.

I look back at the register, then them. Food or awkwardness? I can't tell if it's goodwill or masochism that makes me go to them.

"Hey, guys," I say.

"Hey," Luc says. "I stopped by your apartment the other night, but you weren't there."

"Yeah, sorry." I pull up a chair and steal a hash brown from his plate. "I've been busy with Nico."

"Luc said something about that." Circi squints at me, grimacing with disdain. "How'd he wrap you around his finger?"

I cross my arms. "I'm just working with him. You know, to hopefully stop the end of the world? No offense, but that's kind of my main priority right now."

"There's no other way?" Luc begs.

I roll my eyes. "What's wrong with this one?"

Luc and Circi send daggers to my shoulder. One of the bruises has yellowed but lingers, regardless. Annoyance flutters in my chest. *They mean well,* my conscience reminds me.

"Tenderfoot..." Luc rubs his jaw. "I don't like him."

Circi snorts. "No one does. Except Macy, apparently."

"I guess 'shit-tastic soothsayers' have to stick together, right?" I snap, sharper than I intend. Remorse surges through me.

"Seems that way." She sneers.

My remorse fades.

"Cool it." Luc glares at Circi. "Put the fangs away and drink your latte." His eyes cut to me. "And you need to find your common sense."

"Common sense?" My eyes bulge. "I'm a shifter turned vampire turned soothsayer tangled up in an apocalyptic prophecy. *Nothing* makes sense anymore. I'm not going to throw aside Nico's help just because *you* don't like him."

His almond eyes widen before they narrow into angry slits. He's *angry*. At *me.* I'm flooded with more regret, but I'm hardened too.

"Nico's bad news," says Luc.

"*Why?*" I brace my hands on the table and lean forward. "What do you really know about him? Other than *rumors?*"

"You weren't here, Macy! I'm not the bad guy for trying to warn you."

I scowl. "I'm not saying you're the bad guy. Just stubborn."

He carelessly pushes his plate away. His breakfast tumbles onto the table. "You don't get it. Whatever story he's spinning, it's twisted." He tears his eyes away. Under his breath: "You're just like Val. "

"That's the thing." I growl. "You're the only one spinning any stories."

Luc exasperatedly throws his arms in the air. "He's *not* that great!"

"You don't even know him!"

Luc slams his fist on the table. It wobbles. Plates and cups teeter. "*I* know him better than anyone in this coven! Better than Val! Better than Pyera or Cleon! And better than you!"

"All you know is—"

"*He's my brother!*"

Shock cuts me down. I gape at him because I'm an idiot. Luc was never jealous, and their feud has nothing to do with me.

"But... you *hate* each other."

Luc vibrates with rage. His leg bounces under the table and his fists shake. Circi reaches over to touch his wrist, but neither of his hands unfurl. His eyes dart all over my face. I read the betrayal written on his.

"Val and I welcomed him into our family." His upper lip disappears as he bares his fangs, snarling each word. "I took care of him. Every step of the way. He was my little brother."

I whisper. "What happened?"

"He destroyed us."

"Luc... you have to give me more than that."

His glare pierces me. "I don't have to give you anything."

It stings. I rip my eyes away, biting my cheek. "Whatever bad blood you guys have. It has nothing to do with me."

"You don't know anything," Circi bites.

I look at her in surprise. She doesn't permeate anger. All there is, is care. For Luc. Who she loves above everything else, just like he does her. I'm a trespasser, and it's clear I'm unwelcomed.

Invisible storm clouds rush in and pull me deep into their grasp. I don't feel so hungry anymore. Wordlessly, I stand and make my way to the door. It's not until I'm halfway out the door they speak again. I briskly march past the window without looking at them, feelings rubbed raw and sore.

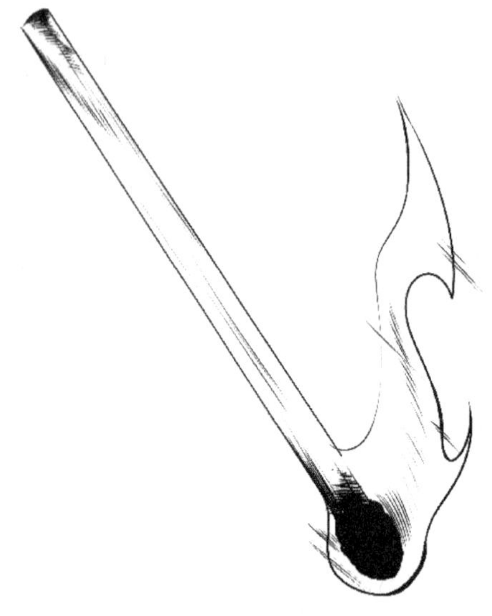

TWENTY-SIX

TRANCE

Valberg lives near the Bridge.

At the base of his porch, a bed of well-groomed flowers demand attention. They're vibrant against the pale gray panels of his home. Nearby, separated by a sparse stretch of trees, is Terces' ramshackle hut, overrun by age and jimsonweed.

I lightly tap my knuckles on the door. After a minute, I knock again. Still no answer. I peek into one of the polished windows. Inside, books have been pulled off shelves, closed, open, or stacked, and papers sprawl across every flat surface.

Is this where Luc and Nico grew up, or did Valberg come here after they moved? Did they huddle close to the Grand Enchanter as he mulled through his books? Race downstairs for dinner? Play hide and seek in the hidden nooks and crannies, outed by groaning floorboards? Did they stare out windows on rainy nights, sharing stories of life before? Sadder is the idea that the version of brothers I know now, connected by the word, not blood or bond, is the *only* version to have ever been.

I go to the other window. There's no sign of Val. I check my phone. I'm on time.

Cupping my hands around my mouth, I call out. "Val!"

"Macy!"

I whip around with a start. Valberg emerges from the direction of Terces' hut. He weaves deftly between the bushes. Not one leaf dares to graze him, and the soft grass hushes every footstep. In the distance, Terces watches behind a window. She shrivels away from it when I spot her. Goosebumps pebble on my skin.

"It's good to see you." His smile is as jolly as ever.

I squint at the shack in the visible distance. "We agreed to meet tonight, right?"

"We did!" His smile grows. The skin around the corners of his eyes crease. "I was sure to clear my schedule. That way, aggravated clients are less likely to beat my door down."

"Did Terces need something?"

"Only an ear." His excitement softens. "And a little guidance."

And what kind of guidance might a Grand Enchanter give to a woman guilty of hacking up innocent animals for their blood?

"Come." Valberg climbs the porch steps. He opens the door and holds it for me. "I've made you wait long enough."

I give him a once over before stepping inside.

Clutter congests all the rooms. Mostly, books, papers, essays. Reasonable clutter?

Valberg guides me down a tightly packed hallway. Photos litter the walls. There's one of Valberg in his youth, taken at his graduation from the Academy of Blood Magic. Another of him accepting the title of Grand Enchanter. There are some of him and Luc, him and Nico, Luc and Nico. In one photo, they're all together and happy.

There's a wedding photo.

"I didn't know you were married," I say.

Valberg's expression softens with love. "I was. He died about twenty years ago."

I suck in a sharp breath of air. "I'm sorry!"

"You're fine, Macy." He touches the frame. "You would've liked Lysander. He was another shifter."

My eyebrows shoot up. I study the man in the photo before looking at Val again. My fantasy of marrying Lilac rushes to the surface. I smile into my chest.

Another photo catches my eye. I gasp and touch the glass. A middle-aged vision of Valberg stands astride Francis Church. Nico had said they were friends once.

His smile is prim, and his hair is neat. His hands aren't gnarled or dirty. They're soft, rested on the shoulders of a young boy I don't know. All the malice is gone. So is the bone-tired exhaustion. This is the man before the monster, the hatred. This is Francis Garret. Of *course*, the Monster wasn't born a killer, but acknowledging that means acknowledging that something made him that way. That something being my people.

"Why do you still have this?" I ask.

Valberg comes to stand beside me. "To remember."

"Remember?"

"Better times."

I brush the corner of a family portrait. A plucky Lucas Walcott grins at the camera. His arm is slung around the devious Nico Navarro's shoulders. Two little boys with massive smiles. Brothers.

"This one too?"

Valberg's face darkens. "Yes."

"Why…" I remember Luc's rage. "… do they hate each other?"

Val winces. "*Hate* is too strong."

"What happened?"

He stares at the picture. He looks much older than he did a second ago. "I told you I helped new arrivals acclimate to the coven before I became Grand Enchanter. Luc was my first child case. He was only six. When he first arrived, he was so… traumatized. This little frightened creature who'd only heard fictitious tales about dastardly vampires, and then seen the rare truth behind those stories. He needed someone, and I… couldn't keep my heart separate from my work. I took him in. Six years later, Nico was brought into the coven. He didn't trust any of us. Not Pyera, not Cleon, not me. Luc was the only one who could get him to open up."

I knot my fingers together, picturing it. One small, broken family that made each other whole. Not like mine; one small, broken family that kept breaking.

"The tension began with Nico's visions," says Valberg. "At first, it was mild. Expected, even. As time went on, it brewed. I had to dedicate more time to Nico, and that took attention away from Luc."

"He was jealous."

Valberg caresses Luc's face with the pad of his thumb. "It reached its peak after I chose Nico to succeed me as Grand Enchanter."

A new apprentice, Luc had bitterly grumbled.

Val nods his head down the hallway. I follow him the rest of the way, leaving the past alone for now. At the very back of the house, there's a room. It must take up half the house, if not more. Papers are scattered about three desks, pinned beneath books, vials, and other miscellaneous jars. They're illuminated by the lamps on the walls neighbored by large, informative placards. There are too many books to count.

Brushing by one of the desks, I turn the page of an open hardcover. "Is this a spell book?"

"It is," says Valberg. "An old one."

"Looks like it." My brows pull together. "I don't really know much about blood magic."

Valberg strokes his chin contemplatively. "It's not *too* complex. Not the basics, at least. Like your people, our magic is fueled by life, but differently."

Very different.

He says, "Shifters use plants, blessed water, and prayer to heal wounds. Your Marrow Marks are an entirely separate magic. Vampires use a motley of plants as well, but blood is our most valuable resource. With it, we cast enchantments on silver. A man could become twice as strong or swift with just a ring. You could look like someone else with a necklace. Or!" He dramatically holds a finger up. "Perhaps you're in need of charisma! A confidence spell could amend that."

I laugh under my breath. "You don't ever tire out?"

"Certainly! We abide by the laws of mortality like everyone else."

"...The laws of mortality?"

"The amount of insurmountable damage one can take before even a papercut is too much. How many punches before you fall? How much blood loss until one last drop is what kills you?" he explains, motioning to his scarred forearm. "The laws of mortality. How much of your life can you spend before you have no more? It's especially tricky for us since we're only allowed our own blood. Restraint and resourcefulness are essential. However, the stronger the spell, the more blood it requires. Fortunately, such costly spells aren't typically necessary."

Terces flickers in my mind. "What about animal blood?"

"Illegal," Valberg says, unflinching.

Turning another page, I stare blindly at its contents. The words come from nowhere. "I've seen vampires use another person's blood before."

A sad look crosses Val's face. "Yes. I... am an advocate for fewer blood mage restrictions, but I understand the shifter's apprehension. Especially when it can be so grotesquely abused."

I don't say anything else. My eyes wander away from the desk. One of the placards catches my attention. The symbols look familiar. They were stamped on Dante Hazel's book.

"What language is that?"

"It's called Lunalian," he says. "The language of ancient vampires. It was outlawed sometime after the covens were built. Nowadays, only the Enchanters, Lords, Ladies, and sometimes Alphas understand it."

Outlawed. Because the shifters wouldn't want to risk encrypted message exchanges. Knowing that only makes me feel worse.

I graze the poster with my hand. The embossed letters send tingles into my flesh, fading impressions of a lost time at my fingertips. They lost too much to the Blood

War, and even more to time. The remnants that have survived are testimonials to their undoctored stubbornness for life.

"I'm sorry so much of it was lost." The apology tastes strange on my lips, but not undeserved.

"There's no reason to apologize, Macy."

I chew my lip. I think of the Monster, Terces, and dead squirrels, but then I think of Pyera, Cleon, and Luc. *I'm not so sure.*

I pore over the arcane lettering once more. What mysteries might they hold, unfathomable to my shifter mind? What if I could understand? Why do I want to?

Eyes dipping down, I skim the open pages of a book, tracing strange shapes. Runes? They're scattered across the sallow parchment. Most of them are small. One, however, is big and emphasized at the center of the page.

It's a large, uneven oval, slashed at the base. Below it, lines of text scrawl across the page. I touch the rune. A shiver skitters up my arm. Whatever spell it's for, it's wrong.

Valberg snakes the book away from me. "I didn't realize I had left that open. My apologies, Macy. That book is for a Grand Enchanter's eyes only."

My gut quivers at his smile.

He says, "Let's get started."

He shepherds me to an ornate door between two bookcases. A staircase awaits on the other side and, at its base, there's a bare and unornamented room. All the noise from the outside world is absent here.

There's a marble table at the center. A circular bed of coals is carved into the console, broken in half by spaces at the peak and trough where two chairs are tucked. The table is garnished by three items: the coals, a box of matches, and a small jar of oil.

I slide into a seat at his behest.

He takes up the cruet and pours the tawny liquid over the stones. "You should know vampire meditation differs from shifter techniques."

"I would assume so," I say.

He circles the table, sure to douse every coal. He reaches for the matches, removes one from the pack, stares at it for a moment, and then at me. There's a severe look in his eyes. "I won't lie to you."

I swallow.

Valberg turns the match over in his hands. "This is as much a ritual as it is meditation. It involves blood magic."

I frown. "What kind of blood magic?"

"No bleeding is necessary."

I chew the inside of my lip. "Okay."

Valberg strikes the match. Its infantile flame competes with the harsher incandescence from above. Then he lowers it to the dampened coals, where the tiny fire becomes a miniature inferno, caged within the rutted walls. Darkness envelopes the room. Then fire is all that's left to combat the shadows.

The Grand Enchanter sits across from me. "In the past, this sort of meditation was used in times of great need. Lords and Ladies, even shifters, amplified their abilities. That's part of the reason I thought it might help you."

"There's a catch though, right?" I ask. "Is it illegal or something?"

"Not with proper permissions."

I eye the way the shadows move across his face. "Do you have those?"

"I wouldn't risk otherwise. Not with a ritual like this."

"What? Am I going to die?"

"Well."

I lean my elbows on the table, gaping at him. "Valberg. I wasn't serious!"

"In order to bolster their skills, those vampires and shifters had to listen to the waves of their soul. Such a task requires a level of tranquility only attainable at the brink of life." He rests his hands at the center of the table, and then motions for mine.

Apprehensively, I obey.

"I won't actually take you to that ledge," he says, "but I'll bring you close. Once there, it's up to you to decide if you want to take the dive or retreat back to the waking world."

My eyes widen. "Pretty sure I know my decision already."

"It may not be so easy," he says somberly.

I sigh a nervous laugh but give him a consenting nod.

There's no smile this time. He gently cups my wrists and massages his thumbs into my veins. A lethargic itch skirts up my arms into the center of my chest, dallying with my core. Slowly, my senses are devoured. Numbness overtakes me, almost like sleep.

"You're going to become tired." Valberg's voice is soft. It gets farther away as he speaks. "I want you to close your eyes."

I hardly need permission.

"In a few moments you'll be taken somewhere deep within yourself."

Something creeps up on me from the depths of my spirit. It saps me of my strength.

"There's no telling what you'll see or how pleasant it will be, but if you feel endangered at any time, say my name. I'll end the trance."

He says something else, but I don't hear it. I float away from my body until it's lost to the void. I'm guided away from the study into a fog, but by what, I don't know. It vaguely sounds like a voice, lilted syllables of an indecipherable language. Aimil?

It becomes frantic and fast. It begs me for something I don't understand. Need flows through my veins like honey. I've never ventured so deep into my own spirit, so I pry my eyes open to witness the glory—to find Aimil.

I'm buried beneath the rubble of a thousand centuries. Eons pass in seconds, too quick and too painful to fathom. I'm thrown from one era to another. Each one attempts to scratch its history into my memory, but it's pulled away so another century can carve its likeness.

There's fire and there's war. There's famine and there's plague. It's misfortune after misfortune, dressed by different ages. Again and again, they war with one another; the brutish culmination of incalculable lives within a few seconds of mine. There's no time to think between every new display, but, in those milliseconds, I summon the image of one person.

Valberg.

My consciousness is thrown into my body. All the air leaves my lungs, so I desperately rake in a gulp of air. It burns on the way down, leaving a shudder.

I can't breathe.

It gets worse.

I can't see.

"Turn on the light!" I yell.

A second later, white brilliance shines down on me.

Caring hands find my shaking shoulders. Valberg stares at me with wide and concerned eyes. He's talking. I hear his soft voice but not what he says.

I failed. Again. *Damnit.*

I rise from my seat and shrug his hands off.

He stands with me. "You're alright, Macy."

I'm not. "I knew this wouldn't work."

"Macy—"

"No thanks." I hold my arms out. "I don't want a pep talk. I don't want a lecture. I don't want to talk at all. I want to go home, so I'm going to."

He doesn't stop me when I head for the stairs. I force myself to walk up the steps, down the hall, and out the door. A block or so away, when I'm certain I'm out of sight, I do what I do best.

I run.

TWENTY-SEVEN

MIND READER

Nights crawl by. Days don't go any faster. I dread every sunrise because it means hours of unending nightmares. They only get worse as the full moon approaches. A small part of me hopes sleep will come easier after tonight, just like when I was a shifter.

Tonight, we're due a vision from the Man in the Moon. Nico's text stares up at me from my phone.

You can come over.

I'd prefer to spend time with Luc, but after our last encounter I can't bear to ask. That leaves me with Nico.

I can't shake the memories of my first vision, alone and terrified, scrabbling desperately away from hellish hallucinations. The premonition may be unavoidable, but if nothing else, I'd prefer not to tackle this one alone, even if it means crossing into the louder, livelier side of town.

The buildings are taller here, and fatter too. They're neighbored by neon clubs, pouring out endless streams of blood-drunk vampires. The wind bristles against me the whole way to Nico's.

I knock gently. When he answers the door, Nico looks rumpled as usual. His beanie is missing, but his hair sticks up in dark, near-black tangles. He swipes his bangs out of his face and smiles at me. It's not as annoying as usual. It's friendlier.

"Hey," he says.

"Hey." I nod at him. "Thanks for letting me come over."

He waves me inside. "*Mi casa es su casa*, Bright Eyes."

"Do you actually know how to speak Spanish?"

"*Un poco.*"

"Uh..."

"A little."

"Where'd you learn?"

"Picked it up here and there."

He closes the door and saunters to a shabby sofa, sitting between it and the coffee table. He aims his pencil into a sketchbook, surrounded by loose pieces of paper, pencil shavings, and erasers. Nearby, the trash bin overflows with crumpled papers. Some are smudged with gray streaks, others with thin blue lines.

When I don't join him, he glances at me. "You shy? C'mon, Sunshine, don't look so scared."

I roll my eyes. "First Bright Eyes, now Sunshine?"

"With hair like that you're lucky I don't call you Strawberry." He taps his pencil against his bottom lip. "I might start though, be warned."

Moving closer, I sit across from him. I rest my elbows against the edge of the table. I glance over his drawings. They're black and white, graphite. Some are half-finished, and others are near completion. Slowly, their details unwind from the dense mass of lines; hazy scribbles become distinct strokes, the result of hard work.

"I didn't know you could draw.", I say.

He peeks up at me with a devilish grin. "I'm basically Van Gogh."

"Van Gogh-Away?"

"Van Gogh-Get-Better-Jokes.

I watch his pencil. This knot of lines and smudge marks blooms into a raven.

"Maybe you are Van Gogh," I say.

"Told you so."

My eyes flutter with annoyance. "Take the compliment, Navarro."

"Thanks." He smirks at me, and I grin back. He turns back to his drawings and says, "Valberg told me what happened."

"Of course he did." I grumble.

He adds value to the raven's iris. "Are you going to try again?"

"It wouldn't work."

Nothing does. At this point, my best chance at stopping the Monster is offing myself. I fist my hand. Eyes clenched shut, I lay my head down on the table.

"That bad, huh?"

"So bad."

I lift my head. Whoever this boy is, he's nothing like the one I saw in picture frames on Valberg's wall. His smile was traded in for a smirk, and the love that was so present between him and Luc has evaporated.

I frown. It's not my secret. It feels dirty to know.

Hesitantly, I venture. "I know, by the way. About you and Luc."

He goes blank. "Val told you?"

"Yes and no." I sit up. "Luc told me first."

His brows shoot up.

"It was during an argument." I explain hastily. His shoulders slump. "He was trying to prove a point. I asked Val about it later."

"You're nosy." He pushes his drawing away. With gritted teeth, he glares at the corner of the page, tapping his pencil. His angry posture quickly dissipates. He doesn't look at me. "What did he say?"

I cock my head. "Val?"

"Luc."

"Nothing good."

He hangs his head, staring into his lap. "He's got this idea that I stole Val from him. And, y'know what's messed up? I wonder if I did. Not on purpose, but the visions..."

I echo our last conversation. "They just came."

"Everyone either loves or hates you," he whispers.

"Val and Luc included."

"There are times I'm favored," Nico says, "and I *hate* it. But how am I supposed to stop it? Any of it? I didn't ask to be Prophet. But no one cares. *Luc* doesn't care. All I do is exist, and he despises me for it. My *brother*."

When his voice breaks, I flinch. I nudge his foot under the table. "You miss him."

His face tightens with pain. "All the time."

"I miss my family too."

His eyes flutter open. "Do you have siblings?"

"No." I toy with the hem of my oversized hoodie. "But I miss my mom. My dad."

Nico looks away. "I miss my mom, too."

The world around us frames our silence. Vampires and gammas alike shout outside, fighting for the right to party, fighting to keep everyone under control. The hum of music from the nearby club rumbles through the floor, a faint quake in my feet. Then there's the wind. It howls above everything, getting louder.

That scares me. A full moon. A vision due.

Nico tips his head back, resting it on the sofa. "The visions get easier."

My eyes widen. "Could you stop that?"

He jerks his face toward me. "Huh?"

"You always do that," I say. "Read my mind. Everyone's mind."

"I just get feelings."

"Well stop it." I scowl. "It's creepy."

A flash of life ignites him. He holds his hands up, and grins. "No promises. I mean it, though."

"How do you know? You only ever had amazing premonitions until I came along."

"Yeeeah. But the first one is always the worst. Not to mention, *your* first one apparently foretold the end of the world. Double whammy."

After a minute, I ask, "What was yours like?"

"My first vision?" His heavy brows sink flat over his eyes.

"Yeah."

"I was fourteen. I spent the whole day with this weight on my shoulders. Like someone was watching me, calling out to me. I was bombarded with scenarios." He draws invisible images with his hands, eyes glazed. "Pictures and voices. I went back and forth between reality and fiction. My mind wasn't ready for it. I kept trying to run."

"But you can't." I sigh.

He bumps my leg with his. "Don't look so down, Bright Eyes. I promise it gets better. Eventually. Besides, that's an ugly face."

I laugh under my breath. "Not as ugly as yours."

A gust of air pushes into the room. It whispers a chill down my arms. I try to rub it away. "Do you have trouble sleeping?"

"I used to."

Another gust rockets in. This one blows his hair into his eyes. He swipes it to the side.

I stand up to close the window. "Not anymore?"

"Not really." He admits. "Do you?"

"All the time."

He motions to his crescent moon necklace. It's tinted red. Enchanted. "This helps me."

"A sleep spell?" I brace my hand against the windowpane and move to slide it closed.

"I made—"

The wind, angry and desperate, plows inside. It heaves the room in all directions. Bookshelves thump against the walls. Novels fall from their mantles and smack against the floor. Furniture jitters and cabinets are thrown open. Nico's drawings get caught in the current, and flap like paper ravens in the wind. It's a turbulent melody with one familiar voice leading the chaos. The Man in the Moon. And he has messages to relay.

His tumultuous wind sweeps me away. I fall and I fall until I'm blind and deaf.

Shards of a shattered red moon dot the darkness. Around me, the desolate landscape returns. A corpse lies at the center of the sterile valley, but not alone. There's another body and the Monster, too. He's covered in gashes. They ooze black mist instead of blood.

The world changes.

Water carries me down a river. There are dying trees on either side. Fire climbs down their trunks and hungrily devours every branch, bristle, and leaf until it reaches the earth and feasts on the grass. Beyond them, twinkling stars replace the blinding sun. Then storm clouds roll in from every direction and smothers them.

...complete darkness of the day, even through the night...

They meet in the middle of the heavens and open a rift. Something rumbles behind the fissure, but thorny bushes extend from either side of the creek to shield me from the sky. White roses blossom among the branches, but they wilt as soon as they sprout. Petals flutter down from their bristly homes. They sit atop the water, making languid ripples. Then they're swallowed. The river bubbles, boils, and transforms into tar.

... the waters turned bitter...

It tugs me lower like quicksand. I struggle, but my legs are trapped beneath the mire. I cut myself on the thorns. Bloodied, tattooed hands reach through the bushes. I frantically grasp for them, but they shove my fingers away and greedily cup the tar. They pull away with handfuls of dripping marsh.

... men died from drinking the taste...

It changes again.

The valley returns. Dry, unforgiving gravel bites into my back. The corrupted sky glares down at me. Cold fingers brush mine. Nico.

I croak at the sight of him.

He lies beside me in two parts: head and body. His skin is pale, his lips blue, his eyes faded and empty. His soul bled from him.

"How does it feel?"

The Monster clutches my throat. He and his impregnable, black mist shrouds me in darkness, leeching my limbs of movement. He wears a smug smile. Those sinister eyes stare at me. They're gray and ghastly. Brimming with enjoyment. Worst of all: they're triumphant.

"*How does it feel?*" He tightens his fingers around my throat. "*You were useless. How does it feel to know it's been that way from the start?*"

Another change.

People push and pull around me. A crowd. At the center of it, a man on the Bridge. He's naked save a pair of boxers. He laughs as he's apprehended by gammas, but I can't hear it. The silence is unbroken.

"*They killed him, and now...*"

It alters again.

A small—*too* small—coffin is lifted out of the Earth by a single pair of muddied hands. A new image takes hold.

Bodies. Alphas. They're organized in one massive row. All their bloodied fingers are twined together like twisted knots. Broken knots. Broken fingers.

It all changes again.

I'm cursed with one last peek at Nico's butchered, bled body.

And then it's over.

The wind whooshes back out the window, leaving us bent over and panting. My head spins, and my ears ring. I can barely breathe.

I lift my head to see Nico. His eyes are alive. They're red, wet, and burn holes through me. I grab a fistful of his shirt just to make sure he's there. It wasn't real. I just need to be sure it wasn't real. He wraps one hand around my wrist, and clings to it. He needs to know, too.

"We need to call Pyera and Cleon." He croaks.

"I-I know."

Neither of us moves. We're too afraid to let go.

Both our phones erupt, ringing too loud and too feverishly. We pry our hands apart, and I fumble to pull my cell out. Ice washes over me. Goosebumps follow. I stare numbly at Pyera's name flashing on my screen. I glance at Nico's phone. Cleon's name. Desperately siphoning courage from the air, I answer the phone.

"Hello?" My voice shakes.

"I need you at City Hall right now." Her words run together in her haste. "There's been another attack."

TWENTY-EIGHT

BROOD OF VIPERS

"By the sound of the third trumpet, a great star called Wormwood falls to the Earth, poisoning the planet's freshwater sources. Men will die from drinking its bitter taste."

The Wormwood League descend down the mountainside of Celastrus like a star plummeting to the earth. If their passions had the capacity to warm their flesh in light, they would scintillate with the might of their desires. They would burn brighter than the moon or sun.

The heavens drum, low like the bass of a corrupt symphony, as they return to their safe haven rooted beneath the Aconite coven.

Their presence there is the culmination of shifter arrogance and clever communications with the radicalized vampires on the surface. Most covens aren't as easily swayed, and thus their connections are limited to a few powerful allies in each.

Aconite, located at the very center of four shifter settlements, is one of the few covens with lax surveillance. After all, what might they do? What could they possibly conspire? It would take immense stupidity to defy the enemy perched from every direction.

Pride. Every shifter's downfall. They're too busy fluffing their furs and staring down their noses to find the holes riddled in the coven. All it took was a few missing people and bloodied paws to inspire the vampires' mistrust. An alliance forged by the promise to make them pay.

That same pride led to the fall of Celastrus.

It's almost disappointing. They were so easily eradicated. After the ashes of Loosestrife settled, the capitol bolstered their fortress for an obvious attack. Misguided. Mother Nature must be ashamed. Her heroes are blind.

Francis strolls the walkways carved beneath the coven. They were built before the Academy of Blood Magic was dismantled. The shifters always worried what a massive population of blood mages were capable of. Most entrances are closed off, hidden, or bulldozed, but Francis knew people from before, when he was just a father, studying his passion. He found a way.

He enters the main hall. The lights flicker. It gives Francis headaches.

"This is the last time." Robin warns Orlando, lounging in a chair. She slides a single cigarette out of a half-empty carton before tucking it inside her coat.

"I'll make it last." He pockets the cigarette.

At the edge of the room, Katherine sits with her back to the wall, her son-in-law's leather wallet unfolded in front of her, all its photos pulled out. She touches every wrinkled one, stroking the faces of her deceased grandchildren. Meanwhile, Tara and Jeremy are huddled by a radio.

A woman's frantic voice vibrates along waves of static.

"Theta Patrols, quarantine any and all drinking water; immediate emergency assistance required at the capitol. Alpha Garth has been incapacitated and total casualties increase by the hour."

Her voice is lost in the static.

Tara wets her lips. "Poetic justice."

"So, she learns." Robin quips with half a smirk.

"All our lives, we've been punished for what we drink," Francis says. "And now, so are they."

"Wish there could've been more fire." Jeremy fiddles with the radio dial, but static is all that responds. "I liked watching them burn."

The others all fade to silence. Robin detaches herself from the rest, shaking her head as she leaves. Orlando, Tara, and Katherine all watch her go before exchanging glances. The scars on their body sting with memories. Reminders of Francis' anger; reminders to never stray. They eye Jeremy, whose hands still, and then their savior.

Jeremy looks over his shoulder with great caution. Francis stares him down. His wrath ices the boy's soul. Jeremy's brittle, splintering ice frosted across a lake. Francis' footsteps are like hammers beating on a nail; they drive Jeremy to quivering madness.

"Such greed," Francis says. Poison drips from each word. "Why undermine everyone's efforts?"

"I-I'm sorry, Francis." Jeremy spews. "I didn't mean it. I was in a stream of consciousness. That's all. I'm so sorry. I meant no disrespect."

"Grovel more," Francis says coldly.

Jeremy's wide eyes water. He frantically throws himself at Francis' feet, stammering incoherent apologies. Not enough. Francis kicks the boy's twined hands apart and places his foot between them. Jeremy worships it with kisses and tears.

Francis bites his bottom lip to keep it from twisting into something sly. "Jeremy."

With a gasp, he looks up. The deadly chill resonating from Francis fades. In its stead, something akin to fatherly warmth brews. Crouching in front of him, Francis caresses his cheek. Jeremy treasures the back of his hand with his own. The others watch on, unease in the air.

As he frames the boy's face, a predacious smile softens Francis' features.

"I understand," he assures Jeremy.

Jeremy stares up at him. Not a man. An angel. He who towers above them all without wings. He saved them from their sorrows and gave their pain purpose. All angels must bear their swords sometimes. Francis is no different.

"I don't deserve you," Jeremy mumbles.

Francis presses a thumb onto Jeremy's quivering lip.

"It's okay," Francis whispers. "You, me, we all want something. I can't blame you wanting more. And I will give you more." He looks at the others. "We began this for our children and grandchildren who died. Our brothers and sisters. Our lovers and friends. Our students and mentors. This has been a demanding journey."

His eyes never stray from Jeremy. A privilege. Their savior's love is private. It's saved for intimate words behind closed doors, where he soothes their fears and doubts. Otherwise, Francis' attention never strays from their objective. It's his second grandest love, exceeded by one other, dead individual.

"Please be patient. It's all I ask." He clasps Jeremy's chin, giving him a tender look. "Though... I do need something more from you, Jeremy."

Ensnared, Jeremy nods. "Anything."

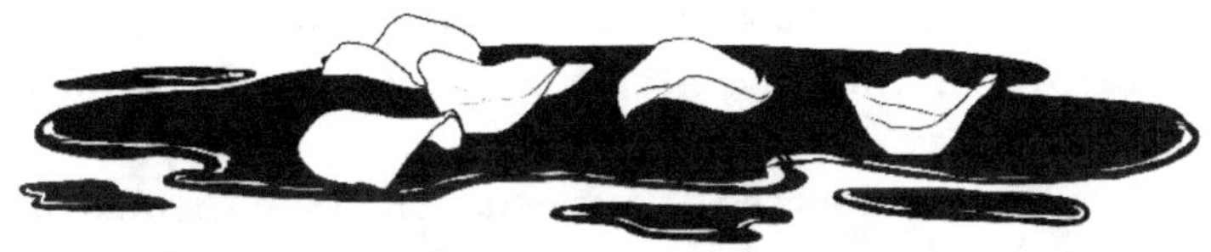

BITTER TASTE

On August 29th, almost half of the population of Celastrus was wiped out beneath a full moon. Male residents and refugees woke from their beds with an unquenchable thirst. It compelled them to the nearby waterway, where they gorged themselves. Even when their bellies swelled, they guzzled handfuls of water until they collapsed. Dead.

Some were spared from the water's spell. No child, male or female, died, and, somehow, a small number of those who drank the water managed to survive, albeit in a coma. One such shifter is Alpha Garth, incapacitated and unable to assist Alpha Althea as she maneuvers the hectic aftermath.

Today is September 1st.

The names of the dead are still coming in. Already, I've recognized too many. Lilac's father was among the first few waves. I haven't seen Dad's yet, but my hope is minimal. Too many names arrive every day. He could come tomorrow, or the day after that, or weeks from now. Mom's, too.

Nico and I are seated at our usual chairs in Cleon's office. He scuttles about the room, gathering things from shelves and tables.

The jokes are missing today. They have been since the full moon. My sense of humor wandered off somewhere, and I'm not in the mood to fetch it. There's too much to worry about, to grieve, to process. There's just too much.

"Alright." Cleon slides into his desk chair. "Let us begin. This is days overdue. We cannot put off the vision any longer."

"Where's Pyera?" Nico asks.

The Lord frowns. "She is handling arrangements with the Packs right now."

"For what?" I ask.

Cleon pushes out a breath. "The Summit has been moved to September 13th."

"That's not a whole lot of time." I grumble.

"Agreed." Cleon tucks strands of his hair back. "At the very least, it gives us a wider gap between then and the blood moon. Apparently, after seeing one of your predictions come to fruition, Alphas Roderick and Kennedy decided our attendance would indeed be helpful. They mentioned it may even be essential."

My hands ball into fists. My knuckles burn white. "It only took 1,000 shifter lives."

A stray hand touches my shoulder. I glance at Nico. His reaches for mine. He twines them together, squeezing my fingers. I squeeze his back. He pulls away.

"Shall we?" Cleon sighs.

He puts his glasses on, prepares a pen and paper, and looks at us warily. Lack of sleep compacted with less time to feed has made him paler, gaunter, older. He and Pyera have both aged since I arrived. These past few months have been more densely packed with turmoil than the majority of my life.

He pushes a Bible towards us. Nico takes it.

"Miss Braddock, we will start with you," the Lord says.

The images replay inside my head for the millionth time. The words don't come as easily, but, slowly, I filter through details until there are none left to share. Somehow, I manage to get to the end without choking. As I recount Nico's corpse, I look anywhere but at him. His dead eyes stare me down in my sleep.

Cleon's swift scrawling comes to an end. A worried furrow wrinkles his forehead, and he looks at Nico. There's an apprehensive flicker of hope in his eyes, and something similar resonates in my chest. It was rare enough our visions aligned the first time, but again?

Nico is white as a lamb. I think he knew all along but hoped otherwise.

"Tell me," Cleon pleads.

"It was almost exactly the same." His voice is tight. "Except I didn't see Macy get strangled. I felt myself bleeding out instead. And..."

He pulls a folded piece of paper from his pocket. Shakily, he opens it up and lays it flat on Cleon's desk. It's the raven he was drawing before the vision, but now it's marred by a single word etched over and over. *Bleeding, bleeding, bleeding.*

Nico's eyes drop to the ground and then back up. "I don't know what it means, but I didn't see this before. I think now… I think Church kills me too."

I hunch forward, burying my face in my hands. Why does everything only get worse?

Cleon takes the page and looks over it gravely. "We will not let that happen."

Nico swallows, but nods. He recovers the drawing—and crumples it.

Eventually, Cleon says, "We know now that the river of tar was meant to warn us of Celastrus."

I dutifully sit up, shoulders slouched in defeat.

Nico opens the Bible in his lap. "That was the third trumpet. Loosestrife signaled the first and second."

He recites excerpts from the Bible. Words whispered in the vision align with those printed on the page. How were we supposed to stop what happened at Celastrus? What could we have possibly done in the seconds between the vision and that phone call from Pyera? Was it really out of our hands?

We have to do better.

I muster the strength to try. "The fourth involves darkness, right? That could be the storm clouds. They blocked out the entire sky." My resolve wavers. "How are we supposed to stop the weather?"

"I don't know if we can," Nico admits. "In the vision, it was happening as a backdrop to everything else, like it's been brewing the entire time. Church set off a chain reaction."

"And we're still catching up." I groan. *Damnit.* "What about you… dying? Is that related to the fifth?"

"No." Nico looks pained. "I think that's just… a side effect of everything. We've changed the future, but not for the better."

"How do we fix it?" I demand.

"The same way we stop you from dying." Nico looks at me with a frown.

"You will not go unprotected, Nico." Cleon says sternly. "I will not allow it."

"The fifth trumpet doesn't have anything to do with me or blood." Nico decidedly switches subjects. "At least, not as far as I can tell. The Bible describes it as 'the first woe.' It says,

Before the trumpet sounds an angel appears, flying in mid-heaven and warns, "Woe, woe, woe, to those who dwell on the earth because the remaining blasts of the trumpets of the three angels are about to sound."

"Angels don't exist," I point out.

"No," Cleon says, "but it may not be literal. In fact, it is most certainly *not* literal. You mentioned something about a man in your vision."

I sit up straight. "There was a crowd. He was standing on the Bridge. Everything was quiet, but there was chaos around me. And he caused it. I know it."

It's one of those feelings. Without knowing *how*, I just know.

"It is a courier's duty to deliver their message," Cleon says.

Clutching the arms of my chair, I careen forward. "Then it *isn't* the same song and dance. It was on the *Bridge*. In Devil's Trumpet."

He nods. "I will have the gammas bolster their guard, and patrol more frequently."

"That's one to one," Nico says. "Let's go two for two. But I'm not sure about the sixth trumpet."

"How so?" Cleon asks.

Nico begins reading from the page again. "It rants about the 'second woe' five months after the fifth trumpet. Then there's all this bullshit with an army on plagued horses, and a third of mankind dying from a blight."

I huff. "So, it's just biblical nonsense."

He holds his hair out of his face. "The blight has to be the ghouls' scourge, but the rest I don't even know. The next excerpt is the final one, and that's all about Christ and Heaven. The end of the world."

"We don't even *have* five months between now and the blood moon," I remark.

"This makes no sense," Nico mutters.

Out of nowhere, Cleon begins to type on his computer. The jarring, rapid *tap* of his keys startles us both. An uncharacteristic cuss leaves his lips.

"Cleon?" Nico asks.

The aged man looks up. "We may not have five months, but there are fifteen days between the blood moon and the Summit."

I count the days on my fingers, and sure enough there's—thirteen, fourteen, fifteen. I count again and again and again until the numbers become meaningless, and the dates become hollow. Fifteen days? Five months? Does fifteen being a variable of five really give it any credence?

The Summit *can't* be the sixth trumpet. It wasn't in the vision. The Man in the Moon wouldn't leave that out. Not if it was crucial.

The final seconds of the vision replay in my head. Dead Alphas lined up. My body heats with anger. "He's going to try and murder the alphas. He knows that, on top of everything else, would destroy us."

"But wouldn't that make them martyrs?" Nico contests.

"It is possible it might affect other nations that way," Cleon says, "but the US packs would be in no place challenge him. First Loosestrife, then Celastrus, then Meadowsweet? That is three of the largest shifter settlements in three months."

We have to do better.

"Alert Alphas Roderick and Kennedy." My wrath cools and hardens; it becomes the stone reinforcing my words.

"Don't let them sit on their asses either." Nico adds. "They can't just think about how important it *might be*."

Cleon visibly digests our words. After a pause, he scribbles in his notes, tears a few pages from the pad, and stands up from his seat.

"I am going to the Embassy," he says, halfway out the door already. "Hopefully Pyera is still there. If need be, I will hunt her down myself."

"They need to spread the word about the attack," I persist as we tail after him. "The Poppy Alphas, the Sage, the Agave, every Alpha on the face of the Earth needs to know."

"I already wrote it down," the Lord says. He doesn't spare a glance over his shoulder. "I also included that preparations for the attack should begin immediately, and, if possible, a closer Summit date."

"What about us?" I demand.

Finally, he looks at Nico and me. "Pack."

THIRTY

THE BEETLE

The next few nights are spent almost exclusively at the gym, from sunset to sunrise. On the track, I run until my legs shake and give out from under me.

Lying there, I scowl at the storm clouds closing in, thinking about a million things, about Mom and Dad.

My chest tightens.

First, they lost me. Then, they lost all semblance of home. My entire childhood is ash. My home is gone. My pack is in shambles. Too many people I knew are dead. There's no telling if Dad even survived Celastrus, but it's painful to imagine Mom all alone. She's cold and calculating; plants are easier for her to love than people, but she's my *mom*. She doesn't deserve that. Neither does Dad. *Mother Nature, protect them.*

And what about Lilac?

With a groan, I throw my forearm over my eyes.

She and Lily are some of Bloodroot's finest, Lily especially. That wouldn't guarantee their presence at the Summit, but the recent deaths might. Who knows how far they've risen in the ranks? The beta pool is already small.

My breath hitches.

What would I say? Would she be overjoyed? *Yes,* my heart shouts, but my mind intervenes. All I hear is: *This is why you're an omega.*

Now I'm even below that. I know how she feels about vampires. I used to feel the same. That night in Hydrilla, it was clear our relationship was doomed anyway.

Deep down, I know it was obvious earlier than that. Our love was fostered from complacency and circumstance. She was there, so she was mine; I was there, so I was hers. Is the history between us, spanning all the way back to our youth, enough?

Lilac wasn't always there. In fact, when things were rough, she never was. Problems were never solved. They were pushed to the wayside, abandoned, as we took late night trips through the woods, to her cabin, to mine, to forget about everything and anything for a little while. Sometimes, that was detrimental.

Sometimes, it made me feel like shit.

My muscles all whine when I sit up. I rub my palm into my forehead.

The Monster must be laughing, like he does in my nightmares, in my visions. The Summit is so close. My

Grounding is a lost cause. The world is ending. I'm going to die. I'm useless. I have been from the start.

Ignoring the soreness in my bones, I stand and break into a sprint. If I run fast enough, maybe I can escape all these doubts, but they're stitched into my every fiber. There is no such thing as *fast enough*; no matter how swiftly I run, those doubts breathe down my neck.

Faster.

My thighs burn. The wind bites my cheeks. Stray hairs fly from my bun and move like ribbons of fire behind me. I swipe strands from my face, and sprint across the long stretch ahead. I pick up speed around the turn, but slow on the second straight. I try to push past the pain, but it drags me into a walk and bends me over my knees. I brace my hands against my thighs. Sweat drips off my brow. It spots the track below.

"Bright Eyes!"

The wind scampers across the track and field. It cools my skin, staying a second too long as if it were looking for me. Nico waves at me from the peak of the embankment, smiling smugly.

"Glad you're still here." He descends down the hill. "Got worried you'd run off as soon as you saw me. I'd have to chase you, and it's too early to go for a jog." He raises a brow at me. "Not that you'd agree."

"It's never too early for a sprint," I say between breaths.

"Now you've lost me. A jog is one thing, but a sprint? I am decidedly anti-run."

I scoff and start walking again. He assumes my side.

"Why're you here, Nico?"

"I could ask you the same thing."

His scrutiny isn't like the kind I'm used to. Mom's was always desperate. Dad's was always blunt. Both were rooted in their hope, but this is grounded in different soils. There's care in Nico's criticism. A bit of concern, too.

I say, "I have to work harder than you."

He doesn't look convinced. "What's your plan? Run yourself into your grave? That way Francis can't?"

"Are you the sacrifice Nico?" I fire back.

"No. But *apparently* I'm supposed to die, too."

I look away.

He reaches for my arm. "Bright Eyes. You're exhausted."

I pull away from his touch. "I'm *always* exhausted."

"This is more than insomnia." He steps in front of me, walking backward. "You're covered in bruises from head to toe. You come here every sunset, and you don't leave until almost sunrise. That's too much time."

"I have to get better," I whisper. "I have to protect everyone."

He frowns. "I have an idea."

"What's that?" I look at him.

He stops waking. I come to a jittery halt. His lips form a smirk. "A challenge."

I glare at him, suddenly very suspicious.

"A sparring match." He clarifies. "If you win, you go about your self-destructive way."

At first, I want to ask what happens if he wins, and then it dawns on me: *he always wins.*

"That's unfair, and you know it."

"What are you talking about?" He's already headed up the hill, toward the gym.

I hurriedly retrieve my things from one of the bleachers and chase after him. "I haven't beaten you *once.*"

"Okay, okay. Good point." He strokes his chin in thought. "In that case, if you *lose,* you go about your self-destructive way. There. Feel better?"

"No. I actually feel worse."

"Do you want fairness or not?"

"I want you to leave." I shoulder my bags with a sigh. "What if you lose?"

"If I lose, then you go home. Sleep. Relax."

I size him up. "And you think because you said that, I will?"

"I'll walk you home."

"I can outrun you."

"That's a risk I'm willing to take," he says. "Besides, you're going to lose, aren't you?"

I roll my eyes. He winks at me. Double eye roll.

Nico holds the door to the gym open for me. We sign in at the front desk before heading upstairs to the sparring room. He tosses his beanie onto the bench and tousles his flattened bedhead. He pulls his hoodie off, over his head, snagging his t-shirt too, exposing the bite marks all over him. They span farther than I thought: scattered unevenly all down the nape of his neck and shoulders. Too many.

His creator must've run out of room and sought more.

His shirt falls over his skin like a fabric shield. He turns and catches me staring. I grimace.

"Like what you see, Sunshine?"

I set my bag down and reach for my boxing gloves. "Not even remotely."

"What?" He faces me. "You aren't stunned by my *exquisite* physique?"

"Don't make me gag." I tighten the elastic around my wrist.

"Now you're looking for a fight." He teases, pulling his own pair on and stepping onto the mat.

I bite back a smirk. "Same rules?"

"Yep."

Raking in a deep breath, I step onto the mat. I abandon everything outside it. Forget I've failed every trial so far. Forget that the world might end in just a few weeks, and that my death would be the cause. Forget it all.

"Don't try to lose this time." He warns.

"Shifters are raised to give it their all or die trying." I shoot back.

"I guess you've been holding out on me then. You're still breathing."

"Bite me."

"Tempting." He brings his arms up to shield his face. I do the same. "On the count of three?"

I nod. "One."

"Two."

He winks again. "Three."

Neither of us moves at first. We bounce on the borders of the mat, hinged for the other's attack. I won't pounce first. He knows that.

I'm always at a disadvantage when we spar, tonight more so than ever. My muscles sting with exhaustion. The ache slowly encompasses my body so that every part of me burns from the slightest stretch. First strike isn't an option. The ball is in his court.

When he takes a sudden step forward, I know not to trust it. It's too random, not calculated enough. A feint.

Sure enough, he leans his weight onto one foot before pouncing onto the other, in the opposite direction. My body aches too much to dodge. Instead, I bounce to the right and block his attack with my forearms. I use the momentum of his swing to put space between us.

He'll expect me to stay on defense, so I don't.

I rush him in two swift strides, jabbing at him. He ducks, and surges beside me. He reels his fist back. I twist out of the way, twirling a few steps back before hurling myself at him again.

Back and forth we go. It's a grueling go-around with no stakes, but it floods my veins with adrenaline. We're caught in an ever-changing sequence of duck, dodge, move, and swing until each of us lags behind, the breathless lull revitalized by spurts of energy.

This is ground level. His brutal blows ring with competition, echoed by the chorus of his exhausted panting. We're both tired. We're both giving it our all. We're equals.

I throw a flurry of punches. Some land, but not all. Better than nothing. I lunge at him, hoping to pin him. He avoids it and rushes me from behind. He seizes my middle, and then we're on the ground. I tear my gloves off to grapple with him. He does the same. In the fray he manages to restrain my wrists, and pins them on either side of my head.

I squeeze my leg between his abdomen and mine. Growling, I extend it and kick him off. I throw myself after him, pin him on his belly, and press my knee into his lower back. My hands are manacles around his wrists, holding him captive. I count the seconds. They whir by and last forever.

Finally, I declare. "I win."

We roll away from one another. I stand with my hands on my knees, catching my breath. Nico sits up, dazed. I'm not much better. When I offer my hand, he takes it.

"You finally beat me." He barely sounds like he believes it.

I huff. "Crazy. I'm going now."

He wipes the sweat off his brow with the back of his hand. "Ah, ah, ah."

Just like that, his grin washes away my pride

"That wasn't the deal, remember?"

... Damnit...

I glare. "Sometimes, I want to strangle you."

He tips his head back and laughs. "You aren't the first person to tell me that."

We take our time to cool down. As the adrenaline seeps from my body, I sit with my neck rested on the edge of the bench. My eyes droop, lids stained red from the lights. Lazily, I glance around the empty room. My imagination paints other young men and women all over, populated as it must've been when Nico boxed semi-professionally. They spar, joke, lounge, and laugh. They do all the things a close-knit team of champions would do in their spare time. Just not anymore.

"Is there a second sparring room?" I ask

"No," he says, settling beside me. "Why?"

I roll my head on my shoulders to look at him. "It's weird that no one else is ever here besides us. You are the champion, aren't you? That implies that you beat at least one other person."

He lets go of a loud breath. "That was a year ago. I'm not on the team anymore."

I cock my head at him. "Why?"

"I got kicked off."

"Again, why?"

He shrugs, staring at his hands as he fiddles with his shoelaces. "I lied. Before."

My mouth is dry. "About what?"

"I hurt someone."

My heart stumbles. "...Who?"

He glances at me, thumbing the mole on his chin. "I don't want to tell you."

"Nico..." I grab his arm and look at him.

He averts his eyes. He barely manages to whisper. "Luc. I hurt Luc."

"What did you do?" I whisper.

For a long time, he says nothing. He takes his beanie off the bench and turns it over in his hands, watching it endlessly. "There are rules. Regulations. The teams travel all over the region, from coven to coven, so the shifters need to trust who they let in and out. No drinking. No history of protesting, disobedience, violence against a gamma. Definitely no escape attempts. You have to undergo a psychological assessment to assure them you're not going to rip into their jugulars while they sleep." His sarcasm is harsh. His one defense. "Any sign that you lack mental or physical restraint and you're taken off the team. Just how it is."

"Nico, what did you *do?*"

"I messed up." His voice is so quiet. "Things were rotten for a while. Luc was angry at me. I was angry at him. When Val chose me to be next in line as Grand Enchanter, it all boiled over. He started yelling, so I started yelling. Then fists got involved. I don't even remember why. Just that I threw the first punch. And the last."

The beanie slides from his slack grip. He rubs his knuckles like he remembers what it felt like to pummel Luc. His face says he wishes he didn't. "I went from his brother to his worst enemy in one night."

"I'm not sure it happened that fast," I mutter. I pull my knees to my chest and listen to the blaring quiet. I shouldn't have said anything.

"I was nine."

I jerk my eyes toward him.

"When I first got here. I was nine. I didn't trust anyone except Luc. He reminded me of my brother..." He turns away. "The one from before I was bitten."

"You had a brother before?"

"Yeah." He snaps and then sighs. "Sorry..."

Time ticks. I wait for more. He waits for the courage to give more.

"He disappeared the year before I did."

I furrow my brows. "... before you did?"

"Yeah." He closes his eyes. "He was killed. I was kidnapped."

I gape at him. My heart twists. *What happened?*

He says, "It was my own fault. I lived in Juarez, Mexico. It's right by the border. My mom was a psychic. Not a fake one, either. She was like us. That's how she made money. But things were rocky after my brother died. I thought I would escape to the great United States, so I wrote my goodbye letter, packed a bag, and headed for the border. Didn't get far. Some rogues found me. They held me captive for days. No food. No water. Barely any sleep. Found out later they were trying to start a family. Vampire fertility rates aren't stellar, and they were desperate to have a child. So, they stole one."

"And no one went looking for you because you left that note."

Pain expands in my chest like a flower with razor sharp petals. His hands are clenched. I clasp his shoulder, grabbing a fistful of fabric, hoping to remind him that he's here, with me, in the present.

He looks grateful. "Maybe they did. I don't know. It was the gammas who found me. They were an American unit. When the rogues realized they'd been followed, they panicked." He traces a scar fading on the knuckle of his thumb. "I spent my last human hours being bitten over and over."

"I'm sorry."

"I have bad dreams sometimes." He looks at me. I expect to see pain, but all I spot is a dull and sullen throb. Time has mended most of the ache. "But only sometimes." After a minute, he adds, "Tell me one of your deep, dark, vulnerable secrets."

"What?" My eyes bulge.

"I don't like to wear my heart on my sleeve." He shrugs, all alone despite sitting right beside me. "Just tell me something stupid. Anything, I don't care."

I pull my fingers away. My skin isn't mutilated like his. Most of my scars are time capsules of growing up. There's the Monster's handiwork on my neck, but that's no secret. The only thing I've ever been ashamed of is myself. There was a time before that, though.

"My mom was almost killed by a rogue when I was a kid," I say. "My dad was a gamma. It took him away from home a lot. We were on our way to visit him when we crossed her path. She was injured by a patrol but lost them in the woods. In her head, we were just another pair of shifters she had to cut through."

For years, that vampire was the source of so much pain. She was to blame for my nightmares riddled with spectral, white monsters lunging from the shadows with blood-soaked claws. She was to blame for Mom's blind eye, her scar, Dad's early resignation, my trouble mastering my Grounding. All of it, I blamed on her.

"Did that patrol find you guys?" Nico lifts me from my thoughts.

"Eventually. I made a light show first."

"What do you mean?"

I hold my hand out in front of us, turning it over to show all the green lines. "Shifter children can't use their Groundings on command like adults. They have to be triggered. Usually, it's a tantrum, hyperactivity, excess happiness. Weak triggers, usually. Just enough to spark a glow. But trauma is a powerful trigger, too."

"Was your mom okay?"

I nod. "We were different after that, though. The healers liked to say I spent all my potential that night. It's actually embarrassing. We spend all our adolescent years learning how to hone our Groundings without a trigger, but I've never mastered it. My girlfriend's sister mentored me for a time. They're both betas."

"I should guess that didn't end well."

"It happened a year ago." My shoulders grew heavy. "I never meant to hurt her, but no one ever means to hurt anyone." *Unless you're a madman, of course.*

"You didn't kill her, did you?" Nico asks, face scrunched.

I laugh despite myself. "No! When we met that day, she had both arms. Afterwards, she only had one."

There's a beat of silence, and then, out of nowhere, he gets to his feet with a groan and reaches for his coat. It makes me jump.

"Are you leaving?" My skin flushes with anger.

"No." He says like I'm dumb. He digs something out of his coat pocket and sits back down with a thud. "You mentioned trouble sleeping before."

He holds his hand out to me. In his palm is another moon pendant. It's like the one around his throat. His is a waning crescent. This is one is full. It's tinted red. He takes my wrist and sets it in my hand.

"This is for you. Life sucks. It sucks more when you can't sleep. I made mine to keep the nightmares away, too." He looks at me like he expects me to say something, but when I don't, he rambles on. "You're my friend, Macy. I care that you take care of yourself. Maybe we might be dead tomorrow, but at least you'll sleep tonight. So, here. Take it, so I can end the mini-monologue."

I clasp the chain around my neck. It hangs higher than my beaded necklace. All my life, the moon has been a treacherous omen. This is blasphemy anywhere else, but here, in Devil's Trumpet, a horrible place to call home, but still mine, it sits comfortably at the hollow of my neck.

THIRTY-ONE

OUT OF MY HANDS

My phone rings, disrupting the unusual tranquility of my room. Groggily, I blink myself awake, mind lagging. There are no flashes of horror or gore. I'm just *awake*. Rubbing one eye, I thumb the moon pendant.

The ringing resumes. I didn't realize it stopped at all. I fumble for my phone, nearly knocking over a lamp in the process. I answer without reading who it is.

"Miss Braddock, I need you at City Hall."

"Cleon?" I sit upright, all traces of sleep sapped. He never calls. It's always Pyera. That sick, foreboding feeling festers in my stomach. "What's wrong?"

"Please, Miss Braddock. Just come."

My heart trips over itself. "Right now?"

"Right now."

We hang up, and I launch out of bed. I hurry into a pair of leggings, flip-flops, and tie my hair up as I dart out the door. I one-handedly text Nico.

Do you know what's going on?

Another attack? We would've seen it, wouldn't we? We saw Hydrilla burn and Celastrus poisoned, even if it was too late. Would it matter, anyway? Tonight isn't a full moon. Church has only triggered his trumpets on the full moon, but is that a requirement? Or is it just a coincidence? Maybe he purposefully misled us.

Night saturates the sky. On the horizon, a thick, smog-like storm looms. Anxiety tightens in my chest. And what about the man on the Bridge? I search every face I pass on the sidewalk, on the lookout for that maniacal smile. My walk hurries into a jog, then a sprint.

City Hall's yellow lights welcome me. All around, the evening's influx of employees flows through an open door, held open by a good Samaritan. I hurriedly squeeze between two people, pushing inward, when someone grabs my wrist.

Luc.

He pulls me to the side of the lobby. His eyes dart all over my face. Our argument at Cinnamon's feels so far away now. After Val's ritual, the vision, Celastrus, and whatever mysterious event brings me here, our anger feels senseless. My fear and his concern absolve any grudges.

"Is everything okay?" His eyes are round.

"I... I don't know."

I tear my arm free. He's right beside me as I race to the front desk. My weight jostles it. The tired receptionist startles, sitting straighter.

She gapes at us before clearing her throat. "Miss Braddock, the Lord and Lady left a note that they were expecting you." She hands me a tablet with a prompt to sign. "Mr. Walcott, are you here to speak to the Grand Enchanter?"

"Uhuh."

Hastily, I scribble my name and slide it back to her.

She takes it, smiling at him. "He's not in yet. Do you mind waiting?"

His eyes say: *No.* His mouth says, "That's fine. Will he be here soon?"

"I'm sure!"

"I'll call him." He frowns, and steps away from the desk. As he scrolls through his contacts, he gives me a reassuring smile. The feeling in my gut keeps me on edge.

The receptionist scans the tablet. She takes her time typing my name into her computer while I bounce from foot to foot, tap my fingernails, being as impatient as possible. Finally, she waves to the gammas. I steal my chance to race down corridors to Cleon's office. I don't knock.

He and Pyera pace, but they come to an instant halt when I enter. Neither of them bothers to wipe the conflicted sadness off their faces. They share a look, exchanging secrets not meant for me. Something terrible happened.

Except Nico isn't here. If the world is one step closer to its doom, why isn't he here? Only one chair has been pulled out. I check my phone.

Nico: *No? What are you talking about?*

My heartbeat accelerates. My pulse wiggles in my wrists as I swallow. "What's going on?"

"Sit down," says Pyera.

I don't.

She glides toward me like a breeze. I flinch away when she takes my hands and guides me to the center of the room. Gentle, she touches my shoulders, no harsher than a feather, and tries to usher me into the chair. My knees are locked straight.

"Macy," she whispers. "Please."

Her mildness is like a punch to the gut. I gag on bile and fear.

"Stop," I mutter.

She parts her lips. I wait for the pain to pour. She stops herself, peeking at Cleon.

"Just tell me," I say.

Her face wrinkles with sympathy. "Just an hour ago...We received another casualty report."

Dad's smile flashes, big and white in my head. His laughter resonates. I feel the coarse texture of his hand as it wraps warmly around mine. Every memory chisels a crack into my heart.

"No."

"Among them..."

"No." I hold my hand out to her, rejecting what she hasn't said. I back away, but I hit the chair. Pyera closes her eyes, the last thing I ever wanted to hear perched on her tongue. She hesitates to say it.

On an inhale, all her doubts show, and then, on the exhale, she lets it all go. "Among them, was your father."

I have no heartbeat, breath, or blood flow. The tattered connections to my life before, holding me up, sawed at for months, quiver. One snaps. I fall into a void.

It's your fault, my pain accuses me.

If I had done something, found a way to intercept the trumpets, or stopped the Monster's ritual before he attacked Celastrus, Dad would still be here. Maybe I would've never seen him again, but he would be alive. He and Mom—*Mom.*

She's all alone now. After every hurdle she leapt for me, for my dad, she's lost us both. Why would Mother Nature punish her endurance? What kind of goddess rewards her servants with pain and self-hatred? What kind of goddess asks for everything but gives *nothing?*

"They're planning a memorial in November." Her eyes are tight. Two sharp lines around her mouth emphasize her frown. "I will bend *every* shifter law so you can attend."

That isn't in her power—and the world might not even exist by then. My legs ache. I need to run. Run away. Run and hide. Run home. Mom needs me.

"Miss Braddock," Cleon says. He's closer than I realized. His hand grazes my shoulder. "I know—"

"No, you don't!" I snarl, ripping myself away.

The venom drains from me as my world crumbles. I should apologize, but a sob claws up my throat. I clench my teeth and keep it inside. Spinning around, I shove the chair aside and dart for the door.

"Macy!" Pyera grasps my arm.

I break away from her.

"Please, Miss Braddock! Stay!" Cleon hurries after me.

I yank the door open. Every hallway blurs into the next. They stretch on like an endless maze. Blindly, I dodge vampires, ignoring their concerned questions. All I can hear is the Monster. He cackles from the shadowy trenches of my brain, plucking at the seams of my universe.

You were useless.

I burst into the main lobby. Everyone looks at me in shock. Luc is with Valberg at the mouth of another corridor. There's pain on Luc's face. Val bows his head. They know.

My soul screams, *Run.*

Luc chases me. "Tenderfoot! Wait!"

I sprint into the night. Devil's Trumpet is fully alive now. If it were day, the streets would be dead. Like Dad. I could curl up on the cement to burn like a piece of coal. I look in either direction. Tears mist my vision. There are colors and shapes, moving bodies without faces. Obstacles in my way. I stagger down the sidewalk, pushing and elbowing. Someone grabs me.

Not again.

"Let go!"

"Bright Eyes!" Nico comes into focus. His eyes dart from both of mine.

I choke on another sob. The wind touches the nape of my neck. It sings a sad apology. I don't care. Letting loose a yell, I shove him away and sprint past him.

"What's happening?" Nico barks behind me.

"Shut up and follow her!" Luc growls.

They can't keep up, but the wind can. It follows me down sidewalks, alleyways, around corners. It howls *it wasn't your fault,* but I know better.

The buildings dwindle. Trees rush to abundance where they're scant; the forest consumes me. I kick off my flip-flops. Soil wriggles between my toes. Sharp pebbles in the grass bite my heels. Overhead, the leaves mock me, and warty, gnarled branches snag my clothes. The river roars riotous laughter ahead. Forget the city. Mother Nature, embrace me. Just this once.

"Aimil!" I scream.

Please, hear me.

She has to listen. I have failed without her every step of the way— but it's not just my fate at stake anymore. It's Mom's, Lilac's, Pyera and Cleon's, Nico's, Luc's, the world's. It all teeters on the brink. Any single misstep could send it toppling over. All – because – of – me.

I'm useless. I need to be stronger and more capable before the Monster takes anything else. Anyone else.

I hear the river. It's close. I vault over a log, tearing my sweatshirt over my head. Goosebumps stipple my skin. Good. I rip off my shirt. The night's icy tongue licks at me. My muscles ache. I push them harder. My lungs burn. I run faster. I hunt the limits of my body, and then destroy them. Maybe the Beast will break free.

A root catches my ankle. Through the bushes, I plummet. Thorns rip my skin, and leaves kiss the scratches left behind. I fall into the shallow creek, scraping my hands on its rocky sediment.

I come face to face with my reflection.

Pathetic. Her hair is a mess. Tears steak both her cheeks. There is no strength or resilience. She's rabid with grief. It should've been her.

It should've been me.

"Aimil! Please!"

I watch my reflection, waiting for her Marrow Mark to glow. It doesn't. I slam both fists into the water. It splashes back, just as angry.

I tip my head back and scream. A gust of wind splits open the woods. Birds erupt from their nests, squawking in protest. The draft whips around me. My hair gets caught in the blast.

"What do you want from me!"

Aimil doesn't answer.

I slacken into the river. It ripples past me, too weak to carry me away. I see the Man in the Moon's reflection in the water. I close my eyes and pretend he isn't here.

I lay there, a sobbing mess, for I don't know how long. The heat and rage seeps from my body, drifting downriver, and the shivers start. Eventually, I'm pulled onto the shore and into someone's arms. My listless attempts at resistance are easily countered by gentle hands.

"It wasn't your fault," Luc murmurs.

I fall apart in his arms.

"It won't stop." He rocks me back and forth. "I know it's hard. I know what you're thinking, but there was nothing you could've done. Nothing. It isn't your fault. It just isn't. Some things... they're just out of your hands."

He chokes on his voice. The sharp, broken edges of something unfamiliar break through his expression. It's pain. And it's ours.

THIRTY-TWO

LIONS EAT LAMBS

"Following the sound of the fourth trumpet, the light that shines from the sun, the moon, and the stars becomes dark. Such catastrophe causes complete darkness of the day, even through the night."

I just want to be alone.

There are several messages from Luc: *Let me know if you need anything.* There's one voicemail from Nico: *"I'm here, Bright Eyes, just say the word."* I haven't called him back. The necklace is on my nightstand. Valberg forwarded me a list of meditation rituals. There are a few missed calls from Pyera. Cleon sent an overly long message. My eyes have been too wet to take it all in.

After three days, the buzzing stops. Then the knocking starts. It's probably Luc. Maybe Nico, Pyera, or Cleon. Whoever it is, I don't care, so I lie motionless in bed.

Minutes pass. The pounding stops. I close my eyes, thankful. And then it starts again, more adamant this time. With a growl, I drag myself out of bed. The blankets plead for me to stay.

I drudge down the hall and open the door a crack. "*Circi?*"

She's the last person I expect to see, but here she is. Her teakwood eyes are resolute, like when we last talked. They're protective, too. Not angry.

"Luc told you?" I ask in an uneven voice.

She nods. Then, she pushes my door open to pull me out by the wrist. Somehow, her fingers are soft and tentative. She embraces me. It's a broken, bleeding hug; she knows this pain better than I do. It's hardened her. I hug her back.

She whispers, "Our fight was dumb. I know I hurt you. I even know it was uncalled for. I didn't want to say sorry, but I'm here now, and I am. I'm *so* sorry... I couldn't let you sit here and rot. You don't deserve this."

She pulls away. Her eyes are intense. They always are. In the heat of an argument or the mildness of an apology, as if every conversation might be her last. During our screaming match, she had roared about the loss of her mother. My own hurt blinded me to hers.

I say, "You didn't deserve it either."

Intensity becomes compassion. Or maybe they're one and the same. Circi, for all her fire, is so much more benevolent than I gave her credit for. She's brave; so brave that she came to me despite all our differences. Just to care.

"You can't stay in this wolf den forever," she says. "Come over to my house. I'll blast away the heartache with hard rock on full volume all night. We can scream at the stars until the moon asks *us* for forgiveness."

The laugh comes out of nowhere. It's needed. "You do this often?"

"My edgy rebel vibe comes with a lot of late nights alone." Her smile is sad and fading. A crease forms between her brows. "Grab your stuff. No if, ands, or buts."

Near total darkness surrounds us when we step outside. The streetlamps barely fend off the icy shadows. Thunder brews in the heavens. A white-hot bolt of lightning strikes in the distance. The Bible verse and the vision play on loop in the back of my mind.

Circi hugs her jacket closer to her body. "It must've been like this all day. I couldn't even tell it was dusk when I woke up."

Uneasy silence envelops us. We shake it off, but it crawls up our spines the farther we walk. Circi edges closer while my eyes scour tenebrous darkness. For what? I don't know. Something, though. *Something.*

We near the Bridge. It's surrounded by a massive crowd. Suddenly, I'm bombarded by sweaty palms and a dry mouth. The shadows are too close. The wind yanks at me.

"Whoa." Circi eyes the crowd. "What's up over there?"

"I don't know."

I don't *want* to know. I don't want to join the onlookers circling something that, without even fully comprehending it, already fills me with dread. I don't want to be here, but something—maybe bravery, but probably stupidity—compels me closer. I push forward.

"I'm not sure about this." Circi admits.

"Me either."

We move through the raucous crowd.

"Just listen to them, kid!" A man yells as we scoot by him.

"Don't make this any worse," a younger woman cries.

The most frequent plea is the scariest: "Put the knife down!"

My entire body tingles. I have to force my way past a barrier of trepidation to reach the Bridge. I almost turn around.

Two hordes of gammas barricade both sides of the Bridge, Marrow Marks alight with danger. At the peak of the Bridge is the man from my vision.

Words and symbols have been freshly etched into his skin. They're obviously self-inflicted, jagged, and nearly impossible to decipher. There are a few, however, that I instantly recognize. The words *angel* and *trumpet* litter his flesh, knotted with all the other signs. Then there's the cross scrawled into his chest. It's the oldest carving, red and irritated from the sutures keeping it closed. This one is perfect, symmetrical, impeccable even. It must've been meticulously carved by another's hands.

"Come on!" The boy mocks the gammas. "Kill me! Kill me! Kill me! *Kill me!*"

"Don't threaten them!" someone shouts.

"Shut up!" He swings his blade in front of him. "Don't you all get it? These wolves are nothing more than lambs! They lock us away because we're the lions! We'd eat them right up! And soon there won't be any more shifters *or* covens!"

"Put the knife down." A gamma approaches him cautiously. On the opposite end of the channel, another shifter mirrors her movements.

He laughs. It's an unhinged jitter from his chest. The blade shakes in his hand. He points it at her. "Or what? Nothing you do will scare me. I've been liberated; and soon so will everyone else. We're going to save all of them."

"Who's *'we?'*" The female shifter distracts him. The other edges closer to the maniac.

I move away from the crowd. Circi grabs my hand. I glance back at her. Her face is white. "This is like 2010. We should—my mom—Macy, you can't."

For that instant, I'm tethered to her.

When I look back, another pair of eyes catches mine. On the other side of the Bridge, Nico inches closer to the gammas, but pauses when he spots me. There's an implicit understanding between us. We have to do something.

The boy on the Bridge takes a bow. "The Wormwood League."

A storm of air blitzes past me. It rips me out of Circi's lassoed grip.

My body operates on a plan my mind has yet to formulate, footsteps falling faster than thoughts string themselves together. I'm pushed by divine and howling winds; the entire planet demands action.

The female shifter gestures to the one sneaking behind the vampire.

"Stop!" I scream.

They don't see or hear me. It's like I'm a ghost.

"What?" the boy taunts. "Scared? Good. I came to deliver a message, so take it to your Alphas like good little puppies. In four nights, anyone who ever wronged our people, the Man in the Moon's ever-abused Children, will be scorned by the sixth trumpet."

The leading gamma makes another gesture. The other pounces. He roguishly apprehends the boy, but he doesn't struggle. His limbs sag in their grasps as they all rush in. They grapple for the knife, but his fingers are practically stitched to it.

"Stop!" My wail is lost in all the commotion.

Sense abandoned, I dart up the Bridge. I clasp the nearest gamma's arm. The heat of his Marrow Mark singes my palms. I grit my teeth and burrow my nails deeper into his skin. An angry growl ripples from his throat.

"Let go!" he snarls.

"You have to—"

His fist is a blur, then a battering ram. It cracks against my cheek and sends me stumbling back. It's numb at first, but hot when I cup my face. My head spins and I watch my feet so they don't twist or tumble. I steady myself on a rail, but a swift kick to my side throws me down the Bridge.

No bones break upon impact, but something deep inside ruptures. A trust I kept so close to my heart, slowly tested, is finally betrayed. I rake in pained breaths. I'm a heap of quivering ache, holding the places that hurt the most. I grab the fabric just above my shirt.

Why? Why? *Why?*

I'm a shifter. I'm a Prophet. The Man in the Moon delivers the future to my eyes and echoes it in my ears.

Why?

More hands clasp my arms. I wince and lean away, until I recognize the freckles, the nails. Circi. She's not so scared anymore. She's angry. A bilious glare oozes hot fire, and her lips curl into a threatening scowl. With that alone, she could burn any shifter alive.

"Who the hell do you think—"

The crowd boils with a wave of appeals, and then detonates. An explosion of screams. It all dulls to silence as I look back to the Bridge.

In the unsettling quiet of my mind, the vampire's lips jabber with laughter. He tips his head back, lifting his knife. His smile never falters, and he yanks the metal across his throat in one brutish gesture. His jaw slackens. His Adam's apple bobs in bloodied hilarity.

Unheard thunder reverberates for miles.

THIRTY-THREE

PAIN, PROMISE, PURPOSE

A cold draft snakes around the forest. It rustles empty nests, abandoned caves, hollow burrows, searching for animals that fled when the horizon burned, and the water sickened. The trees whisper, hushed by fright. Mother Nature's silence is an admission of defeat.

Suffer, Francis thinks to himself.

Another voice quavers like a ghostly echo. Robin. The lilt of her hum guides him to a lofty tower of boulders. At the very top, the moon envelopes her silhouette Her wispy hair bristles delicately, and he remembers every time he ever ran his hands through it. His touch isn't that soft anymore.

Clutching the lowest rocky grip, he climbs to the top, where he hefts himself over the ledge. He crawls across the coarse stone to sit beside her. Their legs dangle.

He says, "Inviting trouble, are we?"

Her eyes cut to him. "You're already here."

She gazes into the charred remains of the North Maine Woods. The cinders have gone cold, guarded by plumes of lingering smoke. Storm clouds cascade on the horizon, bringing with them rain and hail, thunder and lightning, revenge and freedom, promise and purpose.

Robin plucks the unlit cigarette from between her lips and offers it to him. She knew he was coming. With a sigh, he produces his worn zippo lighter from his coat pocket. The glossy metal is blotched and scratched.

He runs his thumb over the name *Dean*, etched across. A name that will forever be a source of pain and grief. A name that spurs him toward the final curtain call, for himself and the world. And, after it all, oblivion will embrace him. There will be no more pain. No more grief. Only peace. Death.

He holds the cigarette to his mouth. A flame sparks, dies. A second ignites, singing the cellophane. His eyes drift closed as he takes a long drag.

"Are they ready?" Robin's usually coarse voice is softer; it's just the two of them.

"Yes." Francis squeezes her knee. From his pocket, he produces a velvet box. "I gave them theirs. This is yours."

Robin opens it. A silver necklace with a ruby jewel. The metal is embellished with black markings. "You're sure it'll work?"

"Only once. No mistakes."

"And the money?"

"There's enough."

After a minute, Robin says, "We won't see each other again."

His heart thuds painfully, reluctant to say another goodbye. They've been together since the start, tethered by pain, separate but similar. He's given everything to reach this point. He has to relinquish this, too. Her. The solace she gives him.

"It's all for the greater good." He tries to channel that confidence he boasts around the others. It wavers.

"Can you not?" She twists toward him and pierces him with her green eyes. Instantly, his fractured armor crumbles. "Can we just be us? One last time. Before it's over and we're gone."

"I'm sorry..." He takes her cheek in his hand. She leans into his palm, begrudgingly letting her body relax.

She's gaunter and frailer than she was five years ago, when this journey was fresh and new, yet to truly begin. Her cheeks have hollowed and darkened. Purple bags cling to her eyes, but she's as sharp as ever. More cunning and fierce by the day. Lethal, except for right now. Right now, she's just Robin and he's just Francis. He presses his lips to her forehead.

"Do you think about it...?" Robin whispers.

"2010?" asks Francis.

"Yes."

"Every day. That massacre, that day... It broke me. And I kept breaking every day after. I thought the grief would kill me. But I'm still here. I'm here and Dean is... gone."

"After..." Robin bows her head. She's long cried all her tears, but her sorrow is bottomless. "After they killed Vivica, I..."

"Shh." He guides his other arm around her and pulls her into his chest. She doesn't fight him.

"Tara reminds me so much of her."

Francis rests his cheek against her hair, holding her tighter.

The 2010 Massacre was the catalyst for everything. Dark, carnivorous grief consumed him. It was a pitch-black shadow that loomed on his shoulders for months. His memory is fogged by depression. Dean's funeral was held on a clear night, he knows that, but in his mind, it's ravaged by a frightful storm and agonized winds. Every night after that runs together, each one the same monotonous routine: struggling to get out of bed, eat, work, and live without his son. His world simply fell apart. He stumbled through the debris as a mournful zombie, devoid of any emotion but the grief that sustained him.

Beneath it all, there was rage. It festered like an infection, hidden under the rubble, morphing into an insidious hunger. This lawless, violent anger unearthed itself. Worse than pain or grief, it grew every day until he was swollen with it.

He hides his scowl in her hair.

His body is taut, brimming with hate. It's always there, driving him forward. Without it, he would collapse under the weight of Dean's absence, fall into the black void his son once filled. He would lose to the shifters.

The shifters. Prideful beasts who sit on manufactured thrones, surrounded by their own vanity, boasting about honor and duty despite how their *honor* and *duty* killed his son—meaninglessly, mercilessly, mindlessly. He vowed to avenge him. It took years to convince the covens that they're strong enough to bring down Mother Nature's tyrants.

Slowly, he discovered souls like his. Others who had been pushed to their limits, unwilling to let the shifters break them down anymore. Others who scrambled at the chance to give their pain back, tenfold.

It may have taken them years, but here they are. One the cusp of retribution.

"That day in the archives..." Robin says. "You broke the law so I could scour those tomes with you."

"The law meant nothing to me."

What sense is there in obeying laws exclusively put in place to *hurt* them? The law is blind. It doesn't care who you are. Innocent or criminal. Young or old. The shifters' world is black and white, and through their lens they have the power to murder. Remorselessly. He could not let that go forgotten, forgiven.

So, as he teemed with malice, he sought an answer in the Grand Enchanter's archives. A single pair of hands was not enough, so he went to Robin, who was another enchanter at the time, and brought her from her grief with promises of virulence and justice. Her pain, like his, morphed into blazing anger.

"I didn't know what we were looking for." She recounts, her mind distant. "It seemed aimless... useless, even. Scouring ancient books for a modern solution. I kept asking myself 'What good has our history ever done us?' But you were so desperate. So I was, too. Then we found Dante's book..."

Dante Hazel had derived much from his visions, putting together wild theories that slowly lost their credibility over the years. A Prophet driven to fiction by his own divinity, all but forgotten, omitted. His writing speculated and hyperbolized. It was easy to dismiss. That said, if there is one thing Francis knows, it's that an inkling of truth is present in everything.

He and Robin followed the trail to the Bible. It was almost laughable. The humans, Mother Nature's *first and finest creations*, worship a God whose mortal texts guard the secrets to undo their secretive guardians. He and Robin sought other vampires damaged by the shifters.

People like Kris, who lost his little brother when he fled, urgently seeking freedom outside the coven walls. Orlando, whose father was riddled with bullets. Tara, who lost her parents to the shifter's bloodlust. Jeremy, a human child with his entire life stripped away, forced to obey a government that wasn't his. There are more. All over the nation. The world.

Robin wets her lips. The cigarette dangles between her fingers. The cellophane burns faint yellow, its fuzzy glow igniting flecks of gold in her gaze.

She says, "Suddenly, my pain had this purpose. All those promises you made; they came true. And I will *never* be able to repay you, Francis."

"Robin." His voice is gentle. Only for her. He rests his forehead against hers.

She chokes out a laugh. "And I thought I'd lost everything."

He cups her jaw. Exhaling softly, he brings her lips to his and kisses her for the last time.

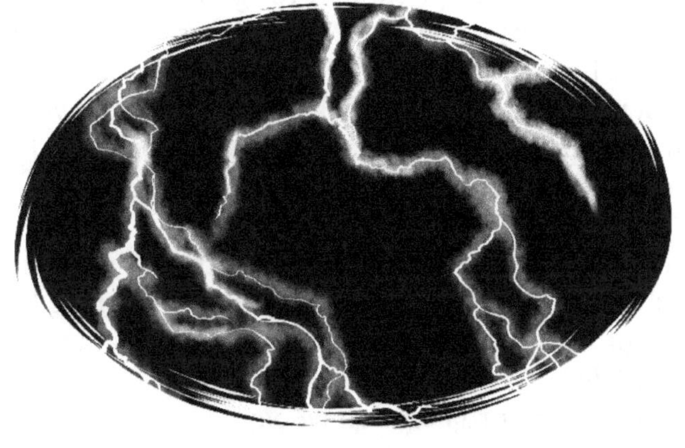

THIRTY-FOUR

TRAITOR

"People don't just appear out of thin air, Pyera!" I bark.

"Yes!" she snaps. "I realize that, Macy. And I *assure* you this bothers me just as much!"

We pace in my living room. Our anger is uncalled for. Neither means it but, after what happened on the Bridge tonight, and with so few answers, it's hard not to lash out.

"He had to come from somewhere," Circi says from my couch.

Luc is beside her.

He came running as soon as Circi texted him. Every time I look at him, he glares at the bruise swiftly forming on my cheek. It's hard enough to ignore the sweltering pain, let alone his scowl. It asks *why did you hold on?* Honestly, I've been asking myself the same thing.

"There has to be a breach somewhere in the Wall." I throw my arms up. "Or maybe he snuck in with the latest blood shipment! He had to come from somewhere!"

"Impossible," says Cleon. He moves away from the kitchen and hands me an icepack. I set it against my cheek. "The gammas are too thorough for that. Every shipment is inspected before it is sent and again when it arrives. We thought the same of the Wall, but it is too well guarded, not to mention *whole*."

"He didn't climb over it." I growl.

"Tenderfoot." Luc beckons to me softly.

I shoot him a sharp look, but the edge dulls. I sigh. "Maybe he dug under. I know some covens have underground passageways. Aconite did."

Pyera's face hardens. "The gammas thought something similar."

"So that's it?" I ask. "He broke in using the underground tunnels?"

She doesn't say anything, staring out my window. She travels a million miles away for a moment. Where she ventures, I don't know, but it scares me. She's hiding something.

I move closer to her. "What aren't you telling us?"

Cleon says Pyera's name, but she glares at him. He may not be taken aback but I am. They're thicker than thieves. Always together, paired up and perfect. He takes her spite in stride, however, and looks at me. I don't like the frown he wears. It's more severe than usual.

"Devil's Trumpet has an emergency evacuation tunnel," Cleon says.

"Right. Doesn't it have two entrances?" Circi says. Almost instantly, she and Luc stiffen.

"What?" I ask, desperate.

"One is closed off," Cleon says, "and the other is guarded by Valberg."

My mind races. I see every time Valberg ever acted odd or suspiciously replay in my head. I don't want to believe it, but—

"Damn right he wouldn't!" Luc jumps to his feet. "He loves Devil's Trumpet. He wouldn't betray us like that."

"There were blood magic runes around his home and the nearby forest." Pyera finally speaks up.

"Maybe it was Terces!" I beg, hoping against my own rationality. "She's a blood mage. She was the one sawing up animals."

"These were not simple runes," Cleon says. His voice quivers. "These were ancient, so old that only a Grand Enchanter could know."

Like the ones I saw in that book when I visited him? I remember a large, lopsided oval with a line through it, centered on a page, surrounded by many more. Val had whisked it shut in a startling hurry. And what about before that? Just before the ritual, he had been with Terces, and before that he'd leapt to defend her.

"Maybe..." I trail off. "Maybe it's true."

"No, it's *not*." Luc hisses through gritted teeth. "Where is he?"

It's hard to tell if he wants to rip Valberg apart or everyone else for considering the possibility. He radiates thick and potent heat, like all the energy his Marrow Mark never got to use oozes off him now.

I place a hand on his shoulder, but he shakes me off.

"He was put under house arrest just over an hour ago," Cleon says. "He is being monitored by the gammas until they decide if he is guilty."

"They're gammas!" Luc yells, throwing his arm aggressively at me. "Look what they did to Macy! Of *course* they're going to say he's guilty! They think we're all guilty!"

His words make me wince. The bruise on my tender cheek is enough to silence my denial once and for all.

Pyera tiredly massages her temples, shoulders hunched. The Lord stands. He crosses the distance between them, and tenderly rubs her upper back. His features are etched with worry, but she eases his concern. The seriousness returns once she looks at us, albeit softer.

"Lucas." Her voice is motherly. "No one here wants to believe it either, but if he let that maniac in..."

"He didn't."

A minute of silence overwhelms the room.

"Do you really think...?" Circi doesn't finish the thought.

Pyera winces. "We won't know until after the Summit."

Luc snorts cruelly.

"When are we leaving?" I ask.

"Two nights from now." Cleon wraps his scarf loosely around his shoulders, and then swipes the wrinkles from his trailing trench coat. Stationed by the door, he eyes his sterling watch. "I must warn you all, the gammas have imposed a curfew. They are not tentative with their lockdowns, so please refrain from wandering out too late. Your status clearly protects you very little, Miss Braddock."

I pull the icepack away from my face. My singed palm sucks up all the cold, but my cheek burns. "They must've forgotten I'm the Prophet, not some zealot."

I don't mean to be so bitter.

"They are cruel at times," he says. "Pyera and I are privileged our names carry such weight."

Pyera crosses the room with enough bravado that she alone could shake the Earth like a stampede. She tentatively touches my jaw and eyes the darkening contusion. Her lips turn down while her fingers map the blue discoloration on my face. I flinch.

"Whoever it was, I will purge them from this coven."

I nod sullenly.

Her scowl remains. "Alpha Kennedy assured me you'd be given extra protection at the Summit. Do you need anything?"

I shake my head.

She joins Cleon by the door, and they leave. I move to the kitchen and drop the icepack in the sink. My distorted reflection stares up at me from the sink's trough, morphed and muddled. Golden eyes dull, the contusion dark, ginger hair dim like Dad's; I don't know *her*. Not like I used to.

"This is bullshit." Luc snarls.

I close my eyes.

"Luc." Circi tries to calm him down, but he won't be swayed.

"Valberg didn't let that psycho in." He paces around the room. "I'm going over there."

"Luc." I plead. "There's a curfew."

"I don't care."

"The entire coven is on lockdown," I say.

He's already on his way toward the door. Circi catches his fingers. "Don't be a dumbass."

"You're supposed to be on my side."

Without another word, he yanks himself free. We yell for him to stop, but he keeps on going. He slams the door behind him, hard enough to rattle the frame. For a minute, Circi and I stare in shock, then at each other. Then, she darts for the door.

"He's not going alone," she says.

I follow her out. A dozen questions fumble on her lips, but they disappear when I say, "Neither are you."

LET ME IN

Black storm clouds growl with thunder. Their white, electric claws lash out on the horizon. Foreign shadows overrun the gaps between buildings. Search lights flare in sweeping waves behind the trees, mounted atop the Wall and its towers. Gammas holler nearby and faraway. They warn any stragglers to head inside before curfew.

At the brink of an alley, we wait until we're sure darkness won't give way to glowing gangs of gammas before we sprint across cement to the Bridge. The river roars as loud as the crowd earlier. A figure runs across it.

"Luc." Circi hisses like he'll hear her.

I take her hand and pull her forward. "Let's go."

The trees surrounding Valberg's house are painted with dark symbols. They're more numerous the closer we get. Runes, Cleon had said. Archaic runes that only a Grand Enchanter could know. A Grand Enchanter, and an ignorant shifter—because I've seen them before. In a book, on a desk, in Valberg's house, right before it was swept away. An uneven oval slashed through the middle.

There's a flash of lightning.

The bushes quiver with the howling wind. Their brittle leaves chatter as they brush up against the gloomy gray homestead, fronted by a withering garden. Lightning strikes again. Luc barrels toward the door, but it's blocked by a wall of gammas already struggling with someone on the steps. Nico, because *of course* he'd come. One angry vampire is bad enough, but two? And they hate each other?

They hurl Nico onto the lawn. He lands on his hands and knees, glowering. At the very top, the gammas let their Marrow Marks smolder, then scorch to life when Nico stands.

"You can't keep me out!" he yells.

They aren't fazed, and neither is Luc. He marches past Nico, up the steps. One of the shifters flattens his hand against Luc's chest. He doesn't stop and tries to push past. The gamma holds him back.

"Let me in." Luc leans into the gamma's hand.

"The Grand Enchanter is forbidden from speaking to anyone," a female shifter says.

Luc spits. "He's my *dad!*"

"He's under investigation."

"I don't care."

He scrambles to get by. He fights them with fists and nails and snarls, scrabbling for the door. They shove him backwards, down the steps. Somehow, he keeps his balance, just barely. Standing side by side, he and Nico are both geared and ready to charge.

Circi and I barge through the trees. I sprint for Nico. She goes for Luc.

I grab Nico by the elbow, pulling him back. A growl lodges in his throat as he wrenches on his arm. I don't let go. Infuriated, he glances back, then hesitates.

"Nico," I say like a command. "You don't want to do this. Not really."

His whole body is tense. He stares at me with knitted brows and tight lips; the last thing he wants to do is listen. The anger, betrayal, and hurt Luc radiated earlier is potent in Nico as well. His looks at Valberg's home.

I step in front of him. His eyes dart all over my face. They search for weakness but linger on my cheek. His rage slackens. Letting go of a sigh, he—

"Macy!" Circi cries.

I whip around.

She grapples with Luc. He fights to break free. She barely keeps him contained. The gammas are awash in purple, blue, every other color, radiant against the brutal lightning, but no less threatening. Luc will never get past.

"I'm *going* inside!" Luc strides up the steps.

Circi grabs his hand. "Just calm down!"

The gammas shove him again. This time he staggers, misses a step, and he and Circi tumble the rest of the way. They land in the mud with a wet thump, splattering droplets everywhere.

The leading gamma unhurriedly descends down the stairs. The bruise on my cheek throbs. I *won't* let this happen again. Nico moves in my peripherals, but I get there first. Face and ribs bruised, fully aware of what the shifters are capable of, I plant my feet between my friends and the gammas, unafraid.

I hold a hand up. The advancing shifter stops.

What are you going to do? His eyes ask.

"We're leaving," I say, ignoring the objections behind me.

For a minute, we stare each other down. Finally, he motions for another gamma, who joins him on the bottom step. "Escort them."

"Yes, sir," the other shifter replies. She moves in front of me. "Get going."

I stay still, watching over her shoulder as the leader retreats back up the steps. I only turn around when I'm sure he won't come back down. Shadowed by the gamma, we retreat into the forest. Circi lugs Luc along, and Nico begrudgingly follows.

Silence is fast to overtake us. We're surrounded by a world of mundane sound: our footsteps slosh through puddles and muck, leaves and bristles scratch, animals scurry for cover. The wind shrieks, and thunder booms.

"Circi," I say. "How far away is your place?"

The rocker eyes me uncertainly. "It's on Maple."

"So closer than mine?" I follow my mental road map of Devil's Trumpet.

Circi scratches her arm. "Why?"

I pull my phone out to check the time, and then nod to our shadow. "Curfew is in less than ten minutes." I motion toward the boys. "And, since we can't trust *them* to behave, our sleepover just got a little bigger."

"What?" Circi gasps.

"You heard me."

"I'm not going anywhere with *him*." Luc grumbles.

Nico tips his head back and unleashes a mean-spirited laugh. "Likewise."

"Prick."

"*Pendejo.*"

Luc gives him a daggered look. "Why are you even here, Nic?"

"He's my dad too."

"Only because you stole him."

"Can you two *not?*" I whip around to face them. Everyone stops walking.

"What the hell is your problem, Luc?" Nico's volume scales higher as he speaks. "I never in my entire life tried to *'steal'* Val."

"Oh, whatever!" Luc throws his arms into the air. "Valberg was the only person I had, and then you came along and wrapped him around your finger."

One of the gamma shoves Nico. "Keep moving."

Nico barely starts walking. He's more focused on Luc. "I didn't pick this! It's not like I woke up one day and decided to be the Prophet."

"You act like it's such a burden!" Luc motions to me. "But, up until Macy arrived, your visions only ever brought you good. You grew up with everyone kissing your ass. Val, Pyera, Cleon. Everyone! You know what I grew up with?"

Nico shoves his hands into his pockets, shoulders hunched.

"Forgotten birthdays, school events, unsigned field trip waivers, half-hugs, conversations that never went anywhere real because Valberg was always so obsessed with *you*." Luc takes a step closer to Nico, who doesn't back away.

The gamma glows. "I said *keep* moving."

"You." Luc reiterates. "Valberg's perfect little Prophet."

Nico's eyes are starless skies. Luc meets them head on.

The soothsayer's lip curls up in a vicious scowl. "Boohoo!" His words mist in the air. "Go ahead, act like nothing good ever happened. Act like I meant nothing to you. Forget the rumors, the insults, forget it all! I have Val, Pyera, and Cleon all because of the stupid visions! It's not like, because of those visions, I lost my *brother!*"

"You never considered me your brother!"

"Yes! I did!" Nico yells—*begs.* "I still do! If I could change things so I was never Prophet, I would. Is that what you want to hear? That I hate this? That I'm miserable because the Man in the Moon chose me but took everything away to do it!"

Nico's shoulders rise and fall with his rage. The anger ebbs, revealing something vulnerable underneath. He quickly glances off to the side. He looks like he wants to take everything he just said back.

"Gerald," the gamma says into a mouthpiece on her shirt. "I have an issue, here. Send backup down the path."

Circi edges closer to Luc. "Hey..."

Looking between them, I demand, "What's wrong with you two?"

Neither answers. Nico buries his hands into his pockets while Luc scuffs the ground with the toe of his sneaker. All the concern from earlier fizzles out. Everything is over. It's just me, Circi, and two idiots.

"Everyone here has had a bad night, week, couple of months, whatever," I say. "Circi and I just saved you two from being pummeled by gammas, and the first thing you want to do is bicker! Why? Because you're jealous, Luc?"

He blatantly avoids looking at me.

"And you're resentful, Nico?"

He too avoids looking my way.

"Because you're both so egotistical you can't just say *sorry?* This is the last thing Valberg wants. You guys know that."

"It's not that simple." Nico grumbles to the sloppy dirt.

I roll my tongue over my teeth. "Bullshit. You told me you missed Luc."

Both boys snap their heads up. Luc stares at Nico, Nico stares at me, eyes round and betrayed. I don't waver. I tip my chin up and meet his shock head on.

Luc sighs. "Nico..."

"Bye." Nico growls, bumping into me as he walks away. "Have fun with your slumber party."

"Nico!" I call after him.

He yells back. "Not tonight!"

Another shifter joins the group. He and the first gamma exchange looks briefly before the first gamma follows Nico. I let loose a breath. It deflates my shoulders.

"I'm sorry, Macy," Luc mutters.

A spontaneous surge of anger bolts through me. I pivot on my heels to face him. "No. You shouldn't be saying sorry to me."

"I—"

"No." I shove his shoulder.

"Hey!" the male shifter snarls.

I don't touch him again. "No. You're being a jerk, Luc. You came to me, trying to get me to reconcile with Circi, and you can't even put aside your own pride to at least *try* and work things out with Nico?"

He rubs the back of his neck, head bowed.

"Look at me."

He does.

"You seriously don't miss him?"

Luc's blue eyes turn sullen and, in shifting shades of vibrant sapphire, flashes a hint of yearning.

"That's what I thought."

Circi clears her throat. "You still coming over?"

I study them. We ran all the way out here to find Luc and keep him from doing anything stupid. He did something stupid, and now, despite all the arguing, I worry about him. Then, I peer after Nico. Why does it always feel as if I'm choosing between them? I can't let him be alone all over again.

I sigh. "No. Someone has to check on him."

"I'll do it," Luc says.

"Wait, what?" Circi says, baffled.

Luc says, "I'll do it."

I give him a wary look. "Are you sure?"

"No." He admits. He unzips and zips his hoodie over and over, before finally settling is hands in his coat pockets. "Not really, but you're right. I miss him."

"Do you want me to go with?" Circi asks.

"No." Luc shakes his head. "Though, if I have a black eye in the morning, assume it didn't go well."

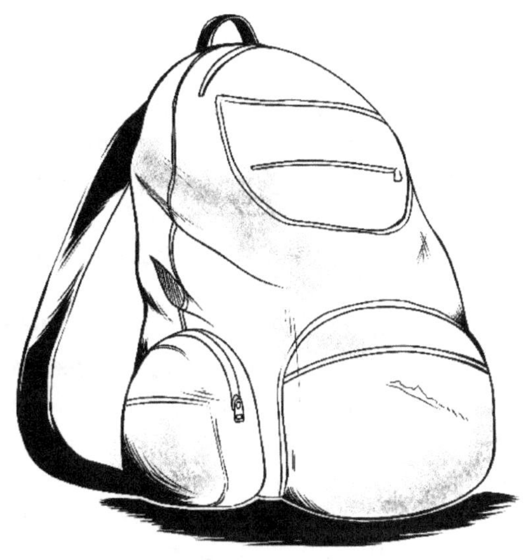

THIRTY-SIX

RASCAL

Gabriel, 10 Years Ago

The gravel crunches under my feet, and bites into my sneakers. I hurry down the road, clutching my backpack straps, alert as I cross the blurry border between Anapra and the middle-class neighborhoods. In between the dilapidated houses, shacks, and stores, darkness leers at me. It's blacker than the raven's feathers, barely contested by the dim streetlights or scarce windowpanes. I hear Mama's warnings in my head.

Abuela brings eggs from the coop for Mama to scramble every morning. When money is good, clients are frequent, and everything else has been taken care of, she buys a pack of American cigarettes from the market down the road to smoke as she cooks. This morning, her last one wobbled unevenly on her bottom lip.

She chided me. "Stay away from those streets, Gabriel, unless you seek your brother's fate."

A grim expression crossed her face, quickly followed by that familiar, painful silence that always lingers between us. It has ever since Nico died. I think that's why she never looks directly at me anymore. From certain angles, I look like him, but I can never be like him. On the nights after her tarot readings or dives into the scrying glass, she often sits beside my bed to tuck me in.

Her knobby hands tremble. Each time, she gazes at me. Her starless-night eyes are haunted. Is it the premonitions or reality? The future or the past? I hope deep down the visions have told her something terrible, but I think I've always known the truth.

She wishes it was me who died in that alley, not Nico.

It would've been better that way. Nico was older, stronger, tougher. He could work longer and harder, and when the streets called to him with promises of money and food, he knew how to navigate the slums and their lowlifes without becoming one of them. Whenever Mama or I needed something, he got it. It didn't matter how long it took; he'd come through. Once, when the rain blustered in, turning the sweaty heat into hard, bitter cold, and my jacket was too small, he gave me his tattered red hoodie. It was too big then. It still is. I wear it anyway.

I'm just his shadow. A little, grimy boy trying to live up to his brother. I wish I had died, too. It would've been better for Mama. A tear beads in the corner of my eye. I wipe it away with my fist.

I just have to make it to the border.

The tatty backstreet opens up into a wider road. The only places open this late are bars, questionable motels, and shady restaurants that look like they belong deeper in the slums. The sky is crosshatched by telephone wires and clothes lines. Shoes hang by their laces, and shirts and jeans sway with the wind. Beyond them, the moon is high and full, ambushed by a pitch-black sky.

My eyes dip to the horizon.

Juarez is laid out in front of me. I follow my mental map, the blueprint I drew out in my head. I'll chase the cracks in the cement all the way to Campestre, weasel through the affluent, rich houses into the Rio Grande. I'll wade across the shallows into El Paso. No bridges, no paperwork, no nothing. And, when I get into America, I'll build my own house, farm my own land, raise my own livestock. I'll draw portraits to make money, and, if I have to, read palms and tarot cards. I've seen enough of Mama's psychic reads to know how to fake it.

"Is that Rosa Maria's baby?" a scratchy, ugly voice whispers.

Across the street, at the mouth of another alley, three silhouettes skulk amongst the shadows. Their cigarettes cast a menacing orange glow across their faces, deepening every crooked line and curve, igniting something terrible in their eyes. One of them smiles at me. Goosebumps scatter down my arms, every hair stands straight, and my stomach twists. A hole opens up inside it. I feel fate loom on my shoulders.

"Yeah...Navarro's rascal."

"Don't he know it's a little late for children to be out wandering?" one of them taunted.

The other blew smoke from his nose like a demon. "He'll learn real quick."

I try not to panic, but it strangles me. I glance up and down the road. No cars, no lights, and the only people around are the ones spilling from bars, surrounded by noise and alcohol. Maybe I could take a detour down another alley. *No,* I hear my brother's voice. *Bad idea.* I don't know the backstreets like he did, but they know him. And me.

Unclenching one hand, I deftly slip it under the hem of my shirt, grazing the wooden grip of Mama's kitchen knife, tucked under my belt. I suck in a breath, trying to be brave, but footsteps creep up behind me. Slow. Confident. I don't have to look over my shoulder to know it's those men.

I almost hear their thoughts like they're a whisper in the night, at my ear, in my head. A promise: *We're gonna get you.* A gust of wind howls angrily. It hears them, too.

Their laughter erupts.

"Hey, kiddo, your mama let you smoke? Come share a cig."

"You don't wanna hang out with us, baby?"

"Don't you wanna be like your brother? We'll teach you how."

My body prickles with danger. I walk faster. The night presses in on my skin, cold, and the cement's chill seeps through the holes in my shoes. The wind blasts past me. It begs *faster, faster, faster.* But if I go any faster, so will they. Their overconfident, lazy footfalls will transform into adrenaline-fueled strides; in an instant, their hunt will take control.

I have to be smart.

They stalk me down the road, around the corner, but when I reach the last, flickering streetlight, I dip into an alley. Their footsteps pick up. I quickly duck behind a putrid dumpster and pull out Mama's knife. My heart thuds. My brain is chaos. The moon hides behind the clouds, so the darkness will protect me. I pull in a breath and hold it.

"This way!" one of the men hollers as he sprints past me. Another man follows him. Just one more... Where is he?

My chest aches, desperate to let loose the tight, panicked breath held inside. I fight the urge, cup my hand over my mouth and nose, prick my ears, and listen for the third thug. The wind sweeps through and hushes the city. Then, in an uneasy pocket of silence, I hear the faint sound of labored breathing, purposefully kept quiet, and the jangle of loose change in someone's pant pocket.

A loud, metallic clatter breaks open the night. I scoot to the edge of the dumpster, peeking around to see the last thug standing over a metal trash bin, knocked over. Its insides are everywhere. Cans and wrappers and tins, half eaten food and rats.

Moonlight slips between a gap in the clouds. I sink deeper into the dumpster's shadow. My body trembles as the man's fat shadow stretches down the alley. He knocks over another trash can, kicks a few boxes. Debris tumbles past me. My fist shakes around the knife's grip, eyes peeled on his monstrous shadow. I see his feet out the corner of my eye. I'm cold all over. I glance up.

"Found you." The thug smirks.

I leap from cover. He grabs my wrist and yanks me toward him. I swipe at him blindly, screaming as I slash his clothes. He fights to grab hold of my other wrist, but I dig my knife into him. He roars, staggering back. Knife in hand, I scramble back out the alley and down the road. Shouts reverberate like gunshots, echoed by threats of all the things people would pay to do to me.

I stumble over my feet, skinning my knee on the pavement as I lurch to catch myself. My legs burn. My lungs ache. They're right behind me. God, I can hear them.

Forget America! I need to get away. I need to go home, back to Mama. She'll protect me, and ward off the sleazy thugs with threats of divine prophetic power. Maybe I'm not Nico, but I'm her son. She'll keep me safe.

One of them breathes down my neck. I can hear him. Feel him. He grabs my backpack and pulls me backward. Crying out, I writhe and break free of my straps. I hit the pavement again. One of them jumps at the chance to grab my elbow. I bite his hand. His blood pierces my taste buds. I clamber to my feet, but one of them tugs on my shirt. He traps me in his arms, so I kick, punch, and scratch! I spit evil words and curses, invoking the wrath of Mama, her ravens, Jesus, and God himself.

"Fire!" I scream at the top of my lungs. "Fire! Burglar! Rape! Someone *help* me!"

A black blur swipes across my vision; a fist against my cheek. My brain shakes inside my skull, and night goes white for a second.

The wind howls all around us. It's loud and desperate, but Jaurez is silent. The city isn't deaf. It heard me. I know it did, but no one pours onto the street to save me. A ghost of a whisper of a thought slips through my head. Everyone agrees: *Better me than them.*

The thugs drag me into the black depths of an unmarked road, ridiculing and taunting me the whole way. Nico died on a street like this, on a night like this, on a month and day like this. There were rumors about the state of his body—stabbed, defiled, and made a mockery of. The local psychic's untouchable son finally shown to be beatable. Killable.

All I can think about is Mama's warnings. They were constant. Every morning. Every night. As if I'm not competent enough to avoid danger. All I can think about how I never listened because I'm too smart to be caught, too clever to be tricked, too cunning to be lured in. I'm too slick for trouble to find me—but here I am, right in the thick of it.

My eyes burn. I don't cry. I swear, I won't cry. I'll bleed out in the dead of night, just like Nico, and I'll do it dry eyed before these men get one tear out of me.

The moon watches, almost sympathetic. Somehow, that's comforting.

Harsh light illuminates the road. They drop me right onto the gravel. The air rushes out of me and I gasp for a breath as they scatter like a flock of birds.

"Police!" one of them shouts.

A sob of joy shakes out of me.

They all dart down narrow side-streets, mangy dogs startled by karma. I laugh—because it's funny. I was so frightened by three men who fled at the sight of pigs with badges. I spit in their direction, lifting myself up into the warm glow of the headlights.

Much softer hands touch my shoulders. Suddenly, that uneasy feeling in my stomach makes a resurgence. A woman. No uniform. Not a police officer. White. *White?* Border officer? I size her up, but someone else comes closer. A man. No uniform either. Their clothes are clean. A little rumpled, like maybe they've been sleeping in their car. The lady touches my face. I lean away like her fingers are made of broken glass.

She's bad. I don't know how I know, but I just do.

"Did they hurt you?"

English. American.

"Déjame en paz." I try to sound angrier than scared.

She smiles at me, unconvinced. "Look at him," she says to the man. "He's so frail. Small." Her eyes move back to me. I cower away from her. "Where's your family, little one?"

"Rosa Maria." I hiss.

Her smile wavers. She glances at the man again.

"We're running out of time," he says. His voice is not gentle. It's gruff and tired. Desperate. "We can't keep looking. He has to do, Sylvia."

"But..."

"He'll be better off with us."

She opens her arms like she's going to scoop me up, so I edge away from her. I have to get home. I have to get back to Mama.

"Please don't fight me, little one." She begs.

I swat her hands away, struggling onto my feet. She's weak. I can get away. But before I can steal any distance, the man wraps his arms around my middle. I yell as he drags me backward. I pound at his arms cinched around my waist. When that doesn't work, I scratch and kick and try to elbow him in the face. I can't reach him. So I try to hit her. She catches both my fists.

Softly, she whispers. English words I do and don't understand. The things I do, I wish I didn't. As the man stuffs me into the trunk, throwing me down every time I jump up, she brings him a set of zip ties. He cuffs my hands, so I kick at him.

The last thing she says is, "Please calm down. It's okay. We'll take care of you."

I flail and fight and scream as they close the trunk.

~~

They tied me to the foot of their bed after I tried to attack Sylvia. The sleek plastic cuts into my skin, bound too tight to the metal frame. No matter how hard I tug, the knots never give.

It's a small room, mostly underground. Like a basement. There's one small window, but it's covered by a thick, black tarp. No matter what time it is, the sunlight is never strong enough to penetrate it.

I don't know how long it's been. I think I've been here for... five days? They don't listen when I beg or snarl. When I start yelling, the man gags me with my old socks. It doesn't matter how many curses I cast or how many prayers I send, God ignores me. I'm stuck here. I'm just... stuck here.

The man is Calvin. An ugly name, just like hers. I hate it. I hate him. Sometimes, he leaves. Every time, I hope he'll bring back food. Anything. Something small. I don't care. Just something to fill this empty hole inside my tummy. He never does.

I think they're hungry too. Every day, their skin is grayer. Their cheeks are thinner. The shadows around their eyes are darker.

Sylvia tries to talk to me. She wants me to confide in her like she's my mother, but I never will. My mother is at home. Where I'm supposed to be. But they robbed her of me.

Sylvia kneels in front of me. Her bony hands always shake, like she's weak and fatigued. She combs my hair with a broken brush, babbling about a little girl she never had the chance to meet.

"But it's okay," she whispers.

Cállate, perra.

"I don't need my little girl. Just my little boy. Just you."

Ojala que te mueras.

"Isn't that right, sweetheart?"

She caresses my cheek tenderly. I snap my teeth at her, snagging her hand and biting down hard on the meaty part of her palm. My teeth break her gray skin. Salty copper splatters on my tongue, just before pain erupts across my face.

Instantly, she withdraws her hand and covers her mouth in horror. "I'm so sorry!"

She reaches for my face. I wince away. I wish she would just stop touching me. With her other hand, she catches my face and cradles it anyway. I want to bite her again, but I don't want to hurt anymore.

"I'm *so* sorry." She says in a rush "There's just...so much happening right now." Her smile is tight. Forced. Ugly. "But it's okay. It'll be over soon. We'll be a family."

I'd rather die first.

There's a stab of pain in my stomach. It makes me slouch forward. My belly is a throbbing, empty pit. It hurts so bad at times I can barely think. I just want to eat.

I look at Sylvia through my bangs.

My lips form clumsily around unfamiliar syllables. *"I need food."*

Her smile wavers. She strokes my cheekbone, my jaw. There's a strange admiration in her eyes, like I'm something new, precious. I don't understand. I don't want to. I just want to go home. I just want to eat. Sleep. When I close my eyes, all I see is Mama. I can hear her voice. Feel her hands. Every time Sylvia hugs me, I try to imagine Mama.

I mutter, *"Por favor, Dios, sálvame. Quiero estar con mi mamá."*

Sylvia gasps. "Yes! Mama!"

Miserably, I open my eyes. Another prayer unanswered.

She grabs my face again. This time I just slump with defeat, listening to her laughter as it twists with sobs.

We jump when the door is thrown open. Calvin charges inside, and slams it shut, bracing against it.

"What is it?" Sylvia asks, instantly terrified. "What's wrong?"

"There's a pack of gammas. Saw them at the gas station we stopped at a few hours ago. They're tailing us. We don't have any more time. We have to turn him."

"*What?* We can't. That isn't how we wanted it!"

Ignoring her, Calvin drops to his knees beside us. He pulls out a knife from his hip, sliding it through the tiny space between my wrist and the zip ties. The tug hurts. I whimper, but soon the plastic is cut open. I immediately try to get away. Calvin grasps my elbow.

"We can't put it off," he says. "It has to be this way."

"But we agreed—"

"It's this or we lose him."

Sylvia shuts her mouth. I try to use her hesitation to my advantage, but when I swipe to scratch at her, she catches my other wrist. She looks at me. For a second, she's swallowed by that deranged, maternal grief before determination turns her into cold, hard stone.

She opens her maw big and wide, and closes it around the top of my hand.

I'm poisoned by fear. Then fire. It shoots up my arm, burning every nerve to coal.

I scream, "*¡Estas hiriendo! Please! Stop!*"

They don't. They're cannibals and I'm a feast they mercilessly devour, biting into any inch of skin available until I'm covered in bleeding, open wounds, all of them burning. Inside me, I feel my muscles and bones melting. Everything is too hot. I can't breathe. The pain is numb but it's not. I rip one of my hands out of their grasps, and claw at the flames inside my chest. I have to get it out.

They take my hands back and tear off my shirt. They bite me there too. I wail in agony, begging in their language and mine for it to stop, for Mama, for God, for death.

THIRTY-SEVEN

BABY BIRDS

Gabriel, 10 Years Ago

I huddle in the corner of the playroom. They haven't been back. Not the fat lady, the tall man, the bearded one, or the glowy people. After I made the mean man bleed, they realized I wasn't some scared lost boy. I'm a feral animal. So, they threw me in here, collared like a dog, surrounded by ugly rainbow colors and toys, with a short leash that tugs back when I yank.

My ears ring in the quiet. I strain to hear footsteps or voices from outside the door or on the other side of the two-way mirror. There's nothing. I feel them watching, though. I glare at them through the glass. My gaunt, bandaged, dirty reflection stares back.

I look at the cameras in the corners. They're all pointed at me. I flip the lens off before wrapping my arms around my knees again.

I can still taste the man's blood. It was *good.* Better than Mama's scrambled eggs, or Abuela's homemade churros. It shouldn't have tasted so good, but the traces that still linger in my mouth make me thirstier. I swallow. My throat is scratchy and desperate.

Pulling my knees tighter to my chest, I close my eyes with a shaky breath.

Mama fills my head. All I see is her. That bent spatula she used every morning to make breakfast in her splotchy, black and brown metal pan, and her calloused, textured hands holding either handle.

Nico took care of things. I tried to be like him, tried to pick up the pieces, but I couldn't. I can't be him. No matter how much Mama or I wished it. He's gone. Now, so am I. She lost us both. All because I didn't listen.

I should've listened.

Just as Mama said, my stubborn pride took me somewhere I didn't want it to. Instead of finding a safe haven across the Rio Grande, I found monsters. Really, *they* found *me.* They *took* me. They *hurt* me. I can still feel their fingers pressing hard into my skin as they bit me. I still feel the fire.

With a whimper, I grab onto my greasy hair and clutch it tight. The sting doesn't make the hurt in my chest go away. I pull harder. I pull so hard my bandages become tight on my slim arms and the bites ache. I keep pulling.

The doorknob clicks open.

My body stiffens. Slowly, I lower my hands to my lap. I glare at the door as it opens without a sound. I miss the way the doors creaked at home.

It's a boy. A kid. Like me. He slips inside cautiously, holding a mug of something steamy. He dawdles at the edge of the room, looking at me, the cameras, the mirror.

The door closes.

Glancing back at it, the boy swallows. He looks at me again. His red eyebrows scrunch upward as his eyes flit all over me. I can see his fear. Despite that, he takes a small step into the room, followed by a larger one. He places the mug on the floor at the center of the room.

"That's for you..." He rubs his arm. "Wh...What's your name?"

I say nothing.

"Ooookay." He sits next to the mug and nudges it tentatively.

I can smell it from here. It smells familiar. Sweet, almost like honey, but not quite. The taste in my mouth intensifies. So does the coarseness of my throat. The mean man's gargled yelp replays in my ears. His blood splashes on my tongue again. Trembling, I turn away from him, hiding deeper into the corner.

"*Aléjate.*" I spit at him.

He doesn't come closer. Neither does the cup.

"Er..." He studies me. "Do you speak English?"

I stare at him. He's not much bigger than me. Only a few inches. He's probably just a year or two older. He doesn't have any magical tattoos like the mean man, and he doesn't smile at me like he's my friend the way the others did. He's soft. If he attacked me, I could fight back. I could maybe even win.

I don't say anything.

He glances at the mirror, sucking his bottom lip into his mouth. He's still afraid. Good. That gives me a better chance.

He looks at the cup, scooting it even closer. I scramble back, but the wall keeps me from getting away.

"It'll help," he says softly. "I promise. It's to make your throat feel better."

I scrunch my nose at him.

He fiddles with his hands. "It hurts, right?"

Everything hurts.

"It'll help." He pushes those twitchy hands into the pocket of his big, orange hoodie. "I'm Luc, by the way. I guess I should've said that sooner..." Luc scans the room, seeing things I don't. "Yeah, I hated it in here, too. It'll be okay, though. You know?"

Did they lock him up in here, too? Does he know them? The adults? Is he their pawn? An ally? My enemy? Maybe he knows how to get out.

I clear my throat. He looks at me. I pull back my upper lip and point at one of my pointier-than-before canines. I nod my chin at him.

He mulls his thoughts for a minute. "You're... different now."

My eyebrows knit together.

"Like, you have a new life."

I don't want a new life. I want my mom. I want my brother. I want to go back to the way things were a year ago.

Frowning, I look at the mirror, then him.

"What? Oh! That's my dad, uh, Valberg. The one with the bushy beard. Then there's Pyera. She's the pretty lady. And then Cleon, the old guy."

I draw a line under my eye, mimicking the tattoo on the mean man.

"That's... the Head Gamma."

I give him a puzzled look.

"He's a shifter. They're like us. Different, just not the same kind of different."

I shake my head at him, making a face.

"No one's going to hurt you," he says.

I'll hurt them back if they do.

"I didn't believe it either at first, but it's true. Everyone here just wants to take care of you. You're... You're safe."

I squint at him. It hurts to speak. *"¿Promesa?"*

"Promise."

Luc looks at the cup. So do I. The stinging burn in my throat demands relief. Apprehensively, I crawl on my hands and knees until my leash pulls taut. I reach for the cup. Luc scoots it into my grasp. I lift it to my mouth. The steam tickles my nose, sending my senses into overdrive. I greedily chug the delicious drink, tipping my head back to drink every last drop.

Slouching forward, I pant as I stare into the empty cup. My lips are wet. I lick them dry.

"Did it help?"

I nod.

"Do you want more?"

I peek at him through my tangled bangs.

"I'll get you more." He reaches for the cup. I place it in his hands. "I'll... take care of you. Okay?"

My eyes cut to the mirror and back.

"I mean it," he says anyway.

Staring at the carpet, I fist and un-fist my hands, thinking about all the things I need to do and the people who need me. Abuela is old. She'll die soon. Then Mama will be all alone for real. I have to get back to her. She has to know I'm coming. The ravens will tell her. They always do. And when I get home, I'll be bigger, stronger, and tougher just like my brother. I'll be the man she needs me to be.

"Nico," I whisper the lie to Luc.
His eyebrows shoot up. "What?"
"I'm Nico."

THIRTY-EIGHT

SON, BROTHER, PROPHET

Nico, A Year Ago

That feeling hits me again. The hairs on my arms, legs, and neck stand straight. My scalp prickles. My gut is heavy. I stare at the unfinished graphite crocodile, hoping the feeling will pass.

Intuition. My mother called it Fate's warning. It's haunted me for as long as I can remember. It's always the same: a twisty knot that burns a hole in my stomach. Sometimes, I think of those balmy days in Mexico when my belly churned unreasonably with dread. Hours before the winds rushed in and the sky darkened, or the night before another body was uncovered in the alleys, or sometimes minutes before another face-off between the dueling cartels. I always knew.

My mother said I inherited it from her. Maybe, if I had never run away that night, she would've shown me how to read shapes in tea leaves, the lines in the palms of hands, and the mists of her scrying glass. Does she know she was right? Does she know I'm alive? Does the moon talk to her like it talks to me? Sometimes, I think the ravens whisper about her.

I set my pencil down. I glance out the window. The Man in the Moon stares at me. Nothing new, except tonight, danger itches my skin. *What is it?* Not another vision. The next full moon isn't for another week and a half.

Uncrossing my legs, I stand up from the floor and walk to the window. The blinds rattle with the wind. I hear the Moon muttering.

Val says to listen. The Moon has things to tell me, but frankly, I'd prefer to keep communication limited to the visions. I'd do away with those too, if I could. Hell, if it were possible, I'd resign from Prophethood altogether. I just haven't figured out where to put in my two weeks' notice yet.

I close the window and lay my hand against the glass. My reflection overlays the woods. *Gabriel,* a ghost whispers my old name. *Nico,* I reply. I squint at myself. The light behind me casts a halo of light around my head. *The Prophet of Fortune.*

A ridiculous title for a ridiculous role. A symbol to all vampires; a beacon of guidance and good will. I'm supposed to remind them of *hope, unification, freedom,* but the Man in the Moon's choice didn't inspire everyone.

Pyera, Cleon, Val, and the like were all delighted. It had been years since the last Prophet's death. They were waiting for someone to come forward, and *what a treasure!* The moon selected one of *their* fledglings. It was their *honor.*

I scoff under my breath, shaking my head, and turning my back on my reflection.

Others were not so happy. I was *bitten.* Not a Pureblood. As if my circumstances couldn't get spectacular enough, I had to be the first non-Pureblood in all of history to be chosen. People don't like change, so they don't like me. Honestly, I'm more aligned with them than my "supporters."

I don't know what I'm doing. No one knows. It's all trial by fire, but they don't say that outright. The Lord and Lady, Val, they all do their best but how do you coach someone on how to read the future? It's impossible. I find it hard to believe every Prophet was as graceful and strategic as they're made out to be. And that's all anyone talks about. No one cares about who they were when they were alone, with their friends, with their family, when they *weren't* the Man in the Moon's Prophet.

That's *my* fate. And I don't need a full moon to see it. I'll either be remembered as a prolific soothsayer, or my mundanity will consign me to oblivion. I think I'd prefer that; to be forgotten for who I am, rather than be remembered as a picturesque portrait of someone who was never real.

Another bullet added to the list of things I never wanted.

Every day, I forget my roots a little more. My mother's face is an old photograph, blurred by the lens of time. My brother's voice is a phantom murmur. Abuela's raspy lullabies sometimes haunt me as I drift to sleep. I try not to think about the fact that she may not be around anymore.

At least, if nothing else, they'll remember me. Not this version of me. The person I was before. And maybe that's all that matters.

I don't think that's true, but, if I try hard enough, I might convince myself.

I sink back down in front of my drawing. The pencil feels heavy when I pick it up. My fingers shake, so I set it down. Gripping my wrist, I glare at my hand. The trembling doesn't subside.

I hear the door slam at the front of the house.

Abandoning my art, I slip off down the corridor. Val and I were supposed to practice enchanting today, but Pyera and Cleon called him to "discuss an issue." Usually, that means one of two things. An unhappy shifter client filed a complaint about their latest shipment of silver, or Terces. She's been especially erratic as of late. Probably the former. Val is rarely bothered enough to slam the door, and even more rarely by Terces.

I check my phone. "Hey, I thought you said—Oh. Hey."

Luc stands by the door. He folds his arms, scowling. The corrosive vapors of his glare erode my melancholic, mildly brooding mood further. Something he's been good for, lately.

Things haven't been good for a while. Not since the Man in the Moon chose me. Luc's never said it outright, but I know that's part of it. Whatever *it* is. What do you call the gradual but certain decline of friendship? Of brotherhood?

Depressing comes to mind.

I'd like to pretend I'm clueless, innocent—but I'm not. I know it. For ten years, I've been his brother, six of which were perfect. Maybe not the version of perfect I would've preferred, but as close as it could be. Under his wing, I felt safer in the new, startling world I had been thrust into.

We shared jokes and laughter, comics and books, counted stars and chased shadows in the woods. Sometimes, when dawn crept across the sky, I would crawl into his bed and we'd lay awake, talking. We talked about what we remembered from our lives before, the things we missed, and what we wish we still had. Then, we'd talk about what we like now. Among those things, we always said each other.

I don't know what we'd say anymore.

I say, "Are you here for Val? Did you need something?"

Luc scoffs. His scowl deepens, anger aging him a few years. "Why are *you* here?"

I purse my lips. "Excellent evasion of the question. You don't normally slam the door, do you? Bad for the hinges."

He narrows his eyes at me. I frown back.

"Bad day. Sorry." Luc pockets his hands into his hoodie pouch. "Where's Val?"

"Talking to Pyera and Cleon." I shrug. "He's supposed to be back later."

He looks at me out the corner of his eyes, eyebrows slowly sinking low over his gaze. "Why... are you here?"

The uncertainty of his tone makes me hesitate. I remember a dozen times before, when the hurt and disappointment crossed his face whenever our two lives and their separate schedules collided. By no choice of my own, it always seems as though I come out on top.

That familiar guilt hits me. *I'm sorry.* And then the resentment. *You can't be angry at me for this. I don't like it either. You're the one making it difficult.* Because he *is.* I get it. It's aggravating how everyone's attention shifted. Their views have changed. The entire universe has seemingly centered itself around me—and it *all* makes my skin crawl.

I swallow my hurt, bury my feelings, and bite my tongue. Those thoughts are not to be said. I can wallow in them another time.

I say, "Val and I are practicing enchantments today."

Luc frowns. "What?"

"Enchantments." I say, motioning around. Ever since I first got here, Val's house has been messy. Notes and papers and books scattered everywhere. The result of his ever-growing workload.

Luc glances about. "Why?"

"Er..." I cock my head at him. "Because I'm training to be the next Grand Enchanter..."

He stares at me for a moment, stunned. I can tell by the look on his face he didn't know. Pain. His face twists with it. He snorts loudly. A mean sound.

"That's just great." He snarls. "Were you guys going to be at it all day?"

I bite my lip. "I think so, yeah."

"Figures. Like always, my plans with Val come second to yours."

"Did you have plans?" I fold my arms defensively. "If you did, I knew nothing about it, Luc."

"Yeah." He scoffs. "Of course not."

"I really didn't," I say.

He shakes his head. His red hair swings aggressively so he wipes it back, out of his face. He stares holes into the ground for several seconds before finally looking me in the eye. A frightening glare. "This gets old fast, you know?"

I frown. "I don't know, no."

"Don't be coy," he says. "You know exactly what you're doing. You take up so much of Val's time, it's like I barely exist. Every time he and I have plans, you find a way to weasel in."

"I don't *weasel*." I snap. "It's not my life's purpose to get in the way of you and Val."

"Yeah? Well, I haven't had a real conversation with my own dad for over a month because of *you*."

"That's between you and Val."

"If I could find the time to talk to him, I would!" Luc throws his arms out in frustration. "Except, he's always too busy with his sparkling, hot shot Prophet son to give a damn about me! Every other word out of his mouth is *Nico*. Nico this, Nico that. Nico, Nico, Nico!"

"Boohoo!" I yell. "What's done is done, Luc. I can't change that the Man in the Moon chose me."

Luc steps closer. He towers over me, pupils swollen, surrounded by a ring of indigo fire. "You wouldn't anyway. This is what you wanted. This makes you *happy*. Finally, everyone loves you. They worship the ground you walk on. And you *love* it."

With a bitter snarl, I shove him away from me. "Back off! You don't know anything about me! You're just a bitter, jealous prick!"

"You're an attention-seeking intruder!"

"No – I'm – Not."

My anger plucks its way through my body, winding every muscle, twisting my joints. I'm tight like a spring, ready to pounce. I clench my fists to contain myself. I try to breathe. I try to calm down. That prickle on my skin is like electricity now. Every nerve is too sensitive. I'm going to explode.

"Yes," Luc says coldly. "You are. It's the only reason you even matter. And you know that."

"Shut up!" I growl.

"Make me."

I glower at him.

"Intruder."

My airflow is tight. I can't breathe.

"You ruined my family." His voice is almost a whisper.

Something inside me pleads. It tries to tell me he doesn't mean it, but I can see that he does. He knows the power behind every word he says, knows the power he holds as my brother, knows that no one can hurt me like him, and he takes advantage of that.

Through gritted teeth, I say, "I'm your brother."

"I used to believe that."

A black hole opens up inside my heart. I see my dead brother. I feel his loss. I see Luc. My brother. I feel the impending dread of something worse than death. It impales me like a sword to the chest.

"Stop it." I whisper.

He spits. "Intruder."

Heartbreak is blind. In that moment, so am I.

I lunge at him. He scrabbles to catch himself, grasping at the wall and knocking picture frames off on the way down. He yelps when his back hits floor. I reel back my fist. His eyes bulge. He looks from my fists to me. Then he glares. *Do it* is written all over his face.

"Take it back." My voice breaks.

"No."

Tears burn in my eyes. "Take it back."

He narrows his eyes. His lips set into a stubborn line.

All I've ever wanted was my brother. *"Take it back."*

He doesn't push me off. He doesn't fight back. He dares me. *Do it. Just do it. Prove to me that we were never brothers. Prove me right.*

Everything inside me screams *STOP!*

I can't.

A scream rips me in half. The black hole in my chest swallows me as I bring my fist down on Luc's face. My pain leaves me as a yell. I hear the gross snap of bone. The gush of blood. The warmth of it on my knuckles. It smatters my face.

My vision blurs. I don't know who I am anymore. I don't know where I belong.

Luc's cry of pain snaps me back to reality. I unfurl my fingers. They shake. I stare down at him. He cups his face. His hands are covered in blood.

"I'm sorry," I whisper. I rip my coat off and try to move his hands away.

He swats me. "Don't touch me!"

I pull my hands back.

I'm not in control of my body when I stand. I watch myself get up from Luc's crumpled body and back away like a frightened puppy. I feel nothing. Nothing at all.

Something drips down my cheek. A tear. I swipe it away.

The door opens.

Shock locks Val in place as he takes in the scene. Then, without another thought, he rushes to Luc's side. He says something as he pries Luc's hands from his face, but I don't hear him. I can't hear anything but my own thoughts, screaming at me.

I'm sorry...

THIRTY-NINE

OUR WINGS ARE SINGED

Luc, Present Day

I don't remember much about my mother, but once she told me that love has many faces.

So does pain.

For a long time, my pain has worn Nico's. Whenever I was low, angry, or bitter, he came to mind. I saw his face. I felt his fist, and the shards of a broken brotherhood embedded in my flesh. Everything was always his fault because everything always came back to him. Maybe it was unfair, but pain is reactionary. Where there's a wound, there's pain, and pain isn't logical.

Neither is love.

I sprint across the coven. Lightning flashes all around me. The rain hammers, hard and ruthless. It soaks into my clothes and saps the heat from my skin. I keep running.

Nico's silhouette is far away. I can barely make him out in the pouring rain. One of the watchtower's lights sweeps across the city, illuminating him briefly. I pump my legs harder. My lungs already sting.

I chase him through empty streets, under flickering streetlamps, and down alleys. He cuts across an intersection. The wet asphalt reflects the buildings, lights, the moon and stars, him. My footsteps slap hard on the streets, sending water everywhere. I run harder. I run faster. He hears me. I know he does, but he keeps going. He's running away from *me* because his pain wears *my* face.

I grasp his arm. He tries to yank free, but the ground is slick. We slip, tumble, fall. Last year is suddenly all I see. His fist and his tears. The pain that shot through my head, and the blood, in my mouth and throat.

Nico throws me off him. Stumbling into reality, I leap up to catch him. I barely grasp the hem of his hoodie. He snarls angrily.

"Let go!" he yells.

"No!" I yell back.

Lightning strikes. His face is lit with ominous white light. I glance over my shoulder, around us. The gammas are sure to descend on us at any moment. I can't waste a second.

I stand up completely, but I don't let go. If I do, he'll run. I'm the last person he wants to talk to right now, and he won't unless he has no other choice. So, I can't give him a choice.

"Nico." I try. "Let's talk."

"About what?" He whips around to face me. "What do you want?" He grasps my hand tight. Too tight. I don't show any pain. "We've said everything we've needed to say. You said everything you needed to say. *I* don't need you to rub anything else in my face."

"I'm not trying to!" Luc insists. "I'm trying to fix things."

"No, you *aren't*."

I wince. My shoulders rise up protectively and I look away. Nico stares somewhere else too. For a few seconds, we're silent, trying to calm the raging emotions inside both of us. I stare down at my feet. My reflection stares up at me from the puddle. The moon watches from behind my head. I lift my gaze to Nico again.

"You have to understand how I feel," I say.

He throws his hands out. "I do! And I've told you... I told you I didn't want this. I told you how *I* feel, but you don't care. You don't care because my feelings mean nothing compared to yours. You don't care because I'm the Prophet. I've been served a perfect life on a silver platter. Everything is *great* in my world!"

His sarcasm sears me. His rage, too. His desperation.

"I was wrong," I say quietly. "I was wrong. Okay? Maybe... Maybe not about everything. But I was wrong for the things I said a year ago, and the things I said tonight."

"I never wanted this." He chokes out.

"I know."

"I only wanted you."

My mind flashes back ten years.

I'm a child. The pain of teeth and fire not forgotten, but the trauma slowly healing. Val tells me about another boy like me. A child ripped away from his life, and he's frightened. He needs someone he can trust because he can't trust Val or Pyera or Cleon. They're too intimidating. He needs a friend, a supporter, someone who can empathize with him. That's me. I'm that person. I cross that threshold.

He's small. His cheeks are gaunt, and his skin is ashy. His dark black hair is greasy. It sticks together in large chunks. He's covered in dirt and bandages. I think about telling him he needs a shower, but maybe that isn't such a good idea. A little rude. Those big, dark eyes tell me they need love, not brashness. So instead, I get to know him, and he puts a little bit of trust in me. Every day after that, he put a little more. I kept it all close to my heart, where it was safest.

And now we're here.

Two men whose love and friendship healed the damage done to them as children, only for them to destroy each other. I've been so angry for so long that forgiveness goes against every grain in my body. My brain tells me *NO*, but my heart needs it. I don't want to feel this way anymore.

I open my mouth. My bottom lip quivers. I close it and then try again. "Nic. I've missed you, too."

He shakes his head. Restlessly, he yanks on his fringe and tries to hide his face from me. Under his hood, he manages. His breathing is unstable.

I reach for him. "I'm sorry."

He shoves my hands away.

I step closer. He steps back.

"I'm sorry." Cautiously, I touch his wrist for a second time. He doesn't pull away. With endless care, I pry his hands from his face to look him in the eye. I feel my own pain contort my face.

I say, "I'm sorry, Nico."

The tears spill over. I haven't seen him cry since we were kids when his nightmares were bad. Those nights, I held him, fending off the horrors of sleep with comic books. It feels like second nature when I go to hug him. He resists at first but gives in. The deep, bottomless holes we carved out in each other's chests start to fill.

I hear the gammas coming closer. Their voices are angry. Their glows are hot on my skin. I hold Nico tighter.

FORTY

THIS IS THE END

Macy

A few nights later, black wisps on the horizon are all that remain of the storm. On the television hung behind the register at Cinnamon's, a newscaster relays the Earth's suffering. Her cold composure is cracked by fear.

The icy tempest sapped life from fertile soils across the globe. Crops withered, flowers lost their vibrancy, and sidewalks are littered with fallen leaves a season too soon. Not even the mountains were spared, none tall enough to pierce the dense cloud cover.

The newscaster's face is obscured by videos of rioters, looters, desperate and panicked people. They assume this is the end. They're right.

The café is quiet.

Everyone's seen the reports, heard the whispers. Francis Church and his league of maniacs are well on their way to worldwide genocide. Whereas the shifters only have one outcome to dread, we're plagued by two frightening possibilities: the Monster's success, *and* his failure. There is no living in the wake of his victory, but in the event of his failure, what are the odds we suffer the punishments he earned? Mercy does not come up often during shifter dialogues about vampires.

Circi and I scurry out, away from the heavy atmosphere.

At City Hall, some staff members escort us to the garage. An assistant takes my things. She hands them to a gamma, who begins a search of all my items, and another shifter pats me down. After they've thoroughly confirmed that I am not trying to smuggle weapons to Meadowsweet, we're shuffled to wait on the side.

At the center of the room, the Lord and Lady discuss some things with the Ambassador and several other shifters—gammas and a few betas. They spare us a glance, unable to wipe the severity from their expressions.

"Luc said Val was supposed to go with you guys," says Circi.

Last night flashes like lightning in my head. The Bridge, the runes, the underground passageway, everything before that. It all impales my heart.

I scowl in pain. "Not anymore."

The door we came from opens. Nico steps inside. Regret for how I exposed him and his feelings throbs inside me. I wave at him with a frown. He eyes me, unreadable, but is quickly pulled aside by the assistants. They walk him through the same routine.

"Have you heard anything about your mom?" Circi pulls me from one bad thought to another.

"No," I say. "But her name hasn't shown up yet."

As if she's the psychic, she says, "She's fine."

I pull my bottom lip into my mouth as I fiddle with my hands. Circi puts an arm around my shoulder. "Hey."

I look at her.

"She's fine." A sad smirk tweaks the corner of her mouth. "You're gonna kick ass at the Summit and save this garbage world from becoming worse."

Scoffing under my breath, I smile. "You're the most pessimistic cheerleader."

"Just another accessory to my edgy rebel vibe." She holds her hands up.

Across the room, Luc slips in. He hides under his orange hood. His reddish-brown fringe clumps together in unusually greasy strands. A brown duffel bag hangs from his shoulder. He clutches it protectively with one hand. *What are you doing?*

He glances up, finds me, smiles tiredly, but asserts his attention elsewhere. On Nico.

Oh no. I rush forward as Luc weasels by everyone. I can see it in my head. Luc will throw the first punch, but Nico will throw the last. The gammas will swarm them, batter them. It'll set us hours behind schedule, thus dooming us to arrive late to the Summit and potentially costing us our chance at gaining the Alphas' support, and my two best friends and their endless feud will cost them both their lives.

As Luc approaches Nico, I hasten my pace. Rather than throw daggered words, Luc's lips move in calm, controlled syllables. They're having a *civil* conversation. Luc hands the bag to Nico, and then a gamma swoops in, snatching it from him. Soon after, Cleon asserts himself on the same shifter and takes it himself.

My name is called. Nico's, too. Pyera. She beckons for me. I don't budge, yanking my eyes back to the boys. Luc stiffly swings his arm around Nico. My breath hitches. Their embrace lasts several seconds before they pull apart.

Nico makes his way to the Lord and Lady, but Luc finds me. His lopsided grin stretches wide at my shock.

"Surprised?" he asks once he's closer.

Beside me, Circi gapes. "You could say that."

"I was expecting a black eye," I say. "Not a hug."

I look at Nico. He catches me staring, and shrugs.

Luc weighs his thoughts. "I don't know how *reconciled* we are, but we're something."

"But..." Circi surveys him up and down. "He hurt you."

His smile is sad. So are his eyes. "I've hurt him, too. There's a lot he and I still gotta figure out. A lot to apologize for, a lot to forgive, but... I'm goin' to try."

She reaches for his hand. "Are you sure?"

He laces their fingers. It's answer enough.

"Damnit." She groans, forehead dropping onto Luc's shoulder. "That means *I* have to apologize too. I hate apologizing."

I nudge her with my elbow. "You had some practice with me."

Not encouraged, she thumps her head against Luc a few times. "Does he accept bribery?"

I tap my chin. "Cater to his ego, and you're in the clear."

She grumbles.

Cleon calls my name again. They've all climbed into the SUV. Still, I linger.

Luc beams at me, arms spread open. "I'm sorry about last night. Truce?"

I clamp my arms around him and squeeze tight. Into his chest, I say, "Truce."

He nuzzles his mouth against my hair, and chuckles. Months ago, when I arrived, he was the only person who understood me. He was my first friend here. I could gladly spill the contents of my heart to him, and he would listen. I don't want to leave without him.

"Stay safe, Tenderfoot." He pulls back and tucks a tuft of hair behind my ear.

"You too."

He smiles. "Deal."

As Cleon yells for me once more, I tear myself from Luc. Quickly, I squeeze Circi. It's short but sweet. "I'm not sure cellphones work in Meadowsweet, but I'll call you if they do!"

I scramble to the SUV. Cleon holds the door open. Hands braced against it, I stare inside. At Nico. *I'm sorry* gets trapped at the back of my throat.

His expression says: *It's okay.*

Hesitantly, I climb in next to him. Cleon joins Pyera in the row of seats between us and the wheel. The SUV rumbles to life. I duck lower to watch the garage door pull upward, clattering as it did three months ago. This time it isn't so scary.

The tires lurch forward, roving from smooth concrete to gravel. We're flanked by two other vehicles. They're filled with soldiers I once aspired to be. Now, with my cheek bruised, a severed connection to my Grounding, and eyes blessed with prophetic visions, I'm grateful I'm not among them.

I touch my two necklaces. Lilac's beads. Nico's enchantment.

I glance at him. He stares out the tinted window. "Nico?"

He looks at me.

"About what I said last night, I'm sorry," I say. No fumbling.

"It's okay."

I don't believe him. "No. It's not. We're friends. You trusted me with that, and I blew it."

"Bright Eyes." A smirk tugs at the corner of his mouth. "You don't have to worry."

I chew my lip, still uncertain. He nudges my foot with his. "You ready?"

"Always."

"Macy?"

"Yeah?

"We'll do this together." He stares at me, unwavering. If there was an inkling of doubt in my soul, it would be abolished by his conviction.

I manage a smile. "Like usual."

FORTY-ONE

SUMMIT

Our drive from Arizona to Michigan's Upper Peninsula is long. I watch Nico draw, or, when his wrist hurts and he opens a book, I read over his shoulder. We flip through some of my comics and play a few games of hangman. When daytime comes, a thick barrier slides over the glass to protect us. Nico falls asleep on my shoulder.

We navigate landscapes of every kind, each of them wounded by the storm. The already barren deserts have dried to hard gravel, and their resilient bushes and brambles to weeds. In the cities, streets are scarcely populated.

Looters are the only ones out, rifling through abandoned bags, cars, bins, and stores.

A dense forest surrounds us on the final leg of our journey. The woods may not be as devastated as the deserts or human hearts, but they're battered. Trees hunch forward in exhaustion, and others are collapsed. Their branches have fallen to the swampy earth.

We traverse a rocky pass between two cliffs. Meadowsweet waits on the other side. The car slows to a muffled halt.

Hydrilla was built like a canopy of leaves. Huts were hidden in the foliage, and larger homes neighbored commercial necessities on the forest floor. Our space was limited. Not theirs. Everything we were scant on, they possess in plenty.

Meadowsweet hugs the base of Mount Milo. Both are cradled by Hiawatha National Forest, barred from outsiders by uncharted pathways and constant patrols. Lanterns radiate twilight hues onto the city, masking midnight hours with illusory daylight. Dying flowers are dappled orange, red, purple, and deep blue. They race along windowpanes, door frames, and Meadowsweet's famous archways. Atop each of the bends is a garden bed. What once bloomed wilts.

Nico whispers. "I've never seen anything like this."

"I've only been here once," I say.

"There aren't any cars? Or roads?"

"Some. Not many." I pat his knee. "We try to intrude on Mother Nature as little as possible."

"Whoa."

A lighthearted smile dances across my mouth. "Hippy bullshit, right?"

He tips his head back and lets out a loud *hah!*

The SUV slows to a stop. The engine's rumble abruptly ends, and the gammas filter out of the van first. Around us, Meadowsweet's standing gamma squadron surrounds us. Our escorts meet with them and the local Head Gamma.

We're seen out one at a time. Pyera, then Cleon, then me. A tall, wide man pats me down, not caring to be gentle. After thoroughly jostling, as if a knife is going to magically fall out of my pocket, he shoves me toward another pair of shifters.

"Name?" he asks.

"Macy Braddock."

"Do you possess any knowledge of blood magic?"

"Uh, no?"

"Have you or have you ever wished violence upon a shifter?"

Would anyone answer yes to that? "Nope."

About a dozen useless questions later, I'm finally allowed to pass through the next wall of shifters. Pyera and Cleon wait, surrounded by gammas. I see shifters lugging my bag down a path, along with everyone else's. Great. I want to yell: *Don't steal my batman comics!* Only because I personally think it would be hilarious.

"Braddock?" A stern but feminine voice grabs my attention.

A beta. She dips her head. Her sleek brunette hair falls into her face. Her skin is covered in shadowy birds. There's another woman beside her. She's not as... All business, and yet much less approachable.

"You're my... guardians?"

"We are."

They herd me into the same line as Pyera and Cleon. Nico joins behind me, and we're steered toward Mount Milo.

"What time is it?" Nico asks.

"About 4 AM," the brunette beta says.

"Most of the deltas and omegas are asleep," says the other beta. Tree branches skirt down her arms and legs. "The last of the Alphas arrived earlier today, and the Summit is tomorrow night."

"Pyera and I will walk you through it beforehand," Cleon says.

I glance down at my hands. "What about my Marrow—"

"The Alphas know of your kind," the brunette interrupts. "As do most betas. Those who are unaware have been sworn into secrecy as of today. None of the civilian ranks are permitted to attend."

I don't know which is stronger: relief or sadness. I would prefer not to undermine the faith of thousands of people with my mere existence but being treated like a secret is far from ideal. A secret only acknowledged because the Alphas couldn't afford to ignore me or the visions any longer.

Milo's doorway opens with a gust of air. The interior walls have been smoothed, sanded, and decorated with miniscule, filigree patterns. An omega with an affinity for art must've spent hours detailing these walls. The somber thought makes me frown. I hope it was someone else.

The shifters pad quietly down the hall, barefoot on flat stone, while we vampires are followed by the *tap tap tap* of our shoes. Pyera and Cleon are supplied a chamber to share. Nico and I have our own separate rooms.

A heavy fur blanket covers the bed. The bedframe itself was carved by a practiced hand. It reminds me of Lilac and her beads. The bedside consoles are home to green candles, also evenly spaced on the walls. It's all remarkable...

But the lack of personality strikes me. Everywhere in Devil's Trumpet is imbued with the essence of its owner, builder, creator. Such simple, modest living catches me off guard. Would it be different if I never turned?

There's a mirror on the wall. *She* imitates me. I keep myself from staring at her too long, but her eyes pierce me regardless.

"My name is Miranda, by the way."

My attention snaps to the door. The brunette beta stands there. Her eyes are fierce emerald, blazing like a forest on fire without the flame.

"My partner's name is Bethany," she says. "Late introduction, I know, but your life is of higher priority than pleasantries."

I let out a crisp laugh. Silence follows. We stare at each other. A crease folds between her brows.

I stand straighter. "You're serious."

"You don't think it's a serious matter?"

"Well, no. I mean, yeah, but you're just so..."

The furrow in her brow deepens.

"Nevermind." I avert my eyes for a moment. "Er. Thanks."

"You're welcome."

The awkward silence is agonizing.

Mercifully, she breaks it. "Alphas Marcus and Rosemarie assigned us to you until the Summit ends. Depending on what's discussed, our guardianship might be prolonged."

I regard her cautiously. Where I expect to find prejudice, I only find neutrality. She was given a task, and, like all shifters, she will complete it to the best of her abilities. Even if I am a *bloodhound*.

"I appreciate it," I say.

"If you need anything, let us know." With a bow of her head, she vanishes from the doorway.

Not long after, Pyera carries my green bag into the room. She tosses it onto the bed before flopping down as well. Lazily, her eyes drag toward me.

She smirks. "From one prison to another. You must feel at home."

"Not really." As I sit next to her, she pokes my leg. "Some things I missed, yeah. But not everything."

She rolls onto her side, propped up on one elbow, cheek in hand. "I didn't expect that."

I stare at my hands. "Me either."

She sits up all the way. Studying me, she caresses my arm. Her touch is gentle, caring. It understands. She wraps me up in a hug and squishes me against her.

"You've come a long way," she whispers.

"This is *definitely* a long way from home."

"Not what I meant." She laughs then sighs. "I'm supposed to debrief you on how tomorrow will go."

"I'm listening."

"The Summit itself will take hours," she explains. "You and Nico will only be asked for a short statement. You'll then be escorted out. I've been told you have the freedom to explore the grounds with your guards."

"What about Nico?"

"He's been given the same privileges," she acknowledges. "He's being shadowed by a pair of gammas."

"You and Cleon?"

Her smirk appears. "He and I were *graced* with seats from start to finish."

"Lucky, lucky." I mirror her grin.

"Do you remember what you're supposed to say in front of the Alphas tomorrow?"

I trace the markings on my hand. "My name is Marcine Bellace Braddock."

Pyera approves.

"I am a resident of Devil's Trumpet, Arizona."

She arches a brow. "And what's not allowed?"

"Sass." I drone.

Her grin says I'm correct.

"Don't address that you were a shifter," she says. "They already know."

"Wouldn't want to insult them," I say derisively.

"I want to every day, but I prefer my lavish life." She stretches her arms over her head, and yawns. "Sunrise is in a few hours. I suggest you get as much sleep as possible. Shifter politics are grueling enough; you don't want to tackle them with less than 12 hours of sleep. I promise."

I give her a half smile. "I'll take your word for it."

"I've been dealing with it for years." She cups her cheek. "I didn't have a single wrinkle when I first became the Lady of Devil's Trumpet. They *age* you."

Her face softens as she stands. She leans over and presses her lips into my hair before she bids me goodnight.

I lie back on the bed.

Thoughts of Lilac dig themselves out from under my Doomsday To-Do List. I close my eyes.

She'll be at the Summit tomorrow. As I desperately try to preserve the world, hers will crumble at the sight of me. When the Summit was first revealed, it was easier. I had a plan: find her, hold her, love her, and convince her to somehow use her status to help me back into the pack. That all feels so stupid now. Not only am I dead to her, I'm a vampire. What's worse? Resurrection or transformation? Which is harder to believe? The bruise on my cheek stifles any hope. Not to mention, our last conversation wasn't exactly kind.

I stretch my arms above me. The jagged, multicolored lines of sediment ripple from wall to wall on the ceiling. They paint ridges between my fingers. I rotate my hands, surveying every crease and crevice in my skin.

Months ago, these hands knew what it was like to love Lilac. I memorized the shape of her fingers as they slid between mine, the smoothness of her cheek as I cradled it in my palm, the bends of her body at midnight. Now, all I feel is faint craving. Other wants, too.

The desire to go home—because Devil's Trumpet *is* home. It's named after a poisonous weed. It is everything I learned to hate as a child. It is the untrodden path I never meant to take, but now that I've wriggled my toes in those soils, I yearn to go back.

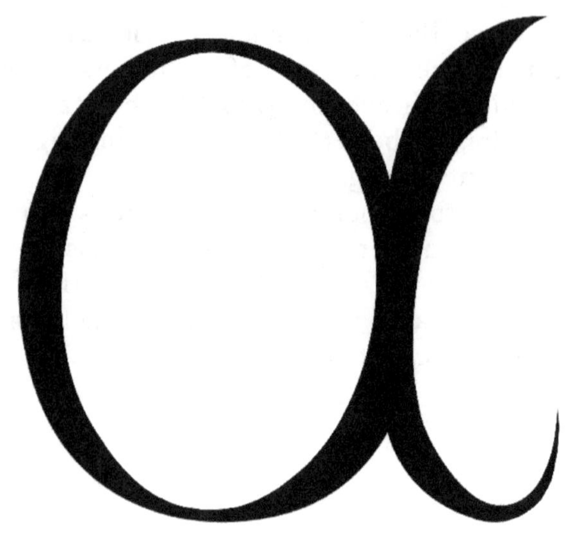

FORTY-TWO

I AM ALIVE

By the time Miranda wakes me, the Summit has already begun. I try to ignore the prickle of my reflection's eyes as I scurry around the bathroom.

"Where's Nico?" I ask as I tie my hair up.

"Sleeping, I assume," says Miranda, waiting outside the door.

"Still?"

"His statement is due after yours." There's a pause. "Which is expected in seventeen minutes."

I stop midway through buttoning my pants to glance at the door, brow arched. "Because saying twenty minutes was too vague?"

"By the time you're done, it'll be ten minutes."

Oh, Nico will just love you.

After pulling on a backless top, I glance over my shoulder, down my back. My Marrow Mark is visible. My people refuse to acknowledge that I even exist, but I will not be overlooked. Anyone that sees me will know. Still, I want to yell it at the top of my lungs. This has to be enough, I remind myself.

Pulling in a breath, I steady my heart and follow Miranda and Bethany out. Two gammas flank us. Down the winding corridors, shifters gush around us. They weave around us like we're boulders moving upriver. I catch snippets of orders, questions, and clarifications flung over my head, or spoken into comm-devices.

The visions replay in my head. I see the Alphas bodies lined up. Dead.

"Have you boosted your security?" I ask any of them.

It's Bethany who answers. "Yes."

"How so?"

"There are several squadrons patrolling the city." Miranda supplies, startling Bethany. "They're circling the city from various distances. We've stationed lookouts to call home our forces if needed, and the city itself is teeming with gammas." She motions around us.

"That's why we were screened so thoroughly?" I ask.

She glances at me. "It is."

We round one last corridor, and an imposing set of doors come into view. Half of a doe's face has been carved into them. She peers into me as if it were Mother Nature herself, not just her symbol. The shifters' centuries-old adage is carved across the top. *Beast, Breath, and Body for Her.*

The gammas take post on either side, and Miranda and Bethany follow me in.

The Summit is held in a gargantuan, circular amphitheater. It was built to accommodate global events like this. There's one in every continent. The walls are lined in rows of ascending seats, where nearly 300 Alphas are assembled. Above the final row, a balcony wraps around the entire room. The betas watch the Summit from there.

The Poppy Alphas are one of two pairs not amassed in the pews. Alpha Rosemarie Bridges, the pack's elegant doe, is seated beside its vulture, Alpha Marcus Pierce, in their throne-like lounges. Alphas Roderick and Kennedy stand humbly before them, Pyera and Cleon at their side.

When we enter, a hush sweeps the room. All eyes are on me. Neither of my wardens falter. They're shameless among their peers, despite who they guard. The Prophet of Misfortune is here. And I'm one of them.

I scan the Alphas. My Alpha, Althea, is seated somewhere among them. On the overlook, the betas rouse the silence with whispers. They hiss and toss questions, trying to understand what I am.

Yes. I'm real. Yes, our leaders lied to you, and I'm sorry.

I search for Lilac, but I can't find her.

As I come to the center of the room with the Knotweed Alphas, Miranda and Bethany pause a few steps behind. The Poppy Alphas are seated before us.

Rosemarie was born with the soul of Sahar; a previously underwhelming Grounding that garnered recognition thanks to Rosemarie's prowess. Her Marrow Mark is the white symbol of a doe. It covers her aged body from head to toe.

Marcus is Grounded by Wenceslas. It's a name so renowned, the healers knew he was destined for something grand when he was born. And in 1960, at age 20, he became the youngest US shifter Alpha in history. He wears an ivy vulture as his Marrow Mark. It's as prominent as Rosemarie's.

"Introduce yourself," he commands.

Out the corner of my eye, Pyera catches my attention. The corners of her mouth turn up. *Like we practiced.*

I say, "My name is Marcine Bellace Braddock."

I am a resident of the Devil's Trumpet, Arizona, I should continue—but I'm more than that.

The Alphas hide my existence. Their betas are complicit. The gammas call me bloodhound, and, to the deltas and omegas, I am not real. To some of them, I'm dead.

We, shifters turned vampires, are stains on their reputation kept clean by lies, manipulation, institutionalized elitism, and the hubris of those in power who would rather embolden their own agendas than make change. Worse, is me. I am a smirch made dirtier because I will not bend to a path not carved by the Moon, the Mother, or myself.

Mother Nature sent me into the night. The Man in the Moon kissed my eyelids and wove in them endless, ever-changing futures. In my hand, he placed a knife with which I was chosen to whittle fate—not just my own, but the world's.

Even after I was banished from the day, I held onto my roots. Harder and harder, with every upheaval and twist. Progress has been slow. It's been non-existent at times, but I never turned my back on the Earth, the Sun, or my people, not even when they worked against me. More than anyone else, I have given everything to Mother Nature.

I hold my chin high. "My parents are Kathleen and Rochester Braddock, deltas of the Bloodroot Pack. I crossed paths with known rogue vampire, Francis

Church, two months ago. Afterward, I was sent to live in the Arizona coven, Devil's Trumpet."

The room erupts with hundreds of languages. Questions and translations are flung about in a hurry while the betas hurl words at me, lost in the chaos of too many voices. My hands tremble, but I don't waver. Not even beneath Pyera and Cleon's needled glares, or the Knotweed Alphas'.

I am alive.

Marcus lifts his hand, and silence befalls the room yet again. He glares at me. His eyes burn, too. Less like a sunset and more like an inferno. "*You* are the Man in the Moon's second Prophet."

He says *you* like I'm not worth the air.

I say, "Macy," because I know I'm worth more.

"Macy." He rolls his eyes. "In the past, the soothsayers have always relayed two different futures. Yet, your visions have exclusively matched the first Prophet's."

"Yes," I say. "We believe that Francis Church is orchestrating a Biblical ritual that could destroy the entire world."

"As of yet," Marcus says, "we've seen nothing but acts of terror. I don't see how this could spread beyond the nation."

My eyebrows shoot up, then furrow. "*I've* seen it."

"Yes. In visions. Which, historically, have been known to show only one of infinite possibilities. Of which the ones shown are never the ones fulfilled."

"Our visions have already been partially fulfilled." I argue. "You've seen the carnage."

"Acts of terror." Marcus frowns. "Acts of terror that cost us a great deal, yes, but that can be handled internally. What need is there to involve foreign Packs?"

"There's a madman on the loose. That isn't enough?"

Marcus sighs, dragging his eyes to Rosemarie.

"Please." I take a step forward. "We need to do what's best for our people."

"*Our people?*" he booms. "They are not *your* people."

I grit my teeth. Someone, I don't know who, hisses at me but I don't care. I didn't ask for this. Not the fangs, not the nightmares, not the visions, and not the responsibility. But I'm here now, and I refuse to be overlooked.

"Francis Church burnt the North Maine Woods to cinders. He killed half of Celastrus overnight, my father included. He summoned a global storm that stole the sky for days. The Earth is withering, and hundreds of shifters have died already. I saw *all* of it in visions. And I've seen more. Church is a threat to your people and mine. And as protectors of the Earth, it is your job to stop him. I shouldn't have to tell an *Alpha* that."

"Macy!" Pyera snarls.

Someone grabs me. I don't resist when they pull me back in line, but I don't back down. I stand tall and straight, meeting Marcus' glare head on as he slowly rises from his throne.

The world is an endless mass of noise. The betas shout, the Alphas chatter; it all swirls in deafening echoes around me. Then, the noise is brought to a jarring halt when Rosemarie lifts her hand.

Reluctantly, everyone settles. This new quiet holds a grudge. Marcus sinks back down.

"Enough," Rosemarie says. "Macy, please share your prophecy with us."

I stare at her for a moment. "Thank you."

I've relived my visions so many times, I know every detail by heart. As I speak, I know, in my gut, in that way I always seem to know, that this is where I'm supposed to be. In every lifetime, realm, dimension, and alternate reality, I am meant to be here.

The Alphas frequently ask me to pause so others can ask questions, or the translators can catch up. I'm asked to clarify, interpret meanings, and repeat snippets. And, after what feels like an eternity, I'm released.

I respectfully bow to Rosemarie and Marcus before retreating. The Knotweed Alphas give me a grateful nod and Pyera and Cleon break protocol to pat my arms as I leave. Although, Pyera looks at me with a honeyed smile that makes me feel like I'm in trouble.

Sapped of heat and anger, my hands and legs start to shake as I go. Miranda and Bethany are waiting for me by the door. The former bows her head at me. She looks almost impressed. Almost.

As we exit the Summit, Nico enters. He's shadowed by guards, too. Our barriers of shifters prevent us from sharing more than a glance. Still, I mouth: *Good luck, Navarro.*

His smirk is more nervous than usual. *Thanks, Bright Eyes.*

Joined by my gammas, we manage to cut through the crowd to a nearby stone bench. I slump down with a big, relieved huff. The other shifters glance at me as they pass. People peek and nod at me, urging others to steal a glace. They whisper out of earshot. Their mouths curl in condescending snarls. *Yes!* I want to yell. *I am the one you heard about!*

Dropping my head, I close my eyes and bite my tongue.

"Northeast? All four?" one of my gammas says.

When I glance up, I see that he's talking into his ear device. He looks at the other gamma. Worry cracks their composure.

Miranda is as calm as ever. "Go on. We'll look after her."

I scoff. None of my guards react. The gammas briskly leave our sides, hurrying off to whatever task came through their comms.

"What's going on?" I ask.

Bethany looks at me but it's Miranda who answers. "They've been asked to help investigate a perimeter breach outside the capitol."

I sit up straight, heart thrashing.

Miranda frowns. "It's not what you're thinking."

"What is it then?" I ask.

"Some shifters went missing over a week ago. We found them."

I relax. With a big breath, I rub my eyes with the heels of my palms. I keep replaying Marcus' indignance. If I had a hard time winning him over, Nico's a goner. I'm at least twice as charming as he is.

They have to listen. I'm not sure what will happen if they don't. Mom always said not to put all your eggs in one basket, but when you're the Prophet *and* the sacrifice, just how many baskets do you have? There's no Plan B. If we fail, it's forever. We only have one—

"Macy!"

My head, heart, and lungs stop working. The universe and its perils come to a standstill. Daylight breaks across the long, endless night of the past two months. She's color and happiness. She's warmth and love. I see the sun. *Lilac.*

GHOST

The world creeps back to life. My pulse beats wildly in my arms and legs. I'm standing before I realize it. I break into a sprint. So does she. We collide like two meteors. Gravity mashes our lips together. Our broken pieces scatter.

The last two months are eclipsed by the rest of my life. My childhood spent chasing butterflies across fields and clumsily stumbling over my own four feet as a pup. The dark haze that surrounds the night of Mom's attack, the bumbling that followed, and my escape: a girl.

A smile that revived mine. Curious eyes, beckoning me closer. Her untamed hair—tangled, frizzy, stuck around my fingers. Her mouth, and the first time we kissed. Lilac petals fluttering through the air; her skin burning gentle violet as we undressed.

A pocket of reality unfolds around us. It's me and her. Together again.

She cries my name into my mouth. I whisper hers back. She presses her blunt, callused fingertips anywhere she can. Every inch of me is hers, and she takes her time remembering, making sure I'm not a ghost.

I break away to gasp. "I'm real."

A sob shudders out of her. I swipe her tears away, my own fighting to spill. Cupping her face, I drag her mouth back to mine. She clutches my wrists. With all the gentleness in the world, she pulls away and sets her forehead against mine.

"You died," she whispers.

I murmur back. "I'm alive."

"I saw him bite you." She shakes her head. "I *carried* you to the healers, but they said there was nothing they could do. They said you were dying."

"Lilac."

She clenches her eyes shut. I touch her cheek, so she opens them.

"I'm alive."

She looks at me, gaze glossy. She frantically tries to unknot her voice from the mess in her head. The regret and shame are there. It's palpable.

"I'm sorry." The skin around her closed eyes tightens. That night plays out in her head. It twists her face in pain. "I'm so sorry, Macy. After you... you... All I could think about was what I said to you."

This is why you're an omega. It doesn't sting the way it used to.

I drag my thumb across her bottom lip. "I forgive you."

"This whole time... you were. I can't believe..."

"I know. It took a long time for me too."

Her body shakes. "And you're a Prophet now, too? I didn't even know that was a thing."

"Neither did I."

"There has to be a way to fix this," she says.

It almost makes me laugh. All my life, Lilac has been the only person I could count on. She's flawed, but so am I. She's the beauty and energy of life, epitomized—ready to help me put the world back together before it falls apart completely.

"We're trying," I say. "It's been an uphill battle. We've been beaten down and shoved away by the gammas. Just getting here was a struggle. Hopefully, the Alphas will listen to what Nico and I have to say. And now that you're here you could…"

I take in her expression. Slowly, she lifts her eyebrows, creasing her forehead. Reluctance hardens her stare. All our happy memories collapse under the weight of the world. Our pocket of reality folds in on itself. I feel exposed. Dread slips its claws around my shoulders. He cackles at my ear.

"That's not what I mean," Lilac says, puzzled.

"What?" I exhale.

"I meant there has to be a way to *cure* you."

"There *is* no cure, Lilac." The love pulsing in my chest starts to hurt. It's familiar. I remember this. "And even if there was, it wouldn't matter."

"Of course it would."

"Not right now."

"You need to come home, Macy, to your family, to me."

Home. I see it in my head. The lush, endless forest all around me. Birds chirp, wide awake, singing. The sun blazes overhead. Its heat is a kiss across my cheek. A breeze tumbles through the trees and cools the sweat on the nape of my neck. Lilac's snout, wet and cold, as it nuzzles my palm. Her fur as she brushes by my leg. Us. Together. Every morning. Every night. Dinners with Mom.

Mom.

My throat closes. I want it all. More than anything, but I can't keep running, hiding, pretending it'll all go away if I just let it be. It doesn't matter how badly I want it, I can't have it, and even if I abandoned everything to run away with Lilac, it wouldn't last. The Monster would win, and it would be my fault.

"I need to protect the Earth." I say, strained. "That's why the Man in the Moon chose me. I'm his Prophet."

She pulls away from me, clutching me by my elbows. "You're a shifter, Macy."

"I'm more than that," I say. "I'm a vampire, too."

"You're a *shifter.*"

"I was bitten, Lilac." My heart races. It thumps in my ears. My thoughts run together. I untangle them slowly. "I have fangs. I drink blood. Daylight burns my skin. Every full moon, I see into the future. I fought it too, at first. I wanted to trust the Alphas, believe they had good reason, but they misused our faith. They fed us lies and secrets, and we—Please, don't look at me like that."

She hesitantly retracts her hands. She takes my heart with them. I follow her as she backs up a step, reaching out. She holds her hands up defensively like I might hurt her. "You've turned your back on Mother Nature."

"How can you say that?" I gasp. "You heard me in there. I've fought tooth and claw to be here. The Earth needs me."

"You've embraced *this.*" Betrayal glows in her eyes.

"This?"

"*This!*" She gestures frantically to the whole of my existence. "Being one of them. A vampire. A monster."

"We aren't monsters."

"Don't you remember what they did to your mom? To *you?*" Her eyes dip to the scar on my throat. I swallow. "They're the same people who set our home on fire. My sister nearly died in the flames. My dad *did.*"

It's like looking into a mirror. I see myself in her hate, her anger, her desperation. She clings to age-old teachings because she's scared. Change has been cruel to her. It usurped her of her home. It took her father away. Pain and bitterness guard the gates of her heart, protecting her from any more atrocities. It's safe inside those walls.

I would know. I once hid behind them, too.

I take a step toward her. The world hurt her, just as it hurt me. But there were people there to show me truth in the form of love.

So I try to show her. "I'm sorry. None of this should've happened. The people who hurt you are evil. They *have* to be stopped. But they're just a few people. I'm a vampire, too. You know I would never hurt you. Most wouldn't."

"They breed evil."

"Everyone is capable of evil."

"You're *blind.*" Her voice quivers. "They all deserve to burn."

In between her words, I hear, *Even you.* I grimace because it hurts, but I can't let it hold me back. Not anymore.

"No." My voice is strong. "They don't. There's been too much death. Too much pain. We don't need more. I'm *sorry* you've been through so much. I'm sorry I wasn't there. This isn't the solution."

Infuriated tears shimmer in her eyes. She searches my face, prying me open in hopes of finding the person I used to be. The malleable girl who was willing to twist and bend and break just to be loved. That person is gone.

When Lilac realizes this, she whispers. "You've changed."

"We both have," I say softly, "and it's okay."

She sucks her bottom lip into her mouth. Bowing her head, she glares at the ground. Denial and fury wreak havoc in her body, winding every muscle tight. She looks at me one more time, but our love is old, faulty. It's not strong enough to keep us together. It never was.

She backs away like a frightened animal. At the precipice of another corridor, shifters pushing around us, jostling us, she meets my gaze. Every part of me aches. I want to love her. I want to be loved. Mother Nature, I want it so bad, but I refuse to undermine myself to get it.

I touch my beaded necklace. "I'm sorry."

She cracks like glass. Then she shatters. Broken, she disappears around the bend. I stare at the empty space she left. Part of me wants to chase her. Our withered love thrashes in my chest. Wild and desperate, it wants to live but I know, if circumstances were different, we would've squandered the chance to thrive. Our souls are not compatible. They never were. For a long time, we overlooked that to stay comfortable. I can't do that anymore.

I am the quintessence of everything she needs to heal from. Before I was thrown back into her reality, ripping open her stitches, she had begun to. *She will again,* I tell myself. It's time we both let go. Eyes closed, I turn my back on Lilac and everything we had.

I navigate the many hallways, followed by my betas, until I reach Mount Milo's entrance. As I step outside, the cold Michigan wind slaps me in the face. I look back at Miranda and Bethany. They search the branches of cedars and maples, survey between every tree for any threat, and smother me with their constant, watchful nearness. I just want to be alone. No more spying cameras, critical looks from other shifters, or constant surveillance. I need space.

"I'd like to walk alone."

They focus on me.

I cross my arms. "I know you're going to follow me, but can you keep some distance? Just for a little while."

The duo shares a silent exchange. Bethany shrugs. "We'll be close."

With a sigh, I traverse down the monument's steps. I pause on the final stair, looking at Meadowsweet's swampy woodland.

There are no walls or roads here. The trees are thin, but they stretch on forever. Tall grasses tickle slender tree trunks while bare branches scratch at the night sky. Their leaves the capitol's soils from end to end. Meadowsweet was not unscathed by the storm, but it stands strong, free, resilient.

Chewing my bottom lip, I sit on the final stair and un-lace my tennis shoes. Cool air kisses my heels. I extend my leg and wriggle my toes. Freedom. I'm not sure when I'll feel it again.

I burrow my feet in the mud. The wet ground gives and slips as I trace a worn, almost indistinguishable trail away from Milo. I rub my chest. The omega markings don't burn like they used to, but the memory of Lilac kissing them does. I pull in a breath.

The air is clean, scented by pinecones and sweet bark, not pollution. From the shore, a rush of freshwater wind whistles as it wiles, wandering happily. Until it skirts past me.

It prods me lightly at first, urging me off the trail. It nudges me again, and when I don't comply, another, fiercer push almost knocks me off my feet. I catch myself on a tree. Thudding, wet footsteps come closer.

"Braddock!" Miranda calls.

I glance her way but another ferocious wind rips through me, turning my attention deeper into the forest. Silhouettes move in the shadows.

FORTY-FOUR

DOWN TO THE RIVER

Shifters, I tell myself. A distant gamma patrol, or maybe a few deltas, lusting after nighttime adventures like I used to. Unease slithers up my spine.

The wind pushes me again, urgently. It chases noise from the woods, hushing every tree and animal. Hollow, the silence echoes inside itself.

In my head, I see the Alphas' corpses. My chest throbs.

"Braddock." Bethany hisses, beside me.

I narrow my eyes. "Do you see them?"

Miranda leans close to me to track my line of sight. "The shadows?"

"The Alphas were murdered in one of my visions." I whisper. "We thought maybe tonight..."

"That can't be possible." Bethany insists. "The entire city is being patrolled by multiple units from several distances."

Yet the wind demands. I say, "They infiltrated my *walled-in* coven."

She hushes at that.

"These people are slick," I mutter. "We were expecting a blatant approach. They know that. They would've found a way to weasel their way in."

"How?" Miranda demands.

"We've known about the Summit for months," I say. "So have they."

"There's been an influx of dead animals since last week." Miranda ruminates. "And those missing shifters..."

The grass of her irises meets the fire of mine. "You know I'm right."

"Miranda..." Doubt tinges Bethany's voice.

Paying her no mind, Miranda searches my face. I don't waver. Abruptly, she decides. "Bethany, climb Milo to Howler's Perch. I'll take Braddock. We'll check out whatever's going on. I'm sure it's nothing, but I'll signal you if it's not."

"But—"

Miranda glares at her. Whatever she was going to say disappears. She inches backward before she transforms into a reddish wolf, and darts the opposite direction, kicking up leaves as she runs.

Once she's gone, Miranda looks me up and down. "Don't make me regret this."

The wind rides low to the ground, sneaking with us toward the shadows. It could be anyone; a gamma, a delta. But the wind has never led me astray. Neither has my intuition.

Humans? Miranda mouths.

I shake my head. It's never just humans.

She grimaces, then ducks behind a tree and presses herself into it. I do the same to the one nearest to me. She mouths, *Follow me,* before she skips to another cedar. I take the one she abandoned. Hopping from tree to tree, she leads the way and I succeed her place each time.

As we get closer, the moon breaks through the cloud cover. It shines light on a barren tree, revealing a strange symbol. My stomach sinks.

It's just like the one in Val's book, and on the trees near his house when Devil's Trumpet went into lockdown. The moonlight shifts, skimming several other trees. All of them wear the same mark. Val *couldn't* be here, but this can't be a coincidence.

Miranda peeks cautiously around her tree. She motions for me to pause.

"How far?" a soft female voice asks.

"Past the northern border," says a gruffer, deep voice.

"Jeremy would've liked the light show," she says sadly.

A third voice says, "We'll see him soon enough."

"Not if we don't get this over with." The man grumbles.

"Katherine rigged the mountain." The older woman says. "As soon as the sacrifice leaves, it'll blow. And one by one, all the others will go off too."

My breath hitches.

For a moment, I can't move, but, rapidly, my rage thaws me. It's them. These are the people who bit me. They're the ones who incinerated my home. They slaughtered my people. They murdered Dad. Now they're here, and they want to kill everyone else, too. Then, an epiphany: *I already left.*

Miranda pounces from cover. Those birds fly from her skin and into the air, a tornado of squawking crows. They rustle the branches and blot out the stars, the moon, the night. In the distance, a wolf howls.

By the time her feet touch the ground, they've turned to jet-black paws. Miranda snarls at the nearest rogue. A man. He brandishes his knife without fear. He brings his blade to his crosshatched wrist. Miranda lunges. She opens her mouth, those big, white teeth slobbering for his throat, but he twists away.

He shouts, *"Scatter!"*

He staggers deeper into the forest. Miranda pursues him. The women flee in the opposite direction, seizing their chance at escape. I spring from the trees to chase after them. Clumsily, they hurtle through the mud, but it grips their shoes, so they slip and slide. The blonde catches herself on a tree, frantically urged forward by the other woman.

Soggy leaves stick to the bottom of my feet. I grip the mud with my toes and use the trees to propel myself faster. I can't lose them.

A root snags the girl's foot. She falls with a wail. In the muck, she clutches her ankle. The woman hurriedly tries to haul her up, but she lets out another cry. She glances at me. There's panic, and then furious denial. She lifts the girl up, supporting her body with her own, and carries her weight as they run.

There's a whisper. It grows into a roar. A river. They hear it too, desperately picking up the pace. They break onto the shoreline. I'm right behind them. They're too slow. The girl's pain is too much. My feet slap loudly in the mud as I charge toward them. Glancing over her shoulder, the woman hurls the blonde away, and spins around. I throw myself at her.

We plunge into the rapids. Water rams into us, so icy it scalds. We tumble with the waves, sediment and stone biting our skins. She swings her blade at me when I try to pin her. A line stings across my nose. Numbness follows. I grip her knife-hand, pinning it underwater. She clutches my hair with the other, rolling herself on top.

I shout. It gets lost when she submerges my head. Water rushes into my nose and throat. It burns. Desperately, I push my head above water, sputtering for air. She pushes me back under. This time, I hold my breath.

Water glazes my vision. She's muddled and messy above, misshapen. She reels her arm back. My death flashes before my eyes—a knife embedded in my face.

Adrenalized, I grab her wrist with my hand. She tries to push against my grasp. Using my other hand, I push back, fighting with all my strength. The blade trembles. My chest feels like it's going to explode. I need to breathe. She releases my hair to press on the knife with both hands. I buck her off.

I roll onto all fours, coughing raggedly. My hands and feet are shaky, but I manage to stand. The current snakes around my ankles. Looking along the shore, I see the blonde trembling. The woman steps between her and me. She glares at me. It's colder than the water.

"*You.*" She snarls. "You won't take her too."

I eye the knife in her hand, cautiously taking a step closer. "Just stop fighting."

She doesn't move. Scowl locked on me, she says, "Tara. Go."

"Robin—"

"Go."

Tara's eyes bulge. She struggles onto her feet. She looks at Robin one last time, before limping down the shoreline. A trail of blood follows her. *You'll never make it,* I think. *Just stand down.*

Miranda leaps from the trees, cutting off Tara's path. She screams and stumbles, falling onto the shore. Miranda looms closer, her lips drawn back, revealing her bloody teeth. She growls warning. Tara scrambles away.

"No!" Robin yells.

She slices into her arm. A vine of blood slithers from the cut. Those chunks of bloodied soil levitate. Tara's damaged ankle gushes more, thick globs floating alongside clumps of dirt. The cut on my nose starts to bleed profusely, little red ribbons drawn to Robin. They take the shape of spears; all of them aimed at Miranda.

I flash back to that night in the clearing.

My legs carry me faster and faster and *faster* until my fists connects with Robin's cheek. The clean, wet smack of flesh on flesh cracks loudly. She twirls away. Around us, the blood falls.

She peers at me through her messy fringe, then charges. She tries to scratch me, so I grab her wrist. Her knife flails in my direction. I grab that wrist too. We grapple for power. The scent of curdled blood is thick this close to her. It fogs my brain, makes me sick, but I don't give an inch.

Then the Earth shakes. I feel it vibrate in the soles of my feet. She totters away, eyes bulging as a symphony of howls energizes the night. One turns to two, and two turns to four. The entire forest quakes from paws pounding closer.

Wolves spill from the river. Too many to count. Too many for them to fight. I fade away as the wolves corner the rogues, bloodlust glittering in their eyes.

"Robin..." Tara's bottom lip quivers.

They cling to each other, bloody fingers laced. Tara shakes. Robin is unbreakable.

She glowers at the wolves, then me. Her hate eats me like acid. It shouldn't. She helped the Monster kill my people, kill Dad. Yet, no matter the harm she did to us, my animosity for her and what she's done does *not* match that which she holds for me. I would never destroy her world—but maybe that's because someone destroyed it before I ever crossed her path. Not just someone. A shifter.

She hides her face against Tara's hair, nuzzling her like a mother would a child. She whispers something to her. Tara closes her eyes, reaching into her pocket. Together, they lift their blades. Holding them out, they show us. Robin's meets my eyes.

"No." I whisper. "No, no, *no.*"

That grudgeful look dares me to watch as they bring the knives to their throats. I can't. I close my eyes tight, hunching my shoulders. My face scrunches when I hear the gargle of breath and blood. I cover my ears.

FORTY-FIVE

WITH ALL YOUR (CALLOUS) HEART

"...four angels are released from their binds to the great river Euphrates. They command a brute force of 200 million mounted troops, whose horses dissipate plague out of their mouths, most notably fire, smoke and brimstone..."

All the covens are the same. Oppressive, joyless cities bound in matching chains: surveillance, violence, elitism, and centuries of murder. Pain stacked on pain. And every coven is brimming with walking corpses, half aware of their own subjugation, but too afraid to fight it. They'd all be better off dead.

Devil's Trumpet is no exception. Francis reveled in tearing it down.

They bit the gammas and crammed them into the Sunlight Chambers. Their screams reverberated down every street as venom undid their pride. Come daylight, the wails got worse. All that's left of them are putrid piles of rotting flesh.

Most vampires were spared. All but those who refused to submit. They were thrown in with the shifters and left to burn. Any residual flames of rebellion were stamped out by their enchantments. Through them, Francis feels their hearts beating.

He circles the library tower. The archway reads *History*, tastelessly dedicated to a vile chronicle of abuse. The skylight bleeds iridescence onto the memorial at the center of the room.

As he runs his fingers along the edge of the table, he peers at photos, frames, lockets, watches, letters. One earring sits beside a shattered phone. A book with frayed edges hides under a yellow handkerchief. Mementos of the people they lost, arranged atop a small casket. A symbol.

There's a photo of his son. He picks it up.

I just want to hold you.

He's prayed. Too much. For things he can never have. Dean is dead. No amount of prayer will bring him back, nor will it trade their places.

He's ready for it to be over. All of it. He's exhausted. The grief is too much, anymore. His rage is dwindling, the end of a long, drawn out battle finally in sight. His body begs him to collapse.

Long ago, Francis could endure anything for his son. Any injustice was manageable. His anger at the unfairness of the word could be set aside. So, although Dean isn't here anymore, he can endure this for him, too. He deserves that much.

Francis shakily flattens the picture on the casket. He looks at the sky. The moon glares down at him. He scowls back.

"They killed him." Francis snarls. "And now I'll kill them."

"Francis."

He walks around the memorial.

Valberg Marshal's head hangs low, blood dribbling down his chin. Dried blood crusts his cheeks and in his beard. He weakly yanks on his hands, bound to the memorial. He has no strength to free himself.

He was the first vampire to fight back. Unsurprising. For as long as Francis had known him, Valberg has always been too valiant for his own good. Francis would've killed him with the others, but he needs him.

"Imagine," says Francis. "We could've stood together if you hadn't shunned me years ago. Now, here we are."

Valberg lifts his face. His eyes are dark. "You're a madman."

"And you're weak."

"Weak?" Valberg laughs through pain. "You've lost your mind, friend, if you believe *this* is strength."

"This?" Francis echoes. "This isn't strength. This is *justice*."

Valberg bows his head in disappointment.

"How many of us have they *murdered*, Valberg?" Francis demands. "You don't want to avenge Lys? For what they did to him?"

"Avenge? I want to *honor* him, And his roots!" His eyes plead for Francis to listen. "I know 2010 was traumatic, but this isn't justice. This is blind rage."

"Who said they were different?"

"This won't heal you, my friend."

"And *what* would you propose?"

"Sense?" Valberg spits the word. An insult.

Crouching in front of him, Francis lifts Valberg's chin. His face is scabbed and mottled in uneven bruises; dark colors that make his glare burn brighter. But Francis burns, too. His eyes are made from thunderstorms and lightning, brilliant white and black all at once.

"Dean wouldn't have wanted this." Valberg whispers.

Francis sneers. "Don't tell me what *my* son would want. He's dead because of *them*. And soon, yours will be too."

Valberg stiffens. "You won't touch my boys."

Francis purses his lips, eyes narrowed. "No. Not both. Just one. He'll come running home to you. All I need is a drop of blood, and it'll all be over."

Valberg warns, wrists writhing against rope. "You're wrong.

Francis' eyelids flutter. "I'm never wrong."

"It said day-kissed." Valberg insists. "He's not—"

"A shifter? That's the point."

"Macy—"

"Is that her name?" Francis drops his hand. "The red-headed mutt? Yes, Terces told me about her. The second Prophet come to foretell doomsday five years too late, but you read *The Primal Ages*. Did it say *earth-bound* or *day-kissed?*"

Val's ragged breaths scrabble frantically up his throat. He yanks on his arms, but the rope bites into him. Francis strokes Val's forearm. New cuts split the old, puckered scars, ugly and irritated.

Francis careens closer. "This has been in the works for years. I knew the day Nico was chosen. It was always him."

Valberg's body vibrates as if the Earth beneath tremors.

"Francis." A familiar voice comes from the archway.

He turns to see Terces. Her sagging face is ghost-white in the dark. She is one of the few self-aware shifters; a puppet who cut her strings. He knew her before she was scorched, before her hair had faded, and before 2010. After, she was one of the first to join him.

She glides into the moonlight.

"Terces!" Valberg hisses.

She looks at him dryly.

"What are you *doing?*"

She clenches her jaw.

"Terces, *please.* You know in your heart this isn't right."

"You're a fool, Valberg," she replies.

His shock evolves to anger. He's shaking again. "It was you! You let that madman onto the Bridge. Even after I defended you! Helped you! I kept the shifters, and the Lord and Lady off your back. But they were right."

"Shifters are never right," Francis says. He waves for Terces to follow.

As they leave, Valberg thrashes against his bonds, screaming, yelling, and cursing them. His voice ricochets against the library walls.

"The assassinations failed," she says.

Francis grimaces. "What happened?"

"The second Prophet."

"Again?" Should he really be surprised? He sighs. "What of the other covens?"

"Taken."

"All of them?"

"Some more easily than others." She toys with the earring. A gift from him. "Your enchantments made it easy."

Francis closes his eyes. He can taste freedom. It's right there, teasing his mouth. Soon, everything will be done. He'll be able to rest.

I'll be with you soon, Robin.

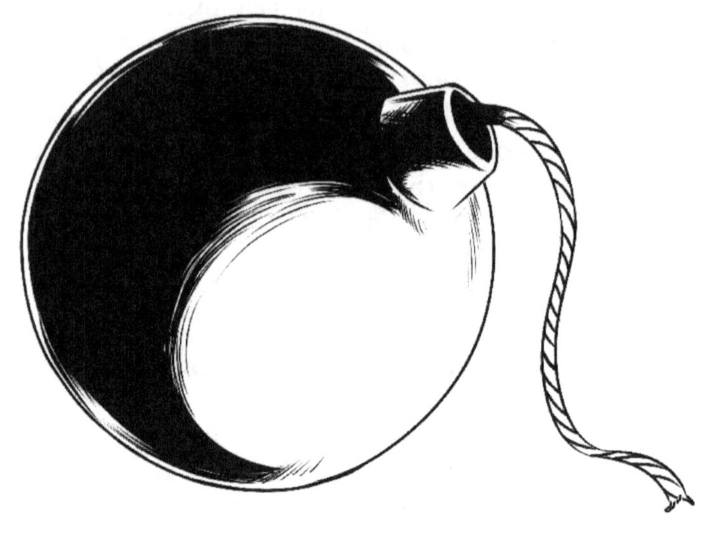

BEFORE THE STORM

When Miranda said they found those missing shifters, she didn't mean alive. They were hidden under a shattered rock formation northeast of the capitol, fully drained. Their faces were mangled, features stretched and slid around, like a photo taken mid-movement. A hideous black etching was carved into their foreheads. Glamour spells meant to steal the face of another. Pyera said it's a forbidden hex.

None of the rogues lived through the night. The memory of Tara and Robin holding knives to their throats makes me shudder, and Robin's vengeful glare haunts me, even now.

After our run in with the rogues, the Alphas finally agreed to send their support. It's the first real, tangible shred of progress since the first vision. Not only that, but we finally stopped one of the trumpets. If all seven have to be fulfilled, then we stopped the ritual. We prevented the end. All that's left is to find Church.

The Poppy Alphas invited us to dinner as a show of gratitude for saving their lives. It was awkward after my pissing match with Marcus. However, as per Pyera's request, I was on my best behavior. Nico and I were asked about our opinions on Vampire Ambassadors and offered positions as a boon. Nico laughed. Pyera and I both swatted him. Alpha Roderick invited Nico to the Knotweed capitol, Wolfden. He could study with the healers there. All the while, Pyera and Cleon had a ball bragging about us.

Apparently, Miranda spoke highly of my combat abilities to Alpha Rosemarie. She alluded to possibly training with her after Church is apprehended.

That night, as the gammas rushed to save the rogues from bleeding out, Miranda put her arm around my shoulder and led me away. She took me far enough that I couldn't see the vampires and their ghosts couldn't see me.

She said, "You're shivering."

The sounds Robin made played on full blast in my head.

"They told me you were an omega," she said. To herself or to me, I couldn't tell.

I said, "I was about to be."

"You don't fight like one."

At the time, I didn't think she meant it.

Nights later, Pyera and Cleon are whisked away to formulate battle plans. Nico and I converge in my room, hiding from the strange, somber celebration. Four shifters died, but their killers did, too. I watched two women slit their own throats so they wouldn't be apprehended, and the image of it still haunts me—but we won. It just doesn't feel like much of a victory.

Nico sprawls across my mattress. His head hangs over the edge, and he tosses a shifter-made hacky sack into the air. He pestered one of his gammas with fifty different levels of sarcasm until he bought it for him. It falls back into his hand with a soft thump. He manages to distract me from the odd aura around Mount Milo.

"Are you kidding?" He sends me a look of a scorn. "You ruined my winning streak by pure luck. Now that we're actually equals—"

I manage to laugh. "Oh, shut up!"

"—Now that we're actually equals, we have to keep sparring. End of the world or not, you've wounded my fragile ego. It's in desperate need of inflation."

"I don't know. I kinda wanna quit while I'm ahead."

He rolls over and jabs a finger at me. "Listen here, Sunshine. I get it. You're the hotshot Prophet who just saved, like, 400 Alphas, but that's all the more reason for us to keep sparring. *Someone* has to take you down a few notches."

My heart is heavy, but I suck air between my teeth, eyeing the floor. "What's at stake?"

"My dignity?"

I peek up at him. "You still have some?"

He snorts and chucks the hacky sack at me. I duck. It thuds against the back wall. Smiling, I lean back to grab it.

"Okay fine," he says. "What do you have in mind?"

"If I lose then I'll go on a one time, strictly platonic date with you. That'll be a blow to *my* dignity."

"You are such a—"

I throw the hacky sack back. "And if *I* win, you have to go on a date with... Circi."

"*Nooo.*" He emphasizes. "She is *not* my type."

"Desperation has a type?" I raise a brow.

"Redheads." He winks.

I roll my eyes. I open my mouth.

He holds up a hand. "Yes, I know. *You're gay.*"

He tosses the sack bag to me with a grin. I catch it between both my hands, chuckling.

Someone pounds on the door. We jump to our feet as Miranda and Bethany rush inside. All the color has drained from their faces. Their chests puff in and out. My heart stumbles over itself.

"What's wrong?" I demand.

Bethany shakes her head with tearful eyes.

Miranda says, "You need to come with us."

She urges us out the door. The weight of the world rushes in, trying to smother us. It gets heavier and heavier, worse when we reach the western half of the mountain. A door is guarded by six gammas. They look like statues. Their stone faces are the image of fear.

I want to run, but I know I can't. Whatever lies on the other side of the door, it's meant for me.

I look to Nico. He's fighting his own apprehension. He tries to replace his fright with strength. So do I, but neither of us is comforted. The shifters move out of our way. I splay my fingers against the door. Nico does too. We take a breath and push through.

The U.S. Alphas are gathered around a large table strewn with maps, notes, and blueprints. They throw fiery words, their fingers knotted in topographical maps and red-ink records. A screen behind them scrolls through endless reports. They fill the screen.

They glance at us as we enter, but few linger. My Alpha, Althea meets my gaze. I spot an apology hidden somewhere in her intense stare. *Sorry*, I would assume, *for severing you from the pack.*

The Lord and Lady are closest to the door. Their eyes are puffy and red.

Worry swells like a bomb in my ribcage, waiting for something, anything, to strike its fuse so I'll explode. I want to explode. I want to break into a million pieces and pierce the stifling world.

Nico's hand grazes mine. I reach for it. Our fingers twine together, and courage sprouts between our palms.

"What's going on?" My voice trembles.

"We did not stop the ritual." Cleon whispers. He speaks quietly like he can lessen the blow of each word, but they skewer me anyway.

Nico clutches my hand.

"That's wrong," he says, *pleads*.

"We thought the same." Cleon hides his eyes behind his hand.

I break away from Nico and march up to the Lord. I pull his hand down, searching his eyes for everything he won't say. He breaks.

The bomb inside ticks louder. "What. Happened?"

"Cleon." Nico whispers.

Pyera finally rips herself away from the Alphas. Her mascara runs down her cheeks. She wipes her tears with the sleeve of her coat. It smudges her makeup: inky storm clouds under her eyes.

"The covens have been taken." She looks away and bites on her knuckle to suppress a sob. "All of them."

The universe tilts too far on its axis, whirling around like a spinning top. The Alphas are alive. Their would-be killers have been captured. We toasted to the victory. What did we get wrong? What did we miss? What details got lost along the way? I traverse weeks into the past, listening to Nico recite Bible verses and witnessing the premonitions again.

...a plagued people...

Vampires?

...mounted troops and armies...

It all crashes down on me at once.

There was never any mention of a massive assassination effort in the Bible; it was only alluded to in our vision. Church sent his lackeys, his Angels, as decoys so he could overthrow the covens.

"No." I beg the Man in the Moon, Mother Nature, the Sun Herself. I *want* it to be a nightmare.

"The Poppy Alphas launched a search unit to find any survivors from Pagoda," Cleon mutters.

Pyera's breath is warbled. She looks the same as she did a week ago when she refused to tell me Valberg betrayed us. A flame inches toward my fuse.

"There's more isn't there?" I shake my head. "What is it?"

She still can't look at me. "We've received word from Snapdragon."

"That's by..." Nico trails off.

Tears well in the Lady's eyes. "A few gammas escaped the assault. They reported that Francis Church was in Devil's Trumpet the night of the rebellion... during the Summit."

Boom.

My stomach drops, and I nearly follow it to the floor in bits.

"I'm gonna be sick." Nico shakes.

"Me too." The words tumble off my lips like putrid vomit. "We've been here for *days.* We've been *celebrating.*

And the whole time, he's been in our home? Murdering people? Destroying us?"

The hard lines of Cleon's face deepen. He fell apart before we even got here. I don't mean to drive the knife deeper.

"What are we going to do?" I demand because we have to do *something.*

Pyera places one hand on my shoulder and the other on Nico's. I don't like the look on her face. Too scared. Too shaky.

"We... we have to wait for reinforcements." Her voice cracks. "They'll be here in less than a week. We're leaving as soon as they touch land."

My nails dig into the back of her hand inadvertently, but she doesn't flinch. "What about the coven? We just let them rot?"

"No one's rotting." Pyera chokes.

"Macy," Cleon says. "We are as wounded as you, but... the reports say the vampires have been locked in their homes and kept alive unless there is no other choice."

Unless there's no other choice?

Circi wouldn't go quietly. She would fight by the skin of her teeth until they killed her. And what about Luc? Could he have calmed her? Would he have? He's always so level-headed, hates conflict. He would try to persuade her, wouldn't he? Or would he join her? He tried to barge through a wall of gammas to get to Val...

What about Valberg? Would he even have to fight? Did he really help curate this disaster?

Pyera cups my chin. "Church is trying to lure you back to Devil's Trumpet, Macy. He needs your blood to trigger the final trumpet."

Her face is seeded with tacit implications.

I shake my head with pursed lips. "I am *not* staying here."

"We—"

"No." Nico's voice cuts through hers. He's a steel blade, glinting and sharper than all of us. "No."

His hand finds mine. Solidarity surges through us when we look back to them.

"I will *not* be tied to this place." My soul rumbles. These are the right words. "I'm going. You either let me or I find a way myself."

Cleon and Pyera share a look. If Devil's Trumpet has been burnt to nothing, then we're the only tokens they have to cherish. But it's our fight. too. They wrap their arms around us.

Whatever waits on the horizon, it's ours to face together.

THE BUTTERFLY

No howling wind or forest song is strong enough to penetrate Mount Milo, but more is missing than the call of the wild. I strain my ears. I stupidly hope to hear the incessant hum of overhead lights, the chatter of a hundred voices, the brassy vibrations of a distant club, or the rev of engines rumbling alive with the night. Nothing. It's all gone, muted by the stars.

I am surrounded by complete and total silence.

That makes perfect sense. Meadowsweet is everything a shifter settlement should be: humble and restrained in its use of technology. A break in the pervasive industrial culture humans are known for. Still, I ache. Devil's

Trumpet sang an opera all its own. The quiet closes in, and my regret overwhelms me.

I peer at my reflection against the wall.

She sits atop her bed in a nest of blankets and shadows. Her glare is fiery. I scowl right back at her. She's the same pathetic girl she was last I saw her. She is months of dedication amounted to nothing.

Impulses. Batter the mirror until it shatters. Step on the shards until they turn to dust, and then sweep them away like every other mess. If I can't squash my imperfections from inside, then I'll destroy them with my hands!

I look at my hands. I ball them into fists. These are the same fingers Nico held onto like they could fix the universe. They're the same fingers that throw punches powerful enough to rival his. They could shape the fate of the Earth. They're calloused and dry with hard work. It doesn't sit right to undermine them, to undermine myself.

I drag my eyes back to *her*.

None of the differences I desire frame me like striking wings; I'm no butterfly.

New and old bruises clash against stark white flesh pulled taut over muscles never defined before I was bitten. Tireless determination takes root as dark circles and bags, skin creased around her eyes. A wrinkle folds between her brows. A sign of stress. Maturity.

I trace the green marks beneath my eyes. She does the same. My hands trail down my throat to touch the scar. Her fingers dawdle like mine. I stroke the full moon hung at the base of my neck. She twiddles with it too.

Staring at the door, restless vapors twist and turn inside my belly. I climb out of bed and open the door. It huffs a sigh, and I peek my head out.

Miranda comes to a stop a few feet away from my room. A gasp falls from her lips. It gets lost under the voices of other gammas down the hall, around the corner. Her dark brows set in a flat line above her eyes, which ask *what are you doing?*

I glance at Nico's door. She does as well. Knowingly, she looks back at me, then over her shoulder. Chatter rumbles down the hall.

I open my mouth, but she shushes me. In her head, she wrestles with something. Orders, probably, or indulgence. My lungs burn with a wild breath, and I gaze at her, hoping. Her eyes soften, and her frown fades.

She nods her head at Nico's door, and mimes, *Go.*

I mouth back, *Thank you.*

Dipping her head, the beta retreats back down the hall.

I tiptoe toward Nico's door. I rap my knuckles against it, but don't wait for him to answer before slipping inside. His back is toward me, bent over his lap. He casts his eyes toward the door, unsurprised. He knew I was coming. Of course he did.

"Hey," I say quietly.

"Hey."

"Do you mind if..."

He shakes his head. "I don't want to be alone either."

"Stay out of my head, Navarro." The tease is weak. His smile is weaker.

He extends his hand to me, beckoning me closer. I sink onto the mattress next to him. The fur blankets crease beneath my weight. Small mountain ranges rise across the bed, and my hand scales each ridge to get to his. My fingers lock around his wrist like a bracelet.

He looks at me the same way he looks at me whenever we spar. Worried. Concerned. Now there's fear.

"I'm fine," I say under my breath.

"You're not." His frown deepens, dimpling his cheeks. He pulls in the biggest breath, puffing out his chest, and deflates as he exhales. "Neither am I..." Resting his head on my shoulder, he mumbles, "Do you think we can stop him, Bright Eyes?

I want to be brave, fearless, and courageous against all odds! But I sound meek when I say, "I'm not sure."

"Me either."

He leans on me. I close my eyes, head rested atop his.

He smells like old books, graphite, and pencil shavings. He smells like sweat and friendship and love. He smells like *home*. Above everything else, he's my best friend.

"I keep replaying this one vision," he says.

I study his hair from under hooded eyes. "Which one?"

"You weren't around. It was the night you were bitten. I knew it was coming, but it hit me *hard*."

I turn my hands over in my lap. "What did you see?"

"You."

I stiffen.

"You were just a few flashes between everything else." He sounds faraway. "I saw you in the library with Luc and Circi. The moonlight lit up your face. I knew you, but I didn't. Then you were there again, under a streetlight. And again, but... you were glowing. You were so bright everything else disappeared."

My mouth is dry.

"None of us knew why you were so special." He smirks. "Won't lie, I thought you were supposed to be my girlfriend."

Miraculously, I sputter out a laugh as I lean away from him.

He laughs too. "Listen! The Man in the Moon doesn't show you a pretty girl in a vision for nothing."

"That explains so much." I smile.

"I... I don't know if we can stop Church." He glances away, gripping his stomach. "But I have this feeling.

Intuition, you know? Fate's warning. Like, somehow, I just *know*, against all odds, that we have a chance because you're here."

Nico turns his face to me again. His eyes burn darker than two black holes. He nudges my knee with his as if that will wash away what words can't; the fear, pain, and dread. It can't—couldn't—but he inspires hope and something sterner.

"No."

He looks surprised, then hurt, but that's not my intent. He stands up, but I catch his arm. For the first time, I have him caged.

"No," I say again. "It's because of *us*. We're in this together, Nico."

The hurt in his heart recedes. He stares at me, unblinking. It's not that *I* make *him* stronger. The odds have been against us since day one, and *both* our backs bore that weight.

He nods, and I know he understands. "Damn right, Sunshine."

I smile.

He lies back onto the bed, and I do, too, space between us. Our breathing keeps the overpowering silence at bay, but one thing keeps bothering me.

He said I was glowing.

"Nico?"

"Yeah?"

I look at him. "How was I glowing in your vision?"

He arches a thick brow. "You were bright green and glittery."

"What's that look—oh."

He bolts upright. It shakes the entire bed.

"I can't glow anymore." I sit up too, chewing the inside of my cheek. "My Marrow Mark..."

"*Oh.*" He throws himself off the bed.

He rifles through one of the bags haphazardly tossed into the corner. His hands are fast like lightning. They throw aside everything that comes between him and his objective—an objective that completely eludes me.

I stand behind him and stare over his shoulder.

"What are you—" I start, but pause abruptly when he produces a twine sac, tied closed by a green ribbon. The bow is wrinkled and torn, as if it was tied, untied, and tied again by nosy shifters.

Nico undoes the tether and empties the contents onto his bed. I've seen them all before. Coals. Matches. Oil. There's a note too. I snatch it up and read it with hungry eyes.

May the Moon guide you, Macy, and may the Earth listen.

-Valberg

Warmness brews in my eyes as I race to comprehend the words inscribed in all too familiar writing. Val was never a traitor. In my hands is real, legible proof that he is so much more than I made him out to be. Hands that felt as fatherly and protective as his could never help sow the apocalypse.

I flash back to that day in the garage. Luc entered with a bag strung over his shoulder and a message no one but Nico heard. The duffel was handed to the shifters but intercepted by Cleon. The Lord dispatched their typical search routine and stuffed it in the back of the SUV with no problem.

Tied, untied, and tied again. Not by shifter hands, but a Lord's. A Lady's. A Prophet's.

"The trance..."

"You have to try again," Nico says in a rush of breath.

He runs to the other side of the room towards the dresser. He clutches it by the corners and starts wobbling it. I run to the other end and help him tip it over. We try to set it down as gently as possible, but it clatters loudly. I clamber to the door. The handle rattles, then the locking mechanism clicks. It's quiet, yet it booms.

A second later, I'm with Nico again. His hands shake, splaying the coals out atop the marble bureau. I take over because he's too frantic and spread the stones out in two parentheses. Nico fetches the ampule and matches from his bed.

Just like his father, Nico douses each coal in an ample amount of oil, and then strikes a match to ignite their dampened bodies in blazing flame. He and I cover opposite ends of the room to blow out all the candles. Light is dispersed bit by bit from the room until all that's left is fire. We then slide onto the ground at either end of the dresser.

I flatten the backs of my hands against the cold stone, looking at him. My conscience seethes at our stupidity:

This is illegal.

We don't have the proper permissions.

There are shifters just down the hall.

I don't care.

He doesn't either.

His fingers are almost as scalding as his expression. The veins on the inside of my wrist burn even hotter. Every piece of me aches to do this one more time, but his thumbs pause at the heel of my palm.

He stares holes through me. "I've only done this once."

"Then we're on the same page."

He smirks. Those dimples reassure uncertain segments of my spirit. "Say my name, Bright Eyes, and I'll bring you back."

He gently kneads my veins.

A familiar sensation lazily sweeps up my arms. A sleepy presence seeps into me. My eyes are impossible to keep open. I'm enveloped in milky darkness. The same hint of a voice whispers at the edges of the fog. Its words are a leash, undecipherable verses strung together to lead me. This time I don't open my eyes.

It's like a dream. I'm unsure how long I float on its waves when those strange, foreign words begin to resemble English.

Be calm.

My heart rate slows.

Be still.

My breathing shallows.

Find me.

I know her voice. Aimil.

Without opening my eyes my vision is restored and the world rushes to meet me where I stand. The blackness is replaced by a blustery landscape.

I've been here sparingly in the past. It was easier as a child, before my potential was contorted into weakness. After that, I only spotted it in glimpses as I slumbered, a faint but ever-present world just out of my grasp.

The terrain is mostly flat beyond a few hills in the distance, and blanketed in dense, white fog. It creeps across the grounds with lecherous slowness. There's isn't a mountain or tree within miles, only a meager slope waiting on the horizon at my back. In front, is a ferocious but bewitching sea.

The words *find me* echo from the depths of my mind.

I venture toward the ocean.

It laps at the base of a snow-white cliff. It's kept company by a hulking mass of land in the distance and a lighthouse whose luster barely breaches the haze. I listen for the voice that led me here, but sound has been exiled.

The waves roll, voiceless against limestone, and the wind careens in silence.

I pivot on my heels with a frown. If the voice isn't here, then it must be nestled in the hillside. That's where I'll go. But when I drag myself inland, I find *her* instead.

The ethereal white wolf approaches. Her paws pad closer with both swiftness and slowness. She sparkles as she grows. All her details disappear in the light, and out of the brilliance appears a woman.

The field of light around her shatters into millions of scarabs. They swarm her flesh and meld together into silver armor plates. They're decorated in designs and dents alike, the results of admiration and battle. Once her body has no more space to spare, the scarabs branch off her hip as a sword and a shield forms on her back. Her white braid sways behind her.

"I've been waiting." Her voice is like water: fluid and melodic, but it could drown me.

"Here I am." I hold my chin high.

"You were so close before." She frowns. "But you were too eager. You saw and felt lives that were not yours to experience."

"I know better now." I step closer. She eyes my approach curiously. "I've been working hard to find you."

"I avoided you."

"It was obvious."

A ghost of a smirk flashes on her lips. It's hidden behind a scowl. "I cannot give you a power you cannot control, lest I wish to see it tear you apart."

At first, I have no idea what to say. How do you talk to the soul of a warrior who's guided countless, worthier shifters before you? My heart whispers to my mind.

"I've been torn apart over and over because you haven't given it to me." I take another step towards her. She places her hand on her sword. "And I understand why. I wasn't strong or smart enough. I didn't have a reason or a need to use it."

Her blade laments a metallic hiss when she unsheathes it. She directs the claymore at me. I don't stop.

"It's different now." My words are ironclad like her limbs, sharpened like her saber. I hold her glowing stare, relinquishing all self-loathing and pity to stand at her level. "Mother Nature knew my future when she gave me your power. So, bind me to her Earth. I need you more than ever."

"You are a child."

"Maybe," I say. "But I've seen the future, and it's bleak. If you don't help me, then there's no stopping it. I have to be complete. Ground me again, *Aimil.*"

I utter her name with enough power to blow the fog to the horizons. The ground quakes and the skies shudder. The entire galaxy trembles, and somehow, I remain surefooted before her. I touch the tip of her sword, and, where my skin meets metal, the scarabs scatter all over again. This time they crawl up my arm while my hand glides across her weapon. The miniature crafters build armor around me until hers disappears.

The warrior stares at me with that ever-hardened grimace; but even her last line of defense is surrendered to my proximity. Rage and bloodlust have contorted her face over countless lifetimes. But tonight, an inkling of awe trespasses her blasé expression. I brace myself for her cutting words. They don't come.

"You were meant for this."

She frames my face in her hands. Her thumbs trace the skin beneath my eyes while she gazes into my spirit. Her touch communicates messages I can only fathom as mystical memoranda relayed by flesh, bone, and passion.

The light fades from her flesh. Her face blurs: familiar strangers flash past, instant after instant, until one face lingers. My own. Then, that too fades.

Faded blonde locks and olive skin frame her vivid green eyes. She's decorated in stains of war, old and new, big and small. Her muddy hands are scraped and scabbed. Freckles lurk beneath the muck. She's tall like I am, if not taller.

The severity in her eyes fades. "I protected you when you were but a babe. I tested Fate, but my interference cost so much. You're right. The Earth and the Moon chose you long ago."

She pulls me closer.

"There is purity in your heart, strength in your limbs..." She sighs. "I hope your words are matched by action."

She leaves a kiss on my forehead. It calms the disarray around us. She pries herself from me, and reluctantly backs away. Like before, the specifics of her existence vanish in the radiance. The light comes together to create a different creature: the wolf. She howls at the sky.

You are not as strong as you need to be, but it will have to do.

Far more suddenly than the journey here, I'm jolted back into reality. This time, the flames have a competitor. My skin gleams, Marrow Mark alight with lime green effulgence. I let out a shaky gasp. It's halfway between a laugh and a sob.

I pull my hands out of Nico's. I turn them over to stare at my livened Marrow Mark. Is it too good to be true? Will control fluctuate into chaos? I try to water down the luminosity. Sure enough, they dim and then finally stop gleaming all together. I stare in disbelief.

Nico clasps my shoulder.

I swivel toward him, eyes bulging, and wrap my arms around his neck and pull him into a hug. He holds me back. His grip is tight and protective like I might float away, but I can shield him from the cosmos with just my arms.

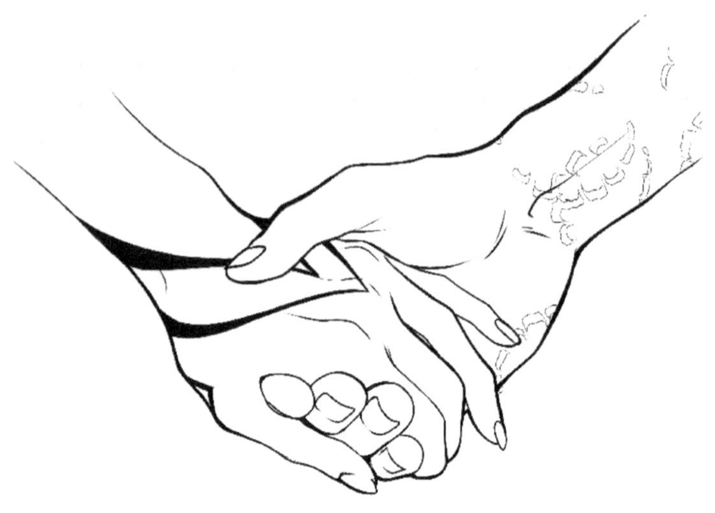

FORTY-EIGHT

WHO I AM

"Here's how this is going to work," says Miranda. "I won't leave your side, and you won't leave my sight. We're a unit."

All around us, people organize. The Alphas call out orders. Gammas and betas alike scurry to obey as sunset fades and night takes hold. They load bags into their trucks and vans. Armor and knives.

They hope to recruit what vampires they can against the Monster and his followers. The ones who know blood magic. The ones who are still alive. I close my eyes and try not to think about Luc, Circi, or Val.

Miranda grasps my arms. My eyes shoot open. Her grip is strong, unyielding, and her emerald eyes are inescapable.

"Your life comes before everything. I will not let anything hurt you. I've sworn that to the Mother herself. You need to trust me."

"I do," I say.

She's a stranger. I know next to nothing about her save this: her job is her everything. Tonight, I'm her responsibility.

"Okay." She dips her head. A strand of her brown hair slips from behind her ear. I have the urge to tuck it back into place. "One more thing."

I nod.

"If everything goes south, you run."

My upper lip curls back instinctively. I start to say something, but she cuts me off.

"No. If you want to play hero, the most heroic thing you can do is stay alive. Understand?"

I purse my lips. Through gritted teeth, I say, "Yes."

She lets me go. "I'm going to check in with the Alphas and Bethany. Head to the van."

I turn away from her, beckoned by the Lord and Lady. They're both in body armor, just like me. Because we're expecting bloodshed, wounds, death. Because this might be the last time we see each other.

The night feels darker as I walk toward them. The shadows on their faces are gloomier. I can feel the Man in the Moon's eyes boring into my neck. I glance over my shoulder at him. A gust of wind rushes up behind me. *Onward,* it tells me. *This is your path.*

But I'm afraid. My entire body is wired tight. My traitorous heart pushes dread through my veins. This is my fate. I think it always has been. Mother Nature put me in that rogue vampire's path when I was only a child, but I dodged fate. Maybe all those nightmares growing up were just the moon calling out to me. I wonder what would've been if I was never bitten—but that reality doesn't exist.

This is who I am—and I'm afraid. I'm afraid for myself, for my friends, for the future. I'm so scared that everything inside shakes, but that's okay. I'm breakable, but I'm tough. I'm not invincible, but I'm strong. I'm afraid, but I'm not defeated. This is who I am, and I will do this.

Pyera welcomes me into her arms. I don't resist. I hug her back, squeezing her as tightly as I can. She holds her lips against my hair, and then rests her cheek there, too. Cleon wraps his arms around both of us.

My family was never perfect. My love for Mom and Dad will never wither. I want it so much in this moment, but what I receive from Pyera and Cleon is more than enough.

Pyera breathes shakily as she pulls back. No makeup. She's barefaced and ready for battle. Her hazel eyes are watery. I touch her cheek.

She cups the back of it. "I love you, Macy."

"As do I," Cleon whispers. He's so much gaunter than he was a few days ago. I touch his face too.

"I love you guys, too." I swallow the pain in my throat. "You've only ever shown me love and compassion, even when I was difficult, even when I failed. I feel like I've found...I've found a home with you guys, and I..."

"Shh." She massages my knuckles and then kisses them.

Cleon cups the back of my neck. His smile is so small. "You have been nothing but a joy, Macy."

I bite my quivering lip and nod. They pull me back into their arms and we hug for a little longer. Eventually, they let me go.

"Inside the van," Pyera says softly.

Cleon holds the door open for me, so I climb in. Nico is already buckled inside. His cheek rests against his fist, and he stares out the window, at the trees, the shifters, the past and the future. He's dressed in the same black gear as everyone else. There's a blade strapped to his hip. It's not his. He doesn't look right without *his* knife.

"Hey," I say.

He glances at me. "Hey."

The silence chokes me. I stare into the seat in front of me. I fist my hands on my thighs. I watch his hand slide over mine. He squeezes it tight.

"I'm scared too," he admits. "I don't want to die."

I look at him. I feel tears coming on. "Me either."

"I won't let you die if you don't let me die?" he whispers.

It's childish. But I don't care. I unfurl my fist so he can slide his fingers through mine. We hold onto each other, unsure of what the night, the Man in the Moon, or Mother Nature has planned for us.

BLOOD MOON

The Man in the Moon looms close to the Earth, hinged on the edge of his crimson throne, alone in a starless sky. Burdened by the weight of his eyes and his even heavier hopes, the Earth emanates only one sound: the delicate, bated hiss of a planet holding its breath.

I study him through the skylight of the van.

Mother Nature's many futures are laid out before him. Whatever their atrocities, he's yet to share them tonight. I worry silence means all hope is lost, but another, potentially naïve piece of me believes this is a sign. Maybe we have more time. My blood hasn't sullied Mother Nature's soil. I refuse to abandon my faith until it does.

Our vehicular cavalcade creeps toward Devil's Trumpet.

It's an emaciated ghost of its former self, guarded by a dying forest. Trees that once stood resilient and solid, clad in iron bark and leafy helms, have withered and bent. The gentlest breeze could break any one of them. Around it, the wall has been reduced to rubble, and the watchtowers to ash.

This is our home. I will purge the Monster from it. We're backed by shifters across the nation, of every rank. As one, cohesive army, we will tear down the kingdom Church built with our despair and take back what's ours. Each of them made a promise: no innocent vampire will be killed. This is liberation, not genocide.

We approach the gates.

"It's..." Nico whispers. "... open."

I murmur. "He's inviting us in."

Pyera and Cleon glance back from the middle row of seats. As they turn back, they share a look. Our anger crackles like electricity.

"Vultures, start circling the wall." A man's graveled tone rumbles from our earpieces.

Wolves move in the dark outside the car.

"Received," another voice replies. "Lone Wolf?"

"On the approach," Miranda says, sat at the wheel of our van. "Doors open. We're pulling up now. Descent on Apex's signal."

The van stops at the gate. The terribly still night taunts us.

Pyera's voice infringes on the brazen silence. "Macy. Nico."

She doesn't take her eyes off the coven.

The streets and buildings wear shadows like scars. The glass of abandoned storefronts twinkles at the bases of windowpanes, refracting the light of the moon and a scarce few, surviving streetlamps. Most don't even flicker, but there are some that attack the dark in weak bursts. Devil's Trumpet fights off the end even after being swallowed whole.

"Do you remember the plan?" Pyera asks.

"Diversion," says Nico.

Cleon speaks, cold but not pitiless. "Elaborate."

To Pyera, I say, "You and me are going to look for the vampires while Nico and Cleon make a run for the venom."

"After that?" she asks.

"We find Church," I say. "And when we do, I distract him. Apex surrounds the area. Miranda shoots him once he's in range."

"Do *not* do anything we do not explicitly say." Her voice is metal—but it bends. It threatens to break. She stares us down with sleepless, glossy eyes.

Cleon bows his head, and then looks over his shoulder. "Please."

We both nod.

"Lone Wolf." Alpha Kennedy's voice severs the tension. "Descend."

The van starts moving again. Into the mouth of the coven we go.

Miranda says into her comm, "Shadow, in 10."

"Received." Bethany's voice comes through. She drives the vehicle behind us. It takes our place at the entrance.

Inside the coven, we split into groups. Three gammas go with Nico and Cleon. Two go with Pyera and me. Miranda joins our squad to make up the difference. They're headed east to the hospital. We're on our way south.

According to the gammas who fled to Pagoda, amongst the chaos and death, most of the vampires were herded into City Hall. That's our first destination.

Along the way, figures move in and out of windows. They never step into the moonlight, but their eyes flash like cats in the nebulous shadows, visible only in my peripherals. Darkness swallows them faster than I glance their way, but I catch glimpses. They're malnourished and sickly. Not quite alive, not quite dead. They've been tainted. In them, I see the worst possible fate of Vampire-kind.

The Ghouls are upon us.

They stalk us all the way to City Hall. It's half-crumbled and covered in soot and blood. I try not to think about whose as we creep up the steps. Cautiously, we move down the dark halls, our Marrow Marks glimmering, Pyera's flashlight leading the way.

She stops at the corner of a hall, staring down another. We all pause a few steps behind her.

"...Pyera?" I whisper.

For a moment, we wait—for what, I don't know. Pyera wordlessly takes a single, cautious step into the lightless room. Then she rushes in. The gammas and I hurry after her, but a putrid stench punches us to a standstill. My stomach gurgles and claws its way up my throat. I fight it down. Covering my mouth and nose, I clutch my stomach as I hastily push through the smell to Pyera's side.

She crouches beside a woman. In the bright, white beam of Pyera's flashlight, the woman's copper hair pools around her head. A chill makes me shudder. Her hair isn't brown. It's blonde and matted with dry blood.

"Is she...?" I trail off.

Shakily, Pyera rolls her onto her back. The weight of her body comes all at once. Her back thumps heavily on the cold floor as her head rolls limply to one side. She looks right at me with those foggy, dead eyes.

I gasp and stagger back, into Miranda's arms.

"Braddock." She whispers harshly. She holds me tight.

Pyera jumps up and pivots toward me. Her flashlight casts a wave of light down the hall behind her, illuminating bodies scattered all the way down. My eyes jump from one corpse to another. Shifters. Vampires. So many. *Too* many. Darkness falls over them again. All I see is Pyera.

She grabs my face. "I know."

"They're all—"

"Shh." She strokes the soft skin under my eyes.

"We have to find the others," I whisper. *If anyone's left.*

I bat that thought away. Forget fear. I'm not afraid. I'm *pissed.* Church took my life, my home, my father. He can't take Devil's Trumpet too.

After calming down, Pyera gently detaches from me. We carefully navigate through the narrow graveyard. I try not to look at them or their faces or their milky white eyes. I just follow Pyera.

At the very end of the corridor, there's a demolished archway. The walls are barely standing, save for the metal support beams. Pyera shines her flashlight. We all gasp.

They're here. Herded into the center chamber, they sit on the floor with their heads bowed. An unseen weight sags from their shoulders, slouching them forward. Their wrists wear bruises from long-removed cuffs, but their scathed hands are folded neatly in their laps anyway.

They're alive. Mother Nature, *they're alive.* But they're covered in blood. Wounds? Or the remnants of a battle we weren't here to help them win?

I spot a familiar head of blond hair.

"Circi!" I say as I rush past Pyera.

Miranda clasps my arm, and pulls me back. I glance at her, then at Pyera. A deep furrow forms between her brows. She shakes her head, expressionless, and mouths *stay*. With that, she spares measured steps toward them. I wring my fists to stay still.

Miranda's voice is close to my ear. "Squad A, we've located the coven residents. The reports were right. They're in City Hall."

"Received." Cleon's disembodied words flitter from the device. "We're on our way now. We've retrieved the venom."

"This is Shadow," Bethany buzzes in. "We're near City Hall; ETA five minutes."

"Received." Pyera lowers her hand. She looks at me from over her shoulder. "Macy."

I go to her.

"Do you see the necklaces?" She points.

They've all been fitted with a silver medallion. Each trinket glimmers with a faint, red tint. I grasp the moon pendant around my neck. "Enchantments?"

"Yes." She holds a hand up to lure the gammas closer. "I'm going to release them from their trance. Comb the halls for any others."

The shifters disband, all save for Miranda. There's a frown on her mouth as Pyera readies her blade. It bends like a snake. A serpent slithers where the fuller should be. It slices the skin of her palm.

She clenches her fist. Blood drips from her hand, but each bead levitates. They're meticulously arranged in the air like constellations. She fires them. They're trailed by a cacophony of hisses, and a second discordance of gasps and sobs.

Dozens of heads jerk up. They call our names. They cry out questions, pleas, and blessings. Woken eyes and minds search mine, dazed as if they've come to from a thousand-year sleep.

Pyera scabs the cut on her hand, and steps forward. Fear banished, she is strong for the people who need her. She's a mother to every person in this room—and a mother bears the heft of the universe for her children.

"I know you're scared." She stands tall and sturdy for them. "We're here now, and I'm sorry it wasn't sooner."

"Macy," Luc wheezes from the first row of vampires.

His voice stitches me to him. "I'm here."

He clutches an orange pocketknife. The blade is stained in blood like everything else. Like him. I place my hand over his, and, with my fingertips, climb the stepladder of scars on the underside of his arm. He fought—and it broke him. I can't save him from the past, nor can I lift him from the harrowing pits he's fallen into. I hold onto him like I can.

"I couldn't keep the wounds closed." He trembles.

"What are you talking about?"

He looks at me, but not completely. He's somewhere else. I dig my nails into his skin, so he'll come back to me.

The skin beneath his blue eyes is wet. "My magic wasn't strong enough."

"We did what we could," a shell-shocked Circi mumbles. She was magnetized to her friend the instant the charms were broken.

"What wounds?" I search him up and down. "Are you hurt? There are healers on the way. You'll be okay!"

He shakes his head. His voice is strangled. "That man? The Church guy? This is all his fault. We were with Val when it happened. They came from Terces' house and dragged Valberg to the Bridge. They..."

My chest hurts.

"I couldn't keep the wounds closed," he chokes out. "They dragged him off. We couldn't stop them."

"He'll pay," I promise. "We didn't bring a whole shifter army for nothing."

Finally, he focuses on me. His bottom lip quivers. He doesn't believe me.

Footsteps rumble from the end of the entryway. Growling, I tear myself away from my friends. My Marrow Mark oozes neon green fronds of light. Pyera joins me, blade ready. We glare into the dark mouth of the hall, from which Cleon, Nico, and Bethany's squad emerge.

They come to a sudden stop. Nico's eyes find Luc behind me. Every barrier he had up crumbles. Nico runs to his brother.

I catch him by both arms.

He grasps my biceps. "Macy!"

My lips tremble with a million warnings. All I manage is: "Careful."

He pushes me aside. He sinks to the floor, and gently takes Luc's face in his hands. Like that, every bit of resentment, bitterness, and jealousy dissolves completely.

"You're alive," Nico says. He looks at me. "What happened?"

"Church," I say.

His expression darkens. "We have to find him."

Cleon briefly embraces Pyera. He asks, "Where is he?"

"Library," Circi says. "He never leaves."

She's cracked with fracture lines, barely held together. I search her face, but her mind is disconnected from her body. I tentatively touch my hand to Circi's shoulder. My presence doesn't anchor her.

"The Grand Enchanter isn't here," one of the gammas says, having returned from scoping out the buildings.

Cleon frowns. "If not here, then—"

"Church took him," Luc says, voice graveled with rage.

Nico fists his hands. "He's trying to lure us there."

"Then that's where we'll go." Miranda comes closer. She looks at the Lord and Lady. "Bethany's squad brought knives, but…" Her eyes cut to the shell-shocked vampires. "Can we really recruit them?"

"We'll have to," Pyera says sternly.

"I'll radio Apex," says Miranda.

She unholsters her pistol. From one of her many pouches, she produces the clip from the hospital. I read *M. Braddock* engraved on the device before she loads it into the magazine. She catches me watching her and holds my eyes.

Guns. Bullets. Before I was a vampire, the idea of either was far away, inconsequential to me. All my life, I learned to shift, hunt, run, meditate, channel my Grounding. Manmade weapons weren't even on my radar. Yet, Francis will be felled by a round of ammunition laced with my venom.

Holstering her gun, Miranda blinks once very slowly, as if to acknowledge my thoughts, before she turns away, finger to her earpiece. Unshaken. Betas are never afraid.

"Alright," Pyera breathes.

Cleon caresses the back of her neck and brings their foreheads together. Their eyes closed, they find resilience together. Then they face their coven.

"Listen up!" Pyera snags their attention. She sighs. "Everyone here has been through *tremendous* turmoil while we were away. I'm sorry. Cleon and I failed you as your leaders. However… many more are doomed to undergo the same, or perhaps worse, if we don't stop the man who did this. And we plan to. No one here is obligated to help us. You've been through more than enough—but this is our home. We need to take it back."

The room is quiet. All those broken eyes stare back at the Lord and Lady. Pyera looks at Cleon with a grimace.

He motions for Bethany's squad, who carry several hefty bags.

"We have brought armor and blades." He waves at the shifters. "If anyone here is practiced in blood magic, license or no, and is willing to help us retake Devil's Trumpet, *please* join us."

Luc is the first on his feet. It makes my heart sink. A piece of him was lost; the brightest, happiest piece. He is a pillar of vengeful determination. In his wake, several others rise. The librarian I snapped at; a cashier from Cinnamon's; several lesser enchanters; everyday people I don't even know. Circi doesn't stand.

Nico stares at his brother. "Luc—"

"No." Luc shakes his head. "The man killed so many people. My friends, the gammas. Maybe even—" His voice breaks. He jerks his eyes away, and swallows. "Then he burnt down my home, and I couldn't do anything. I'm not letting him hurt *anyone* else."

Anyone else, meaning Valberg. Me. Nico.

"You know blood magic?" I ask.

He's momentarily surprised, and then serious. "Yes."

"You fought these people before?"

"Yes."

"You killed some?"

His eyes rage like an ocean squall. "Yes."

I look at Nico. "This is his fight, too."

Betrayed, he closes his eyes tight and shakes his head loose of all the nightmares inside. He turns his back on us and steals a minute to breathe.

As knives, body armor, and tips are distributed to the vampires, I lead Circi away. I lean her against a wall. She slides to the floor. I fetch a blanket, hoping to stop her shivering but I don't think it's that kind of shiver. I wrap it tightly around her shoulders and wonder if anything will ever be the same. I think we were too late. Even if we win... maybe we lost too much.

"One of them saved me," she whispers.

"What?"

"One of the shifters," she says. "Some vampires betrayed us, Macy, but they were... I don't know. Something was wrong with them. I tried to fight one. She was stronger. I don't know blood magic. She... Macy, I would've died if it weren't for..."

My hand finds her cheek. I cradle it. "You're alive. That's what matters, Circi."

"That shifter isn't, though." She's torn up inside. "What if she had a daughter? And now that daughter doesn't have a mom. And now she has to grow up all alone and scared and it's all because I—"

I hug her close. "Don't think about that right now."

She nods, and swallows. "Are you going to fix it?"

"The world?"

"Could you?"

I stare into her amber eyes. Hope sparks like fire.

I say, "Yes."

FIFTY

LAWS OF MORTALITY

The wolves move in swift and thunderous currents. They weave in and out of alleys, bounding across low-rise buildings, and stalking the shadows as we march in the streets. In the darkest corners, the ghouls lurk alongside us, all the way to the library.

The courtyard is all that lies between us. Everyone tucks themselves into the umbrae of the gaunt buildings across from it. We keep our eyes peeled.

The library's once regal silhouette is now a hungry, emaciated beast, ornamented in a fractured crown. Every window is shattered. They're gaping maws, driveling ash and soot, hungry. The doors hang open, impenetrable darkness on the other side. It beckons to us.

"Lone Wolf." Alpha Kennedy's voice vibrates in our ears. "This is Apex."

An evanescent glint flashes from the shadow of a nearby shop.

"We see you," Miranda whispers into her comm. She's the only wolf obligated not to shift. "Are you in position?"

"Yes."

Miranda gestures. Everyone but us fans out. Pyera and Nico hide away in an alley; meanwhile, Cleon and Luc tuck themselves into the carcass of a coffee house. They're backed by troves of vampires who are in turn backed by wolves.

Miranda unholsters her pistol. With her thumb, she pulls back the safety. Staring down at it, she ponders and then meets my eyes. In hers, I see my safety promised. There's a question, too.

Do you trust me?

After a single nod, I step out of the darkness.

The Man in the Moon's crimson shadow kisses my skin, heavy but certain. He bellows with Mother Nature. Her battle cry binds with his, and the rabid harmony undoes the eerie silence. Their wind embraces me when I reach the center of the quad.

"Church!" Adrenaline is like leaded courage in my veins, giving me strength. It isn't that I'm not afraid—I am—but, for the first time in my entire life, my fright is not my weakness. It's my fuel. I use it rather than run from it.

My Marrow Mark glows. It *scorches.* From it, glimmering ribbons of light wrap around my limbs. They harden into gossamer armor plates around my arms, chest, neck, and head, and two gauntlets shield my hands and wrists.

Each one produces a saber. I am a beacon for Mother Nature and the Man in the Moon.

"*Church!*"

Leisurely, he saunters from the dark depths of our library. The bloody night touches his skin; he holds his pale arms out to embrace it. His head rolls from shoulder to shoulder. His sunken cheeks are corrugated by distended, black veins, which chase down his neck, twitching. He pushes his thinned hair back with both hands.

Finally, he looks at me. "I heard you were coming."

"All according to plan, right?" I reply through gritted teeth.

A look of rapture crosses his face. "Not quite. You're just a cockroach."

"This cockroach rallied an army," I challenge.

"An army that thinks they're much sneakier than they really are."

Heavy footfalls thud the ground as wolves make themselves known, vampires staying hidden. Miranda's softer approach drums closer, too.

"You've two choices," I say. "You can surrender, or we take you and all your followers. Dead or alive."

He laughs. "You're not very threatening."

There's something dark inside me. My voice drips with venom. "Your friends thought so, too. Where are they now?"

"You shifters," he snarls. "You always boast false valiance."

He drifts down the library steps. Goosebumps tremor down my neck. Miranda edges closer as well. Unimpressed, he scoffs and tips his head back, locking eyes with the moon. He heaves a sigh, rolling his sleeves up. His emaciated arms are mutilated with lengthy scabs. They crack open, dribbling black.

Black mist erupts. It swells forward in waves, strong enough to push the largest wolf off its feet. I stagger away, bumping into Miranda. The mist throws us down and holds us against the pavement. The weight of the entire universe squashes me. It's too much. I'm about to break until Miranda throws herself over me, shielding me from the brunt of it. We keep our heads down until the pulses stop.

Miranda rolls off me with a grunt. Both our arms shake as we push up off the ground. She's up first and steadies me when I wobble. We turn in circles, but the fog surrounds us. It's thick. Only pale trails of red light break through.

"Macy?" Pyera's voice jaggedly stutters into my ear.

I spin to find her. The haze hides her away.

"Where are you?" I ask.

Her response comes in unintelligible clips.

I clench my fists. *Aimil.*

The waiflike plates harden with tangible light, fighting back the haze. With that, we dive in to search for the others. Our every step makes the darkness shrivel, but it returns in bulk behind us.

A ragged howl breaks open the quiet. There's another, and another. Too many ricocheting all around, wailing and desperate.

"What's going on?" I shout to Miranda.

"I don't know!" she yells back.

"We have—"

Something grabs me. I'm ripped off my feet and thrown to the cement again. My armor shatters on impact right before a creature launches on top of me. Its skin is saggy, hanging off its body, and its eyes are red with bloodlust. It jabbers mindlessly, flinging spit and black pus. It fights for a chunk of my flesh, clawing at my gear, my arms, my face!

"Get off!" I scream, but it's too strong.

Miranda grabs it by the hair. With a groan, she throws it off of me. It hits the ground, head bouncing. I hear a crack. On my hands and knees, I watch it spasm and twitch—then it rolls over. As the mist dissolves some, clinging to the earth, the ghoul sees me.

And it *gets up*.

Miranda hauls me to my feet. We run. All around us, the ghouls attack gammas and betas. They toss themselves onto shifters, burying them under their writhing bodies, piercing their pelts with teeth and nails. Suddenly, red whips lash through the air. From the boundary of the courtyard, the vampires come to the shifters' aide. The startled monsters are wrangled off their victims, who spring back into battle.

At the center of the storm, I see Pyera, Cleon, and the others. The Lord and Lady move like parallel rivers. Wherever one flows, the other follows. She weaves war with her blood, knocking ghouls back so he impales them with his lances. Beside them, Luc and Nico are a disarrayed duo. They're not equal, but Nico picks up the slack, stretching the thinnest amount of blood to its fullest. He's fast, hard to read, and close to unbeatable.

But... every ghoul that falls gets back up. It's like the legend come to life; invulnerable corpses rising up from the dead, sent on a mad quest to devour life. No amount of damage is enough. No amount of blood lost is too much. They defy the laws of mortality.

As Miranda and I run for them, a ghoul creeps up on Luc. It leaps onto his back, knees hooked around him. Shouting, he stumbles from the momentum before tripping. He falls onto his belly.

I run *faster*. All I can see are its teeth inches away from Luc's jugular. I barrel into it. We skid on the pavement, but I'm on my feet in a second. Pyera binds it with a rope of blood. She swings her arms forward like she's throwing a heavy sac, sending the ghoul into the rubble of a building.

I give her a wide-eyed look. She just pants, a bead of sweat rolling down her forehead.

The last of midnight billows across the courtyard, toward the library. They sail up the staircase back to Church. His swollen veins bulge and quiver, welcoming those sickly clouds into his bloodstream. Soon, all that's left of the dark horror is cords, clinging to the pavement.

Frenzied by its absence, the ghouls attack more viciously. It's war. Everywhere. Noisy. Chaotic. Screaming, yelling, blood and gore. The future collides with the present. If I don't do something, this is the end.

My eyes lock with Church's.

For a moment, there's nothing but him and me. Shifter and vampire. Monster and monster. There's a smirk tucked in the corner of his mouth as he smugly turns his back on me, on the battle, like he's above it all, and glides back up those stairs. My blood starts pumping again.

I barely hear Cleon yell, "We have to retreat!"

Not me. Fate or impulse, I don't know which one beckons me, but I chase after Church.

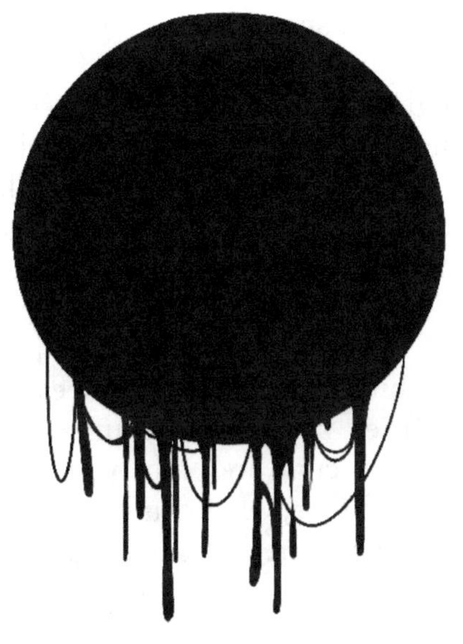

FIFTY-ONE

HISTORY

Everyone yells my name, but I don't stop. Something moves in my peripherals. Nico. Beside him, Luc.

Nico shouts. "Bad idea, Bright Eyes!"

I don't stop for him either. "Then go back!"

"*De ninguna manera!* We do this together or not at all!"

So together we go. As we hurry into the library, the out of place, potent smell of petrol crashes into us. I cover my nose, brow furrowed, and look at the boys. As we tiptoe further in, surrounded by darkness, I notice the floorboards are soft—moist.

"It's doused," I whisper.

"Look." Luc points at *History*.

Red moonlight beams from the ceiling, covering a memorial-like display. Heaped upon a table, trinkets, pictures, and other mementos circle a small, child-sized casket, topped with wilted marigolds. A ragged, bloodied corpse is bound to the display by his wrists, the rest of his body slouched like a rag doll. He lifts his head.

"Valberg!"

We sprint to him. I skid onto my knees, hands hovering over his injuries, shaky and unsure. He's covered in putrid, pus-riddled cuts and crusty bandages. If Luc couldn't seal his wounds, what could I do?

I look at his wrists. The ropes too tight. His hands are deep, bluish-purple. Inhaling sharply, I scramble to untie the knots, but I can't pry them loose. Nico pulls me back, taking his pocketknife out. He frantically saws at the thread, and Luc does the same for the other bind.

I press my fingers into my earpiece. "We need healer's ASAP. We're in the library."

A wave of static cackles in response. There's a voice lost in the buzz, but I can't make it out. Looking over my shoulder, I stare out the library's entrance, seeing war. Shifters, ghouls, blood, and darkness—all vying to win. We can't carry Val into that.

"Nico," Val croaks.

I jerk toward him again.

Nico cradles his cheek. "I'm here."

"We were wrong," he whispers.

"We know, Val," he says. "If I had known Church would've come here, hurt you, destroy our... I would've stayed."

"No... You have to... to leave."

I inch closer "We will."

"All of us," Luc assures him, his hand on Val's arm. "And you too."

"Luc. My Luc. You're here." Pain seizes Val's face. He looks frantic. "My Nico. My boys. You're both here."

"We came for you," says Luc.

He shakes his head, brows turned up, mouth gaping.

"What..." My gut is heavy. "... is it, Val?"

He looks at me. "We were wrong."

I touch his knee. "Val, we..."

"Nico, Nico. Nico. You have to leave." His chest heaves with panic. *"You have to leave!"*

"Not without you," Nico insists, almost meekly.

"The blood! The blood of day-kissed kin—"

"We'll protect Macy."

"Not Macy!" his hoarse voice breaks as he yells. Heartbroken, he stares into Nico's eyes. *"You."*

Nico's head moves from side to side. Slowly, then faster. Frantically, he denies it, but I remember his decapitated corpse. His pale skin. His dead eyes. The vacancy in them haunted my sleep. That night in his apartment, he had blindly scrawled the word *bleeding* repeatedly into his sketch of a raven. A million obtuse pieces abruptly fit. All the things that never added up, do.

But... Francis Church turned me under a full moon. It was my death in the first vision. It was Church's hands around *my* throat. We couldn't have gotten it wrong. It's impossible. Every single unfortunate event between when I was bitten and now, couldn't all be a coincidence.

I fist my shaking hands.

"Day-kissed," Valberg mutters. "Not earth-bound."

"You're lying," Nico snarls. He clutches Val's shirt and jostles him.

"Nic..." Luc covers his hand with his own. "Nic, stop."

"You're lying. You're lying! *You're lying!*"

His spine hunches. His head hangs low, hair in his face. His forehead touches Val's chest. He trembles, splintering little by little, a dozen revelations coming to light. Nico the Prophet fractures into the Prophet, Nico.

I touch his shoulder, trying to mend his cracked shell, but he leans away. "Nico..."

Hurt strains Valberg's voice. "I've never lied to you."

Nico lifts his head. "This whole time. It was me."

"I'm sorry."

"For the first time in *years,* it was someone else. Some-one else was special. Someone else was chosen. Someone else was the puppet on strings. But it was me." He fists Val's shirt again. He quakes but he doesn't shake Val.

I reach for him again. "We have to get you out of here."

He lets out a crisp, mirthless laugh. "I'm just the world's pawn."

"Nic," Luc hisses, "shut up."

Nico growls at him, but Luc doesn't waver. "Being a Prophet doesn't define you."

"It's the only thing that defines me!" Nico yells.

"*No.* You're an artist. A mage. A friend. A son. You're my brother."

Nico opens his mouth as if to protest, then closes it. They share an untiring look, reliving years of good and bad memories. Luc looks at Nico like he's his family, not the world's sacrifice.

I touch both their wrists. "We have to go."

They hook Val's arms over their shoulders as I lock my fingers at the middle of his back. On the count of three, we all heave him onto his feet. Groaning in pain, he nearly topples over me, but I push him upright. His bandages dampen with fresh blood.

"You got him?" I gently let go and back up.

Nico says, "Yep."

The boys lug Valberg carefully, his weak, gaited steps pacing them. I trail close behind. The floor squelches beneath our weight.

Aimil, I whisper to my soul.

I'm engulfed in my Marrow Mark's aura. Its green, shimmery light hardens into exoskeleton-like armor. The gauntlets and their sabers expand, scaring the shadows away.

A gust of wind pushes into the building. It whispers to me. We aren't alone.

"Guys..." I say.

They stop. All three of them look over their shoulders at me.

The wind urges me to turn. As I do, it plucks at a few stray hairs, tickles my cheeks and nose. I sniff away the sensation and breathe in something vulgar. It mixes with the stench of petrol. Something foul. Rotten.

The Monster.

He emerges from nothing. Every hair on my body stands straight, but I don't back away. I'm not the sacrifice, but I withstood the burden, even if it wasn't mine. I will be his end.

I spare a glance at the others. Nico pries Valberg's arm off, leaving Luc to shoulder the weight. The brother's share a second of understanding, forgiveness, and promise.

He tells Luc, "Go."

Then Nico's eyes connect with mine. They communicate, *Together,* and a million other things too. I dip my head: *Okay.*

He holds his pocketknife against his wrist. We face the Monster.

"I see the Man in the Moon sent his Prophets to *smite* me." He sneers sarcastically.

We say nothing.

"Do you remember when we last met, mutt?"

My throat aches from the memory of his teeth. I clench my fists.

A crimson thread lashes across Church's chest, cutting through worn fabric and flesh. Francis yelps and staggers back. Black secretes from the wound. He compresses it with his gnarled hand. The gooey black tar slinks back to its source before fleshy threads stitch the gash closed. He looks at Nico. His face becomes something inhuman.

Nico attacks again, but this time Church extends a hand. His swollen veins bulge. The shadows growl. Nico's blood writhes in midair. The mages fight for control, but the Monster's spell is too strong.

I lunge forward, and duck beneath the string of red when it swings at me. It slithers back for a second assault, but another one of Nico's scarlet tendrils surges into it. Church relinquishes control of the blood, focusing on me when I bring both gauntlets down on him. He evades it. I slash at him again. The tip of my saber scratches his cheek. It too seals itself shut.

His fingers dance like broken dolls, calling upon volatile power.

The darkness descends from everywhere at once. Its spidery legs sweep me off my feet. The Monster pounces at the chance to pin me—but Nico rams him off. On all fours, he snarls.

Surging upright, Nico and I begin our assault. Shadows clash with glowing green blades and bloody spears. The wind howls through the building. The Man in the Moon, Mother Nature, and the Prophets collected to face one ghastly creature. We have each other, but there isn't a soul to save Francis Church. Finally—*finally*—months of anger, pain, and despair are ending.

Until he roars, infuriated. *"Enough!"*

He holds a grisly hand out and the night attacks again. All his gashes break open and trickle ash. Another pulse booms through the building. This time I can't cut through it. Nico and I are both sent flying.

My side collides with the edge of a bookcase. It teeters from the collision, and then plummets to the marble floor with me. I try to move before it crushes me, but a stabbing pain in my ribs makes it impossible. The shelf comes down on my head and body.

An alarm rings in the distance and black blinks across my vision. Ringing screeches inside my head. I cover my ears, but it gets louder. I scream, but can't hear it.

I push against the floor, but a splitting pain in my side tears a howl from my throat. *Endure it,* I distantly command myself. I just have to breathe and get up. Only, breathing hurts. *Try anyway.* The pain gets worse.

Again.

More agony.

Just do it, Macy.

Tears blur my vision. I'm detached from my body, a spirit fastened by the thinnest thread. *Keep trying!* I push and push until my elbows give. I collapse under the bookcase.

I lift my head and narrow my eyes beyond the veil of dizzied vision. The Monster's long, slender legs waltz closer, tattered dress pants dragging along the floor. He emits an eerie chuckle, just like in my nightmares. The veins on his face pulse so thick I swear they'll explode—but not before he disembowels me, bleeds me dry.

I need to move; *just get up!*

My Marrow Mark flickers.

"You're pathetic." He bends at the knees, fingers dangerously close to my skin. Memories bury me—pain, fear, *fire* . "I love it when—"

A red, barbed wire wraps around his wrist and burrows its teeth into his flesh. With one, strong tug, it pulls the Monster back, onto the floor. Francis hollers, and scours the dark for his attacker.

Luc stands in the doorway, rosy light flowing in behind him. He hurls another toothed spear at Francis. It latches his other hand and yanks him farther away from me. Nico sends his own bloody rope.

"Touch her and we'll kill you, asshole," Luc growls.

Francis pushes himself up, and stares at the other vampire with large, dilated pupils. The boys pull their whips back. They revolve around them, protecting them. The Monster advances, but neither Nico nor Luc back down.

"Fine." He focuses on Nico. "*You* are much more important."

Luc sends two spears of blood across the room, but Church waves them away. The Monster strolls closer.

"Nico," Church pleads. "I'm giving you something spectacular."

"Death?" Nico throws his own spell.

Church dispatches it easily. "Transcendence. Vengeance. Retribution. A place in history."

"History won't exist tomorrow!"

"Exactly."

"He's not your pawn!" Luc shouts.

His fingers dance eerily, hurling his blood across the room at unmatched speeds. Too fast for Church. It pierces his shoulder. His jaw tightens and he stretches out his hand. The crimson stream blackens. Corrupted, it swings back around. Its teeth bite into Luc's arm and yanks him away from Nico—into Francis' grasp.

I flash back to the clearing. Except this time, it's not me. It's Luc.

Church clutches Luc's hair, tipping his head back. His black blood binds one hand while he clutches the other. He twists Luc's wrist, making his knife refract light as it slips from his grasp.

"Let him go," Nico growls.

He glares at the Monster, irises like two black-holes ready and willing to swallow the entire universe. He plunges his knife into his forearm. His lip curls with pain, but he draws more and more blood from the wound. He assails Church with a multitude of spells: spears, daggers, arrows, whips. Every assault is imbued with violent might. Nico, vitalized by rage and desperation, is a monster all his own.

Church throws Luc onto the ground. As Luc scrambles away, Church follows him steadily. He sways his hands in water-like movement, calling upon every bead of blood and shadow in the room. Nico's weapons become his. Rather than skewer him, they violently shudder and explode. Blood splatters everywhere.

He climbs over Luc, grips his hair, and holds his face against the floor. He holds the point of Luc's blade against his jugular. They freeze.

"Calm down," he commands.

Nico's whole body is tense. "Don't you dare."

"Look at this boy." His knife traces Luc's scarlet Marrow Mark. "He's a chameleon, just like *her.* Repulsive dogs parading among us like they belong. They were created to *kill* us, and for eons they have. *This* is what they deserve."

"Fuck you, too," Luc spits.

He digs the point of his knife into the base of his neck. Luc lets out a strangled cry.

"Stop it!" Nico screams.

Francis digs the knife in. Luc screams louder.

I wail his name. I throw everything I have into one last skirmish, but the pain in my side seizes, and my body falters. His name turns to a strangled cry caught in my throat, and soon I give up on his and beg for Aimil's. A faint numbness attempts to lift me from physical hurt, but the stabbing in my ribs won't concede.

"*I said stop!*" Nico shouts.

Church wrings one last scream from Luc before relenting. Luc's pants, choking on his own sobs.

"We're better than them, Nico." Church almost pleads.

"I wasn't born a vampire!" Nico shouts.

"But were you born a *shifter?*" Church yells back.

Nico doesn't budge. "Your hate has made you into a monster."

Church loses all light. He looks at me, but he doesn't see Macy Braddock, the Prophet of Misfortune. He sees every shifter who hurt him. He sees a monster. "You did this."

He plunges the knife into Luc's neck.

ALPHA AND OMEGA, BEGINNING AND END

"The sound of the seventh trumpet signals the third woe. Loud voices in Heaven proclaim Christ as ruler forever and ever under the "Kingdom of our Lord."

Luc screams. Gargled. High-pitched. Like an animal. His Marrow Mark burns to life with a surge of frantic, crimson power. His spirit, his Grounding, fights to keep him rooted in reality, in life. Church cuts the connection.

Aimil floods me. My body swells. The pain spreads. For an instant, I am adrenaline, anguish, and anger. I roar, uncaged from my body, growing too large for the heavy bookcase to hold me down. The Earth blesses me with a piece of myself I lost months ago: the beast.

My senses are overloaded. Sensation and sound. Screams, blood, and gasoline. It's chaos, undecipherable, and I am a part of it, a translator. All but one thing is a blur: The Monster.

I rush him.

There is nothing else. Just *him* and my desire to hollow his chest with my claws. They slice through his flesh with a squelch.

We tumble. There's pain on impact. A wave of it pulsates from my ribs, sending me into another transformation. Wolf turns to woman. I clutch my side and curl in on myself. My lungs are on fire. It hurts to breathe.

Seconds feel like eternities as I lie there, swallowed by agony. My head is heavy, weighed down by my undone hair. The world seesaws, blurs. A sharp ringing rattles inside my ears.

A few feet away, the Monster mutely gasps for air. He clutches the gaping wounds in his chest, trying, trying, *trying* to seal them with his foul magic. The black mist doesn't mend them like before. He's too weak.

I did that. A noiseless laugh spills out of me.

Fighting the ten-ton weight of my body, I shakily push myself up. The ringing blares louder than ever before it starts to fade.

"H-Hey! Hey! You're okay." Nico's voice is faraway, muffled, underscored by noisy, wet gasps.

I blink. My fuzzy vision clears. I scan the library for him, and my heart drops through the floor.

Nico crouches over Luc, who weakly compresses the wound on his neck. Nico covers his hand with both of his. Blood gushes between their fingers.

"You're fine." Nico's voice wobbles as he cries. "You're fine. I'll fix it. It's fine."

Luc gags, hacks, and chokes on words, names. Nico's, Val's, mine, *anyone*.

"I'm coming!" My body whines as I push onto all fours, but he *needs* me.

I crawl through pain to be by his side.

His eyes bulge. He doesn't blink. His Marrow Mark flickers, casting twisted shadows across his face. His bottom lip quivers. My name is mangled by another bloody gasp.

"I'm here," I croak.

My hands hover over him with uncertainty, but I have to be better. Stronger. I have to know what to do and how to do it—but I tremble.

I look at Nico. He's gone pale. "You have to close the wound."

"It's too deep," he says. "I can't scab over muscle."

"Try!"

"*I am!*" He looks at Luc, biting back tears. "Why didn't you just go? What's wrong with you?"

Luc opens his mouth but says nothing. There's an apology in his eyes. It hurts us both.

"Hey," I cry, fat tears rolling down my cheeks. "We'll take care of you."

He wraps his freehand around mine, painting my skin with his blood. I squeeze his hand. He holds on tightly, but he's fragile. There's no bravery anymore. He clings to me because he's afraid, and I cling back because so am I.

Resting my forehead against his, I wipe his tears away. My fingers leave streaks of blood on his skin. My bottom lip trembles. I close my eyes, wishing I could wipe his pain away or drown in his sapphire gaze.

Someone yells for us.

I jerk upright. Pyera, Cleon, and Miranda rush inside. Broken wails for help claw out of me. The Lady grabs me by my shoulders and tries to wrestle me away. I fight back.

"Fix him! Just fix him!" I scream. *"Heal him!"*

"Macy!" she cries. "Move!"

With Miranda's help, she pries me off. I grapple to stay with him, but Miranda locks her arms around my waist. They don't understand. *He needs me!* And I need him. I need to be there, so I can wither alongside him. So he isn't alone.

"Nico!" I shout, fighting against Miranda. "Luc!"

"Braddock. Braddock!" Miranda growls at my ear. *"Macy!"*

I slump into her arms. For a moment, she holds me tight before slackening her grip. Then, I sense movement from my right. Church limps toward *History*, clutching his chest and something else in his hand. Numb, powerful fury overtakes me.

"Aimil," I whisper. "Give me strength."

My conscience begs apprehension. Shifting once was hard enough on my body, but twice? *I don't care.*

The pain is worse this time. It's magnified by the transformation, and then blunted when my paws hit the tiles. I am leashed to one purpose.

Digging my nails into the floor, I spring forward with a bloodthirsty snarl. He glances over his shoulder and breaks into a panicked sprint. I'm too fast. I sink my claws into his back. My momentum hurls us through *History's* archway, into red moonlight.

On impact, I pin him. He loses his grip on his dagger, and something else bounces away. A lighter. He fights to break free, shouting and writhing. Leaning my snout down, I open my mouth around his neck.

A sliver of black mist pierces my damaged side. It throws me off Church and expels the beast from my body. Then I'm naked and vulnerable, laid out on the floor.

Church throws himself at me, dagger in hand. I barely manage to roll away. He reels back his arm to stab me. A black blur storms into him. Another wolf. Miranda.

They knock over chairs, tables, and lamps as they grapple. Francis slices his knife at her. She lets out a high-pitched whine. Sidestepping and shifting simultaneously, Miranda staggers away from him, cupping her eye. Blood seeps down her cheek.

He whips around and scans the floor frantically. His eyes lock onto something. The lighter. The acrid scent of gasoline smells so much stronger. The vision flashes. Fire, smoke, and death. He's going to burn everything to the ground. I can't let him.

"The gun!" I shout to Miranda as I scramble after Church.

Just as he reaches the lighter, I tackle him yet again. The lighter slips from his grasp when we hit the floor. As soon as I have him down, he throws me off. I spring to my feet, bumping the lighter. I kick it backward, so that I'm between it and him.

Church stares through my legs at it. His eyes slowly rise to meet mine. "You people are monsters."

"Look who's talking," I snarl. My skin blazes to life. The exoskeleton wraps around me.

"Just roll over and *die* already."

The shadows lash out at me, frenzied. I evade and guard against every attack, armor cracking. Glimmering green scarabs try to rebuild but Church's attacks are too swift and too mighty. I make my way closer, still, un-afraid, and then I plow into him.

His bleeding arms don't have the strength to stop me. He gives up on magic, and slashes at me with his blade. It cuts into my chest plate. The exoskeleton shatters.

He slashes at me. I batter him with punches. I feel his bones crack beneath my knuckles. His ghastly exterior is no rational match for my sturdy muscles, but my body aches. Every swing is fatigued. Agony vibrates in my ribs.

His foreign hands clasp my neck. He swiftly pins me against the memorial. The table bites into my lower back. He digs his nails into the scar, and I let out a strangled cry.

I stare into his eyes. They're empty and burning. I'm burning too. My lungs are burning, huffing and gasping and aching for air.

He pushes me down onto the casket, bending my back at a painful angle. Fruitlessly, I scratch at his hands like I did so many times in the visions, the dreams. I fight harder than ever because this *isn't* a dream. I won't wake up from this with fully capable lungs. I won't wake up at all.

I scrape at his face. His skin burrows under my nails, and red lines chart across his cheek. He tightens his grip. The casket budges under our weights. It slips off the table. Trinkets scatter and break on the floor, and he presses me into the table. I kick and struggle more.

"How's it feel?"

I growl at his words.

"*How's it feel?*" he snarls. "You were useless. How does it feel to know it's been that way from the start?"

The beast howls from the depths of my soul. *Aimil, give me strength.* I feel the tickle of power, but the world starts to dim.

A gunshot rattles the building. White light flashes. He lets go. I gasp for breath as he tears his eyes over his shoulder.

Miranda stands in the doorway, cupping her bloodied eye. She holds the gun anyway. It wobbles. Her aim is off, but she fires again. Church lifts a hand. The shadows around her tremble in response.

I grab him by the hair. With all the power left in my soul, I twist us around and pin him onto the table. He screams as I expose his grotesque neck.

We've been brought to our last resort. Me.

I sink my fangs into his throat. Black mist erupts. It tastes like poison. He swings at me with his blade, but nothing stops me. I fist his tattered shirt and tough out the pain, tough out the taste, tough it all out.

He took everything from me. My family, my life, Luc. He took every chance I had to be happy with Mom and Dad, and any chance to be happy without them. He took my entire world.

I hope my fangs burn worse than fire. Worse than his blade when he stabs my side. That's what finally throws me off him.

I feel like I'm diving off a cliff. The air moves slowly around me. My back presses into the table. The vibrations of the impact don't hurt. Nothing hurts anymore.

Warmth trickles down my waist. My hands wrap around the grip. I try and pull the knife with a wheeze, but I'm too weak. My hands fall slack.

Beside me, he's a mess of spasms, dying from the venom he gave to me. It ravages him from the inside out

Darkness sets in on the edges of my vision. It borders the broken skylight, from which the Man in the Moon gazes down at me. His breeze sweeps down the tower, and dances across my body. It's cool on my warm skin. There's another voice, too.

Mother Nature's wind kisses my skin.

A sob escapes me.

She treasures me. Her touch is so kind. She heals the pieces of my soul that broke tonight and ensures that her love keeps me company as the world fades.

They sing together. My eyes droop, and my spirit is lulled.

I'm sad I won't be there for Nico, Val, or Circi. They'll grieve my loss, and they'll grieve Luc. They'll have to undergo the same pain Mom and Dad did when I was first changed, but they'll be okay. They'll heal like Lilac because, although I am a piece of them, they're whole enough to mend. I hope the same for Pyera and Cleon.

The darkness closes in on the Man in the Moon. Before it's swallowed completely, a butterfly flutters from the sky. A faraway thought follows the beat of its wings. *What are you doing here?* It gently lands on my forehead. A message from the Earth and stars: *watch.*

The red drains from the moon. It fades to orange as whiteness breaks free. Images blind me. Pyera flicks her wrist dramatically, and Cleon hides his grin behind his hand. Luc and Circi laugh together. Red feathers like Luc's Marrow Mark sink through the night to touch fresh, porcelain snow. Nico's scarred hands attend to bandages, gentle. Mom's eyes—her loving eyes.

I croak a teary laugh.

They'll be okay. You did enough, Macy. It's time to rest.

FIFTY-THREE

FLASHES

It all comes in flashes. Colors, shapes, sounds. Faces. Miranda's, Pyera's, Cleon's. Nico's, too. They blur together. I'm not sure where one starts and the other begins. It's all of them all at once. But I see their fear.

It's okay, I want to tell them but I'm too tired.

Their voices tangle. Over and over, they say my name. They say other things, too. The wind sings somewhere far away. Everything runs together.

Hands slip under my heavy body, but the heft of my limbs disappears as they lift me up. The fading red moon gazes at me. The tether that binds me to reality slackens.

I float away. As I drift from the Earth to the sky, a doe shoots across the stars. She turns toward me and bows her head. I smile.

Darkness takes me.

FIFTY-FOUR

BREATHE AGAIN

My throat burns. Every inhale stokes the flames of thirst. It brings me out of a long, lethargic slumber, demanding something, *anything*, to quell the unbearable fire.

I open my eyes. The world is blinding. I wince and shield my vision with a shaky hand. I blink rapidly, dampening the harsh light, and soon reality fades into place.

I don't know where I am.

All I remember is the library tower, blood, pain, and the Moon. I see none of that. Instead, I'm confronted with a large, soft bed and an open room carved from granite. Rivulets of untapped crystals weave sporadically along the walls, glittering brilliantly like a Marrow Mark. On the ceiling, similar veins of sparkling gemstones make the shape of a doe. She was watching over me.

Sitting up, I see my reflection in a massive mirror on the far wall. My hair is matted badly, and I'm covered in bandages. Most are small, save the one on my side. When I touch it, I expect pain but pleasant numbness tingles in its place. I know the feeling. It's the same sensation as those inspired by a healer's magic in the pack.

Someone's been taking care of me.

I swallow. It hurts. The thirst makes me dizzy. I need blood.

Clasping my throat, I push aside the hefty fur blanket and swing my legs over the edge of the bed. They're heavier than usual, but flimsy too, somehow. I tentatively test their strength by gradually pushing weight onto one foot. Then the other. There's a little bit of pain, but when I'm sure I won't fall over, I stand.

The room spins. I stagger and flail my arms before I catch myself on the wall. I brace myself against it for a moment. Bowing my head, I breathe through my nose. That burning itch in my throat persists. I try to massage it away. It doesn't help.

With one hand against the wall, I make my way to the door. As I lay my hand against it, gentle, it opens on its own. I gasp.

The Monster's knife and his fangs flash before my eyes. Panic hotwires my body. I stumble away from the door, but trip over my own feet. I land firmly on the floor.

"Miss Braddock!" Cleon shouts

My entire body unwinds instantly. I croak. "Cleon."

He and Nico rush into the room. Hastily, Cleon shoves his platter into Nico's hands, causing the kettle and teacups to wobble, and crouches in front of me. He cups my face gently.

His icy blue eyes bulge. "You most certainly should *not* be out of bed! Your body is weak, Miss Braddock!" He lets go of my face and lifts me onto my feet by my underarms. "Up, up, up!"

He helps me into bed. Carefully, he inspects my bandages to make sure I haven't opened any of my wounds and, once he's sure I haven't, he relaxes. Nico sets the platter at the foot of the bed. He sits beside me.

"You're up early, Bright Eyes," says Nico.

"Early?"

He nods his head. "The healers said it would be a few more nights before you woke."

I open my mouth to say something, but a sudden, intoxicating aroma pulls my attention to Cleon. He fills two teacups with a steamy brew. The misty vapors smell delightful. My mouth waters. My throat burns. My skin pebbles. Knowingly, Cleon places a cup in my hand.

I greedily guzzle the entire thing in seconds, but the thirst persists. I need more. I hold my cup out to Cleon, who fills it again. I try to drink it more slowly this time. It's useless. When it's gone, Cleon reads my mind and refills it.

"Does that help?" he asks seriously.

"Yes." I gasp after a big gulp.

"Wonderful. It is only lightly spiked. Mostly for flavor. You will require another feed very soon, but for now this should stave off the pain."

"Thank you," I murmur before taking a smaller, more reserved sip. I stare into the rosy brown tea pensively, then glance at them. "How long have I been...?"

"Over a week," Nico says gently.

My eyes fall back into the teacup. "Where are we?"

"Wolfden."

The Knotweed pack's capitol rooted in the northern half of Arizona. Often, this is where healers come to complete the Rite of the Oasis, granting them the divine ability to mend wounds with blessed spring water. No wonder we were brought here.

Memories of the blood moon shatter me. The recollection of white-hot pain sears my side, and images of Luc's crumpled, fading body break my heart all over again. I clench my eyes shut and run away, deep into the trenches of my mind. The cup in my hand trembles with me.

Please, Mother Nature, let him be okay.

A hand touches my forearm. I open my eyes with a sharp gasp, finding Nico's dark gaze staring into mine. There's a frown nestled into the corner of his mouth. My frail, desperate hope withers.

"He's okay," Nico whispers.

I close my eyes again, but this time it's to keep tears from falling. "How?"

"It was close. Way too close. The healers did what they could. Everyone did. For him. For you. For Val. But..."

"You all needed immediate intensive care," Cleon says. "So here we are."

"But..." I swallow. "Luc's okay?"

Nico bites his lip. "Maybe not as okay as you think, but he's *going* to be. That's what matters."

All I see is that knife embedded into Luc's neck, and his blood. It was a darker, scarier red than his Marrow Mark. Nothing erases the sensation of his shaking body under my hands, the image of his blue eyes dimming with every passing second, how he needed me, and how I couldn't fix him.

"I need to see him," I whisper.

"Soon," Nico murmurs back.

I lean toward him. "How soon?"

He smiles at me sadly. "As soon as he wakes up."

I relax against the bedframe. The full moon replays in my mind yet again, slower this time. "What happened to Church? I bit him. He should've..."

My mind races. It won't stop.

"Hey. Slow down." Nico touches my arm again.

I take a deep breath but look to Cleon for answers. There's a deep furrow between his brows.

"Church is dead," he says. "Your venom brought him to his end, although our plan quickly fell apart." He's kind enough not to chastise me for explicitly disobeying his and Pyera's command, and endangering Nico, Luc, and myself. I'm grateful. "We hoped to gather his remains. We thought perhaps it would put his spirit at rest to bury him beside his son, but his body crumbled to ash before we could."

"What about the Ghouls?"

"The same."

I don't know what to feel.

It was his venom that allowed this version of me to exist. Although I know this is the person I was always meant to be, I hold no gratitude toward him. From the moment our paths crossed my fears took the shape of him. Every setback, failure, and pitfall was yet another reminder of the inevitable fate that awaited me. A fate that ravaged many of the things I held dear. A fate orchestrated by Church.

So, I feel rage. I feel pain. I feel grief. But I also feel pity, shame, and guilt because just as I saw him as the Monster, he saw me as one, too.

He was a father undone by loss. *My* people did that to him. He called for action. That call echoed across the covens. It touched the broken hearts of other vampires who felt similar pain. It gave them a purpose. I may not have killed Church's son with my own hands, but *my people* did and for a long time, I supported it. Not anymore.

What Church and his Wormwood League did was unforgivable, wrong. It was skewed and inhuman, but it was rooted in a pain we can fix.

"What will the shifters do now?" I ask softly. "Things can't go back to how they were."

Cleon says, "They cannot. The Packs agree. Things must change. It is tentative right now, but they have disclosed that the walls will not be rebuilt. Those that remain standing will be torn down. I believe that is a hopeful sign."

I sip on my tea for a few minutes. "What about Miranda? She was with me. I saw her eye. It was... It wasn't good."

"They couldn't save her eye," says Nico, "but she needed the least care. She was recommended bedrest but that didn't last long. She's already back on watch."

"Miss King has watched over you day in and out." Cleon swipes a stray strand of his blond hair behind his ear. "As have we all."

"And what about Val?"

He was in terrible shape. Maybe worse than any of us. I know by the grave and pained looks that cross both their faces the news isn't good. My heart drops. My mouth dries. I try not to cry.

"What is it?" My voice trembles.

"He's *alive*," Nico rushes to say. I suddenly notice how red his eyes are. How puffy they are. Like he's been crying. "It's just that..."

He looks away, choked up.

Cleon says, "He was in terrible shape. None of us were sure he would pull through. There is still some speculation. He may never fully recover."

"Can I see him, too...?"

"In due time."

Everything is always in due time. I'm tired of waiting. With a frustrated huff, I rest my cheek on my shoulder and look at the wall. "What happens now?"

"The Packs are still organizing," he says. "There is much to do. Repairs, death counts, lawmaking, and change. It will take time, as most things do, but I do believe that better things are on the horizon. After everything—"

A gentle tap comes from the door. We all look. It's a young shifter girl. A healer. "Sir Lamalcom?"

"Yes?" Cleon turns toward her.

"Alphas Roderick and Kennedy requested your presence."

His shoulders weigh heavily. He drops his head, not wanting to go, before looking at Nico and me. "I will return shortly."

With a sigh, the Lord slaps his thighs before standing. His blond braid sways as he walks out the door, shadowed by the shifter girl. The doors come together with a hushed sigh. Then it's just Nico and me.

"Have you seen Luc?" I ask. "And Val?"

His eyes wander away from me. They're stormy with tumultuous thought. Tears start to form so he closes his eyes. I set my tea aside so I can touch his wrist and be his strength like he was mine.

"Nico," I whisper.

He looks at me. The whites of his eyes are redder. "Everyone's okay but they're not—and I'm just here. I'm just here, Macy. Perfectly fine. Not a scratch on me."

"Come here."

Wordlessly, he scoots across the mattress. The weight he's put on himself visibly crushes him, making him two times smaller, and the struggle of it twists his face with pain. I cup his jaw like he's the brother I never had. All the stress stacked on top of us finally falls apart, and a new, strange grief replaces it. But we did it. Him and me, and a thousand other people.

His bottom lip quivers. Mine does, too. I hug him. He cries into my chest as I hide my face against his hair. For the first time in months, we can breathe again.

FIFTY-FIVE

CLEMATIS

"I wish you were here already," I mumble into the phone. "You'd fit right in."

Luc laughs. His merriment is interrupted by a short, strained hiss. I don't like to think about the pain that plaits his body. Sometimes, when I close my eyes, all I see is his lacerated neck.

He lets out a softer, more relaxed chuckle. It's his way of telling me *I'm okay.*

"Is it pretty?" Luc asks.

My gaze dallies over forested hilltops. A river splits the woodland. Its currents loll over wet, glossy stone, sparkling glitzy silver under moonlight. A thin carpet of snow laps at the shore, and hoods trees in gossamer white cloaks.

My breath mists when I say, "Definitely, but it'd be better with everyone up here."

"What? You jealous the Terrible Two are still stitched to my side?" Luc teases.

I smirk. "No. Not at all. I've needed a break from Nico and Circi since I moved to Devil's Trumpet."

"Try a decade with 'em," Luc says.

"How are they?" I ask, chasing a crease in my leggings.

Luc hums in thought. "Circi has successfully riled up every shifter within ten miles with her political debates. Nico hasn't helped. Apparently, they agree about more than just heavy metal."

I laugh. "That can only mean trouble."

"Rest assured, they still bicker. They just take thirty-minute breaks now."

My smile spreads wider.

Things between Luc and Nico still aren't perfect, but there's something about almost dying that brings people together. I would know. I've done it twice now. Valberg's recovery has brought them closer together, as well. He needs them more than ever.

The healers did what they could, but his hands went too long without blood flow. They couldn't be saved. The last time I saw him, his eyes were dark with sadness.

I swallow, decidedly focusing on something else. "How much longer until you leave Wolfden?"

"The healers say it won't be for another few weeks," Luc admits. "Sucks, since it's been a month already. But hey! I'll meet you in Maine soon."

I scoff lightheartedly. "What about my alone time?"

"Gasp!" I imagine Luc's hand on his chest, exaggerated, offended look on his face when he says, "Macy! I'm still recovering from my heroic brush with death! You can't say such cruel things! I'll die from heartbreak."

Sniggering, I shake my head. "Are you going to make it to the ceremony?"

"Duh!" Luc says. "I am not missing this! It's not every day a vampire is made an honorary member of a shifter pack! I will claw my way out of Wolfden to make it, Tenderfoot."

"No rush!" A gust of wind sighs against the nape of my neck, blowing strands of red hair into my face. They tickle my cheeks before I tuck them behind my ear, smiling. "It's not for another month anyway. Right now, they're still getting everything situated."

The line is quiet for a moment. Luc pulls in an audible breath. "Have you talked to...?"

My nails dig under the stretchy fabric of my leggings. Tense. A sudden surge of worry rockets down to my stomach, making it rumble. "No, not yet. We're supposed to meet today. Soon. Like, really soon."

"Hey," he says softly.

I stare at my shoes.

"It's going to be okay." I know he's right. The line is muffled by indiscernible noises in the background. "Listen, Tenderfoot, I gotta go, the gang just came in." A chorus of hellos reverberates, muddled by static but intelligible. "Call me later?"

"Definitely."

We say our goodbyes, and I lower the cellphone into my lap. I run a thumb up and down the glossy screen. The smudges fog the glass beneath the stars. Another breeze kisses my shoulder, reassuring. It then brushes past me, and dives into the wooded valley.

Celastrus is built mostly underground and within the great alps lining the Canadian border. It sits close to the river, though people are still wary of it after it was poisoned. So far, reparations across the world are underway. When I left the coven a week ago, the city was on its way to health at a rapid pace. Give it a month or two. Everything will be rebuilt and thriving; everything save the wall.

True to their word, the Alphas have officially decided the walls are through. After the lunar eclipse, it's clear to everyone that changes needed to be made, lest we want another Francis Church somewhere down the line. There's still going to be strict in-and-out surveillance, but everyone hopes this newfound freedom will do good for vampires and shifters alike.

Things can only improve. They'll have to. Every vampire with common sense realizes Church's methods were extreme, but it did highlight a specific detail: shifters can be crushed. That knowledge is as dangerous as the hubris of wolves.

One of the biggest issues we've yet to resolve is how the Alphas are going to handle people like me. We aren't many, but we're enough to stir trouble. Do you strip your people of faith in their government by revealing their force-fed lies? Or do you settle for small benefits, and let the shifters spin a story to correct their misinformation down the line?

As of yet, the Alphas have formulated a tale. This is all a gift from the Gods in hopes of inspiring a more united era. There are only a few who will be permitted to know the truth: the immediate family of former shifters.

I stare at the opened envelope in my lap. My name is drawn across its face in delicate handwriting; symbols spun like vines across paper. Gently, I thumb the soft swirl reaching below all the other letters. Pushing the fold upward, I pull the slip of paper out. I admire every word, having spent countless nights reading, rereading, stroking, and digesting each one.

I've spent hours sitting here, overthinking, weeping, denying any of this is real, but I have no words to describe the pain I felt after losing you, and the relief I feel now, knowing you're alive. To say I only want to hold you again, Macy, is a lie, because I want so much more.

"Me too, Mom."

Kathleen Braddock flashes in my head. Alone. Grieving me, grieving the forest, and then grieving Dad. Warm wetness blurs my vision, but I blink back the tears.

I close the envelope and touch my neck. The beads Lilac gave me still reside there. Lately, they've felt out of place. I unlatch them from behind my neck, turning the necklace over in my palm.

I don't know where she is. Our last conversation flashes in my mind. I know, deep down, I was never an essential pillar of her life. She doesn't need me to be strong. I knew it that day we reunited. I saw our paths, how they split away from each other. I chose love. I can only hope she gives up her hate.

The beads slip through my fingers.

I don't need her either.

Mom, though? Blood is different. My time as a vampire taught me as much. It's a terrible, lethal thing, but it's binding, too. I can't leave Mom all by herself. She *does* need me.

The beads tumble down the hillside.

"Ambassador?" a voice asks from behind me.

I glance over my shoulder at Miranda. "Oh, hey."

After the blood moon, Miranda and Bethany were both assigned to me by Alpha Rosemarie, for a "temporary" amount of time after the eclipse. An entire month later, none of us are sure just how long "temporary" is.

Miranda's hair is tied up. Her new eye-patch is leather, embossed with the Poppy pack's symbol of honor: the head of a buffalo, framed by two stems of gladiolus flowers. I touch my ribs. The healers mended my side, leaving only a scar, but they couldn't give back Miranda's sight.

Miranda moves out from under a tree. The snow crunches beneath her boots. Her honey smell rides the wind, dizzying my senses. She edges close. I turn away from the view to gaze up at her. She stares down at me, brow slightly raised.

"Sightseeing?" she asks.

I shrug. "Just catching my breath."

"Have you been running?"

"Are you always so literal?"

"Not always," she says, softer.

"Do you ever get nervous?" I ask, quietly.

"Do you always ask such silly questions?" There's a phantom smirk on her lips.

I grin. "So betas aren't fearless?"

"Not even close." Miranda shrugs. She offers me a hand, and I take it. She lugs me to my feet. "After Loosestrife was destroyed, my brother went missing. He must've died during the assault. I felt very afraid after that."

"I'm sorry," I frown.

"*You* aren't the one who should apologize." Miranda swipes a strand of brown hair from her green eye. "We aren't fearless, Braddock. We aren't even brave. But we never let fear control us."

"*We* as in betas? Or *we* as you and me?"

Miranda raises her chin a little higher. "Both."

Pulling the sleeves of my sweater over my hands, I shake my head. "That might be... the nicest thing you've ever said to me. Careful, I'm starting to doubt how heartless you are."

Her laugh is like music. It makes me proud. She nods toward the capitol. "Are you ready?

No. I'm not ready, but I say, "Yes."

Miranda guides me into the bulk of the city. Along with the destruction of the walls, there's been an increased influx of movement across the nation. Open-minded shifters have taken their wares to whichever coven is up and running enough to have them, and vampire embassies are being built all over. Pyera and Cleon were some of the first vampires given the honor, as were Nico and I. He plans on succeeding Valberg as Grand Enchanter, as well.

Despite this new age of integration, eyes still linger as Miranda and I pass. Fortunately, I've gotten used to the staring. It's basically in the job description at this point. *The latest Prophet of Misfortune: receives nightmarish visions from the Man in the Moon, constant glares from vampires and shifters alike, unquestionably bad luck, and, by the way, required to save the world, occasionally.*

Miranda doesn't waver either. She looks almost proud to stand beside me.

Inside Celastrus' mountain walls, we bustle through mighty corridors. There are several wide, open spaces to accommodate the massive population of shifters, as well as several stories dug below dirt. We carve a path up several staircases until we come to the Embassy.

Pyera commands a room of vampires and omegas alike. She spews surefooted commands, and waves her hands in kind, practiced gestures. People scurry in and out of the room, hastily doing as they're told. Lady Pyera Vandiver, for all her complaints about politics, looks right at home, surrounded by shifters and vampires, dramatically executing well-thought demands. She spots me and breaks away from the hub of activity.

She practically bounces her way from across the room and shakes me excitedly. "You're here! Finally!"

"I'm here!" I agree with a big grin as she whisks me away from the door and leads me further into the Embassy.

"Cleon sends his regards!" Pyera flicks her wrist. "He has made sure to flaunt his immediate access to a shopping mall—though I reminded him he's supposed to be running the coven, not *shopping.*"

"Pyera!" I gasp, "Are you saying you're *against* a good shopping spree?"

Pyera hides her smirk. It's as sharp as her eyeliner.

"Are you jealous?" I whisper.

"That outlet mall was my second home!" Pyera huffs goodheartedly.

Suddenly, she steps behind me and pushes me toward another door. It's tall. The silhouette of a deer's head is carved into the face and split down the middle by a fine line separating the door in two.

"Enough of that! She's been waiting!"

"Okay! Okay!" I shake her hands off. "Stop pushing me!"

Pyera holds her hands up in the air innocently, and retreats to stand by Miranda. The beta nods at me.

I gather all the courage I've built over the past several months and take that one step forward. The doors open quietly. It closes with a soft clatter. The woman at the center of the room jumps.

Kathleen Braddock takes in the sight of me, almost afraid. Then she races across the room. Her embrace swallows me whole. Her chest quakes with her sobs and her arms are tight. They shield me. She smells just like she used to—like the garden and the woods, like freshly cooked meals, and leisurely melted candles. Suddenly, I'm crying, too.

She pulls back to look at me. She traces my face with a feather light touch as if she, my own mom, has to reacquaint herself with the very girl she sculpted from scratch. Her red, puffy eyes dart all over my face as she memorizes me. That's what she's afraid of. Kathleen Braddock, my fearless, cold, calculating mother is scared to lose me *again*. I'm a ghost, but I'm not. I never died like she thought. I'm her daughter. Her living, breathing daughter.

I cover the backs of her hands with mine. "I'm not going anywhere, I promise."

"I missed you so much."

A laugh breaks through all the tears. She laughs, too. It's the most beautiful sound.

"I am so proud of you, Macy." A heartbroken twinge contorts her expression. "Your father would be, too."

A million feelings blitz through me. All I can do is bury my face in her neck and ride them out. Her fingers move through my hair slowly, tenderly. She kisses my temple, brightening the shadows of my heart. Together, we cry, and we cry, but we mend, too.

THE END

ABOUT THE AUTHOR

Michaela is a self-taught artist and passionate novelist who wrote her first book by the age of 13. She's participated in various local writing anthologies, art showcases, and poetry slams. When she isn't slaving away on her latest novel or art piece, she can be found hiding from civilization with the help of a book. Her artwork can be found on her website:

https://artbymichy.squarespace.com/
or on Instagram: @protectivespell1

SPECIAL THANKS

Thank you to my parents who indulged wholeheartedly in my dreams. Not once did you ever doubt. The same could be said for all my family. Every aunt, uncle, grandma, and grandpa. I am so grateful for you all.

Thank you to Mr. Cowley for inspiring me to put my imagination to work when I was only twelve. In fact, thank you to all the teachers who stoked my desire to do better: Nance Louise, Alexandra Strouf, Staci Calkins, and Traci Peugh.

Thank you, Rosemary, for not only mentoring me when I was young and cocky, but for being the most gracious friend. Your feedback is precious.

Thank you to all my friends who suffered through horrible versions of my book and never told me how bad it was. Mostly, thank you to Sophie Thompson. You've been a joy every day since we met, and your feedback helped make *Tooth and Claw* what it is today.

Lastly, thank you to Benjamin Gorman, Viveca Shearin, and the Not a Pipe family for welcoming me with open arms.